image® comics presents

SKULL KICKERS

1000 OPAS and a DEAD BODY

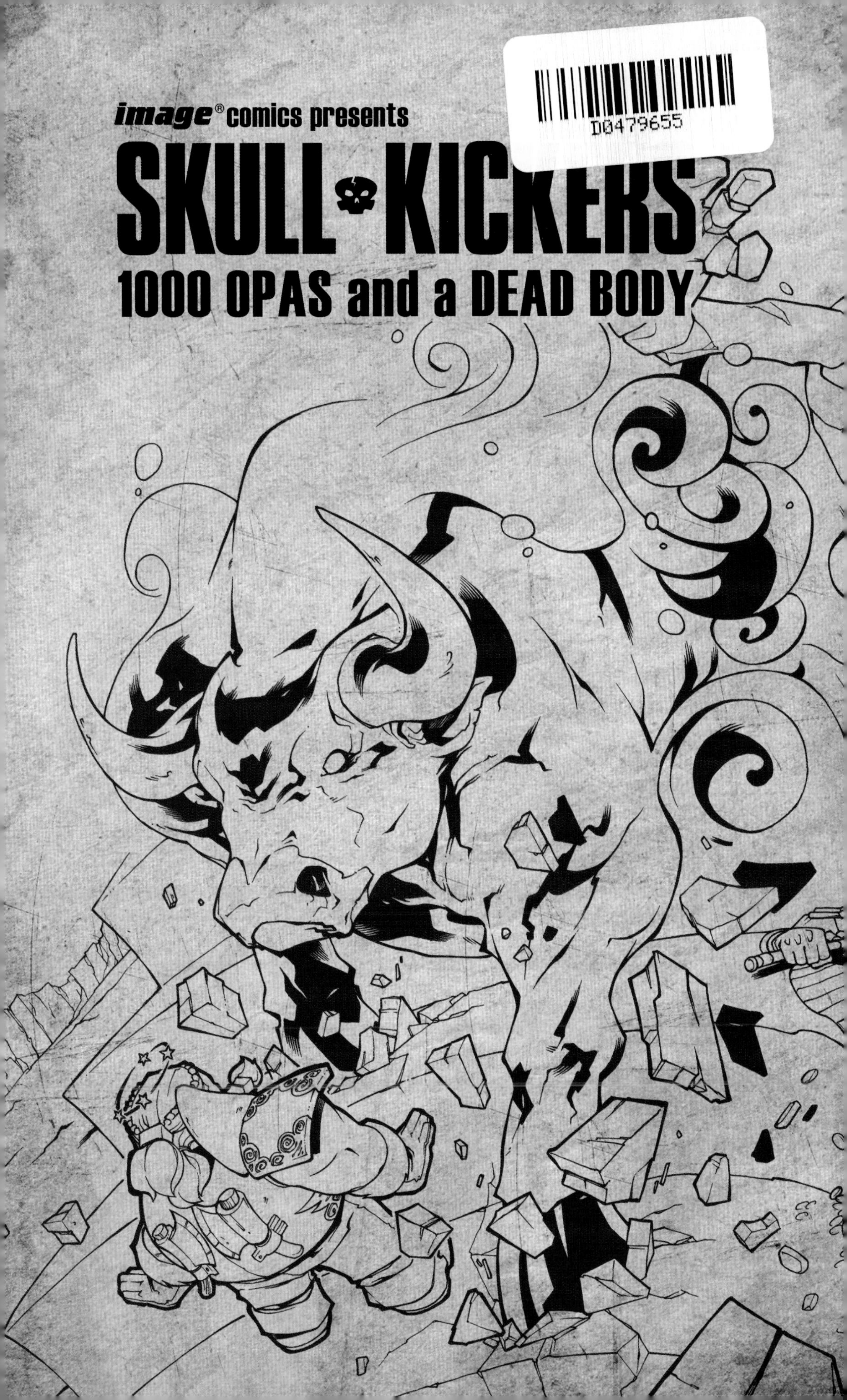

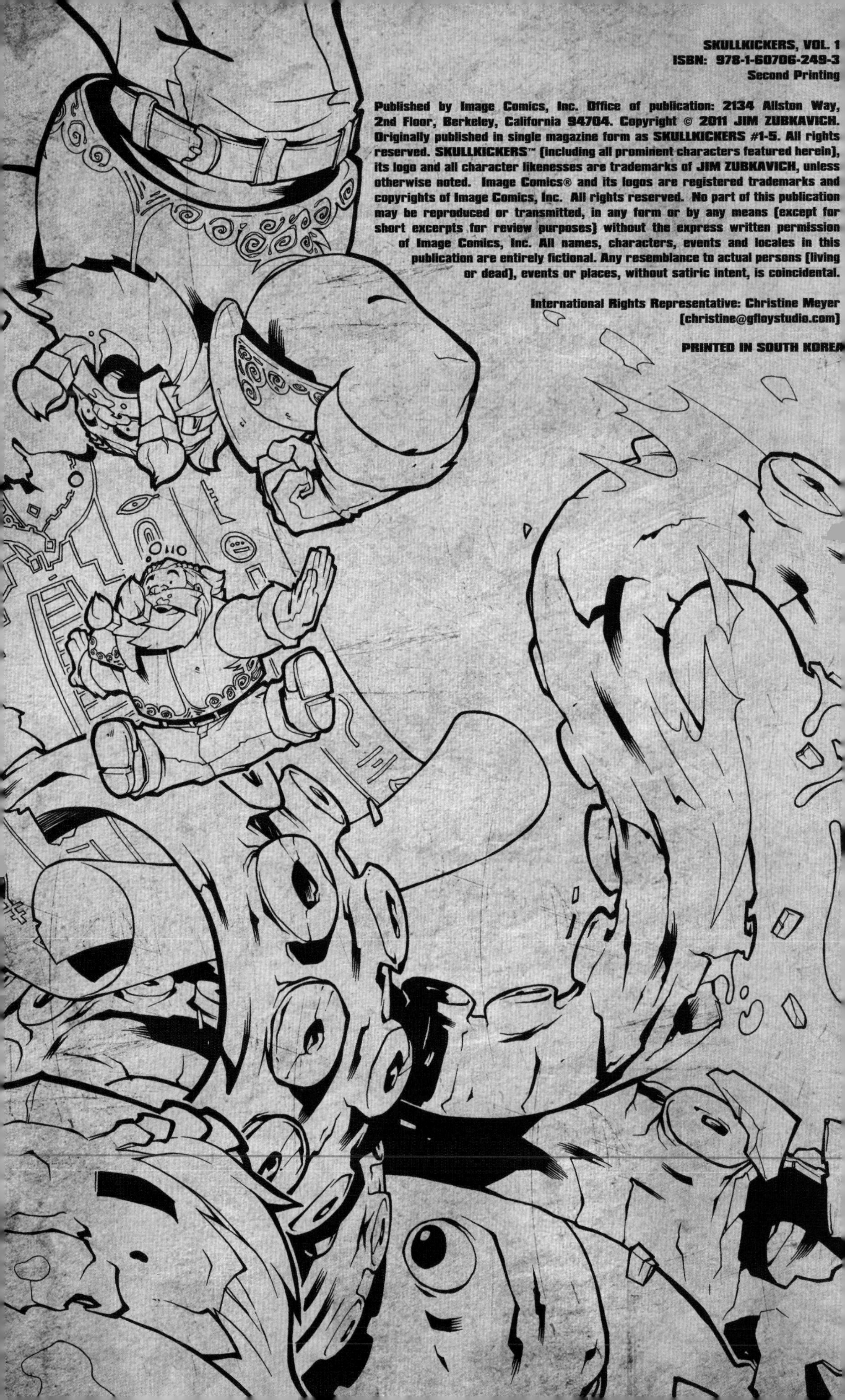

SKULLKICKERS, VOL. 1
ISBN: 978-1-60706-249-3
Second Printing

Published by Image Comics, Inc. Office of publication: 2134 Allston Way, 2nd Floor, Berkeley, California 94704. Copyright © 2011 JIM ZUBKAVICH. Originally published in single magazine form as SKULLKICKERS #1-5. All rights reserved. SKULLKICKERS™ (including all prominent characters featured herein), its logo and all character likenesses are trademarks of JIM ZUBKAVICH, unless otherwise noted. Image Comics® and its logos are registered trademarks and copyrights of Image Comics, Inc. All rights reserved. No part of this publication may be reproduced or transmitted, in any form or by any means (except for short excerpts for review purposes) without the express written permission of Image Comics, Inc. All names, characters, events and locales in this publication are entirely fictional. Any resemblance to actual persons (living or dead), events or places, without satiric intent, is coincidental.

International Rights Representative: Christine Meyer
(christine@gfloystudio.com)

PRINTED IN SOUTH KOREA

IMAGE COMICS, INC.
Robert Kirkman - chief operating officer
Erik Larsen - chief financial officer
Todd McFarlane - president
Marc Silvestri - chief executive officer
Jim Valentino - vice-president

Eric Stephenson - publisher
Todd Martinez - sales & licensing coordinator
Sarah deLaine - pr & marketing coordinator
Branwyn Bigglestone - accounts manager
Emily Miller - administrative assistant
Jamie Parreno - marketing assistant
Kevin Yuen - digital rights coordinator
Tyler Shainline - production manager
Drew Gill - art director
Jonathan Chan - senior production artist
Monica Garcia - production artist
Vincent Kukua - production artist
Jana Cook - production artist
www.imagecomics.com

Writer/ Creator
JIM ZUB

Line Art
EDWIN HUANG
(chapter 1-5)
&
CHRIS STEVENS
(chapter 1 & bonus stories)

Colors
MISTY COATS
(chapter 1-5)
&
CHRIS STEVENS
(bonus stories)

Additional Art/Art Assist
ESPEN GRUNDETJERN
TOM LIU
CRYSTAL REID
and
JIM ZUB

Lettering
MARSHALL DILLON

Issue Covers
JOY ANG,
GRUNDETJERN
EDWIN HUANG
SAEJIN OH
&
CHRIS STEVENS

Trade cover
EDWIN HUANG
&
ESPEN GRUNDETJERN.

Graphic Design
VINCENT KUKUA
&
JIM ZUB

Skullkickers Logo Design
STEVEN FINCH

SPECIAL THANKS:
CHRIS BUTCHER, CORY CASONI, JIM DEMONAKOS, RAY FAWKES, JERRY HOLKINS, STACY KING, ERIK LARSEN, RYAN OTTLEY, JOHN SHABLESKI, GAIL SIMONE, ERIC STEPHENSON, HOWARD TAYLOR, ADAM WARREN, & JOE ZUBKAVICH

Warren—

Mash a million monsters!

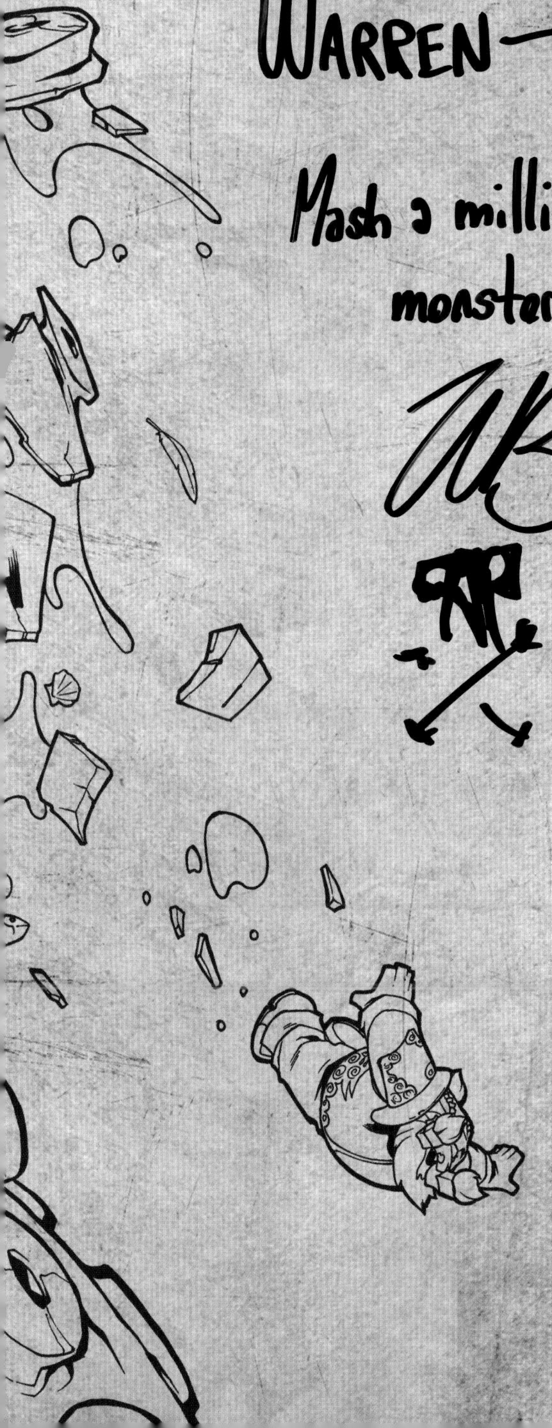

Sneaky-Sneak and Imminent Violence

As they hack and slash their way through their fantastic world of werewolves, assassins and undead servitors, the unnamed skullkickers of Skullkickers follow a long and storied tradition.

The mighty-thewed granddaddy of them all would be Robert E. Howard's Conan the Barbarian. This sorcerer-slaying, maiden-shagging freebooter establishes the anti-heroic tradition of the sword and sorcery hero. He may bring his crimsoned blade down on people and creatures who are way nastier than he is, but he's in it for the money and the conquest. And the shagging. I mentioned the shagging, right?

The nameless dwarf guy and the nameless bald guy who romp through the volume you hold in your hands certainly share a body count with Conan. But in their camaraderie and breezy humor they bear a closer kinship to Fritz Leiber's Fafhrd and the Gray Mouser. In this classic series of stories, Leiber's contrasting pair of buddy thieves leavens the sword and sorcery sub-genre with a wit unseen in Howard's ichor-spattered output.

Another classic fusion of drollery and fantasy appears in Jack Vance's stories of the Dying Earth, especially those featuring the caviling, self-seeking Cugel the Clever. He outwits and is outwitted in turn as capricious fate buffets him through a decadent, expiring world of horror and beauty.

All of these literary forebears come together in the early 70s, swirled in the grid-mapped creative stewpot that is the roleplaying game. As deeply steeped in fantasy literature as they are in military history, a pair of hardcore wargame fanatics, Gary Gygax and Dave Arneson, fuse a series of proto-roleplaying games into a brave new form they call Dungeons & Dragons. At first spreading as much by illicit third-generation photocopies as by legit copies, it rapidly grows into an entire adventure gaming hobby. In the process, it revitalizes the fantasy genre. A whole new audience hunts down its classics. They devour J.R.R. Tolkien's earnestly humanitarian epic Lord of the Rings and its many thin-blooded imitators.

But when they roll up characters and sit down at the gaming table to kill orcs and take their treasure, they behave more like Conan, Fafhrd and Cugel than the self-sacrificing Frodo and his ever-loyal Samwise. They gleefully slaughter, happily pillage, and greedily accumulate gold and experience points. They act, in short, exactly like bald guy and dwarf guy.

You don't have to know what a Con stat is, or how to choose your side in the hotly debated 3E vs. 4E divide, to appreciate the gonzo fantasy action of Skullkickers. Jim Zubkavich brilliantly channels the treasure-hoovering spirit of a thousand marathon dungeon-bashing sessions so that anyone who digs a beer joke or enjoys seeing an evil necromancer get his teeth punched in can join in the fun. Edwin Huang makes ultra-violence cute again, drawing a fantastic world a hundred times cooler than the collective imaginings of any pizza-fueled game group. From purple-cloaked dungeons perilous to scarlet-lit dens of magical diabolical, Misty Coats pops that world with vivid color. That's all you need to appreciate the lunatic fun you'll encounter as soon as you bust down the door on this foreword and charge into the pages that lie ahead.

But as Jim pushes the envelope of comic book onomatopoeia into exclamations that sound suspiciously like the whisperings of an offstage Dungeon Master, or Edwin brings hallucinatory surrealism to what is clearly a narrowly-rolled poison save (dwarves get +2, you know), there's a history at work here. A history that smells headily of decaying pulp and sounds like the plastic clattering of a d20 across a tabletop.

But to Hades with all that, warriors! Let's find some monsters, kill them, and take their stuff! Then to the tavern, to celebrate with ale and wenches!

--Robin Laws
   January 2011

Writer and game designer Robin D. Laws is the force behind such RPG games as Feng Shui, The Dying Earth Roleplaying Game, HeroQuest, The Esoterrorists and Ashen Stars.

D&D players know his work on various supplements, including sections of the Dungeon Master's Guide 2 for both third and fourth editions of that game.

CHAPTER ONE

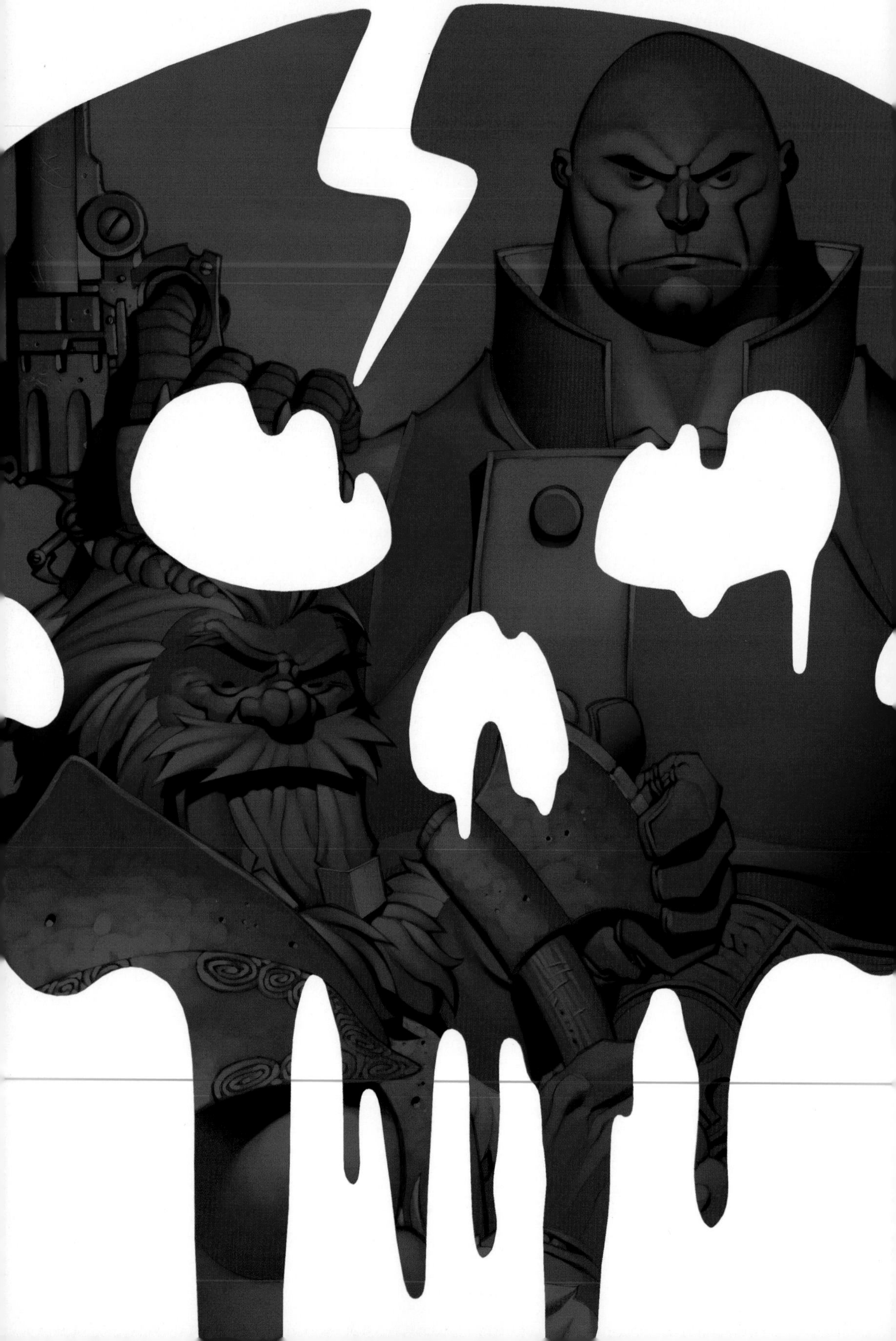

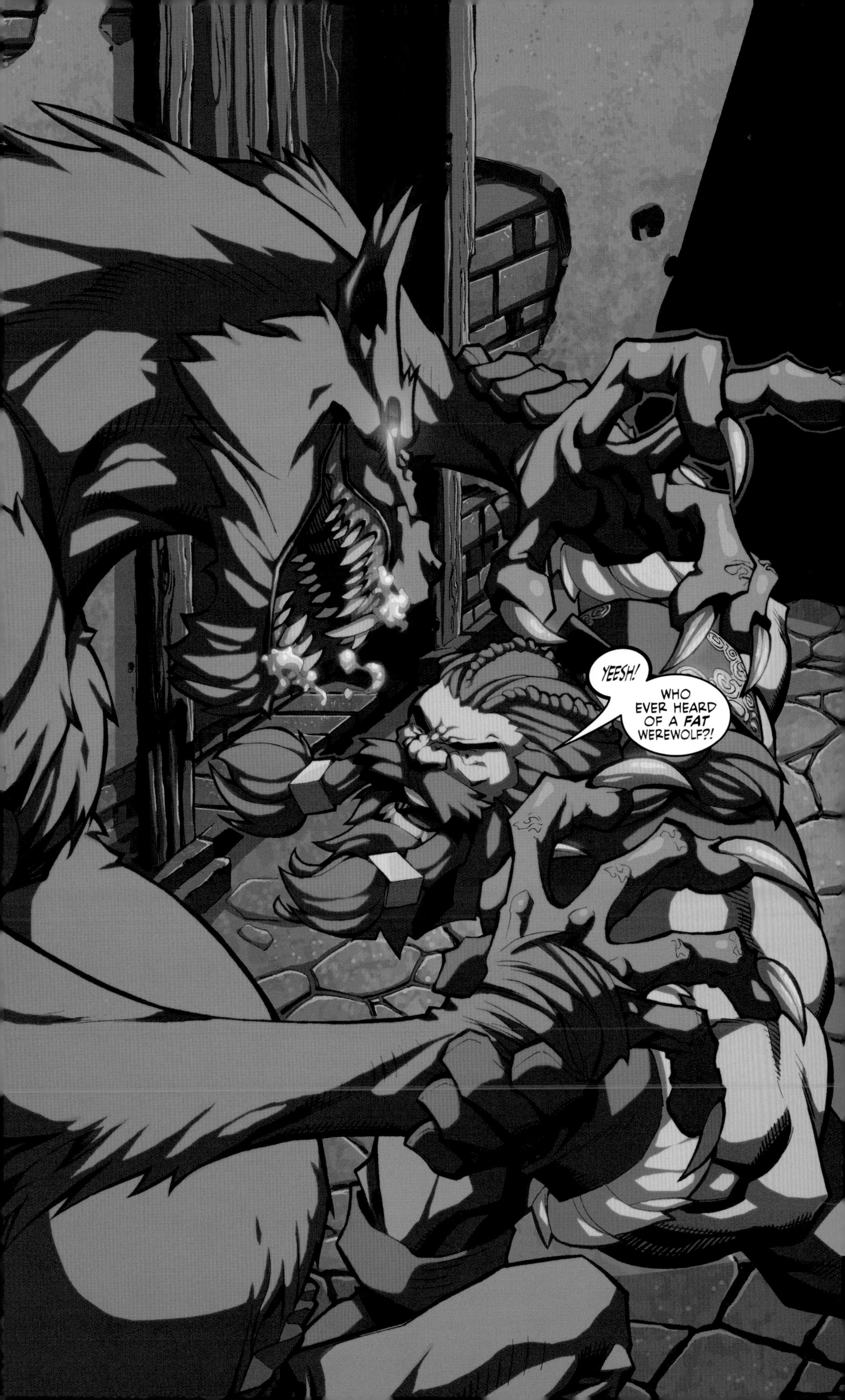
YEESH!
WHO EVER HEARD OF A FAT WEREWOLF?!

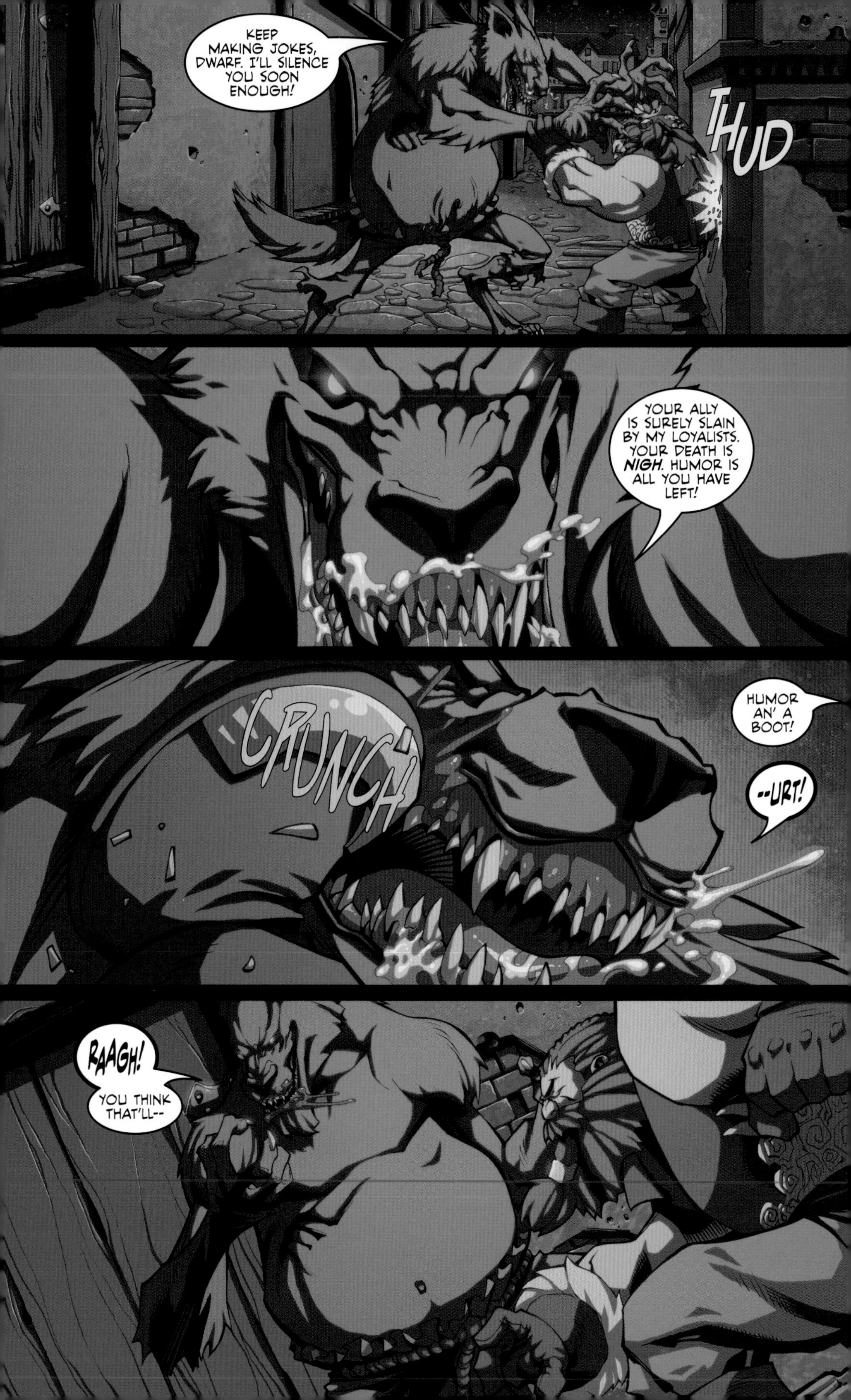
KEEP MAKING JOKES, DWARF. I'LL SILENCE YOU SOON ENOUGH!
THUD
YOUR ALLY IS SURELY SLAIN BY MY LOYALISTS. YOUR DEATH IS *NIGH*. HUMOR IS ALL YOU HAVE LEFT!
CRUNCH
HUMOR AN' A BOOT!
--URT!
RAAGH!
YOU THINK THAT'LL--

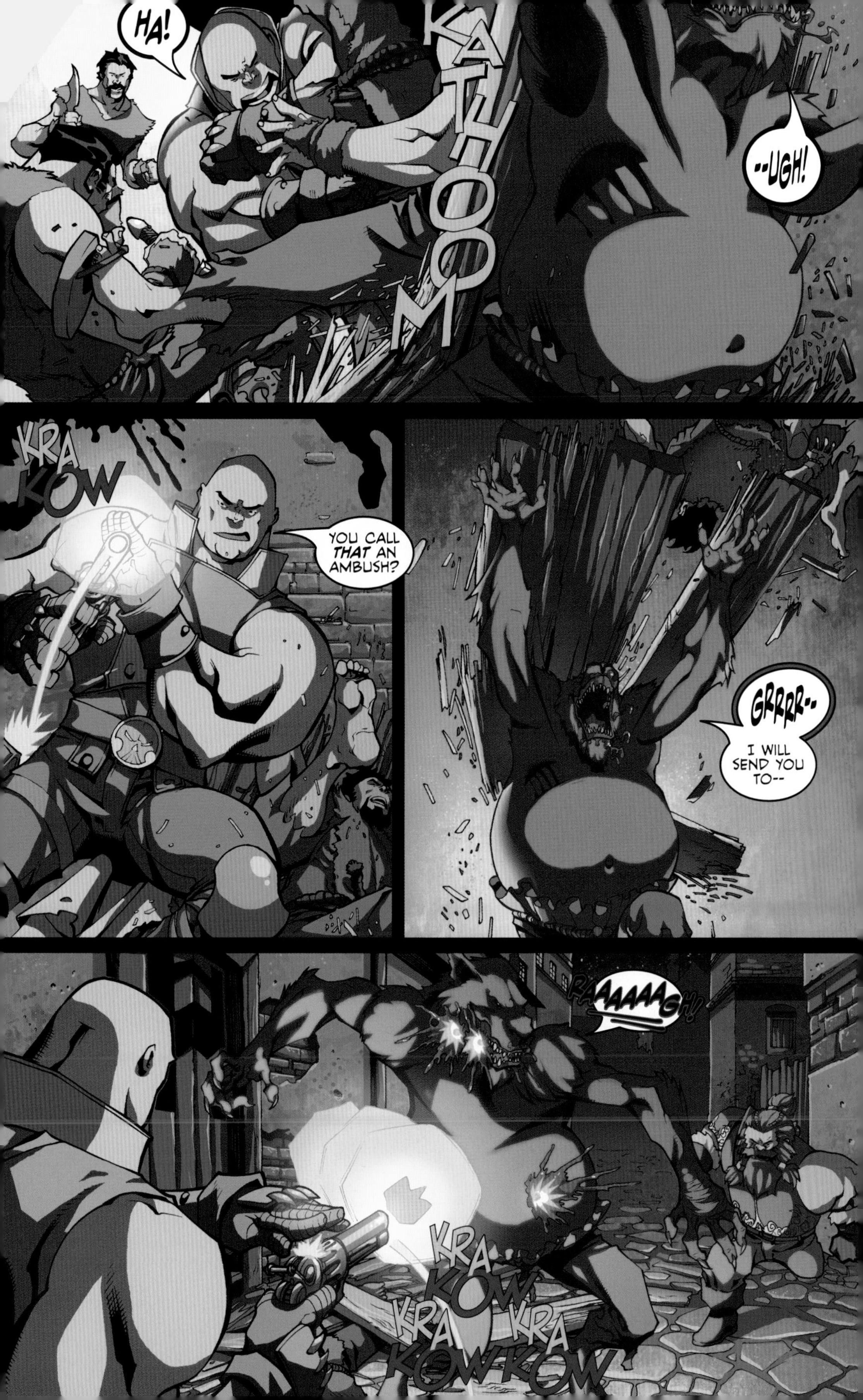
HA!
KATHOOOM
--UGH!
KRA KOW
YOU CALL *THAT* AN AMBUSH?
GRRRR--
I WILL SEND YOU TO--
RAAAAAAGH!
KRA KOW
KRA KOW
KRA KOW

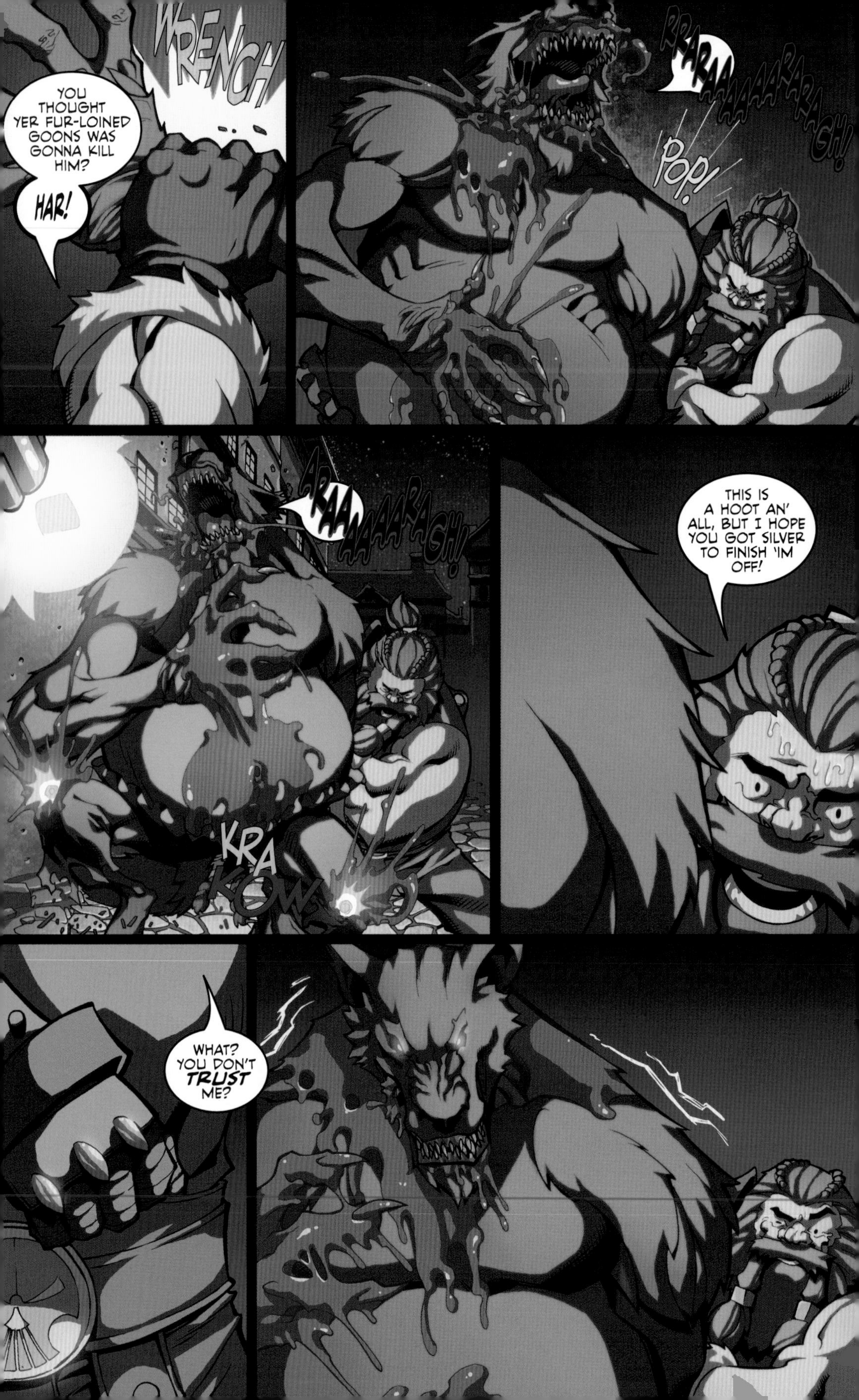
WRENCH
YOU THOUGHT YER FUR-LOINED GOONS WAS GONNA KILL HIM?
HAR!
RRARAAAAAAAARAAGH!
POP!
ARAAAAAAARAGH!
KRA KOW
THIS IS A HOOT AN' ALL, BUT I HOPE YOU GOT SILVER TO FINISH 'IM OFF!
WHAT? YOU DON'T TRUST ME?

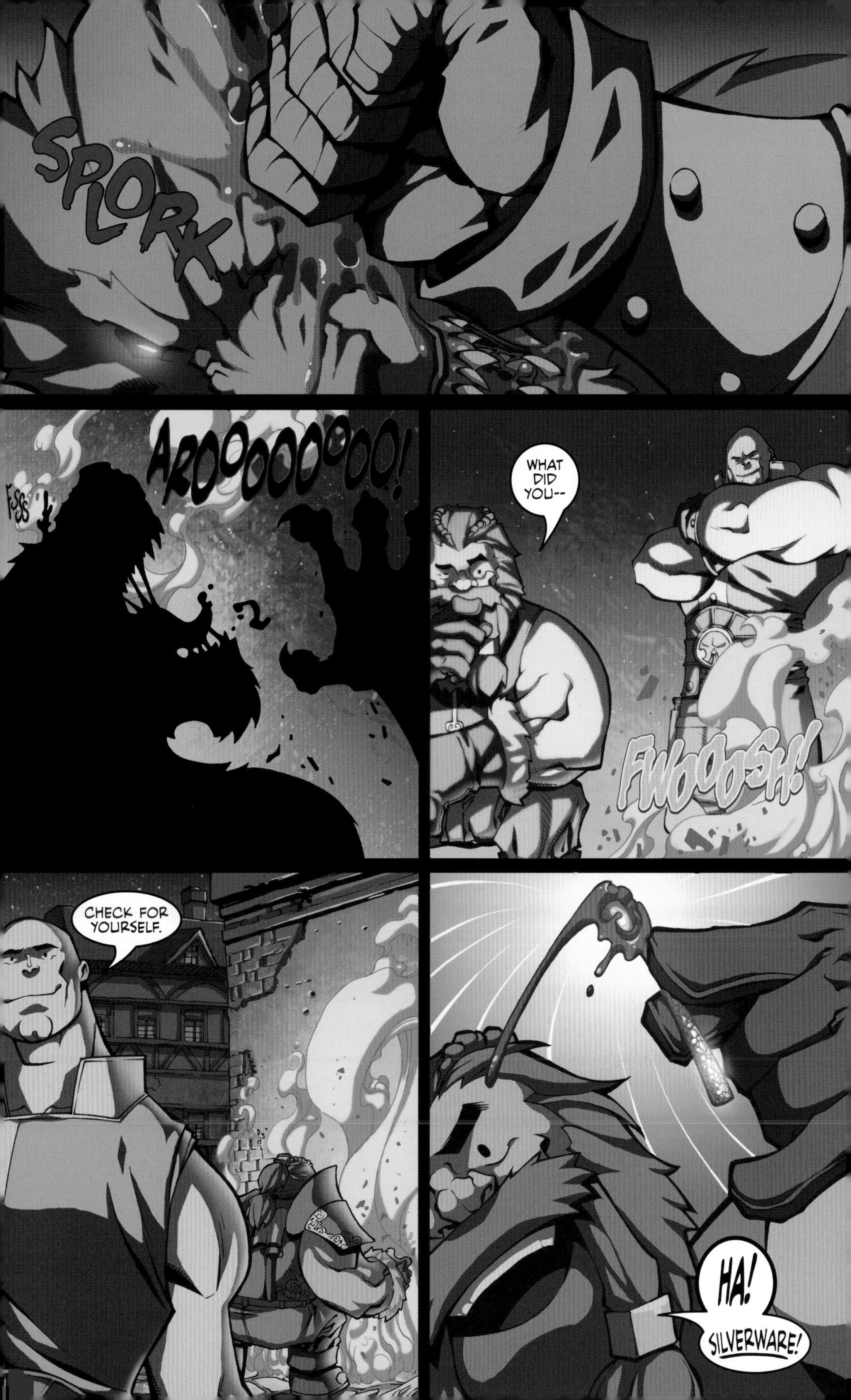
SPLORK
AROOOOOOOOO!
FSSS
WHAT DID YOU--
FWOOOSH!
CHECK FOR YOURSELF.
HA!
SILVERWARE!

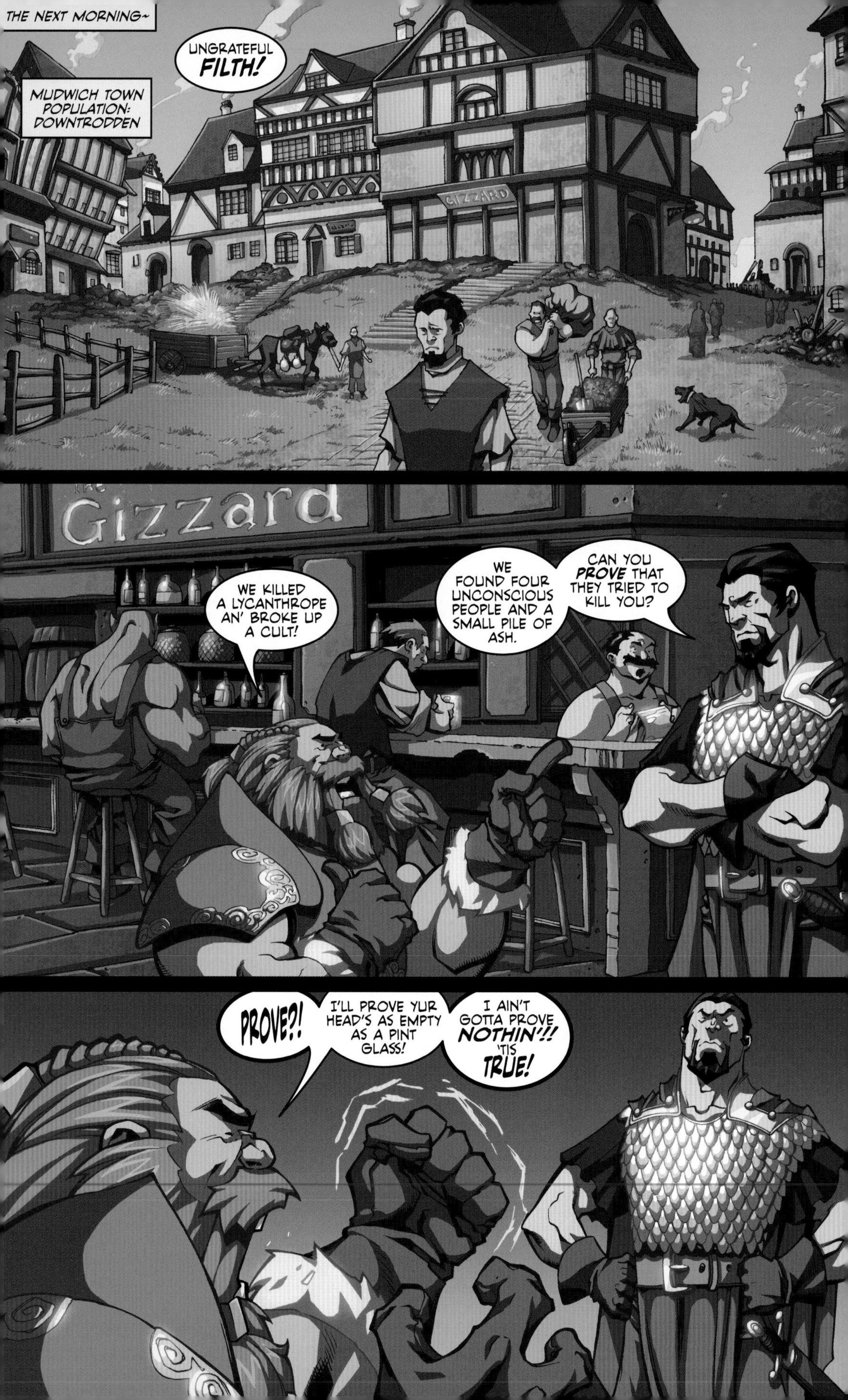
THE NEXT MORNING~
MUDWICH TOWN
POPULATION:
DOWNTRODDEN
UNGRATEFUL
FILTH!
GIZZARD
The Gizzard
WE KILLED A LYCANTHROPE AN' BROKE UP A CULT!
WE FOUND FOUR UNCONSCIOUS PEOPLE AND A SMALL PILE OF ASH.
CAN YOU PROVE THAT THEY TRIED TO KILL YOU?
PROVE?!
I'LL PROVE YUR HEAD'S AS EMPTY AS A PINT GLASS!
I AIN'T GOTTA PROVE NOTHIN'!! 'TIS TRUE!

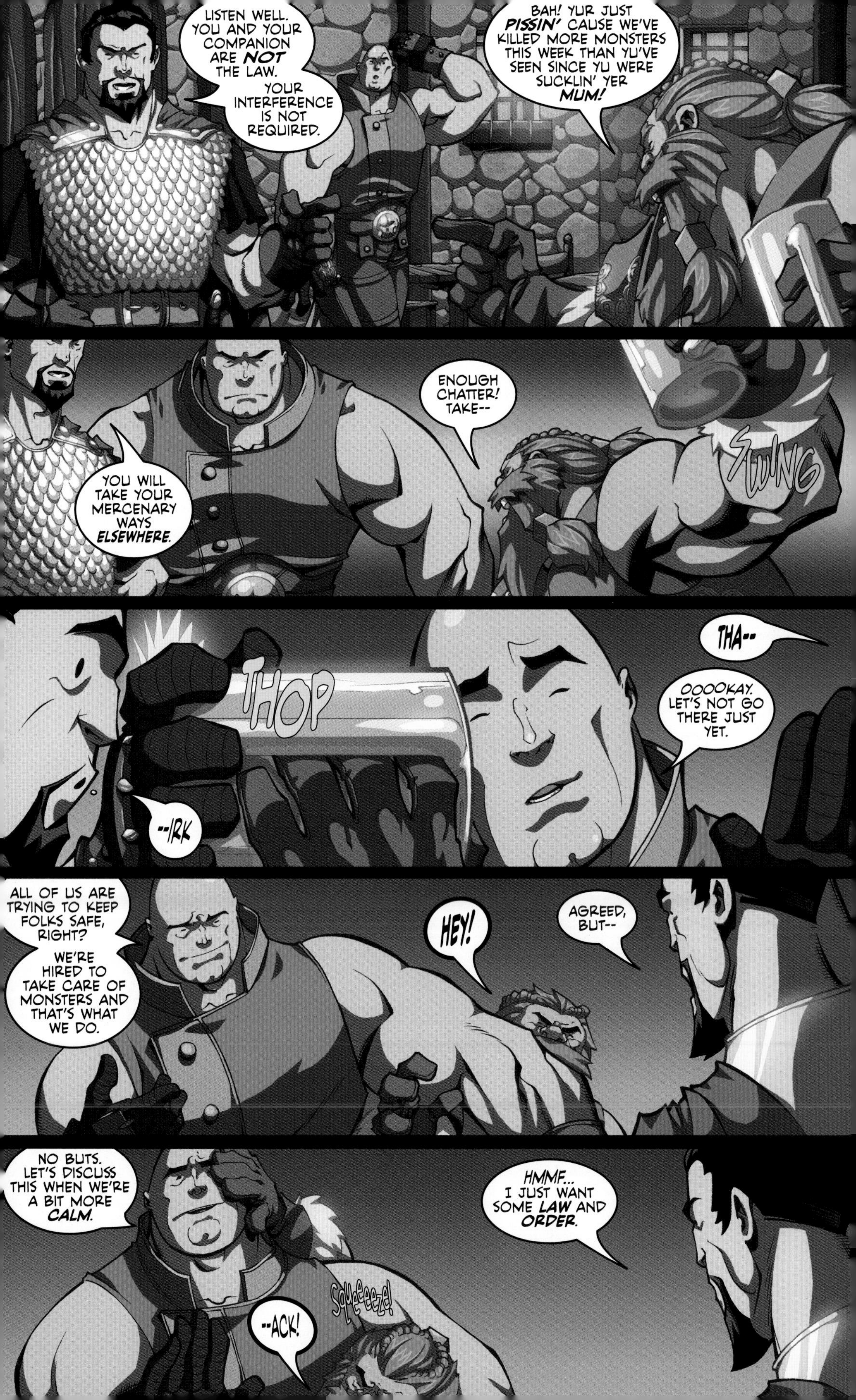
LISTEN WELL. YOU AND YOUR COMPANION ARE NOT THE LAW.
YOUR INTERFERENCE IS NOT REQUIRED.
BAH! YUR JUST PISSIN' CAUSE WE'VE KILLED MORE MONSTERS THIS WEEK THAN YU'VE SEEN SINCE YU WERE SUCKLIN' YER MUM!
YOU WILL TAKE YOUR MERCENARY WAYS ELSEWHERE.
ENOUGH CHATTER! TAKE--
SWING
THOP
THA--
--IRK
OOOOKAY. LET'S NOT GO THERE JUST YET.
ALL OF US ARE TRYING TO KEEP FOLKS SAFE, RIGHT?
WE'RE HIRED TO TAKE CARE OF MONSTERS AND THAT'S WHAT WE DO.
HEY!
AGREED, BUT--
NO BUTS. LET'S DISCUSS THIS WHEN WE'RE A BIT MORE CALM.
HMMF... I JUST WANT SOME LAW AND ORDER.
Squeeeeze!
--ACK!

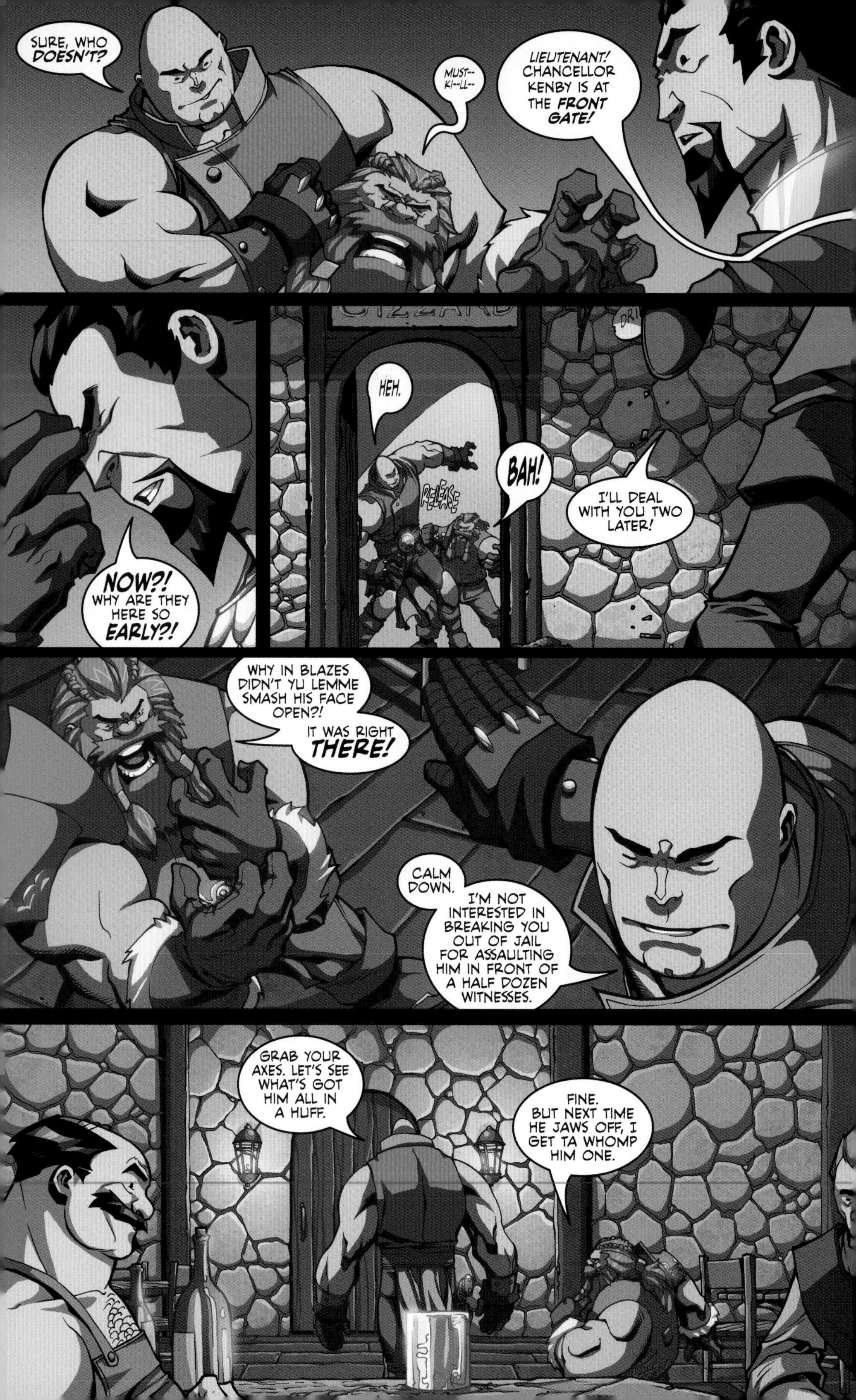
SURE, WHO DOESN'T?
MUST-- KI--LL--
LIEUTENANT! CHANCELLOR KENBY IS AT THE FRONT GATE!
NOW?! WHY ARE THEY HERE SO EARLY?!
HEH.
RELEASE
BAH!
I'LL DEAL WITH YOU TWO LATER!
WHY IN BLAZES DIDN'T YU LEMME SMASH HIS FACE OPEN?!
IT WAS RIGHT THERE!
CALM DOWN.
I'M NOT INTERESTED IN BREAKING YOU OUT OF JAIL FOR ASSAULTING HIM IN FRONT OF A HALF DOZEN WITNESSES.
GRAB YOUR AXES. LET'S SEE WHAT'S GOT HIM ALL IN A HUFF.
FINE. BUT NEXT TIME HE JAWS OFF, I GET TA WHOMP HIM ONE.

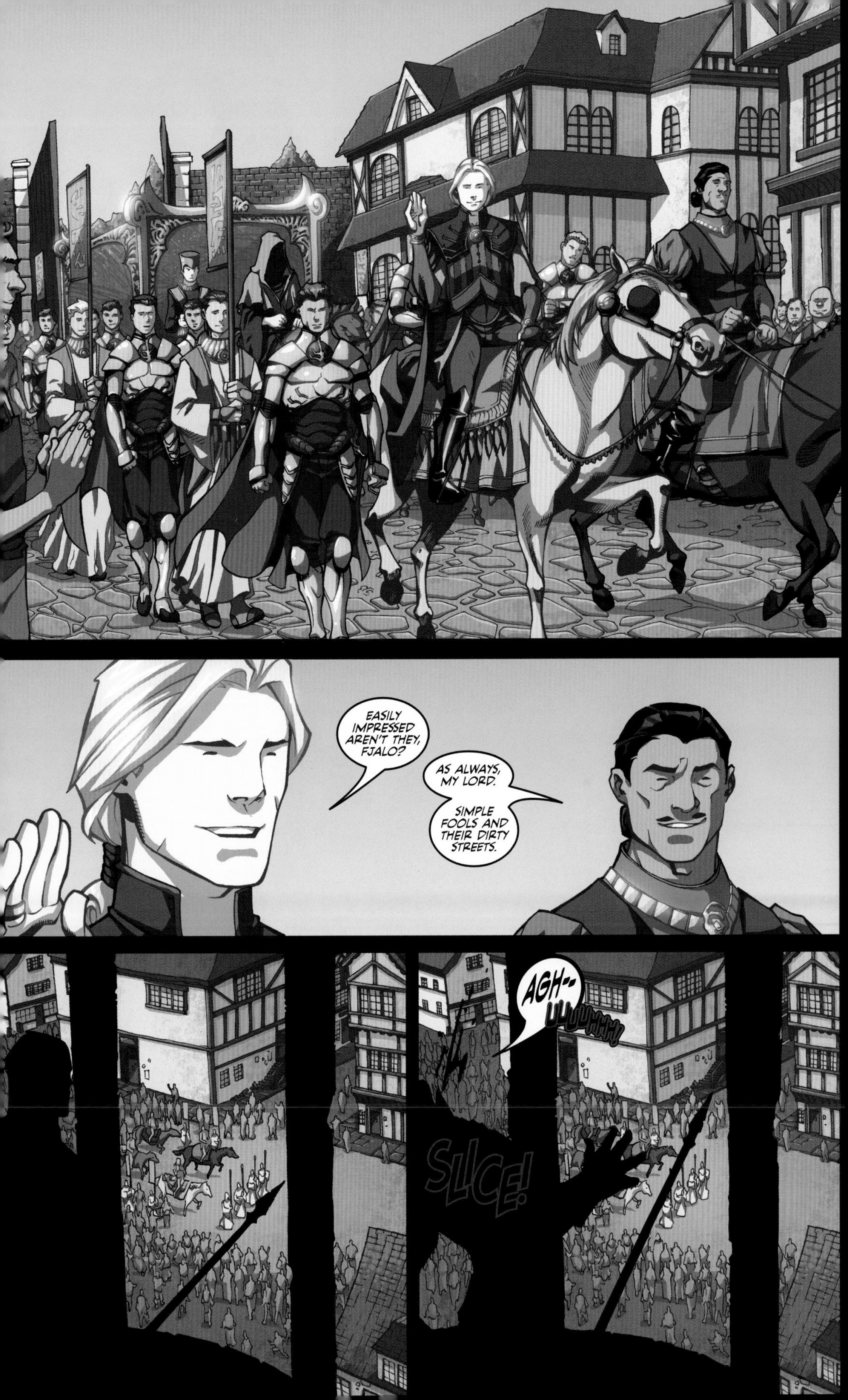
EASILY IMPRESSED AREN'T THEY, FJALO?
AS ALWAYS, MY LORD.
SIMPLE FOOLS AND THEIR DIRTY STREETS.
AGH--UUUUHHH!
SLICE!

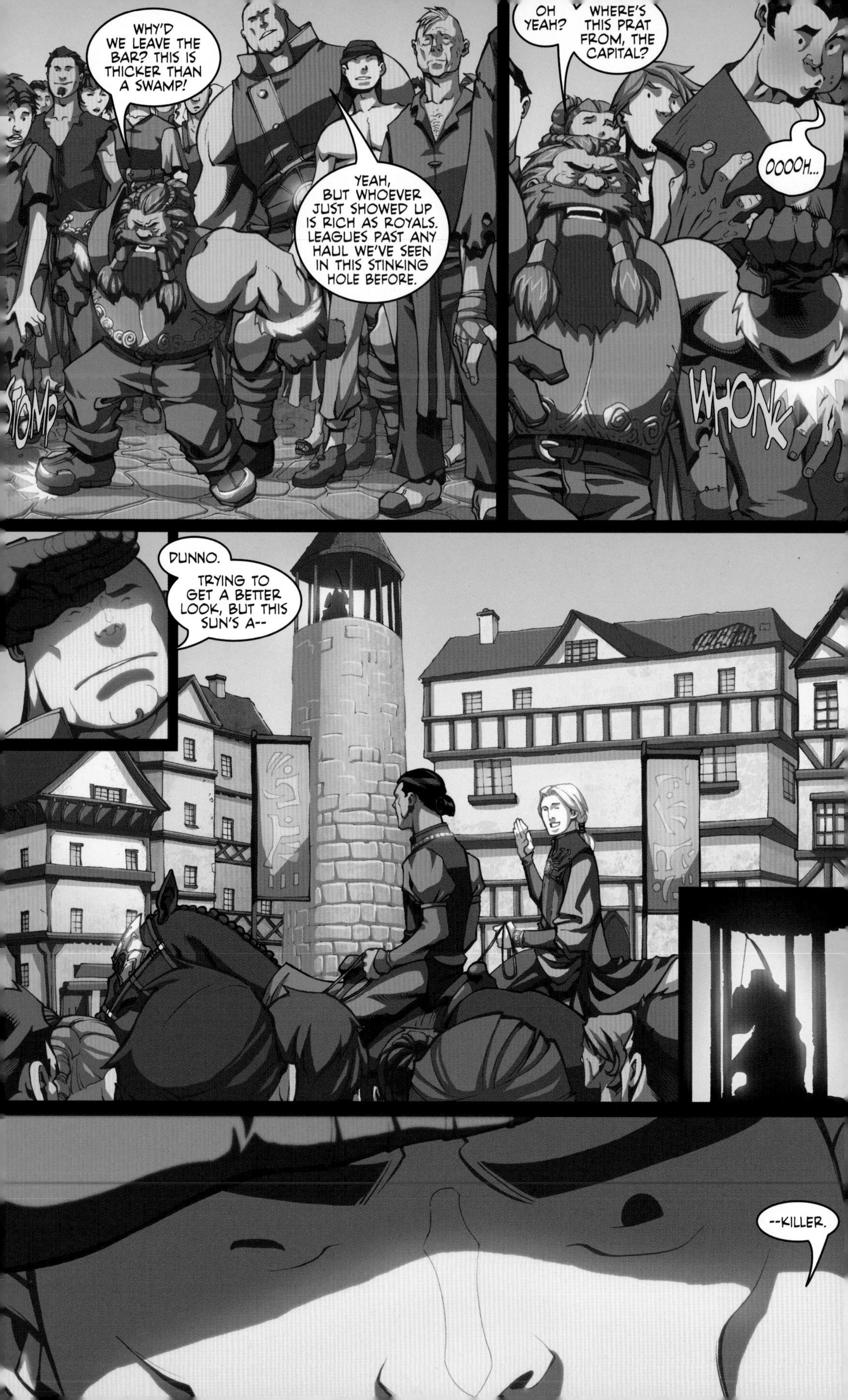
WHY'D WE LEAVE THE BAR? THIS IS THICKER THAN A SWAMP!
YEAH, BUT WHOEVER JUST SHOWED UP IS RICH AS ROYALS. LEAGUES PAST ANY HAUL WE'VE SEEN IN THIS STINKING HOLE BEFORE.
STOMP
OH YEAH?
WHERE'S THIS PRAT FROM, THE CAPITAL?
OOOOH...
WHONK
DUNNO.
TRYING TO GET A BETTER LOOK, BUT THIS SUN'S A--
--KILLER.

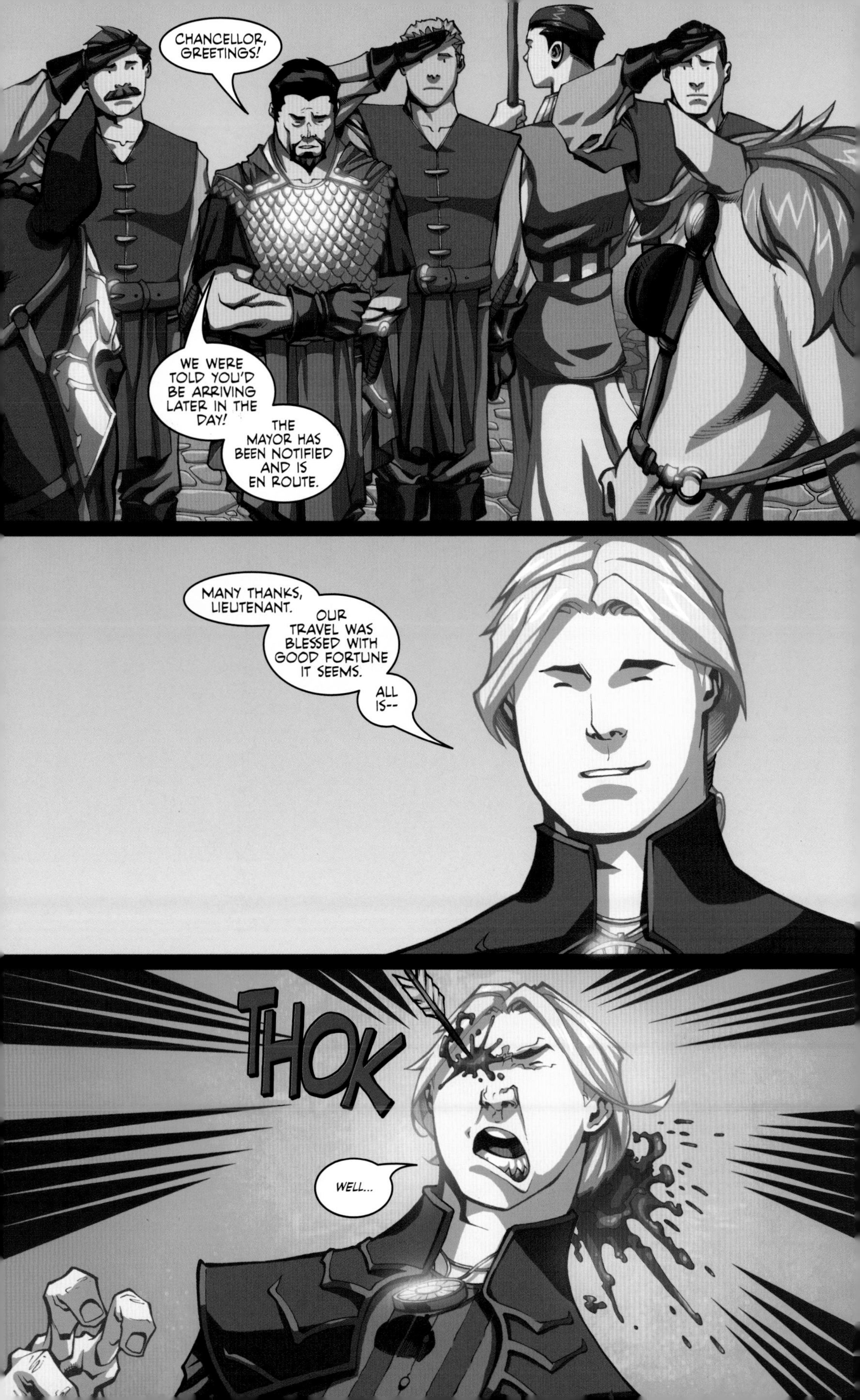
CHANCELLOR, GREETINGS!
WE WERE TOLD YOU'D BE ARRIVING LATER IN THE DAY!
THE MAYOR HAS BEEN NOTIFIED AND IS EN ROUTE.
MANY THANKS, LIEUTENANT.
OUR TRAVEL WAS BLESSED WITH GOOD FORTUNE IT SEEMS.
ALL IS--
THOK
WELL...

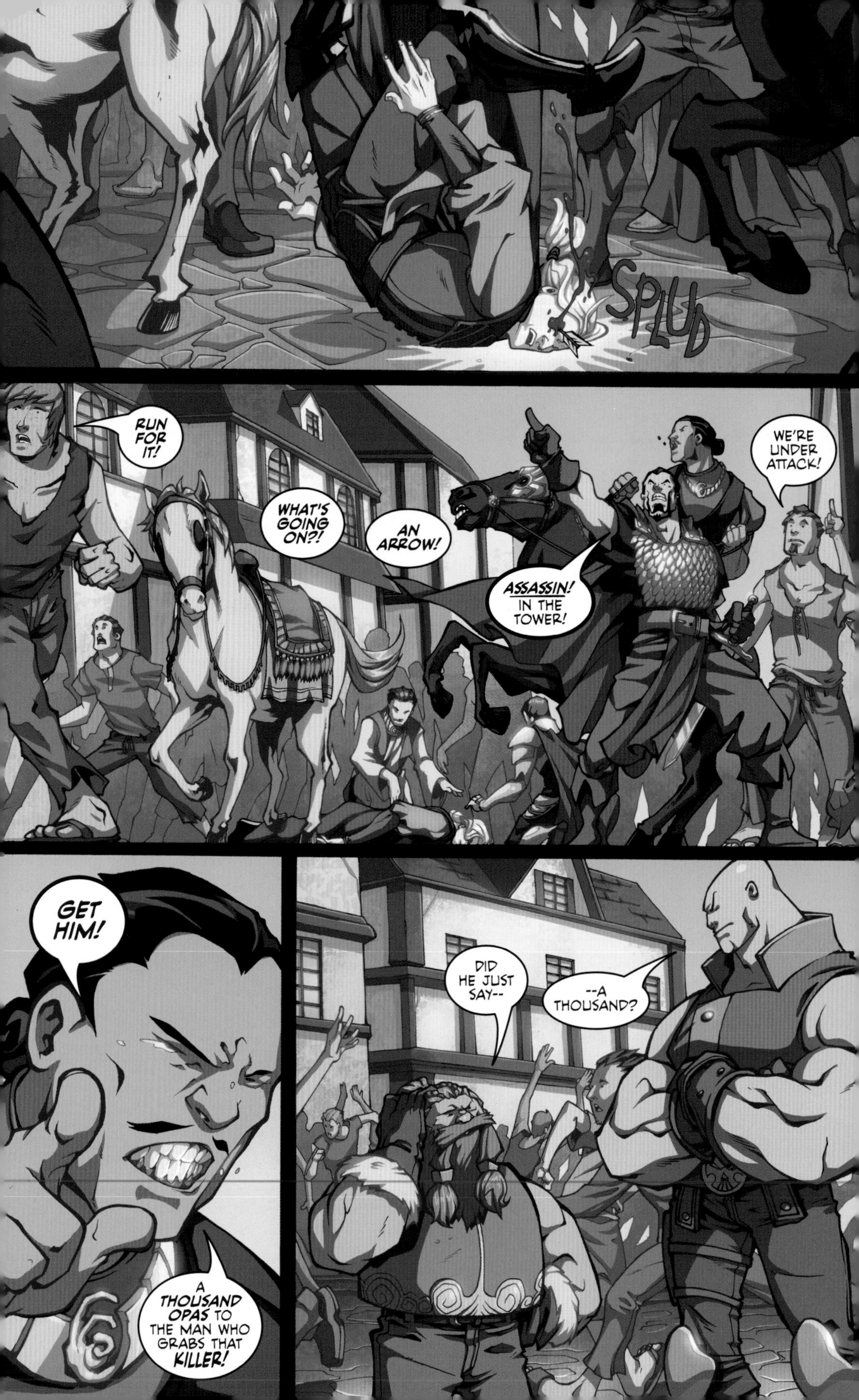
SPLUD
RUN FOR IT!
WHAT'S GOING ON?!
AN ARROW!
ASSASSIN! IN THE TOWER!
WE'RE UNDER ATTACK!
GET HIM!
A THOUSAND OPAS TO THE MAN WHO GRABS THAT KILLER!
DID HE JUST SAY--
--A THOUSAND?

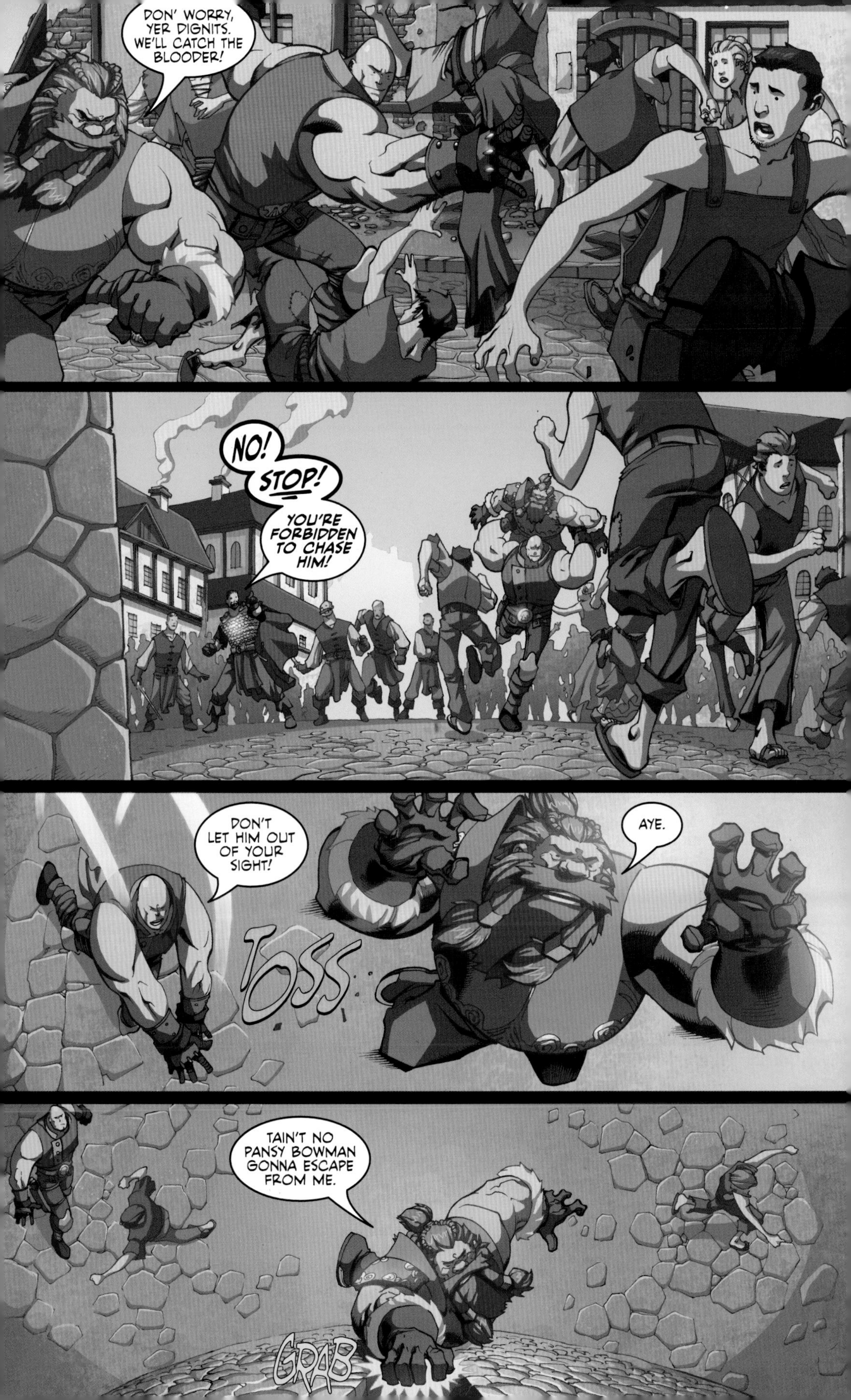
DON' WORRY, YER DIGNITS. WE'LL CATCH THE BLOODER!
NO!
STOP!
YOU'RE FORBIDDEN TO CHASE HIM!
DON'T LET HIM OUT OF YOUR SIGHT!
AYE.
TOSS
TAIN'T NO PANSY BOWMAN GONNA ESCAPE FROM ME.
GRAB

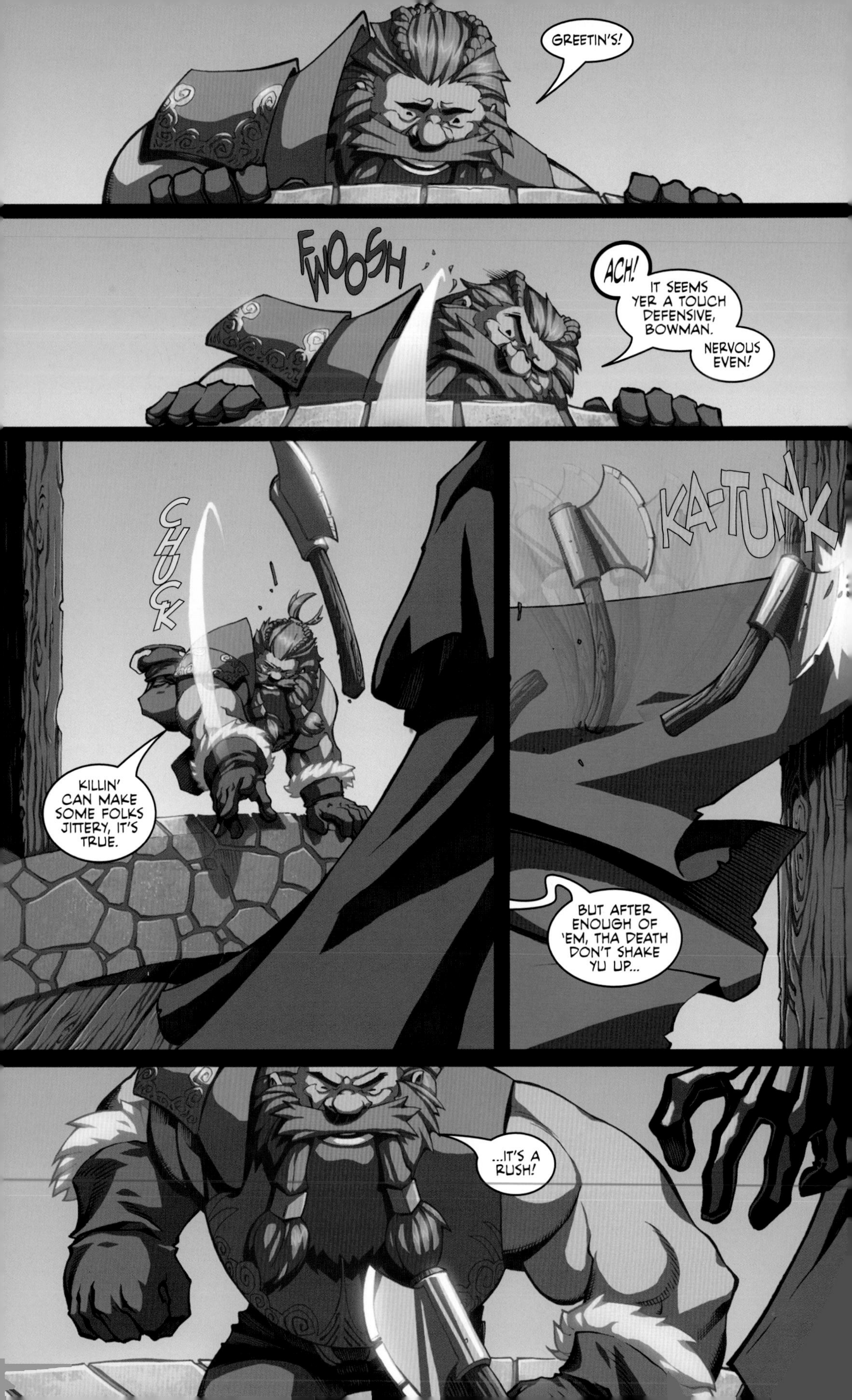
GREETIN'S!
FWOOSH
ACH! IT SEEMS YER A TOUCH DEFENSIVE, BOWMAN.
NERVOUS EVEN!
CHUCK
KILLIN' CAN MAKE SOME FOLKS JITTERY, IT'S TRUE.
KA-TUNK
BUT AFTER ENOUGH OF 'EM, THA DEATH DON'T SHAKE YU UP...
...IT'S A RUSH!

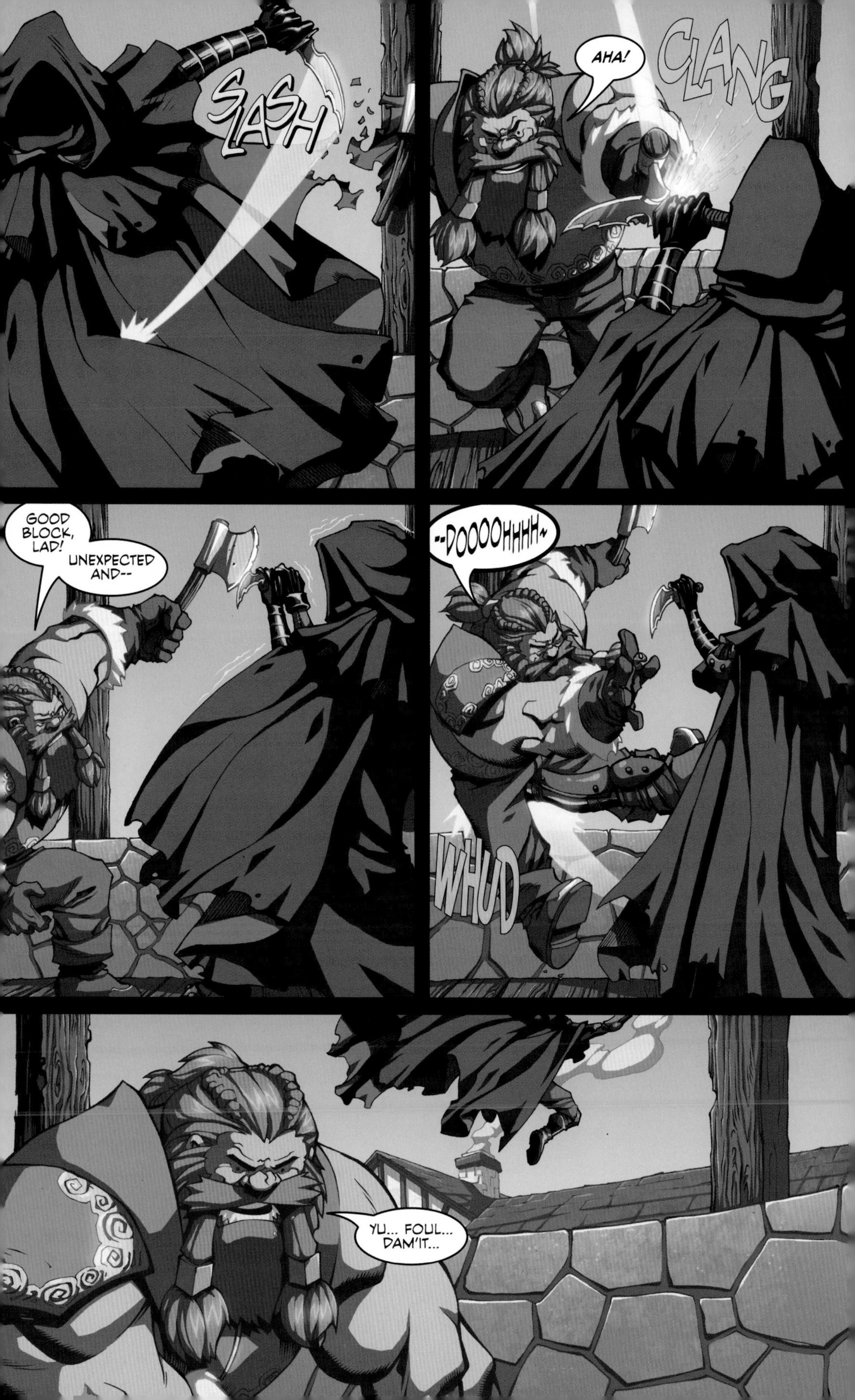
SLASH
AHA!
CLANG
GOOD BLOCK, LAD!
UNEXPECTED AND--
--DOOOOHHHH~
WHUD
YU... FOUL... DAM'IT...

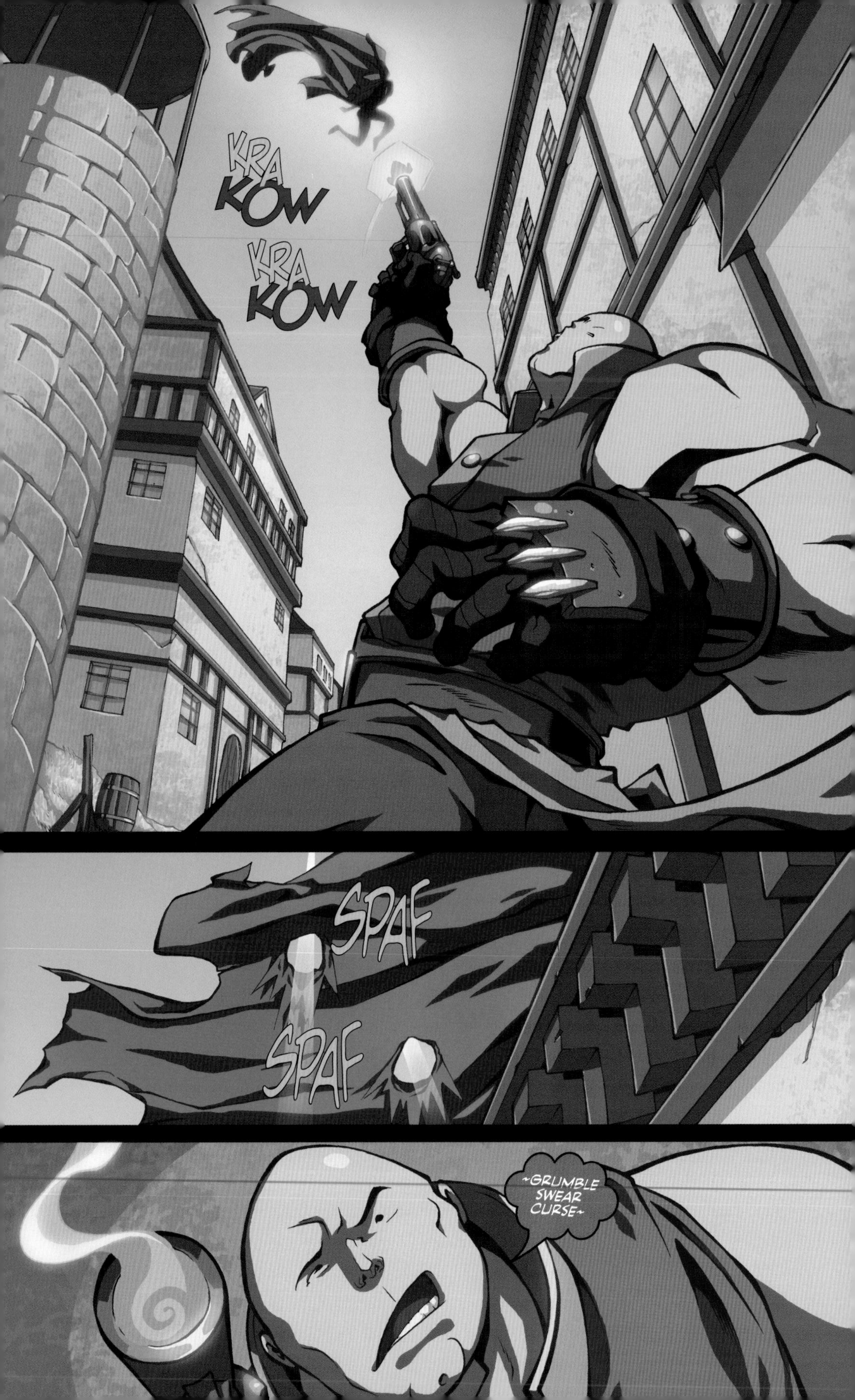
KRA KOW
KRA KOW
SPAF
SPAF
~GRUMBLE SWEAR CURSE~

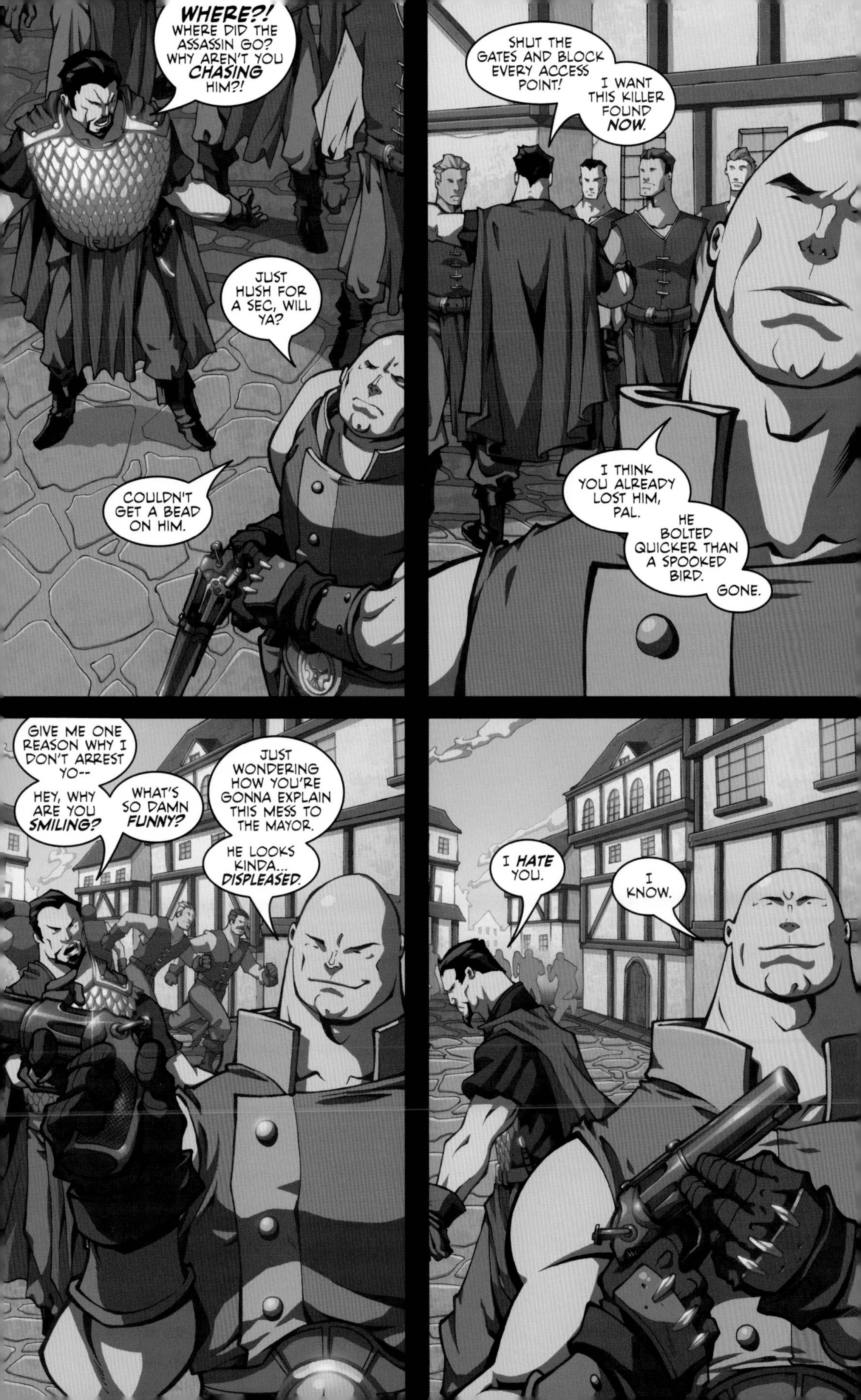
WHERE?! WHERE DID THE ASSASSIN GO? WHY AREN'T YOU CHASING HIM?!
JUST HUSH FOR A SEC, WILL YA?
COULDN'T GET A BEAD ON HIM.
SHUT THE GATES AND BLOCK EVERY ACCESS POINT!
I WANT THIS KILLER FOUND NOW.
I THINK YOU ALREADY LOST HIM, PAL.
HE BOLTED QUICKER THAN A SPOOKED BIRD.
GONE.
GIVE ME ONE REASON WHY I DON'T ARREST YO--
HEY, WHY ARE YOU SMILING?
WHAT'S SO DAMN FUNNY?
JUST WONDERING HOW YOU'RE GONNA EXPLAIN THIS MESS TO THE MAYOR.
HE LOOKS KINDA... DISPLEASED.
I HATE YOU.
I KNOW.

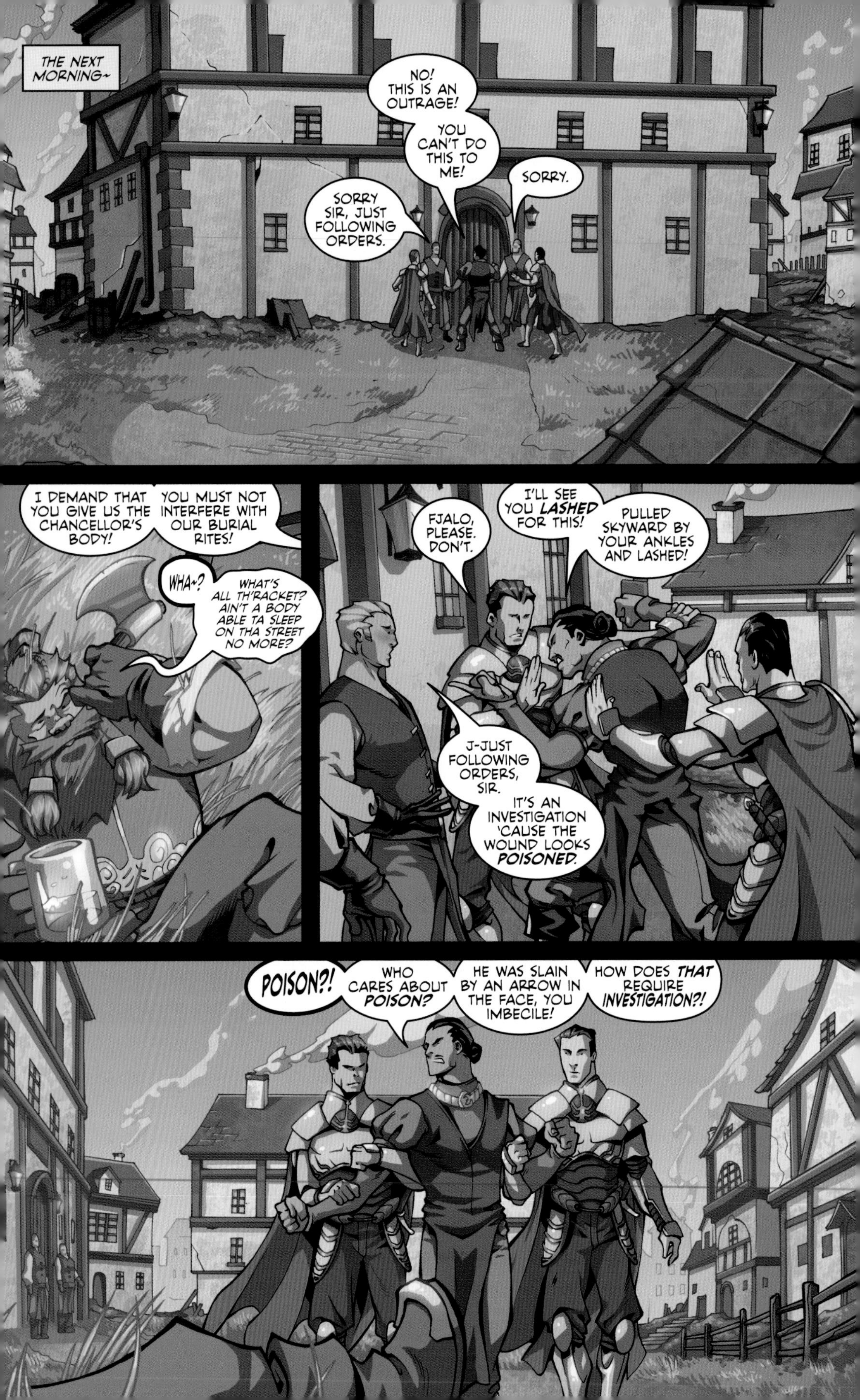
THE NEXT MORNING~
NO! THIS IS AN OUTRAGE!
YOU CAN'T DO THIS TO ME!
SORRY SIR, JUST FOLLOWING ORDERS.
SORRY.
I DEMAND THAT YOU GIVE US THE CHANCELLOR'S BODY!
YOU MUST NOT INTERFERE WITH OUR BURIAL RITES!
WHA~?
WHAT'S ALL TH'RACKET? AIN'T A BODY ABLE TA SLEEP ON THA STREET NO MORE?
FJALO, PLEASE. DON'T.
I'LL SEE YOU LASHED FOR THIS!
PULLED SKYWARD BY YOUR ANKLES AND LASHED!
J-JUST FOLLOWING ORDERS, SIR.
IT'S AN INVESTIGATION 'CAUSE THE WOUND LOOKS POISONED.
POISON?!
WHO CARES ABOUT POISON?
HE WAS SLAIN BY AN ARROW IN THE FACE, YOU IMBECILE!
HOW DOES THAT REQUIRE INVESTIGATION?!

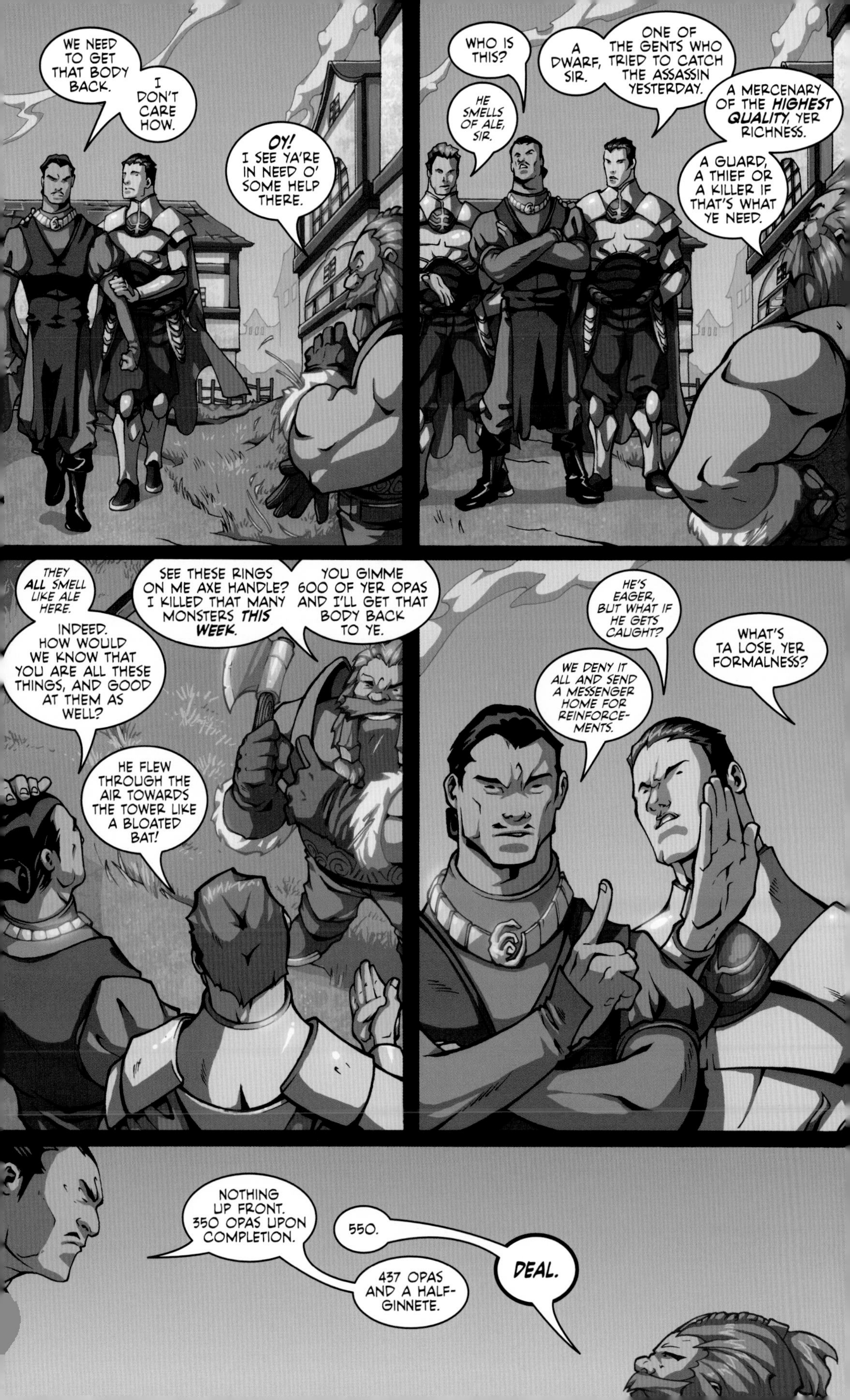

WE NEED TO GET THAT BODY BACK.
I DON'T CARE HOW.
OY! I SEE YA'RE IN NEED O' SOME HELP THERE.
WHO IS THIS?
HE SMELLS OF ALE, SIR.
A DWARF, SIR.
ONE OF THE GENTS WHO TRIED TO CATCH THE ASSASSIN YESTERDAY.
A MERCENARY OF THE HIGHEST QUALITY, YER RICHNESS.
A GUARD, A THIEF OR A KILLER IF THAT'S WHAT YE NEED.
THEY ALL SMELL LIKE ALE HERE.
INDEED. HOW WOULD WE KNOW THAT YOU ARE ALL THESE THINGS, AND GOOD AT THEM AS WELL?
SEE THESE RINGS ON ME AXE HANDLE? I KILLED THAT MANY MONSTERS THIS WEEK.
YOU GIMME 600 OF YER OPAS AND I'LL GET THAT BODY BACK TO YE.
HE FLEW THROUGH THE AIR TOWARDS THE TOWER LIKE A BLOATED BAT!
HE'S EAGER, BUT WHAT IF HE GETS CAUGHT?
WE DENY IT ALL AND SEND A MESSENGER HOME FOR REINFORCE-MENTS.
WHAT'S TA LOSE, YER FORMALNESS?
NOTHING UP FRONT. 350 OPAS UPON COMPLETION.
550.
437 OPAS AND A HALF-GINNETE.
DEAL.

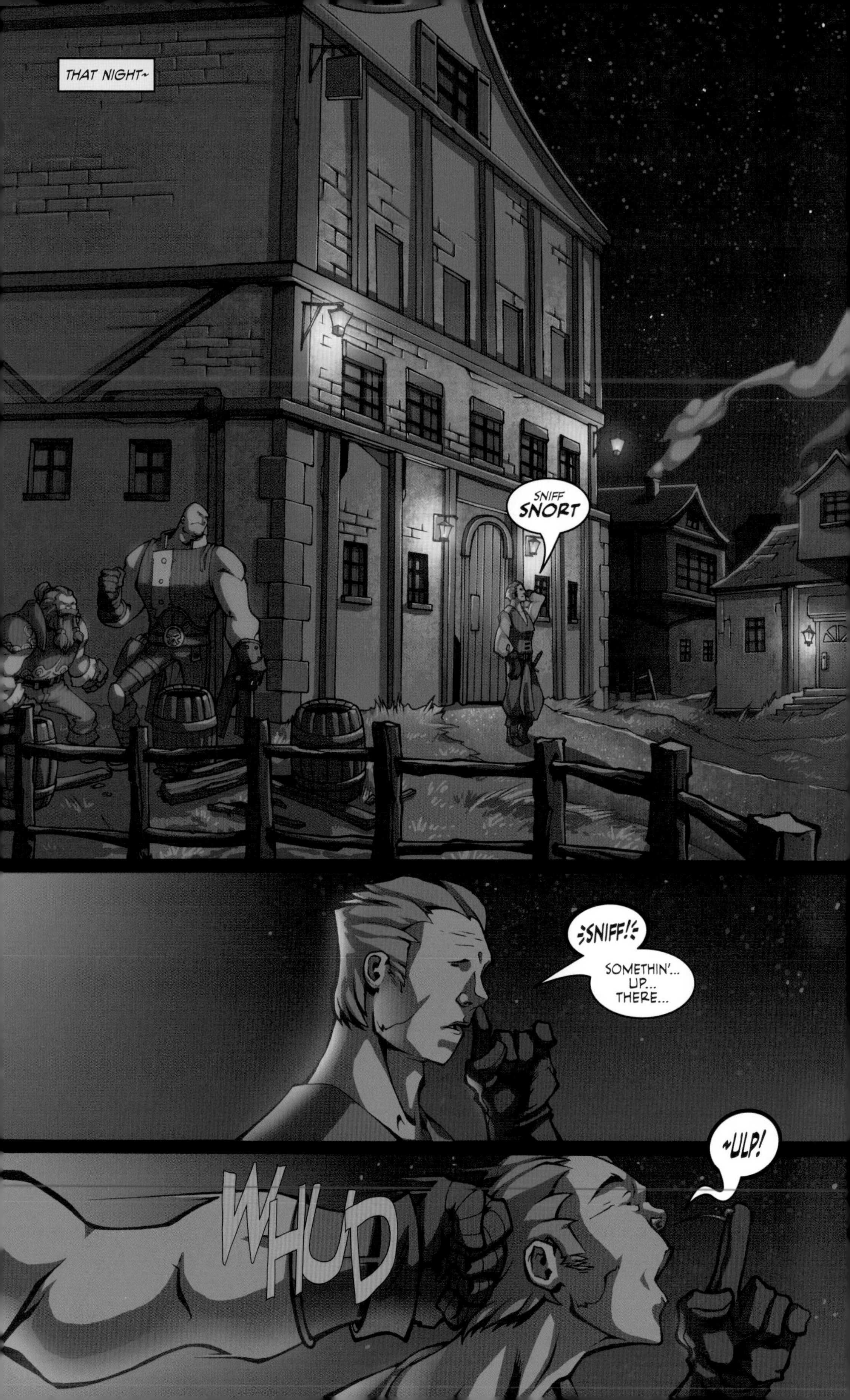
THAT NIGHT~
SNIFF SNORT
SNIFF!
SOMETHIN'... UP... THERE...
WHUD
~ULP!

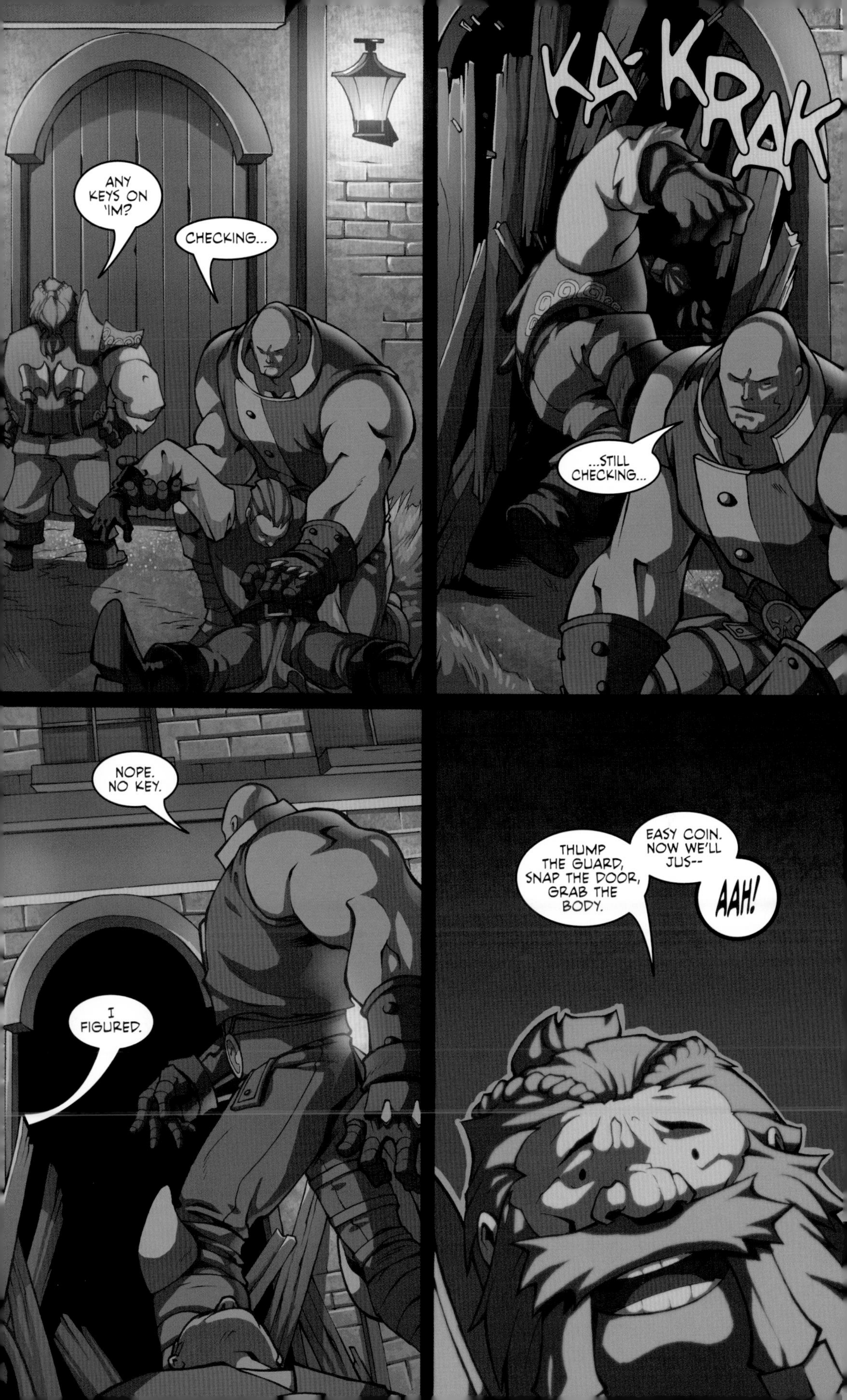
ANY KEYS ON 'IM?
CHECKING...
KA-KRAK
...STILL CHECKING...
NOPE. NO KEY.
I FIGURED.
THUMP THE GUARD, SNAP THE DOOR, GRAB THE BODY.
EASY COIN. NOW WE'LL JUS--
AAH!

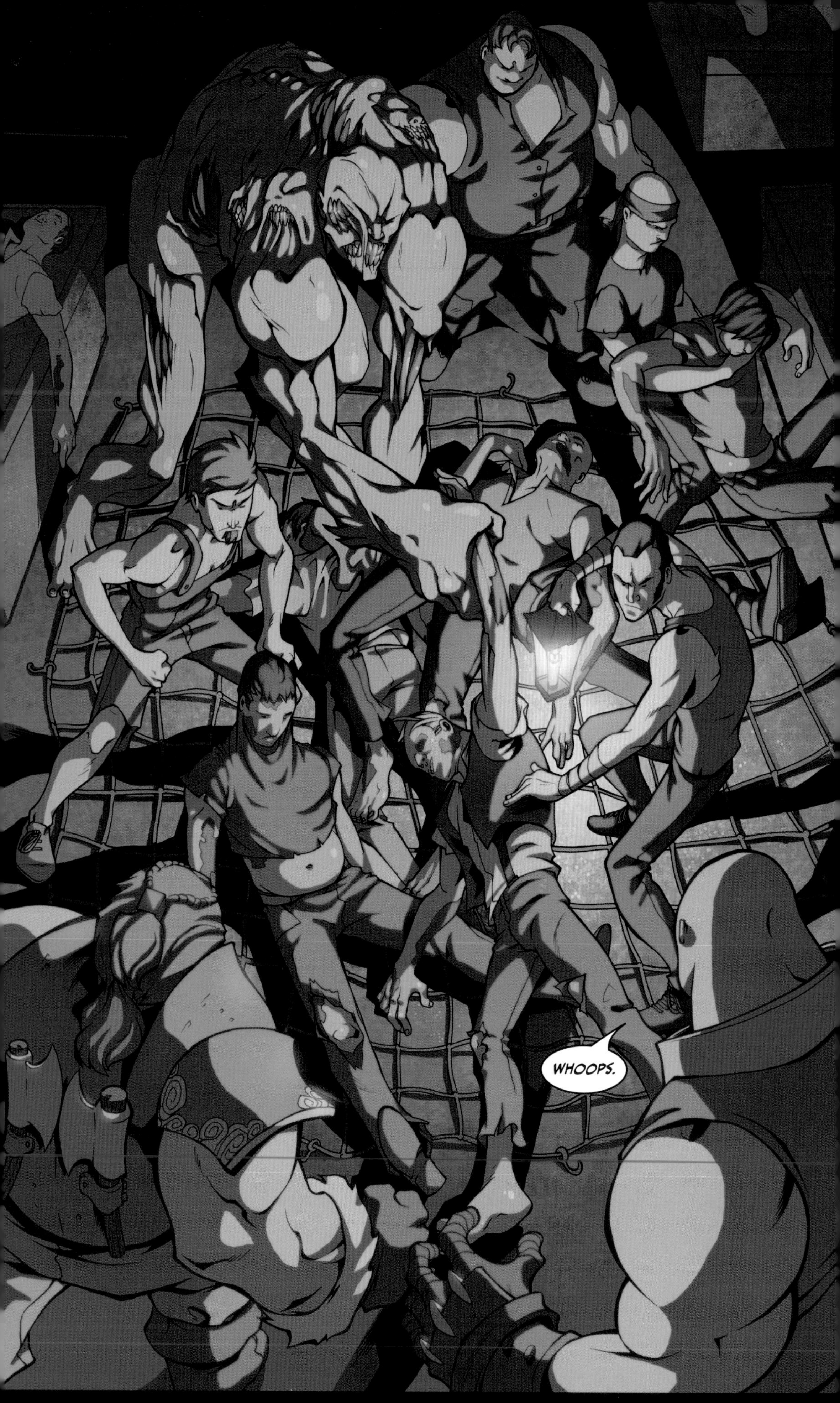
WHOOPS.

CHAPTER TWO

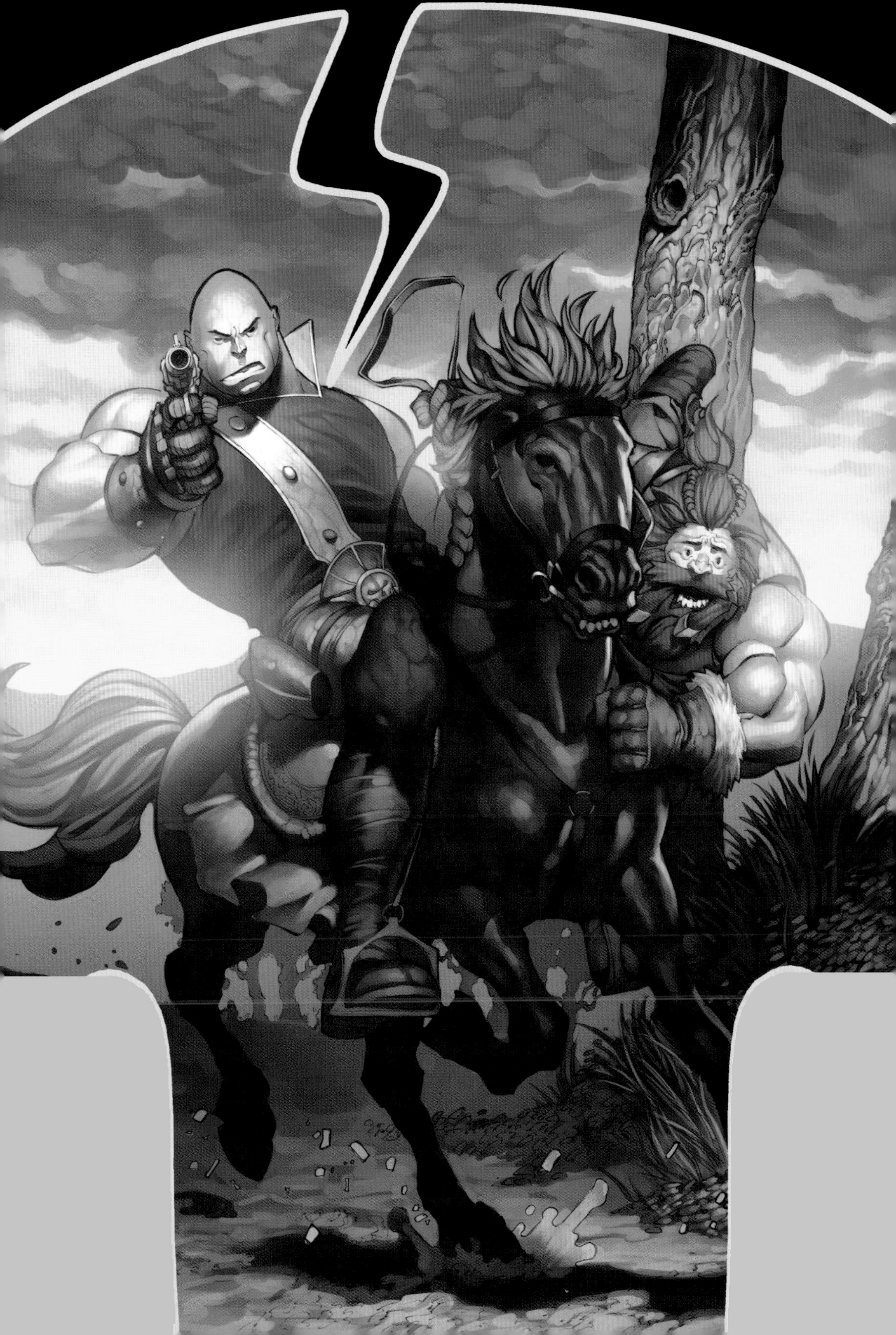

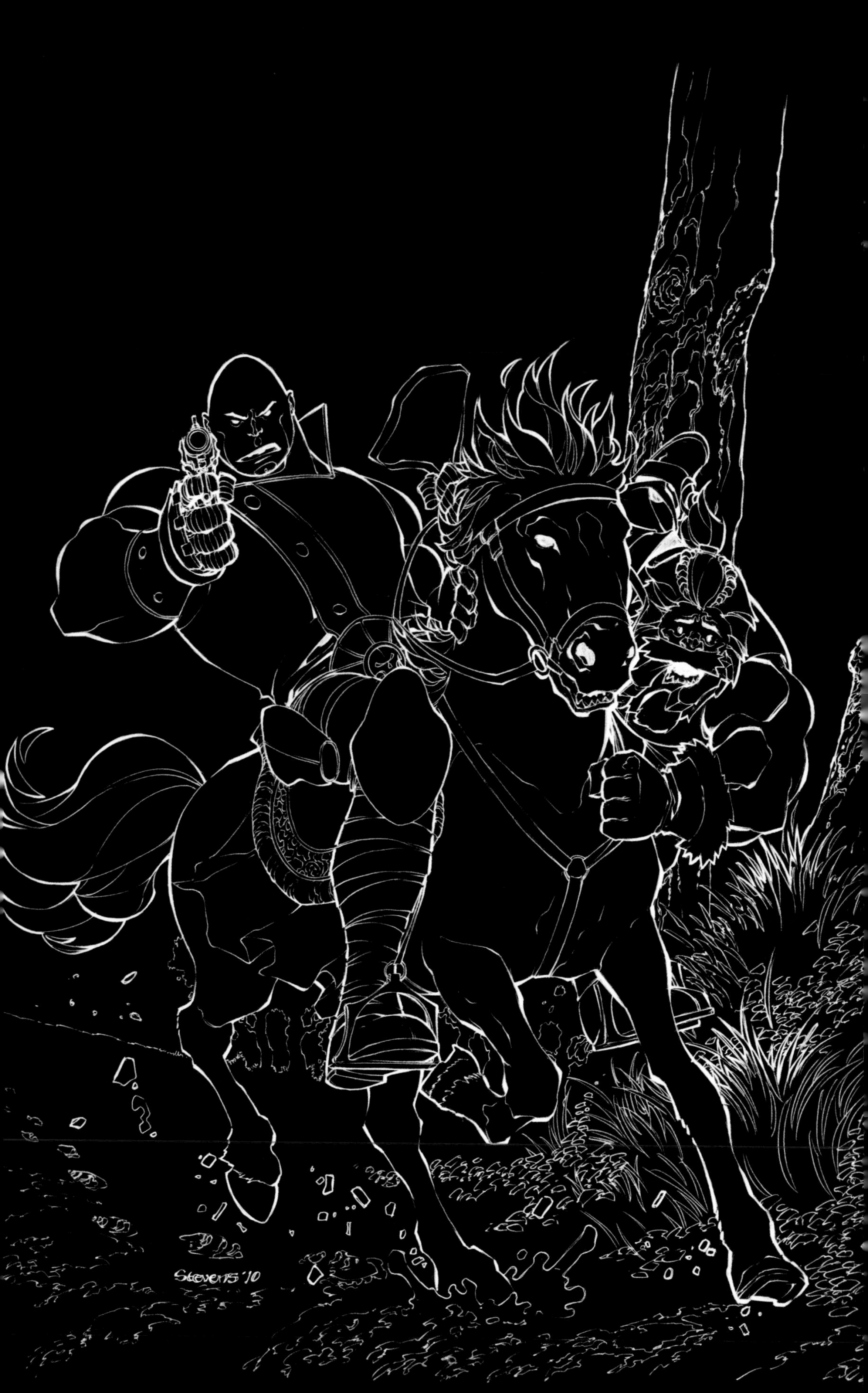
STEVENS '10

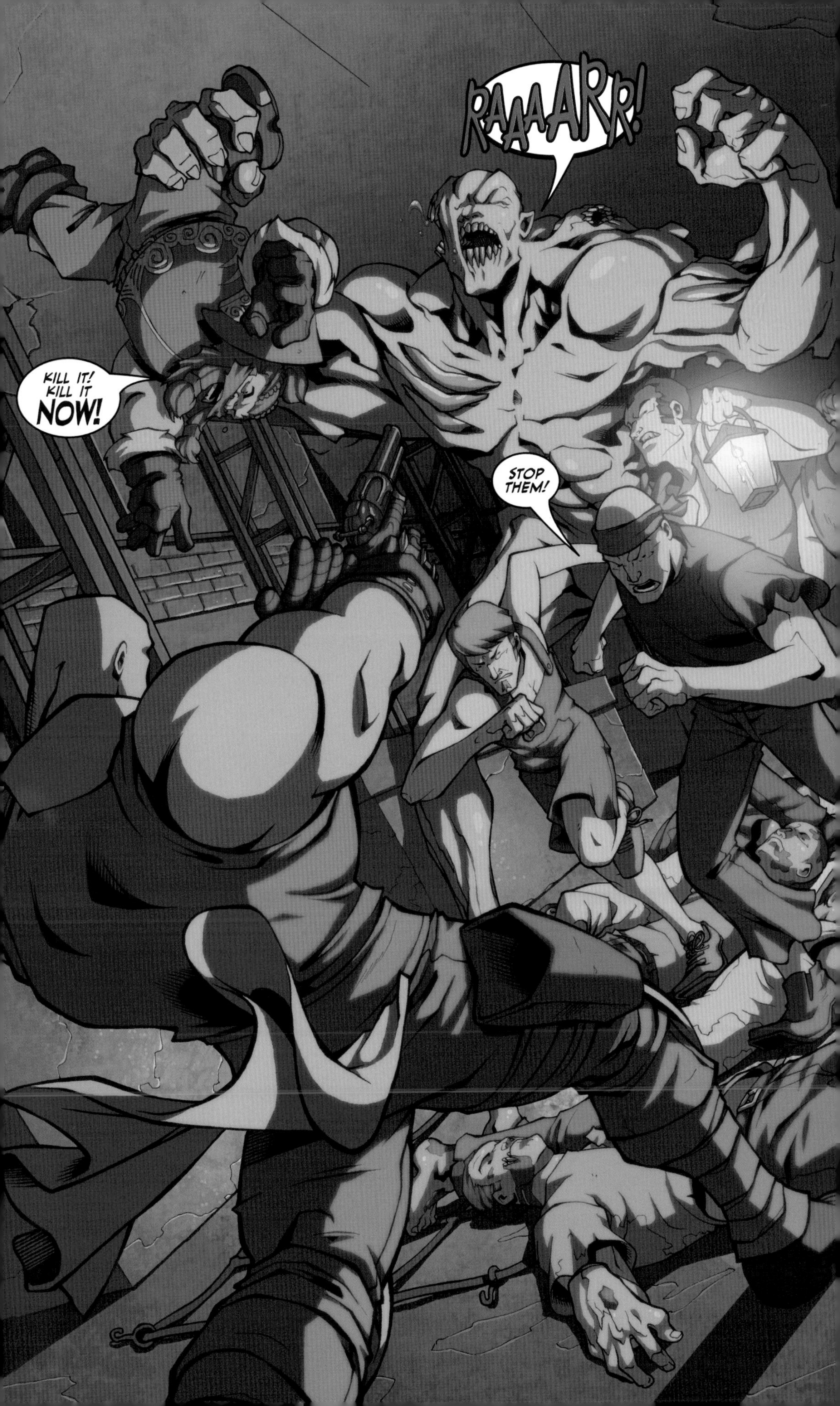
RAAAARRR!
KILL IT! KILL IT NOW!
STOP THEM!

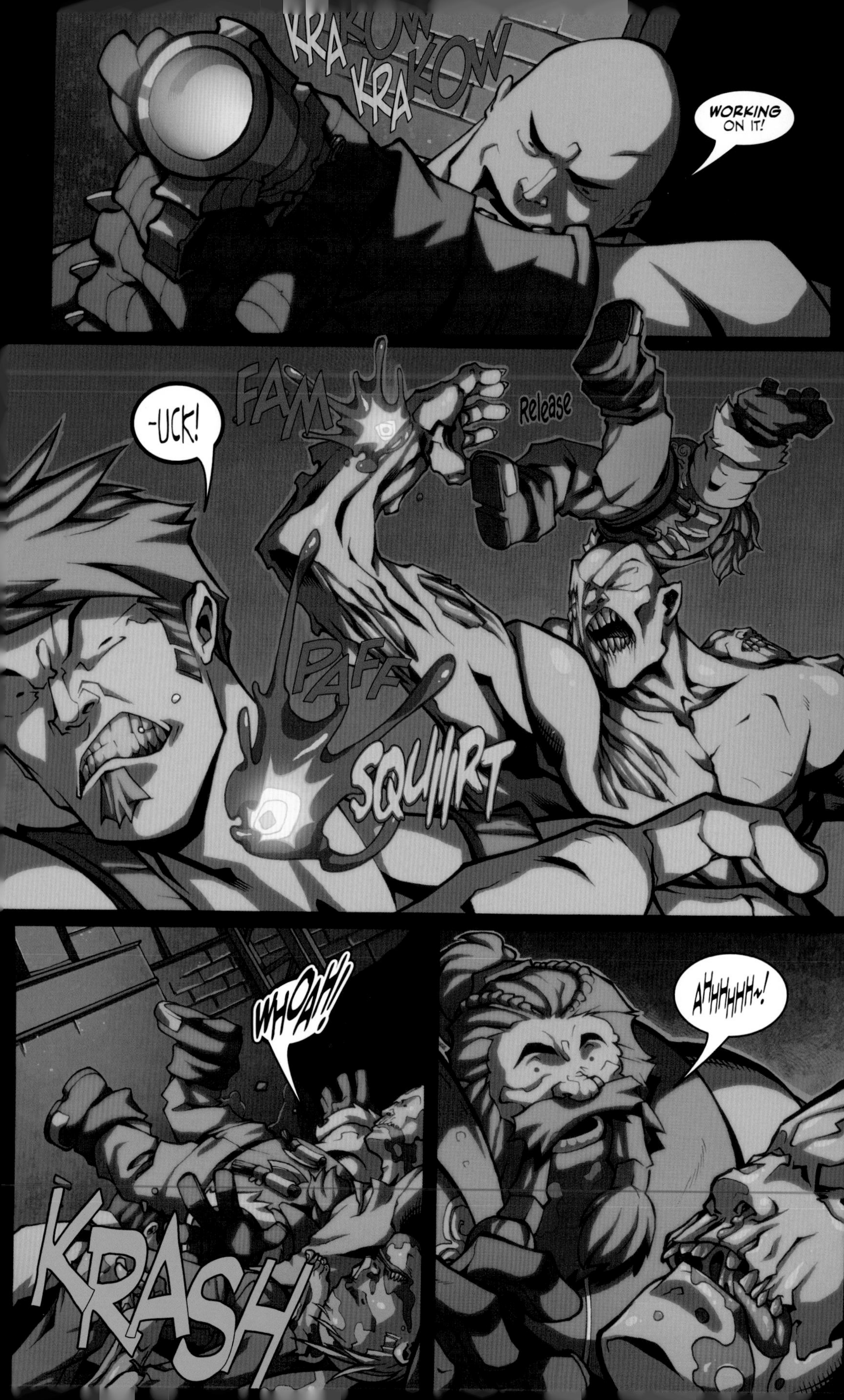
KRAKOW
KRAKOW
WORKING ON IT!
FAM
Release
-UCK!
PAFF
SQUIIIRT
WHOAH!!
KRASH
AHHHHHH~!

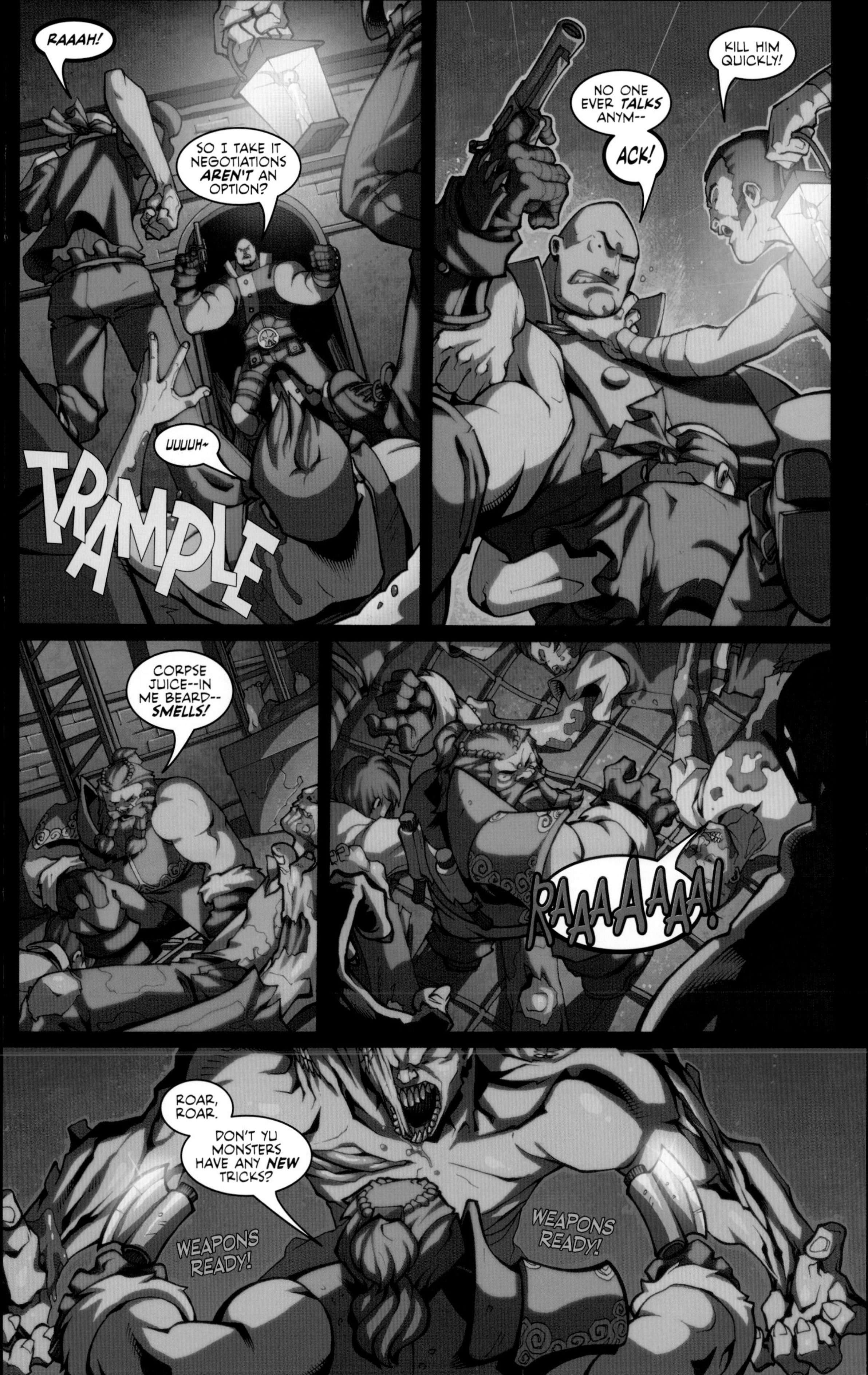
RAAAH!
SO I TAKE IT NEGOTIATIONS AREN'T AN OPTION?
UUUUH~
TRAMPLE
NO ONE EVER TALKS ANYM--
ACK!
KILL HIM QUICKLY!
CORPSE JUICE--IN ME BEARD--SMELLS!
RAAAAAAA!
ROAR, ROAR.
DON'T YU MONSTERS HAVE ANY NEW TRICKS?
WEAPONS READY!
WEAPONS READY!

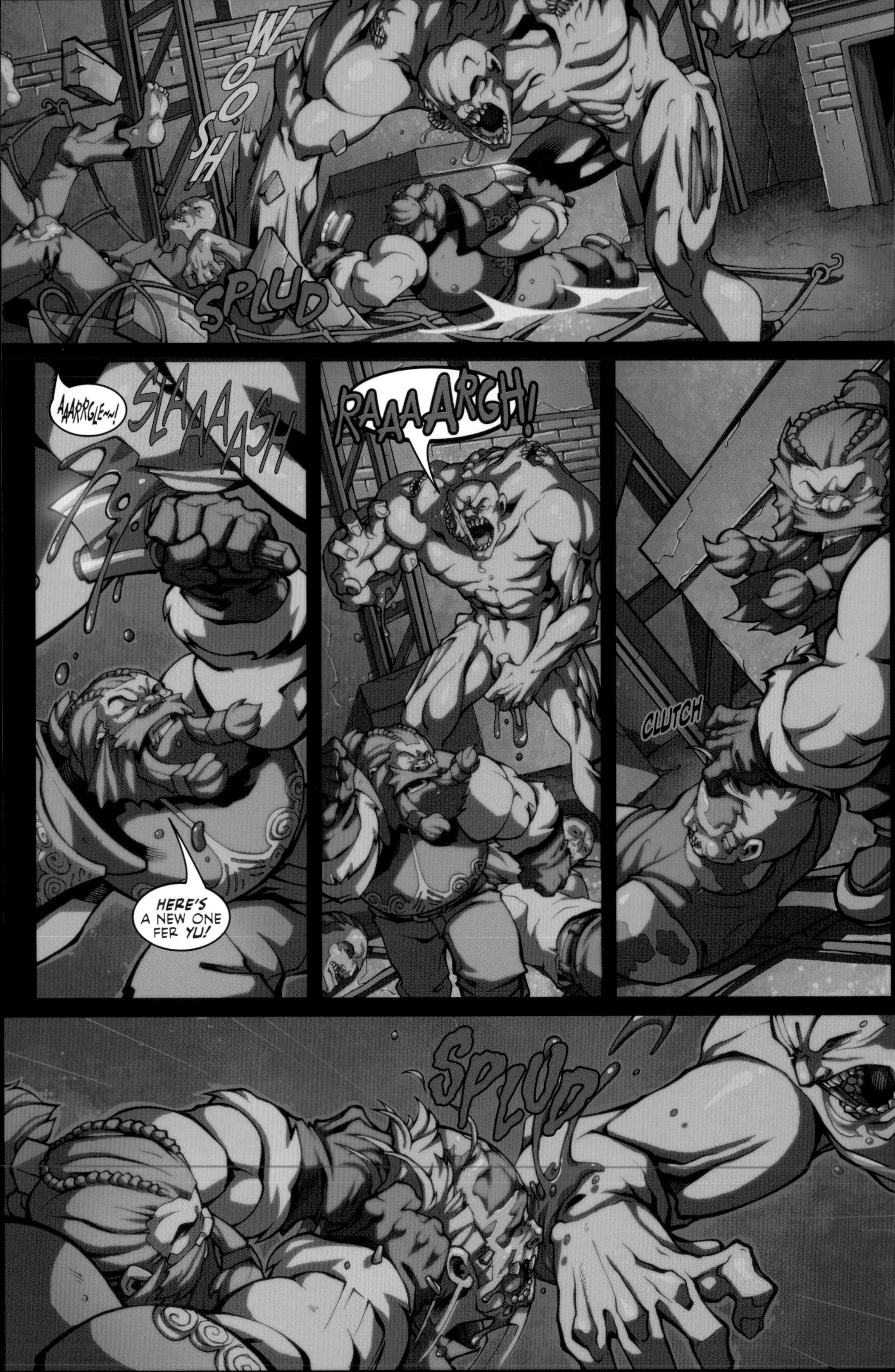
WOOSH
SPLUD
AAARRGLE~~!
SLAAAAASH
HERE'S A NEW ONE FER YU!
RAAAARGH!
CLUTCH
SPLUD

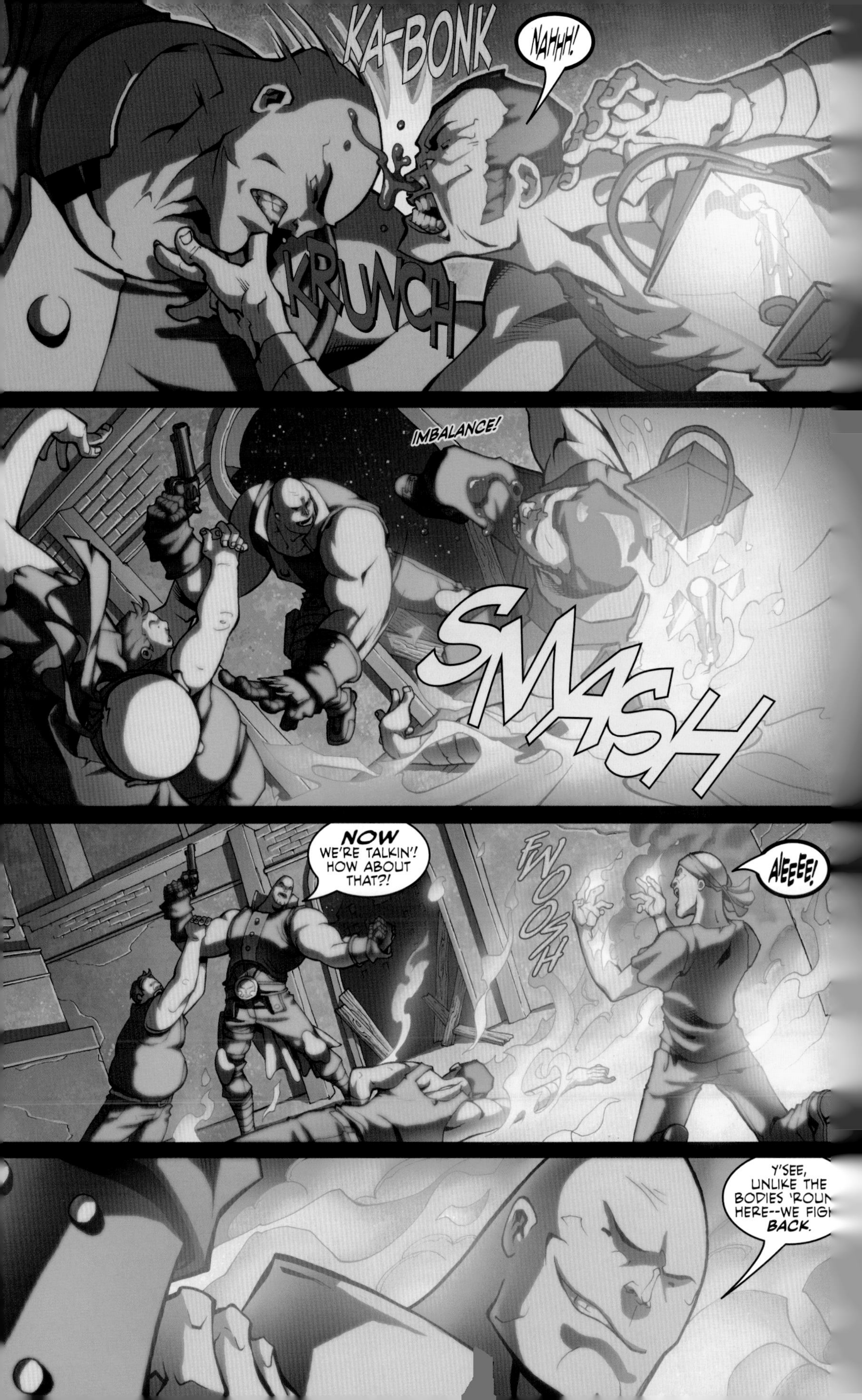
KA-BONK
NAHHH!
KRUNCH
IMBALANCE!
SMASH
NOW WE'RE TALKIN'! HOW ABOUT THAT?!
FWOOSH
AIEEEE!
Y'SEE, UNLIKE THE BODIES 'ROUN HERE--WE FIGH BACK.

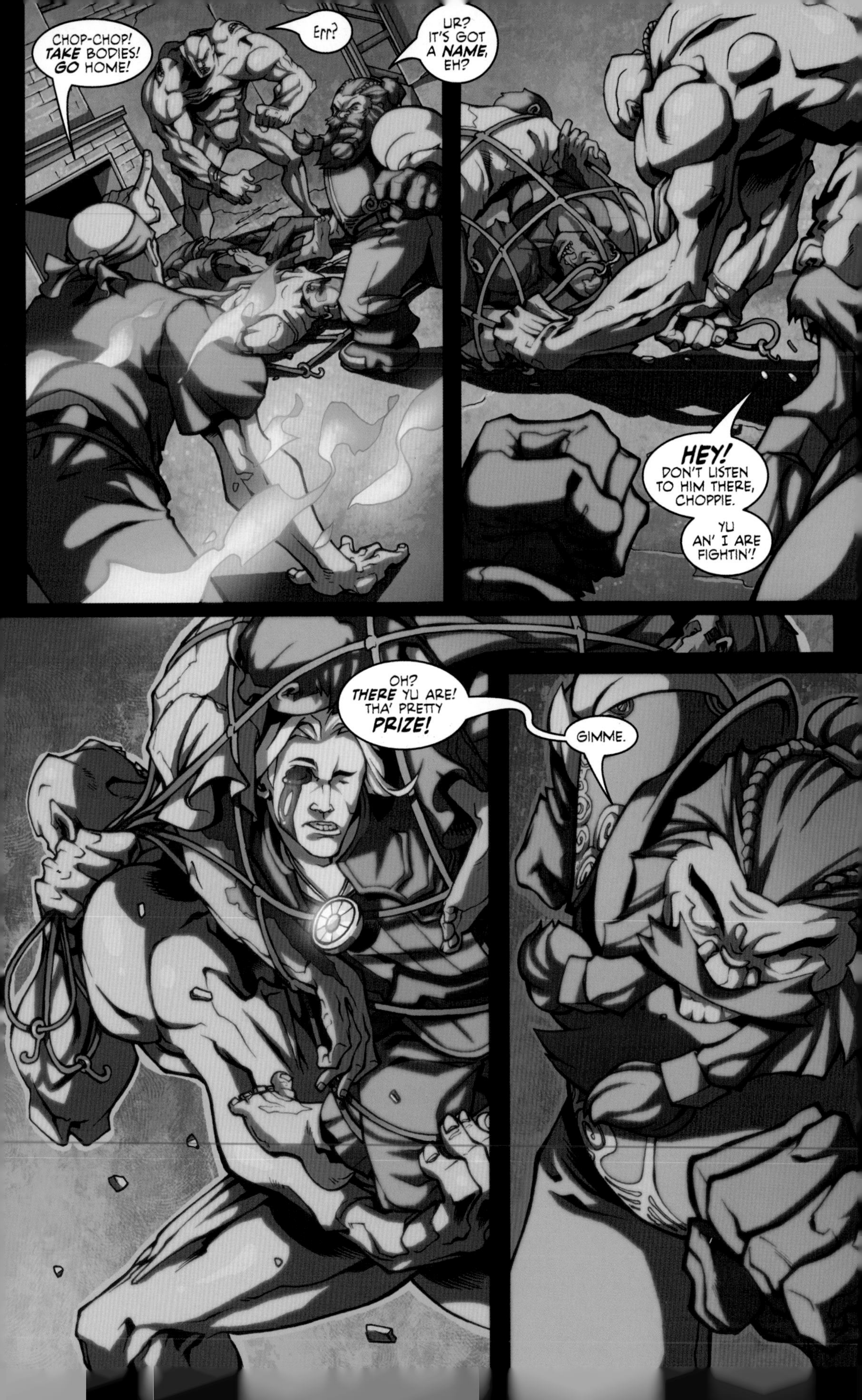
CHOP-CHOP! TAKE BODIES! GO HOME!
Err?
UR? IT'S GOT A NAME, EH?
HEY! DON'T LISTEN TO HIM THERE, CHOPPIE.
YU AN' I ARE FIGHTIN'!
OH? THERE YU ARE! THA' PRETTY PRIZE!
GIMME.

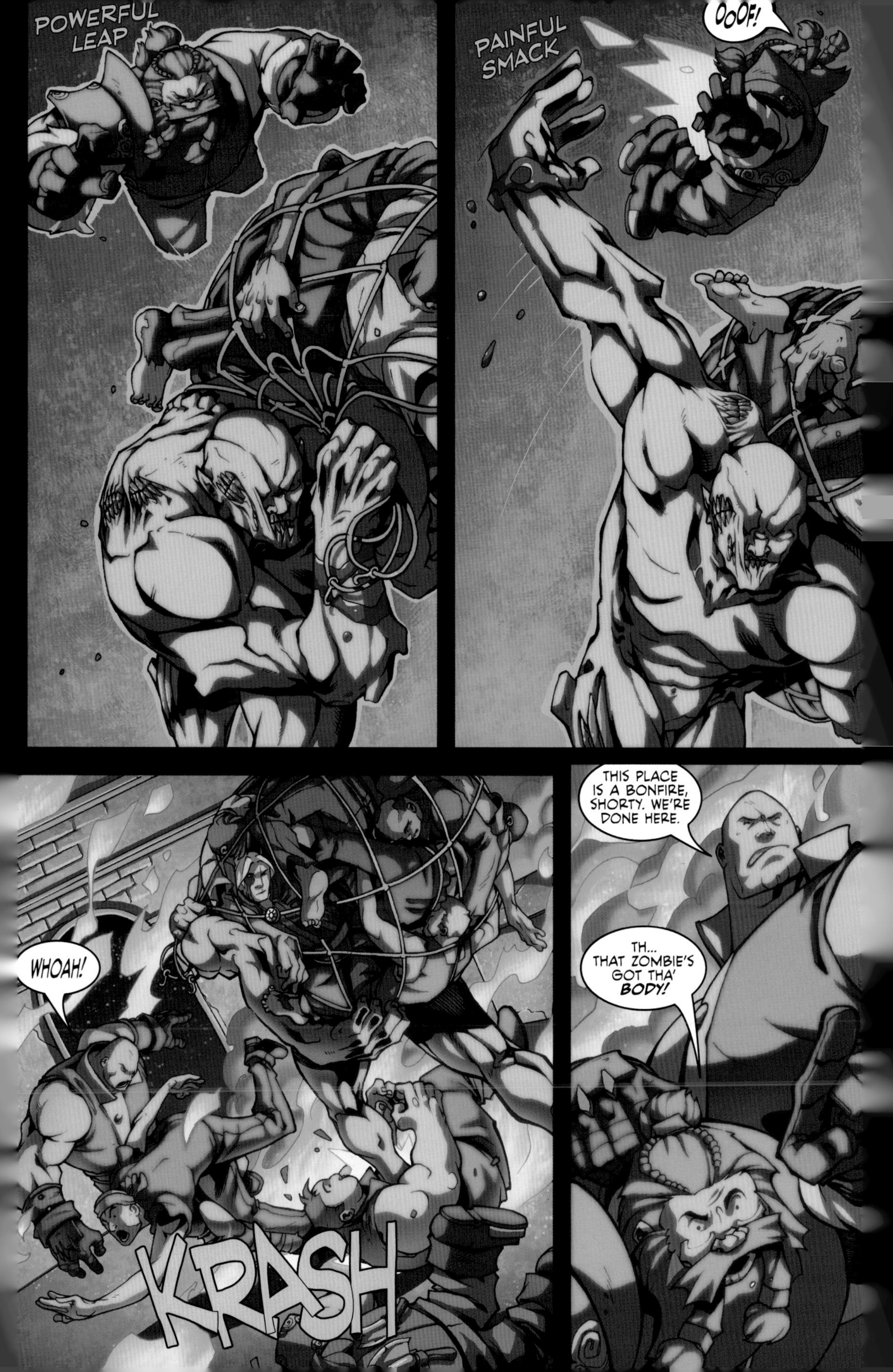
POWERFUL LEAP
PAINFUL SMACK
OOOF!
WHOAH!
KRASH
THIS PLACE IS A BONFIRE, SHORTY. WE'RE DONE HERE.
TH... THAT ZOMBIE'S GOT THA' *BODY!*

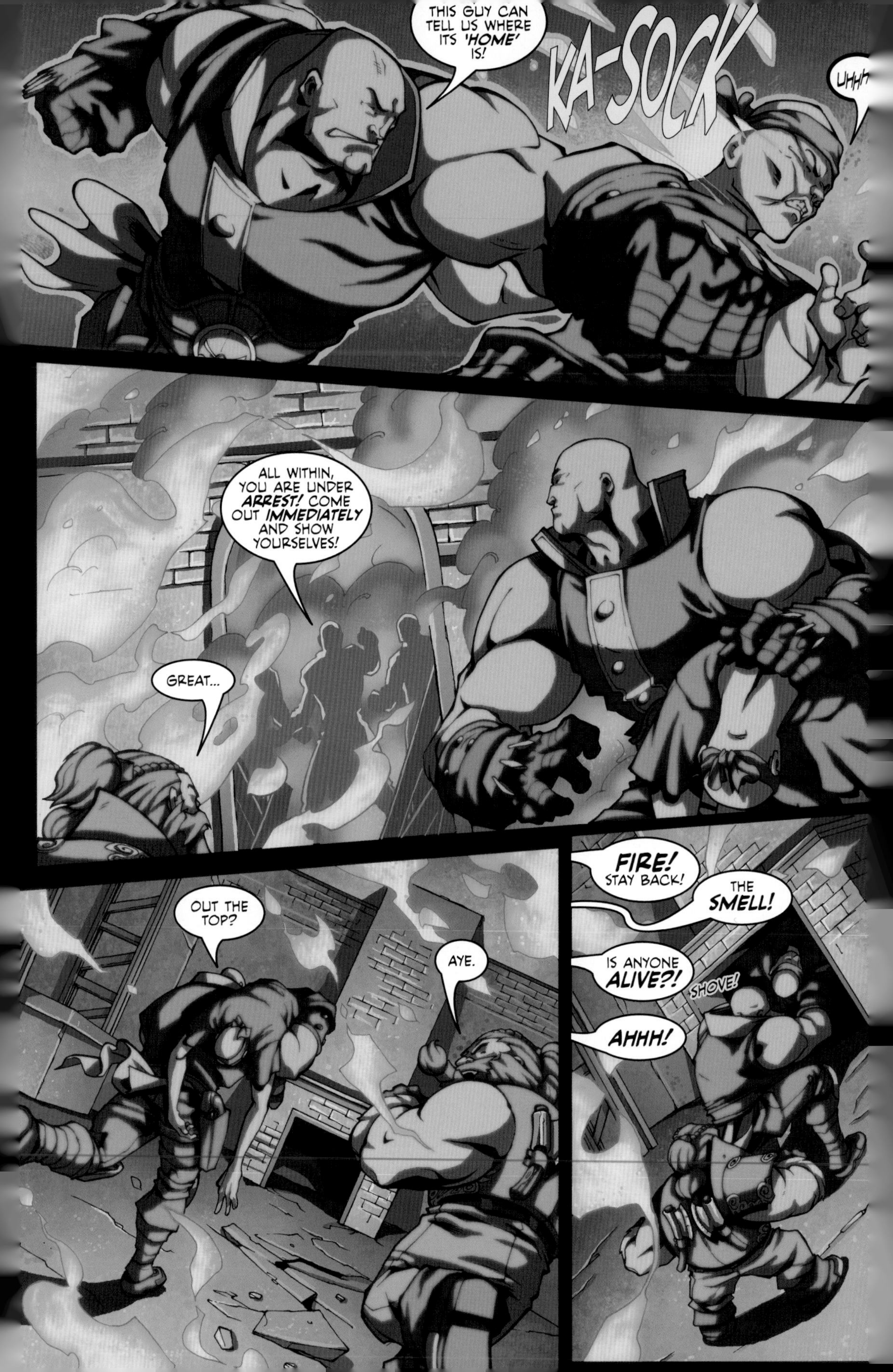
THIS GUY CAN TELL US WHERE ITS 'HOME' IS!
KA-SOCK
UHHH
ALL WITHIN, YOU ARE UNDER ARREST! COME OUT IMMEDIATELY AND SHOW YOURSELVES!
GREAT...
OUT THE TOP?
AYE.
FIRE! STAY BACK!
THE SMELL!
IS ANYONE ALIVE?!
SHOVE!
AHHH!

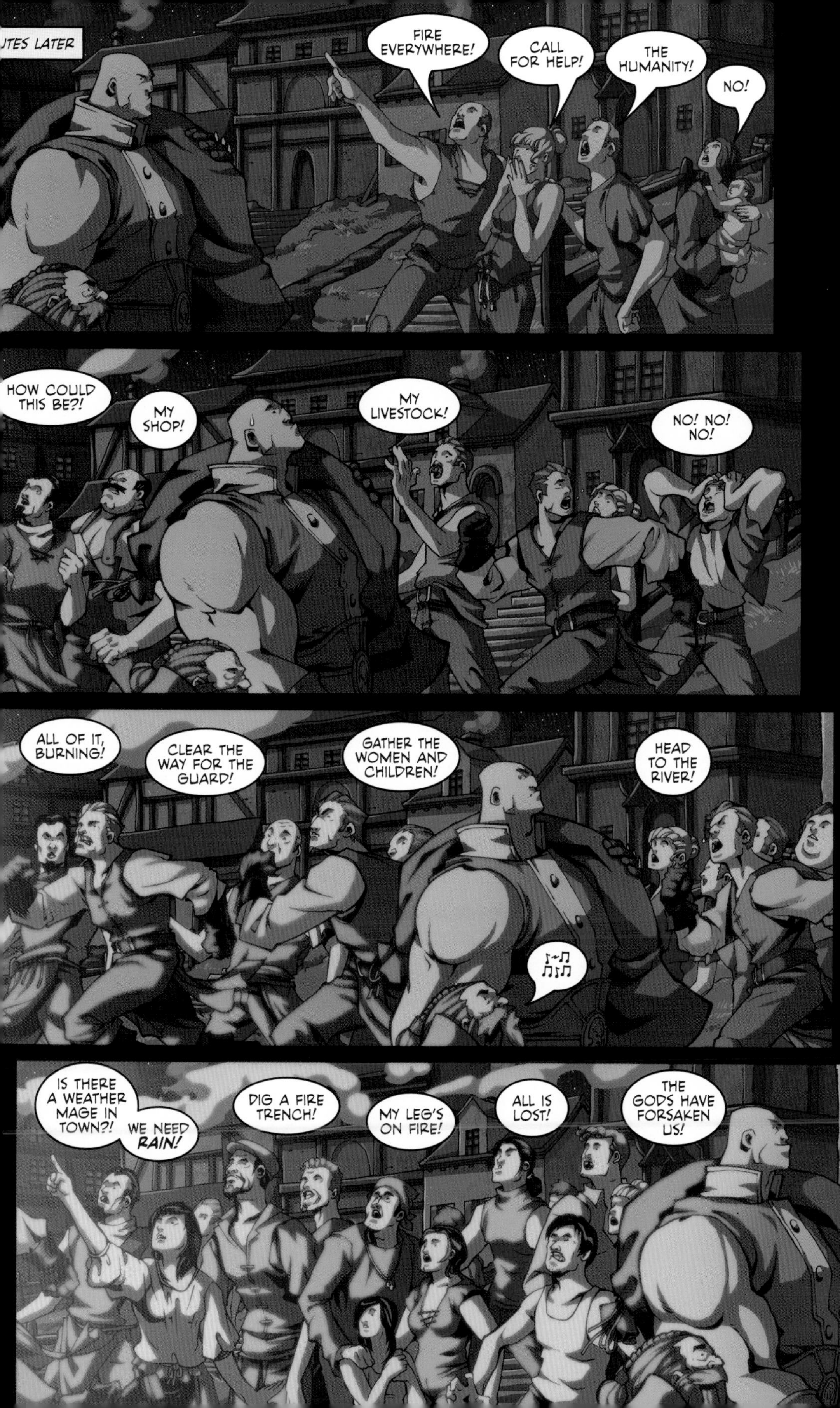

...UTES LATER
FIRE EVERYWHERE!
CALL FOR HELP!
THE HUMANITY!
NO!
HOW COULD THIS BE?!
MY SHOP!
MY LIVESTOCK!
NO! NO! NO!
ALL OF IT, BURNING!
CLEAR THE WAY FOR THE GUARD!
GATHER THE WOMEN AND CHILDREN!
HEAD TO THE RIVER!
IS THERE A WEATHER MAGE IN TOWN?!
WE NEED *RAIN!*
DIG A FIRE TRENCH!
MY LEG'S ON FIRE!
ALL IS LOST!
THE GODS HAVE FORSAKEN US!

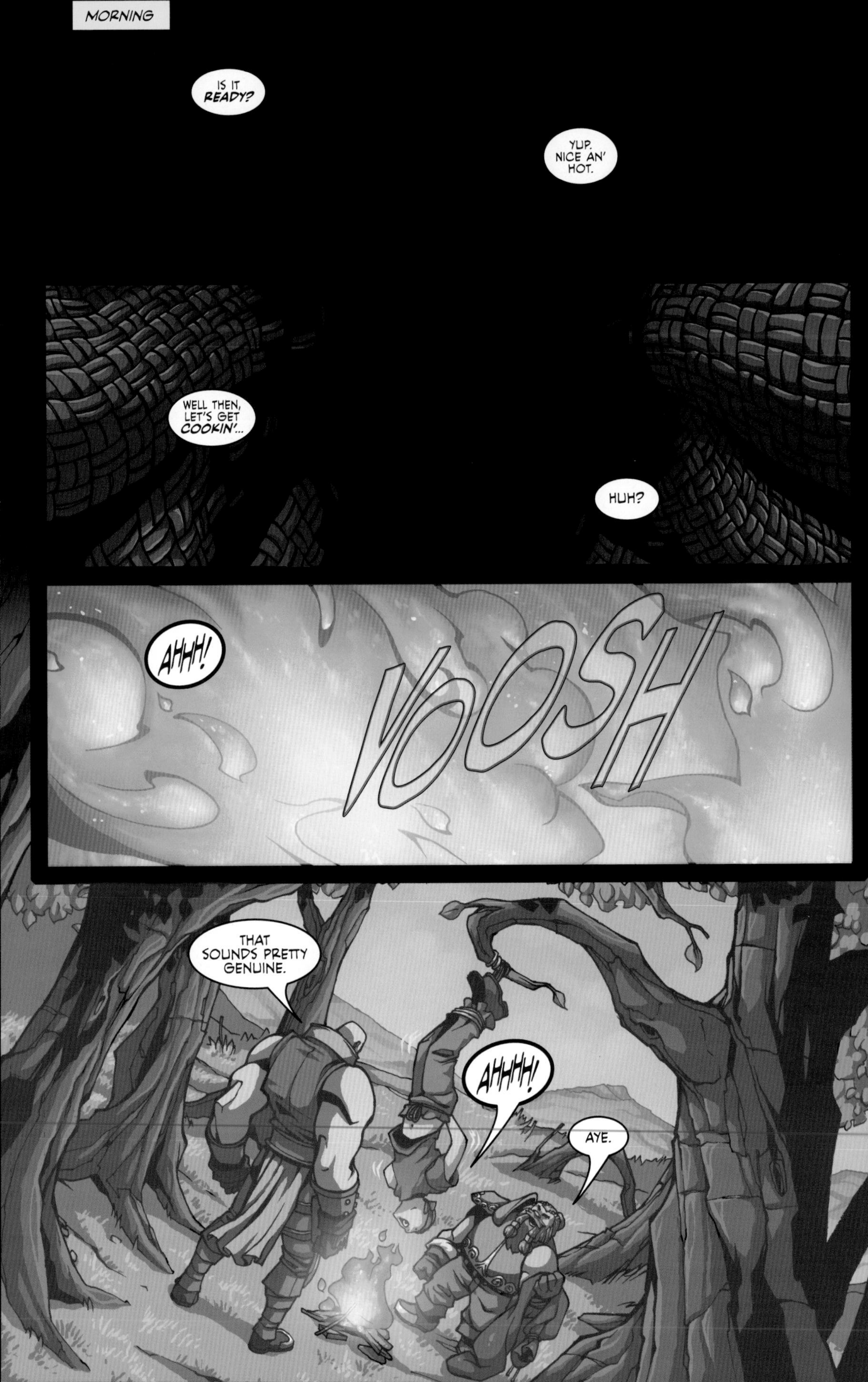
MORNING
IS IT READY?
YUP. NICE AN' HOT.
WELL THEN, LET'S GET COOKIN'...
HUH?
AHHH!
WOOSH
THAT SOUNDS PRETTY GENUINE.
AHHHH!
AYE.

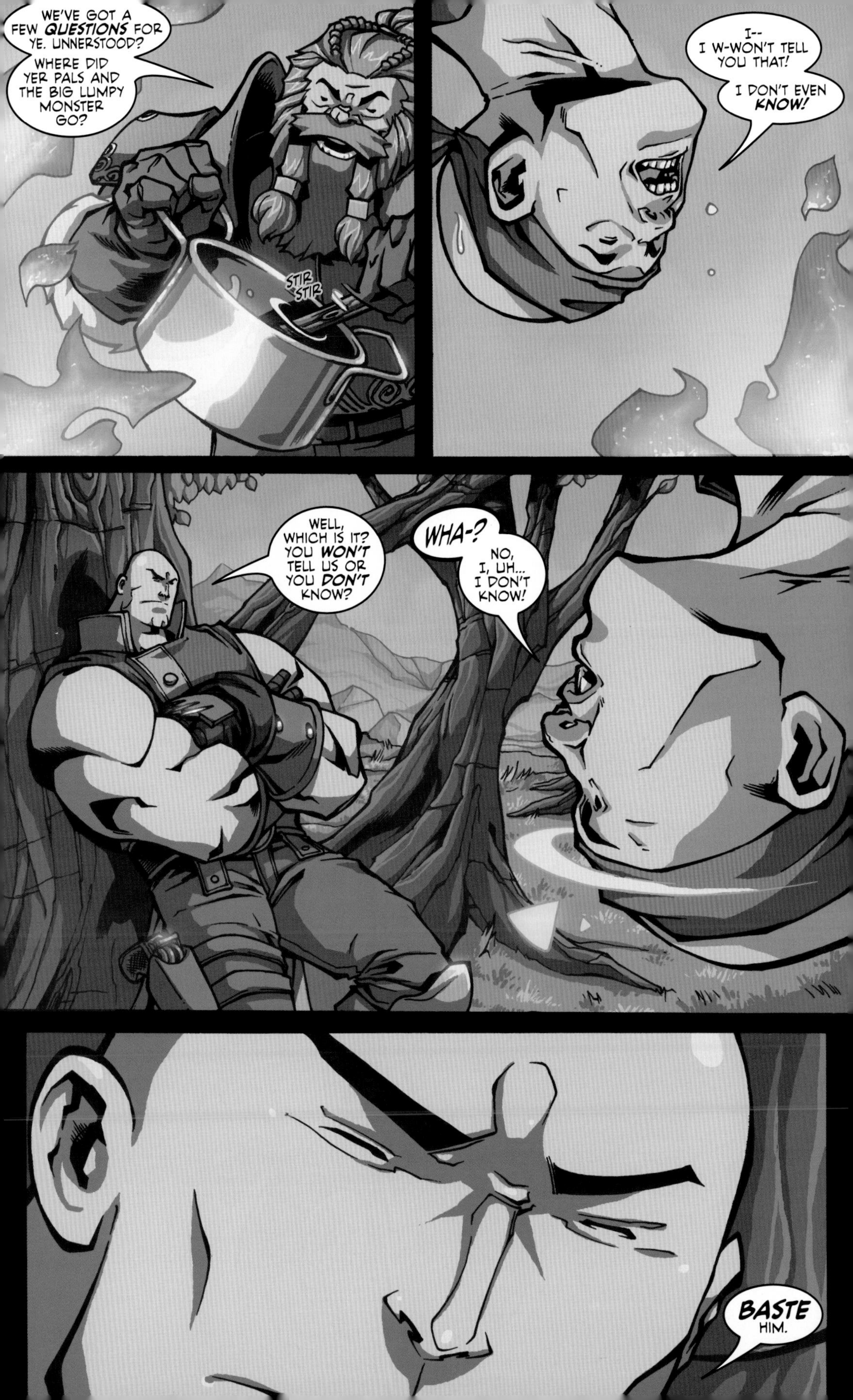
WE'VE GOT A FEW QUESTIONS FOR YE. UNNERSTOOD?
WHERE DID YER PALS AND THE BIG LUMPY MONSTER GO?
STIR STIR
I-- I W-WON'T TELL YOU THAT!
I DON'T EVEN KNOW!
WELL, WHICH IS IT? YOU WON'T TELL US OR YOU DON'T KNOW?
WHA-?
NO, I, UH... I DON'T KNOW!
BASTE HIM.

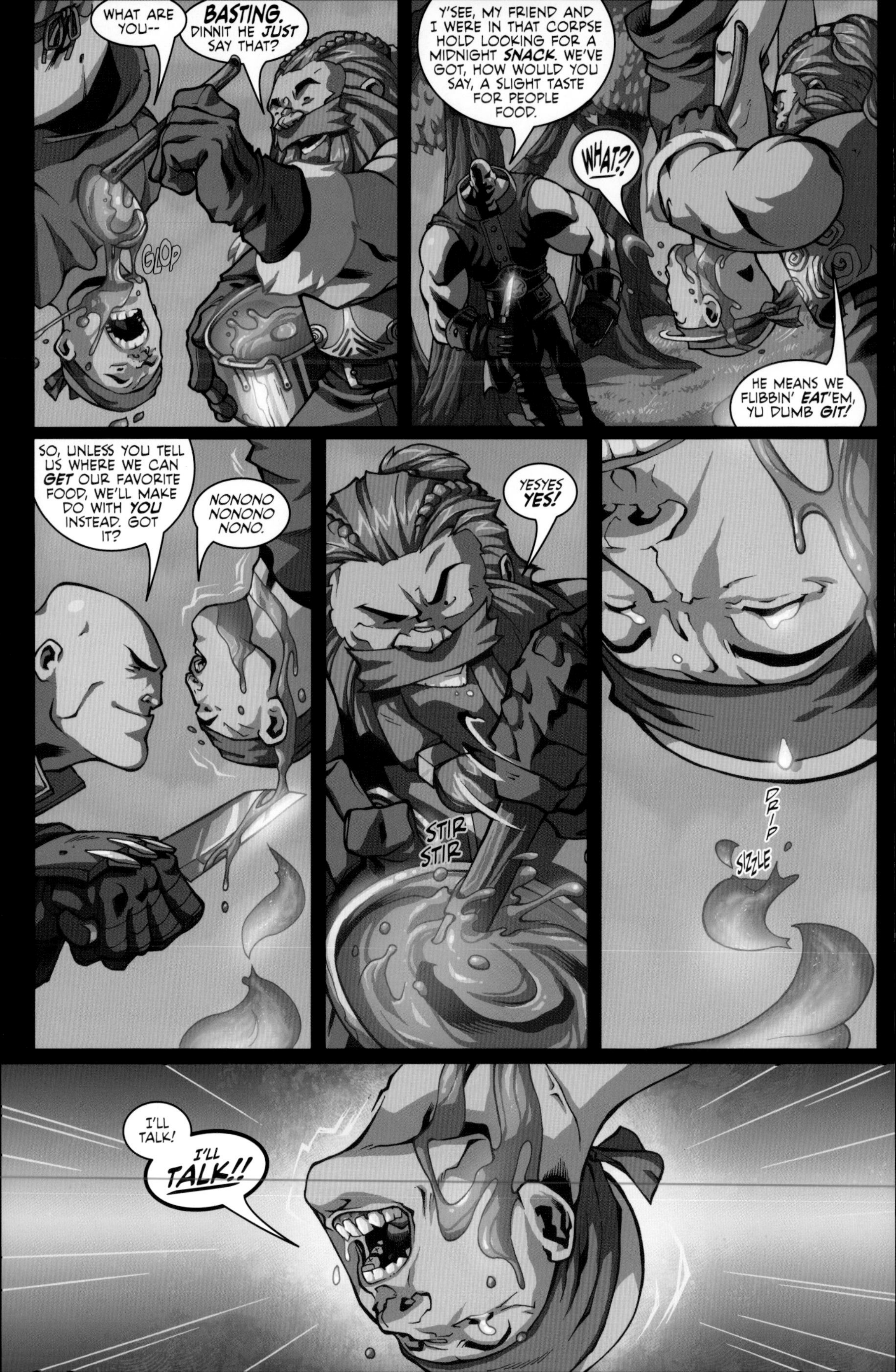
WHAT ARE YOU--
BASTING. DINNIT HE JUST SAY THAT?
GLOP
Y'SEE, MY FRIEND AND I WERE IN THAT CORPSE HOLD LOOKING FOR A MIDNIGHT SNACK. WE'VE GOT, HOW WOULD YOU SAY, A SLIGHT TASTE FOR PEOPLE FOOD.
WHAT?!
HE MEANS WE FLIBBIN' EAT'EM, YU DUMB GIT!
SO, UNLESS YOU TELL US WHERE WE CAN GET OUR FAVORITE FOOD, WE'LL MAKE DO WITH YOU INSTEAD. GOT IT?
NONONO NONONO NONO.
YESYES YES!
STIR STIR
DRIP
SIZZLE
I'LL TALK!
I'LL TALK!!

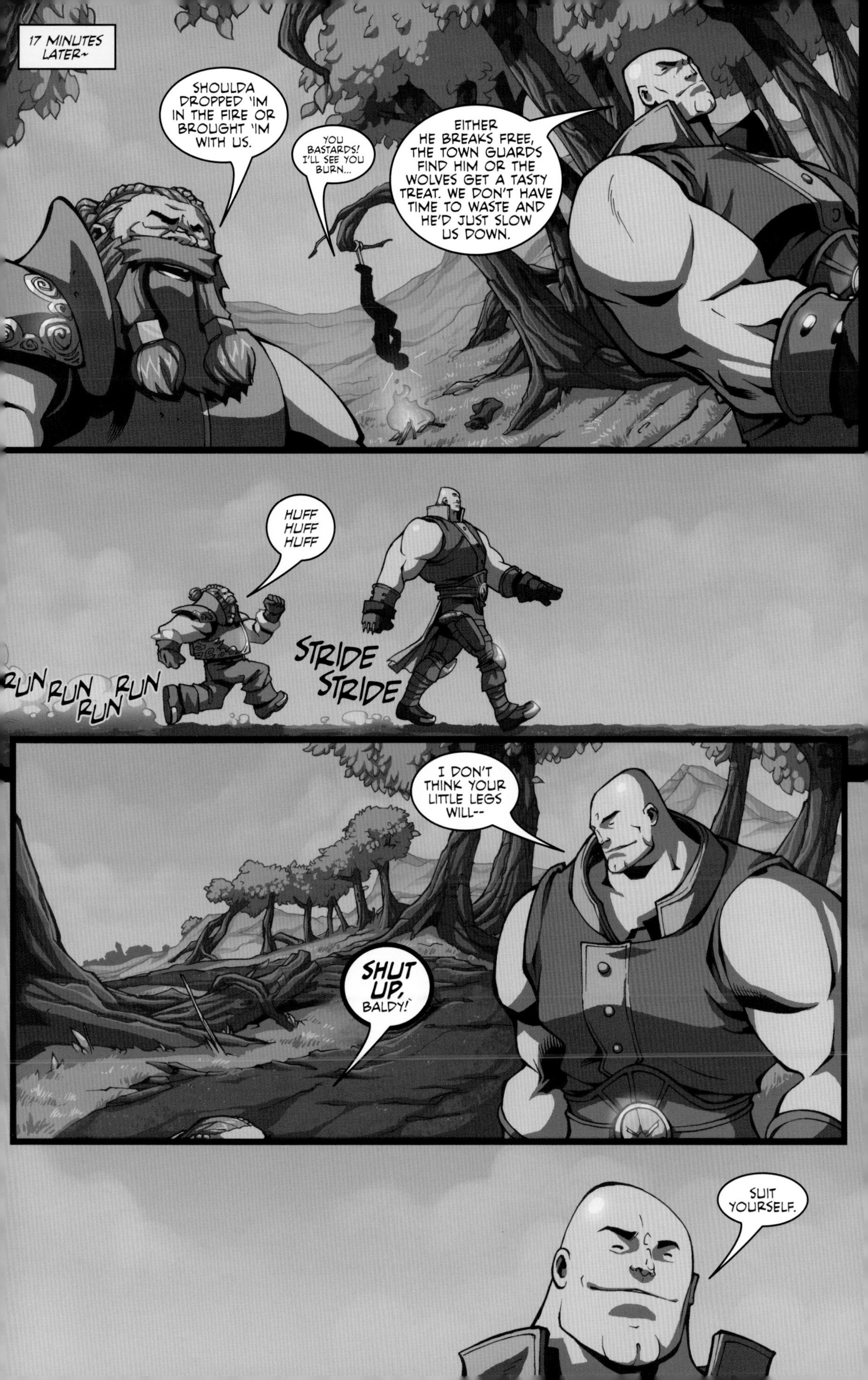
17 MINUTES LATER~
SHOULDA DROPPED 'IM IN THE FIRE OR BROUGHT 'IM WITH US.
YOU BASTARDS! I'LL SEE YOU BURN...
EITHER HE BREAKS FREE, THE TOWN GUARDS FIND HIM OR THE WOLVES GET A TASTY TREAT. WE DON'T HAVE TIME TO WASTE AND HE'D JUST SLOW US DOWN.
HUFF HUFF HUFF
STRIDE STRIDE
RUN RUN RUN RUN RUN
I DON'T THINK YOUR LITTLE LEGS WILL--
SHUT UP, BALDY!
SUIT YOURSELF.

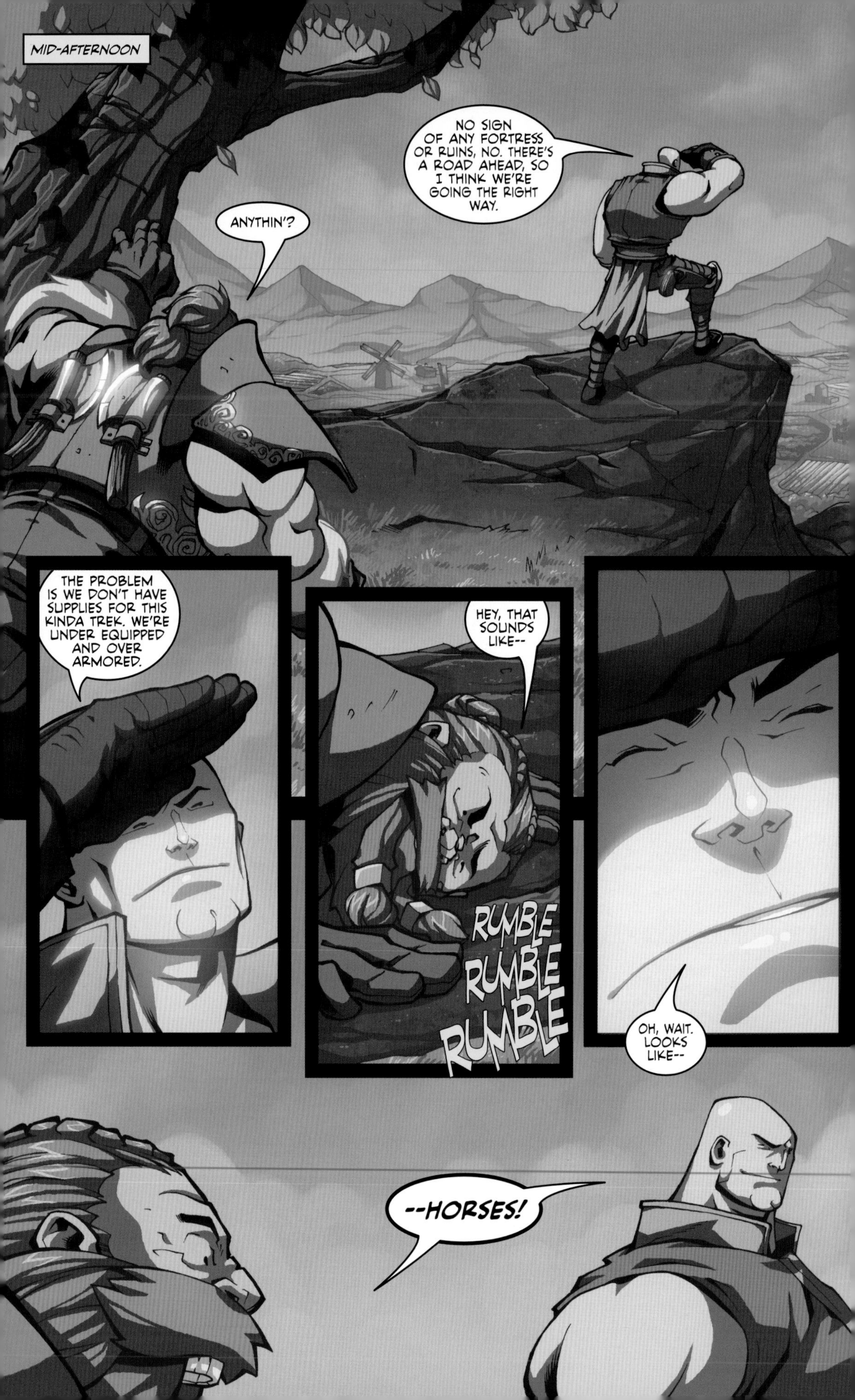
MID-AFTERNOON
ANYTHIN'?
NO SIGN OF ANY FORTRESS OR RUINS, NO. THERE'S A ROAD AHEAD, SO I THINK WE'RE GOING THE RIGHT WAY.
THE PROBLEM IS WE DON'T HAVE SUPPLIES FOR THIS KINDA TREK. WE'RE UNDER EQUIPPED AND OVER ARMORED.
HEY, THAT SOUNDS LIKE--
RUMBLE RUMBLE RUMBLE
OH, WAIT. LOOKS LIKE--
--HORSES!

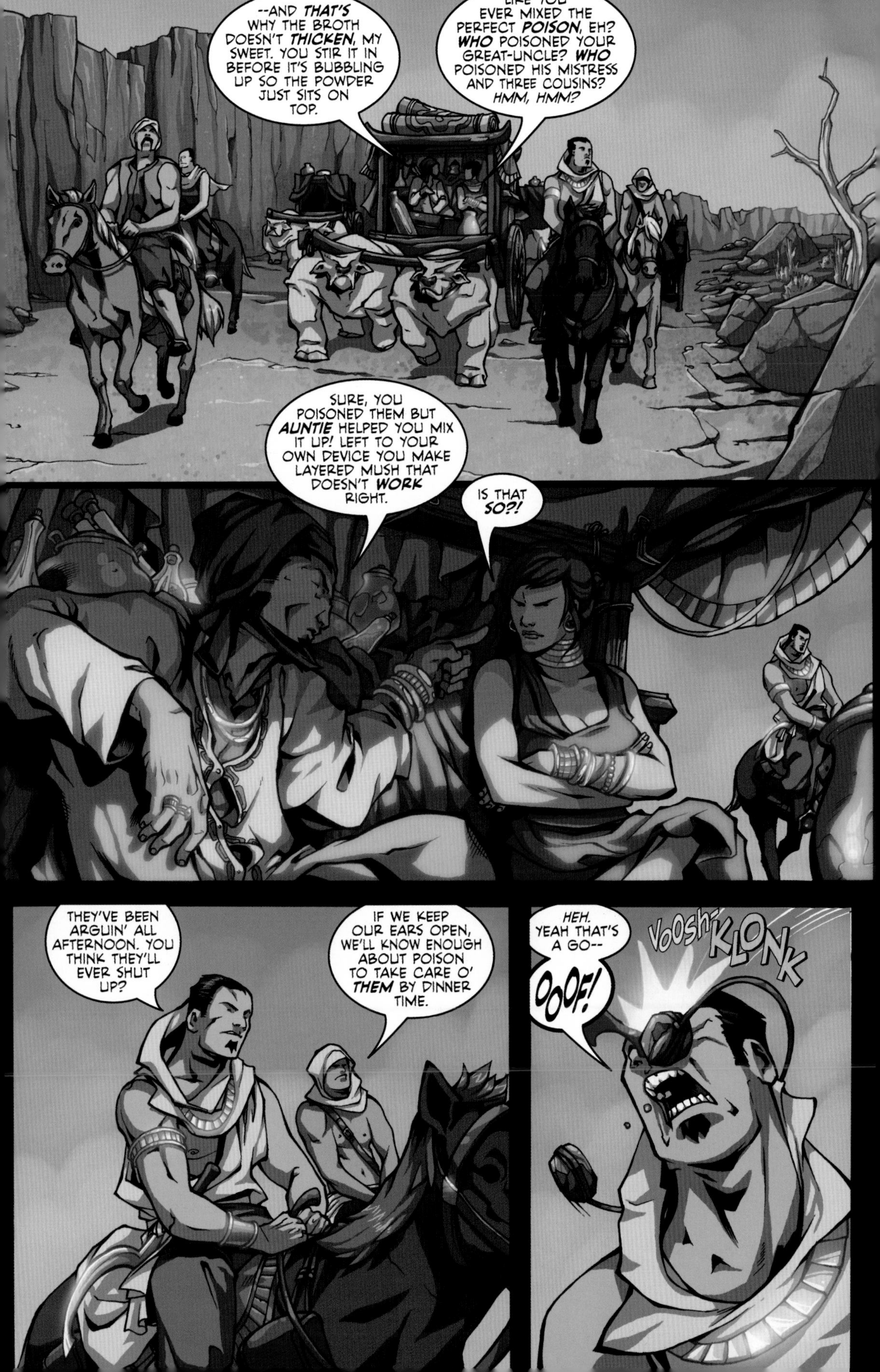
--AND THAT'S WHY THE BROTH DOESN'T THICKEN, MY SWEET. YOU STIR IT IN BEFORE IT'S BUBBLING UP SO THE POWDER JUST SITS ON TOP.
LIKE YOU EVER MIXED THE PERFECT POISON, EH? WHO POISONED YOUR GREAT-UNCLE? WHO POISONED HIS MISTRESS AND THREE COUSINS? HMM, HMM?
SURE, YOU POISONED THEM BUT AUNTIE HELPED YOU MIX IT UP! LEFT TO YOUR OWN DEVICE YOU MAKE LAYERED MUSH THAT DOESN'T WORK RIGHT.
IS THAT SO?!
THEY'VE BEEN ARGUIN' ALL AFTERNOON. YOU THINK THEY'LL EVER SHUT UP?
IF WE KEEP OUR EARS OPEN, WE'LL KNOW ENOUGH ABOUT POISON TO TAKE CARE O' THEM BY DINNER TIME.
HEH. YEAH THAT'S A GO--
VOOSH-KLONK
OOOF!

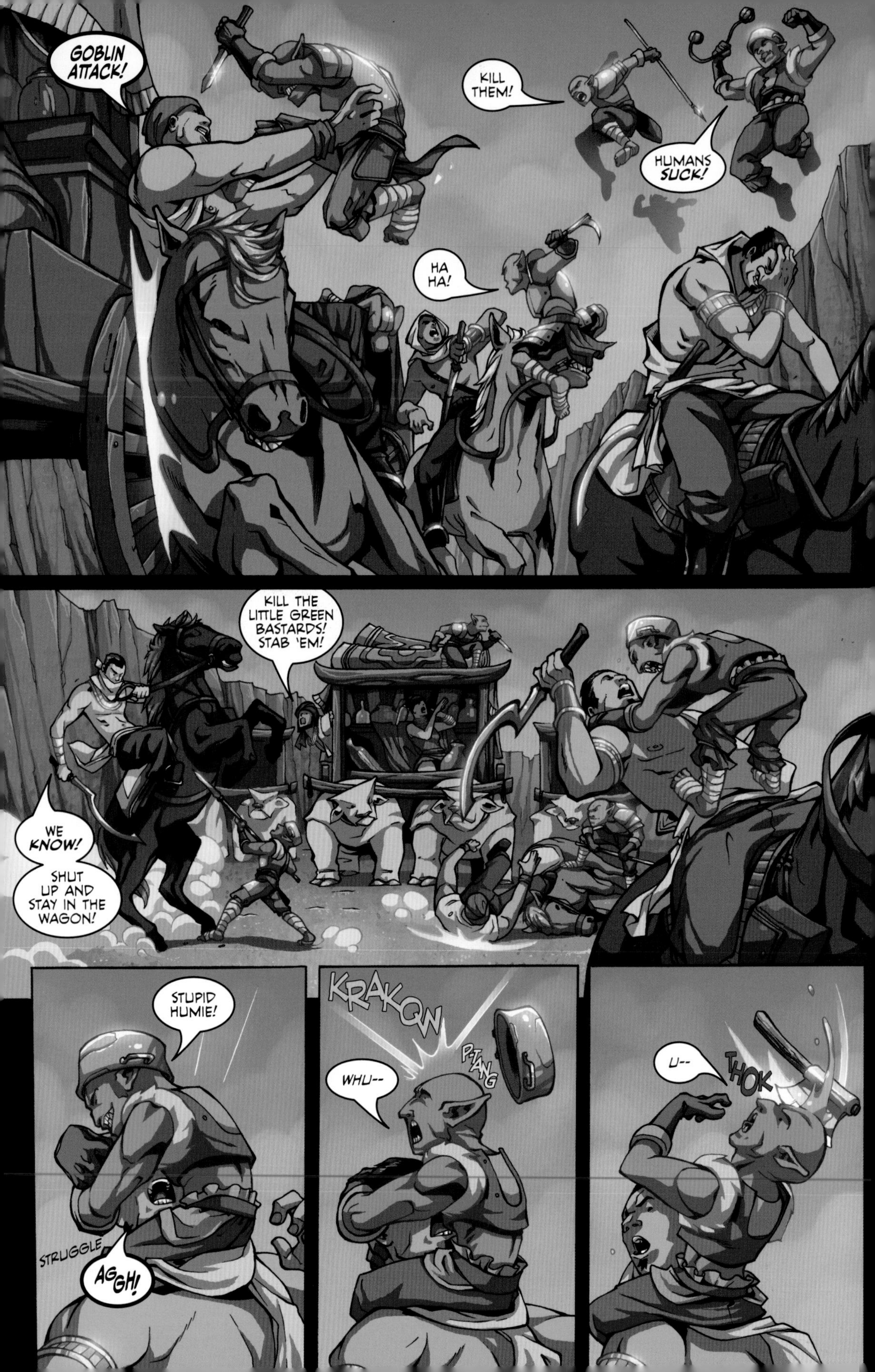

GOBLIN ATTACK!
KILL THEM!
HUMANS SUCK!
HA HA!
KILL THE LITTLE GREEN BASTARDS! STAB 'EM!
WE KNOW!
SHUT UP AND STAY IN THE WAGON!
STUPID HUMIE!
STRUGGLE
AGGH!
KRAKOW
PTANG
WHU--
U--
THOK

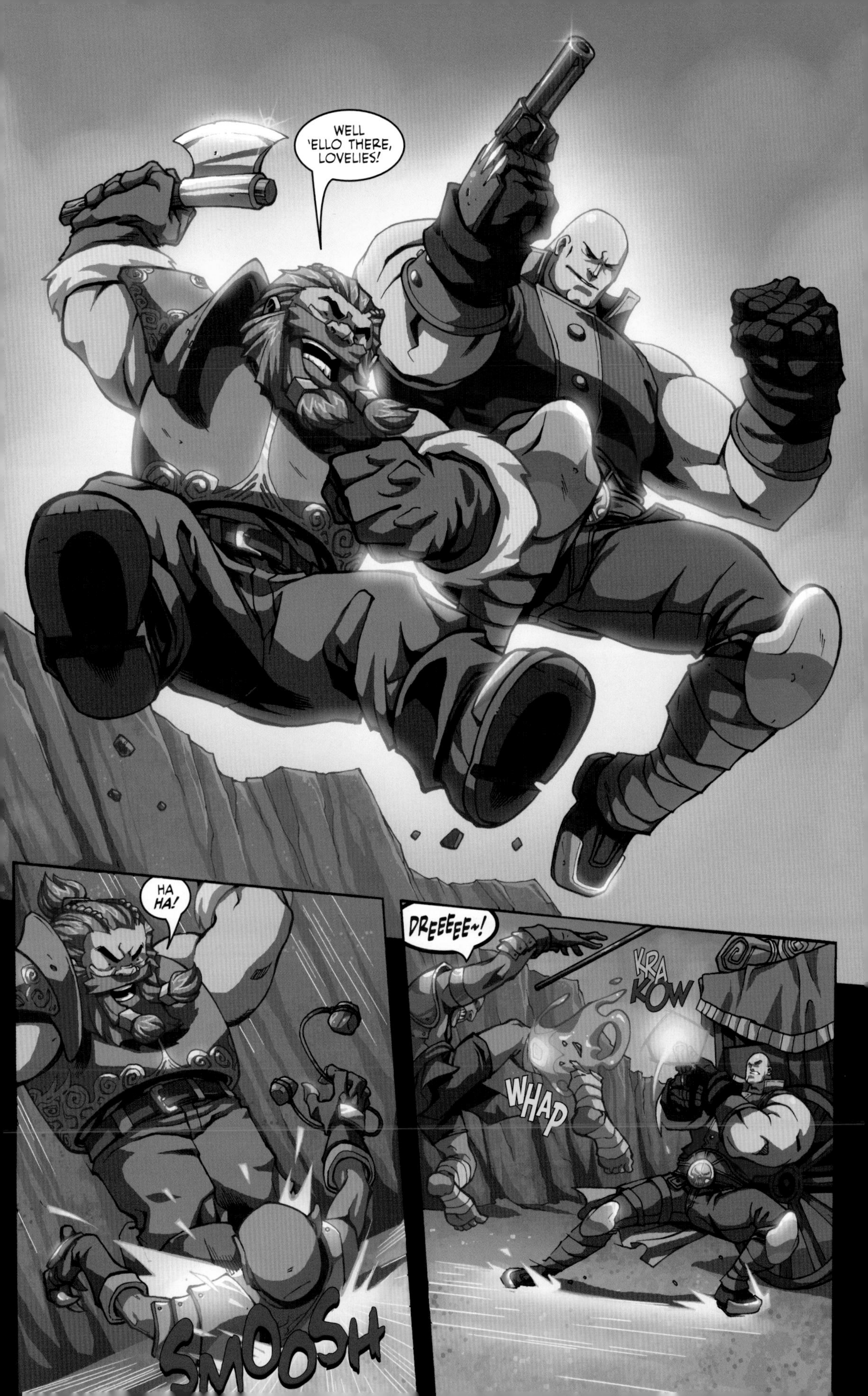
WELL 'ELLO THERE, LOVELIES!
HA HA!
SMOOSH
DREEEEEE~!
KRA KOW
WHAP

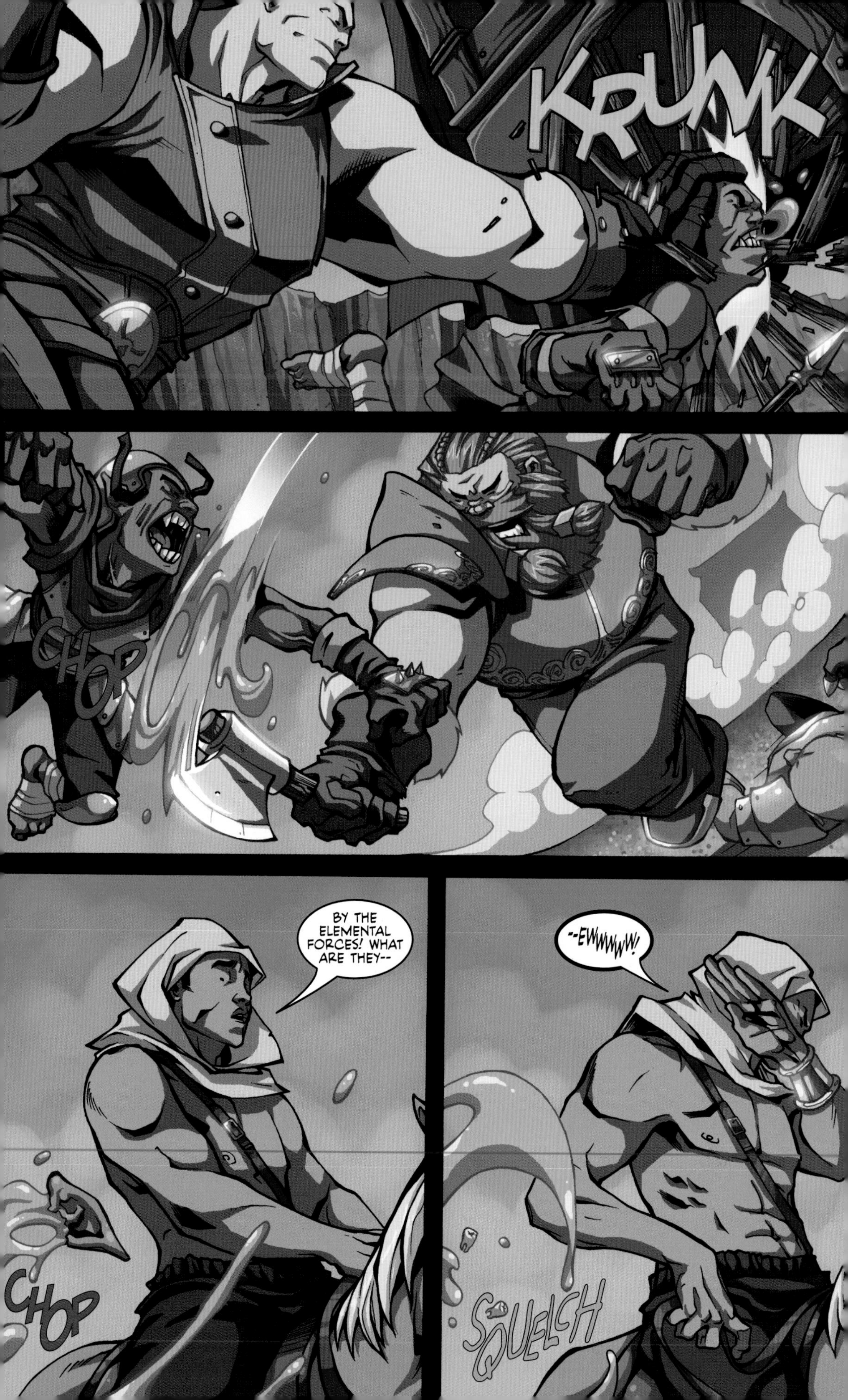
KRUNK
CHOP
BY THE ELEMENTAL FORCES! WHAT ARE THEY--
CHOP
--EWWWWW!
SQUELCH

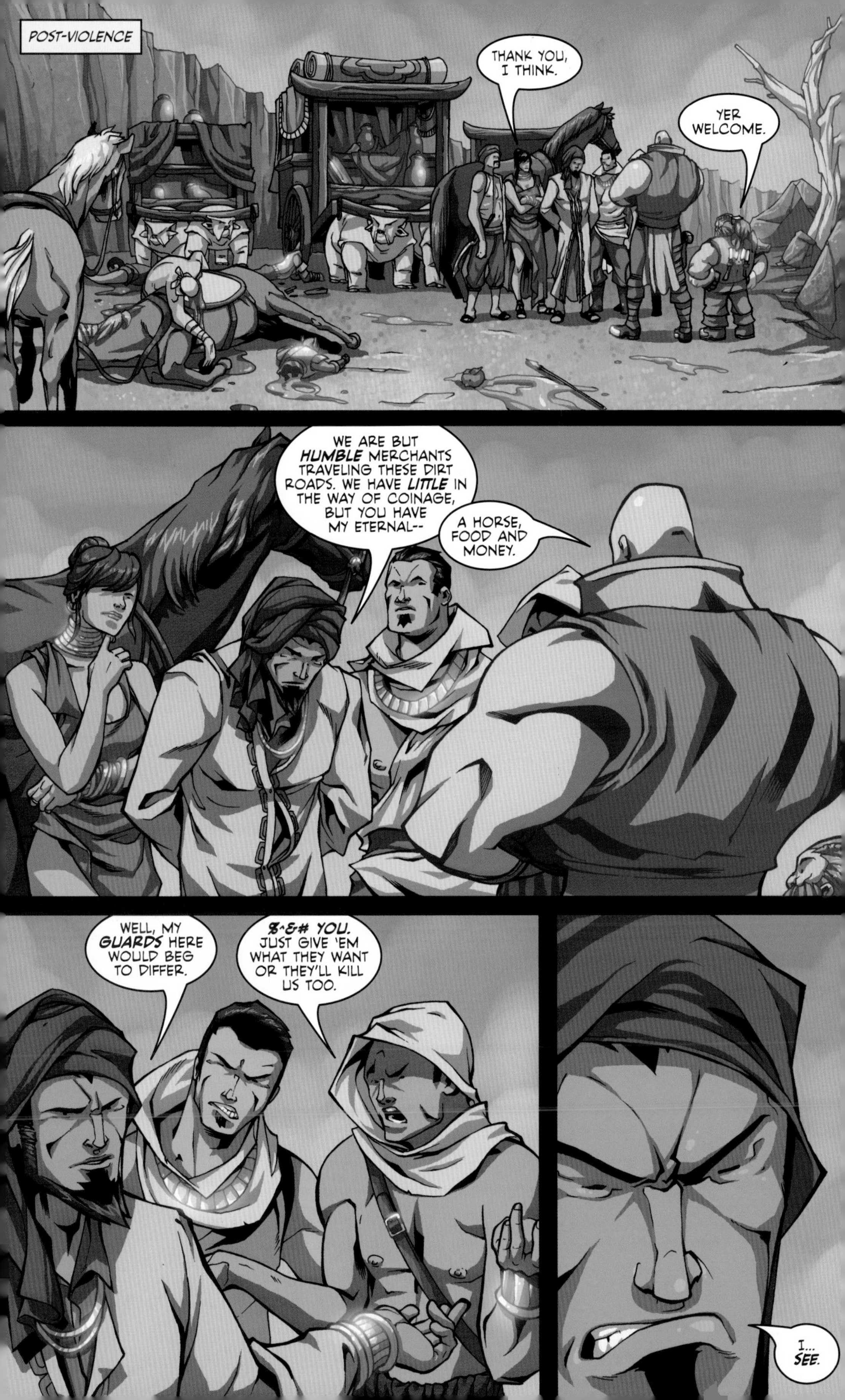
POST-VIOLENCE
THANK YOU, I THINK.
YER WELCOME.
WE ARE BUT HUMBLE MERCHANTS TRAVELING THESE DIRT ROADS. WE HAVE LITTLE IN THE WAY OF COINAGE, BUT YOU HAVE MY ETERNAL--
A HORSE, FOOD AND MONEY.
WELL, MY GUARDS HERE WOULD BEG TO DIFFER.
%^&# YOU. JUST GIVE 'EM WHAT THEY WANT OR THEY'LL KILL US TOO.
I... SEE.

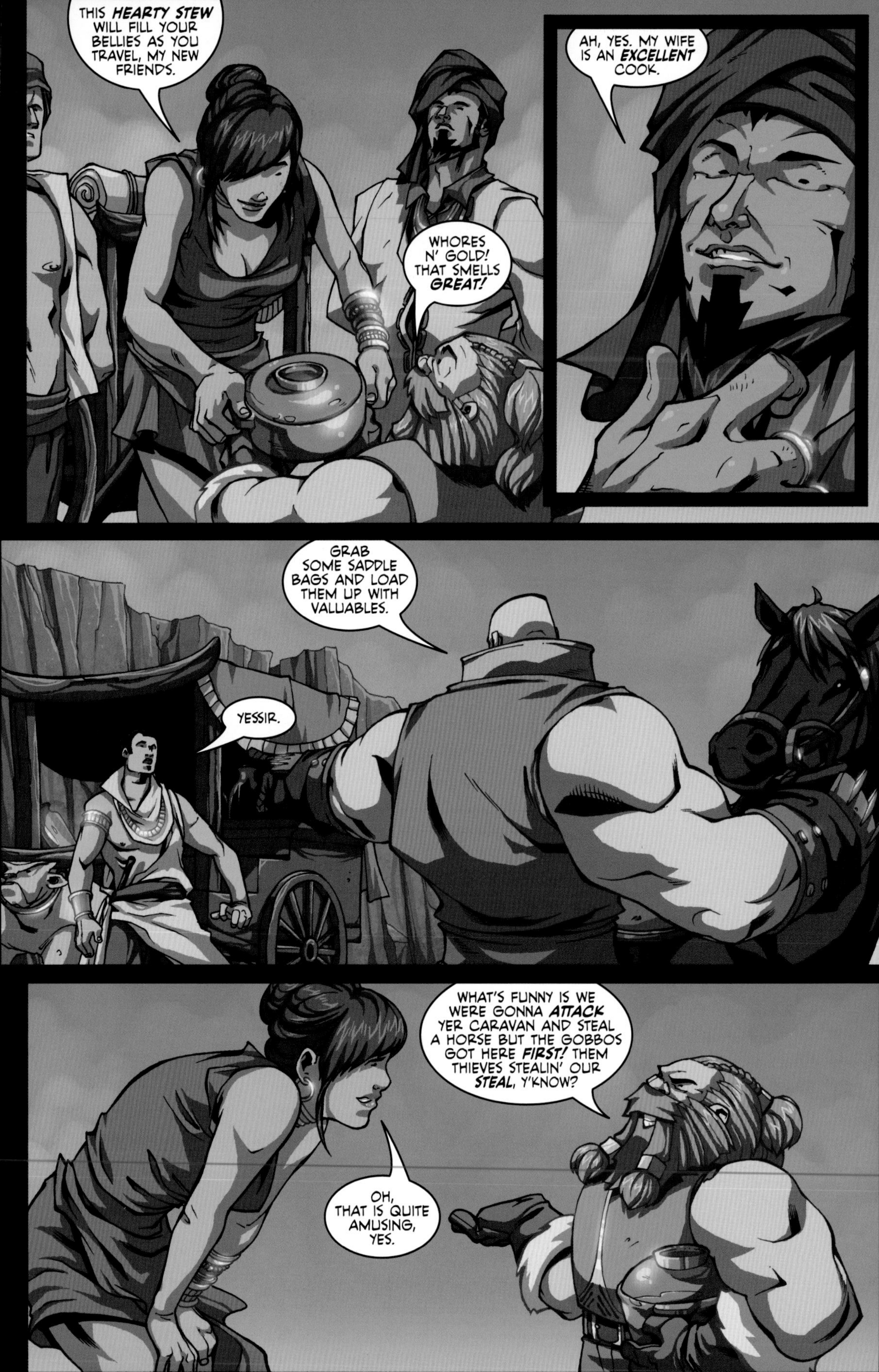
THIS HEARTY STEW WILL FILL YOUR BELLIES AS YOU TRAVEL, MY NEW FRIENDS.
WHORES N' GOLD! THAT SMELLS GREAT!
AH, YES. MY WIFE IS AN EXCELLENT COOK.
GRAB SOME SADDLE BAGS AND LOAD THEM UP WITH VALUABLES.
YESSIR.
WHAT'S FUNNY IS WE WERE GONNA ATTACK YER CARAVAN AND STEAL A HORSE BUT THE GOBBOS GOT HERE FIRST! THEM THIEVES STEALIN' OUR STEAL, Y'KNOW?
OH, THAT IS QUITE AMUSING, YES.

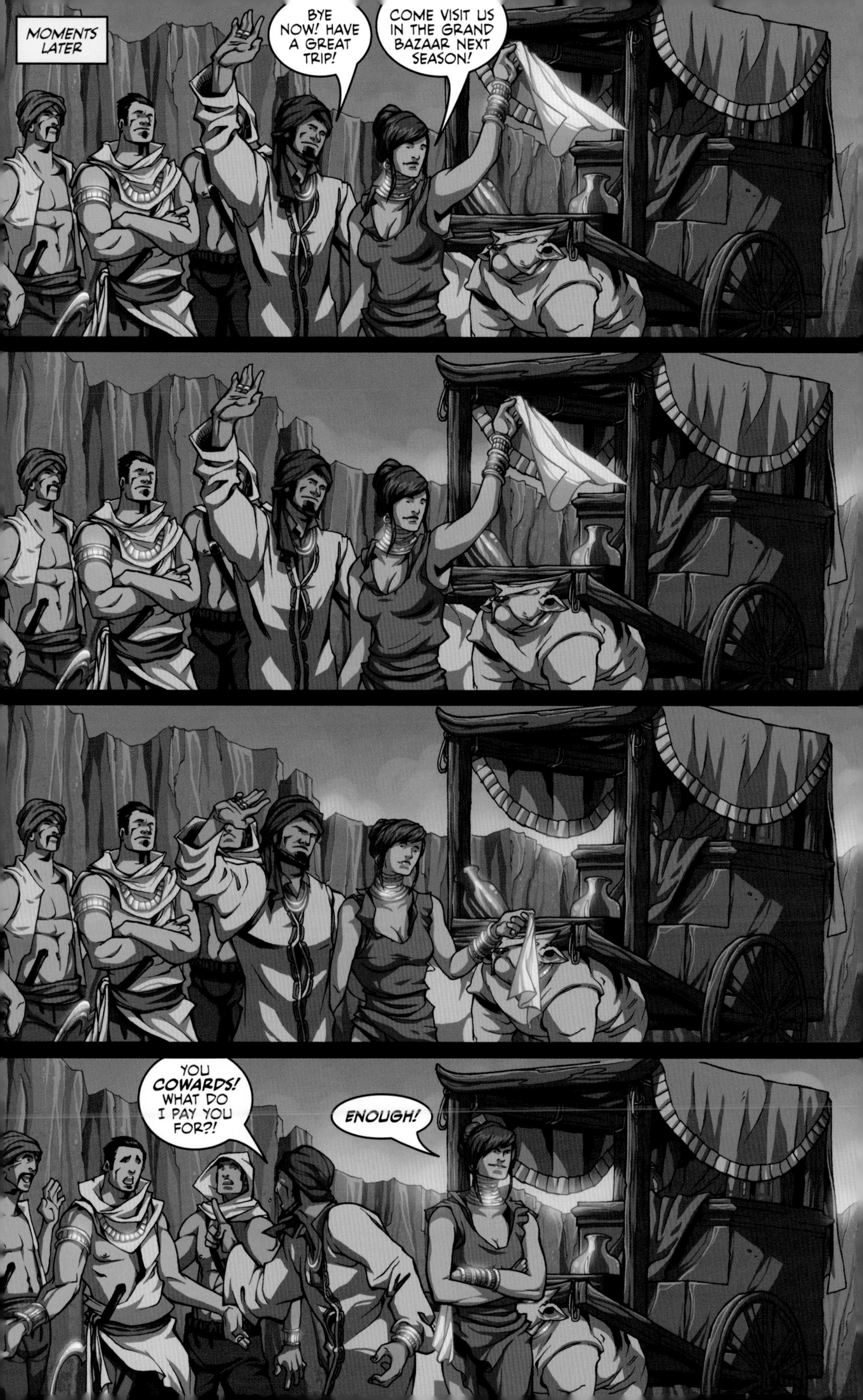
MOMENTS LATER
BYE NOW! HAVE A GREAT TRIP!
COME VISIT US IN THE GRAND BAZAAR NEXT SEASON!
YOU **COWARDS!** WHAT DO I PAY YOU FOR?!
ENOUGH!

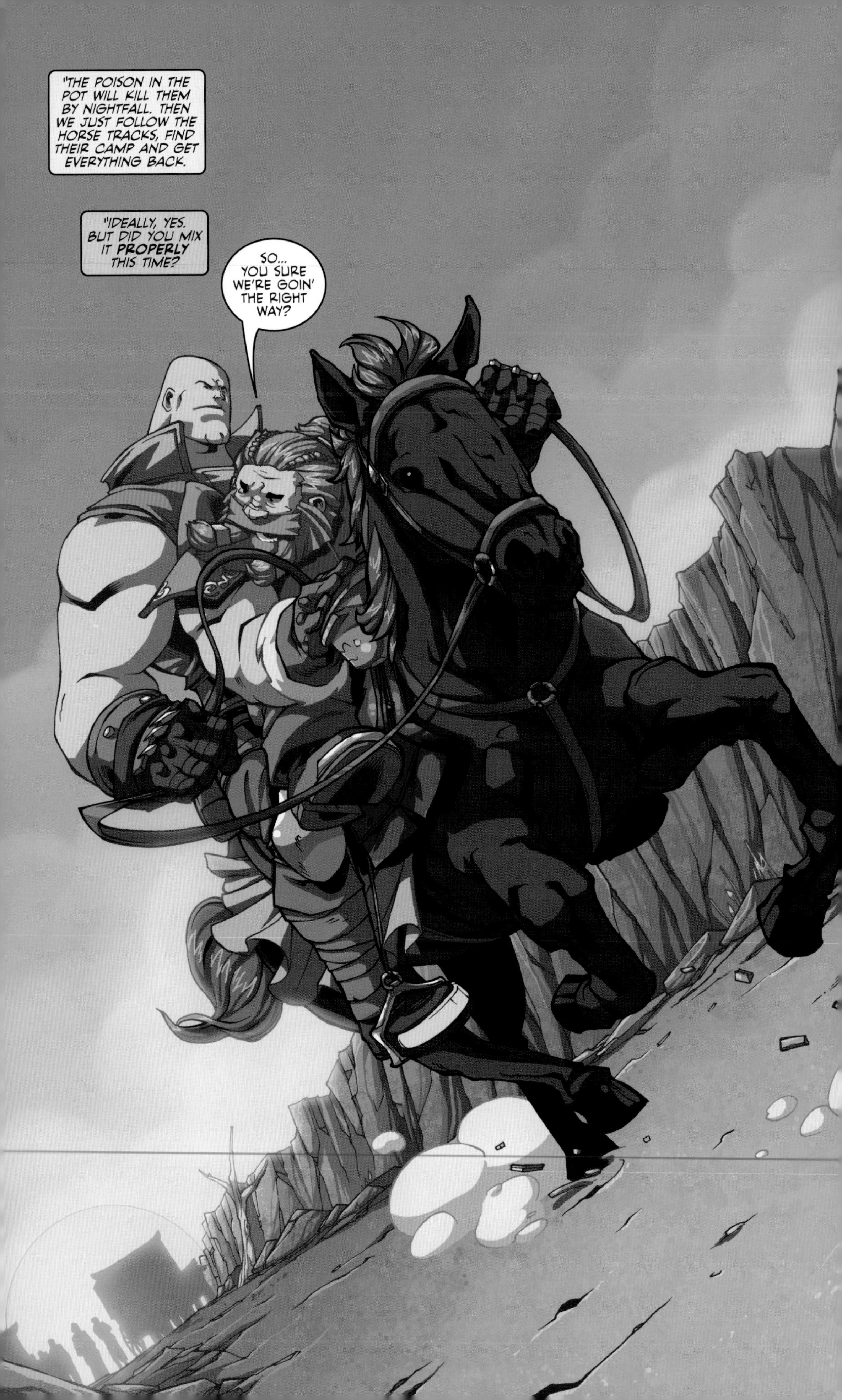
"THE POISON IN THE POT WILL KILL THEM BY NIGHTFALL. THEN WE JUST FOLLOW THE HORSE TRACKS, FIND THEIR CAMP AND GET EVERYTHING BACK.
"IDEALLY, YES. BUT DID YOU MIX IT **PROPERLY** THIS TIME?
SO... YOU SURE WE'RE GOIN' THE RIGHT WAY?

CHAPTER THREE

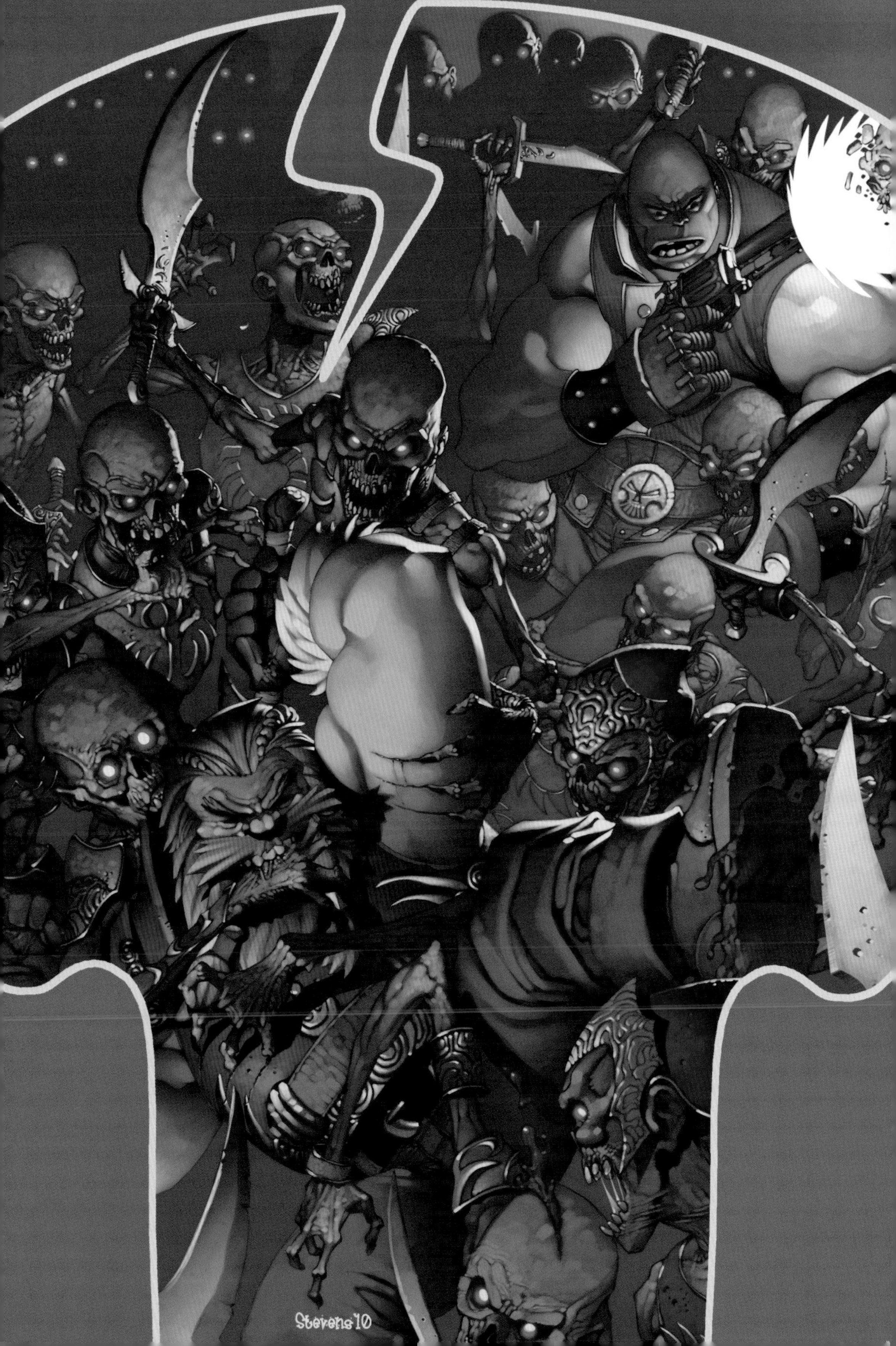
Stevens'10

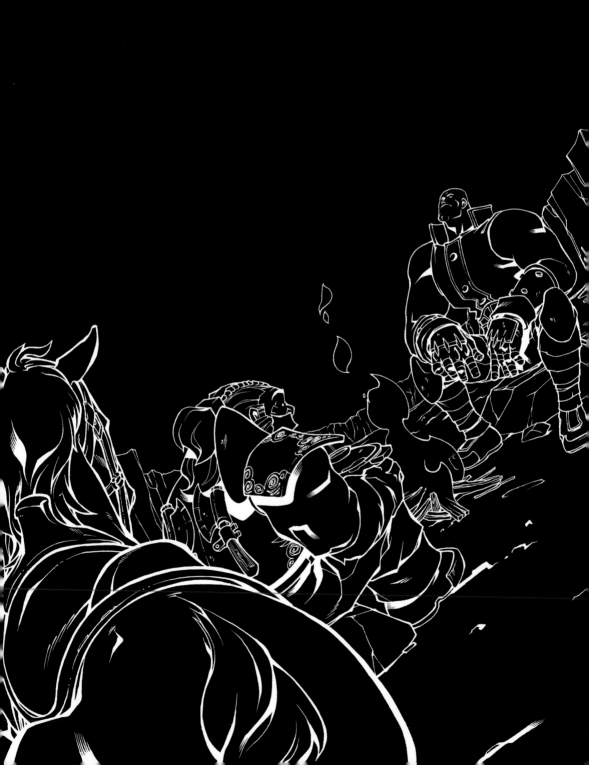

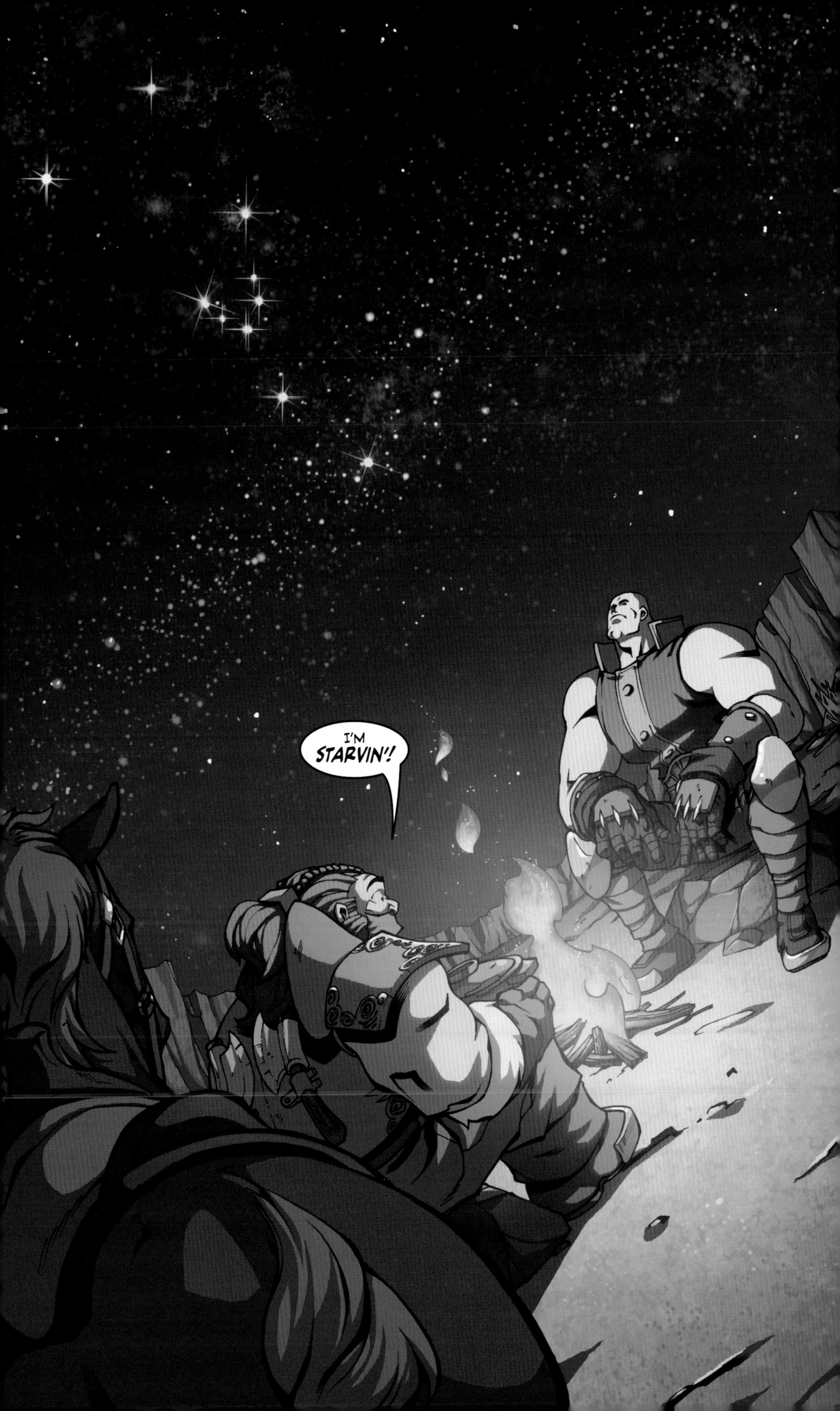
I'M STARVIN'!

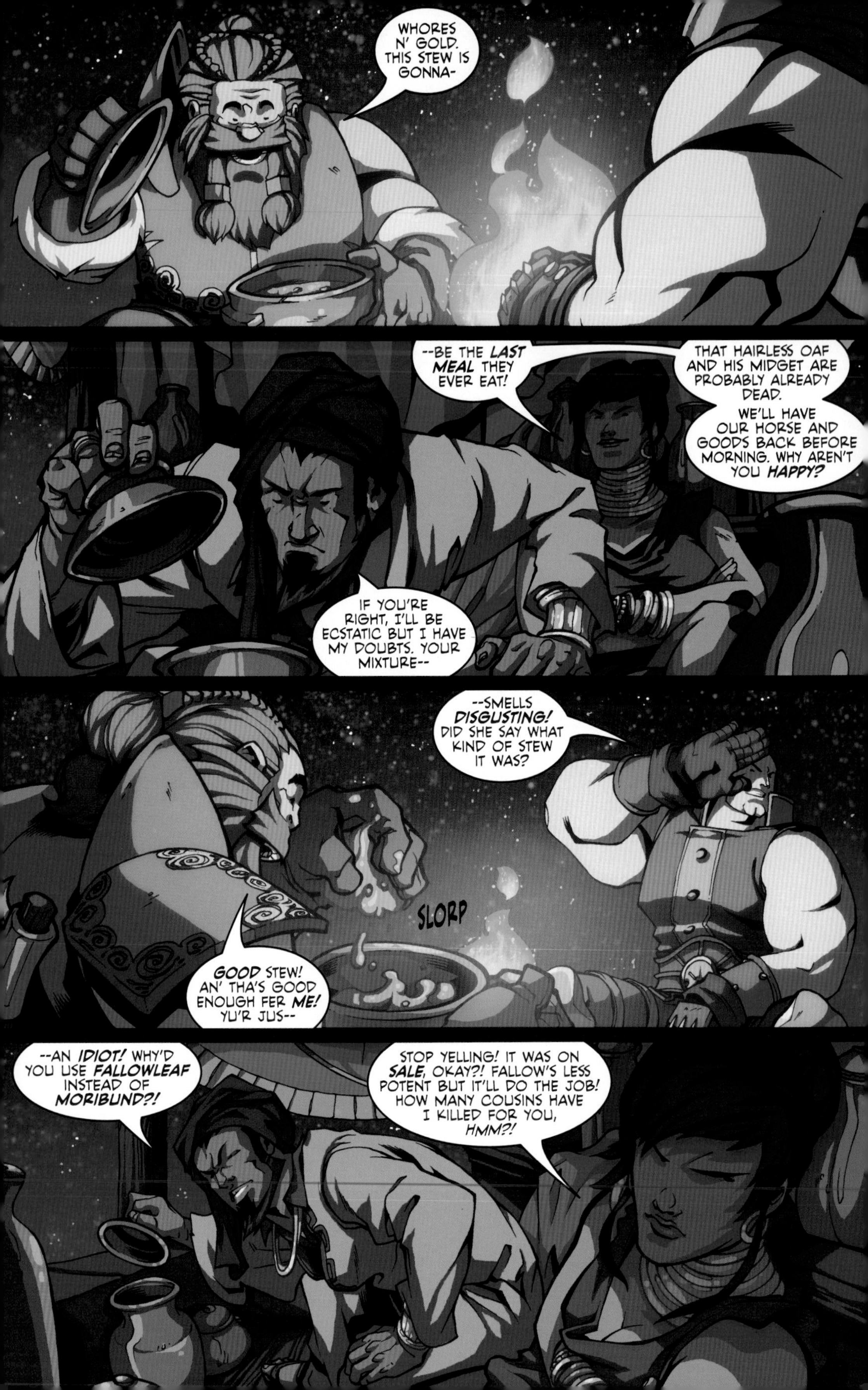
WHORES N' GOLD. THIS STEW IS GONNA-
--BE THE LAST MEAL THEY EVER EAT!
THAT HAIRLESS OAF AND HIS MIDGET ARE PROBABLY ALREADY DEAD.
WE'LL HAVE OUR HORSE AND GOODS BACK BEFORE MORNING. WHY AREN'T YOU HAPPY?
IF YOU'RE RIGHT, I'LL BE ECSTATIC BUT I HAVE MY DOUBTS. YOUR MIXTURE--
--SMELLS DISGUSTING! DID SHE SAY WHAT KIND OF STEW IT WAS?
SLORP
GOOD STEW! AN' THA'S GOOD ENOUGH FER ME! YU'R JUS--
--AN IDIOT! WHY'D YOU USE FALLOWLEAF INSTEAD OF MORIBUND?!
STOP YELLING! IT WAS ON SALE, OKAY?! FALLOW'S LESS POTENT BUT IT'LL DO THE JOB! HOW MANY COUSINS HAVE I KILLED FOR YOU, HMM?!

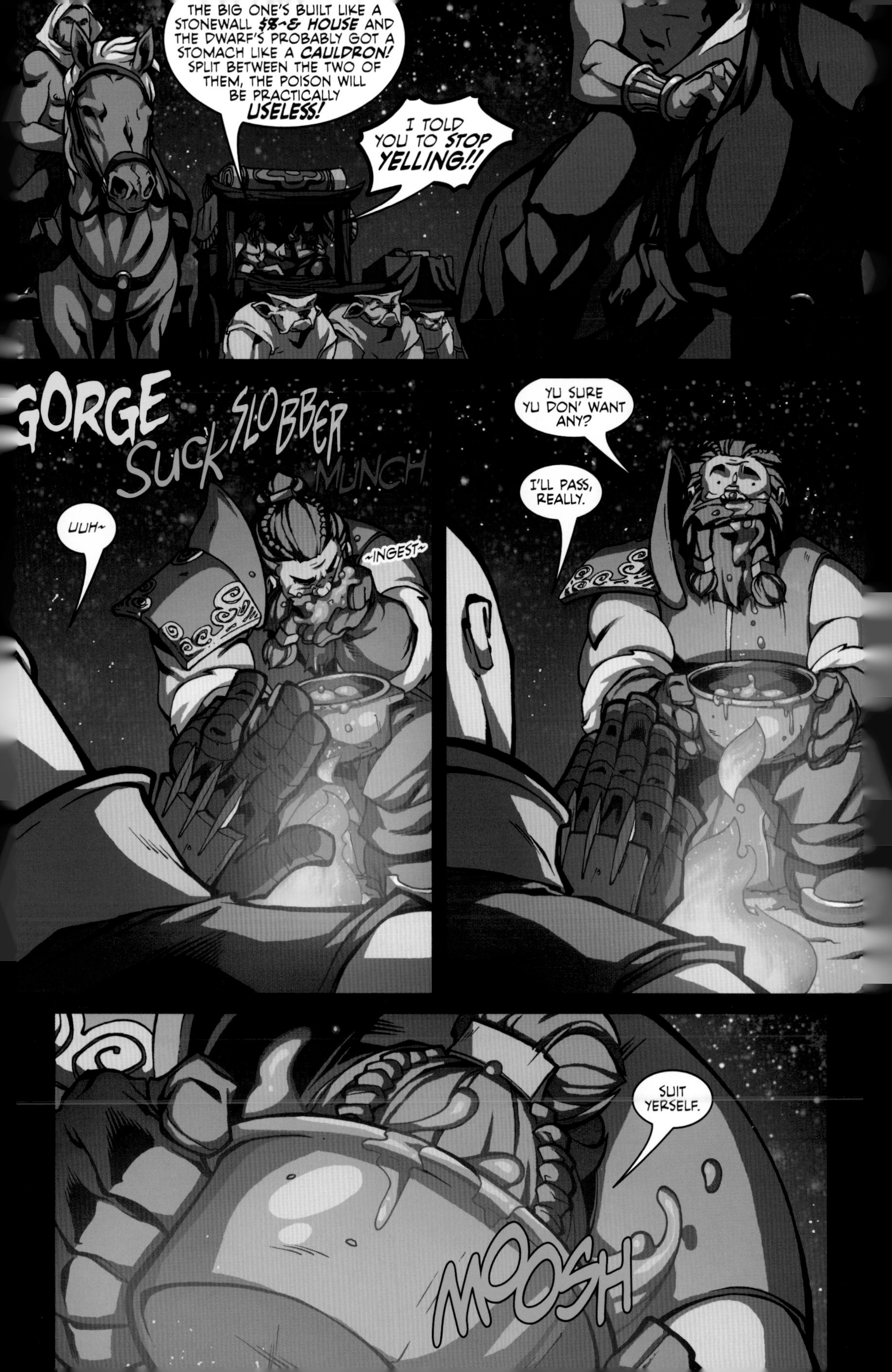
THE BIG ONE'S BUILT LIKE A STONEWALL $%~& HOUSE AND THE DWARF'S PROBABLY GOT A STOMACH LIKE A CAULDRON! SPLIT BETWEEN THE TWO OF THEM, THE POISON WILL BE PRACTICALLY USELESS!
I TOLD YOU TO STOP YELLING!!
GORGE
SUCK SLOBBER
MUNCH
UUH~
~INGEST~
YU SURE YU DON' WANT ANY?
I'LL PASS, REALLY.
SUIT YERSELF.
MOOSH

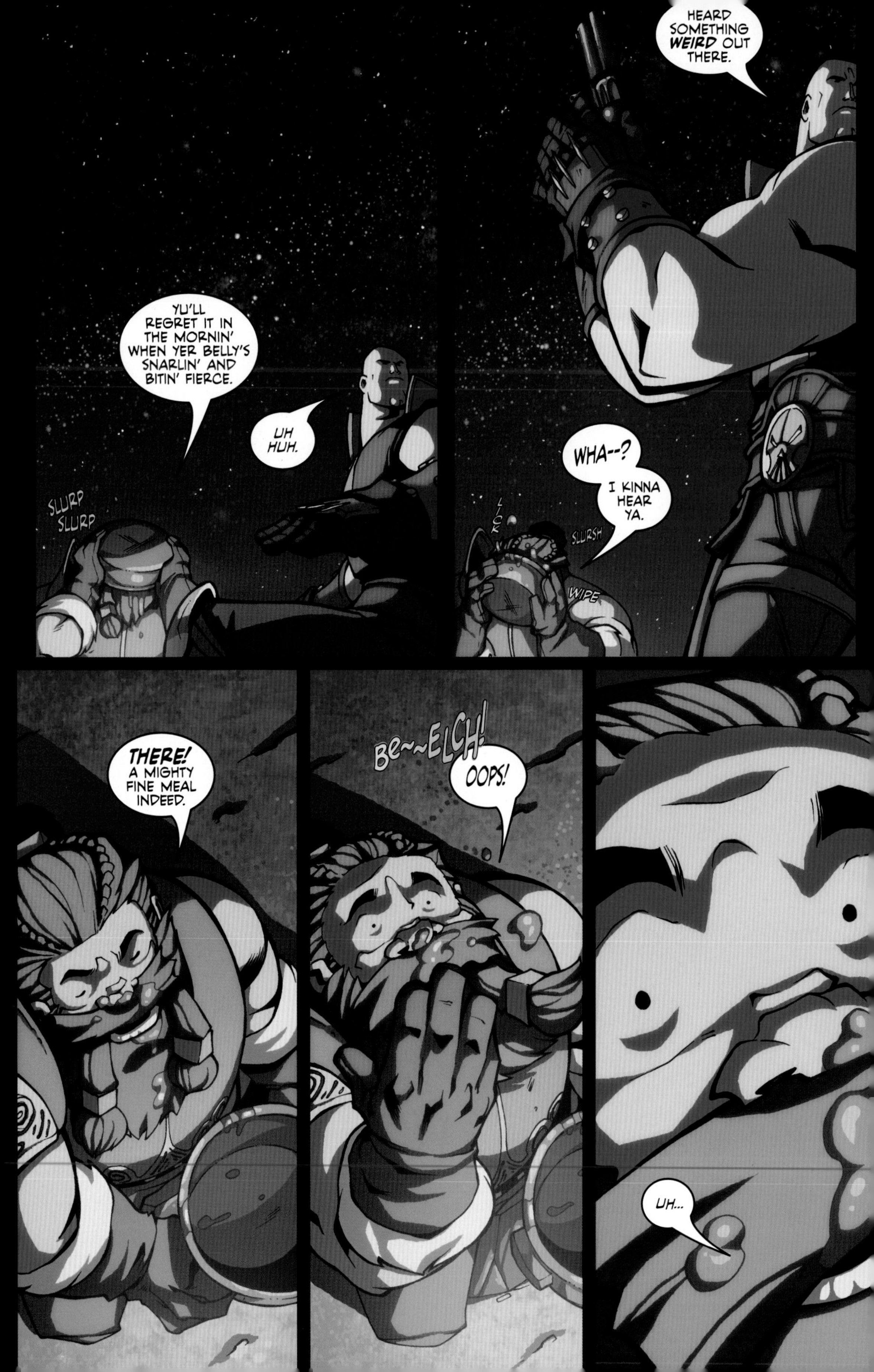
YU'LL REGRET IT IN THE MORNIN' WHEN YER BELLY'S SNARLIN' AND BITIN' FIERCE.
UH HUH.
SLURP SLURP
HEARD SOMETHING WEIRD OUT THERE.
WHA--?
I KINNA HEAR YA.
LICK
SLURSH
WIPE
THERE! A MIGHTY FINE MEAL INDEED.
BE~~ELCH!
OOPS!
UH...

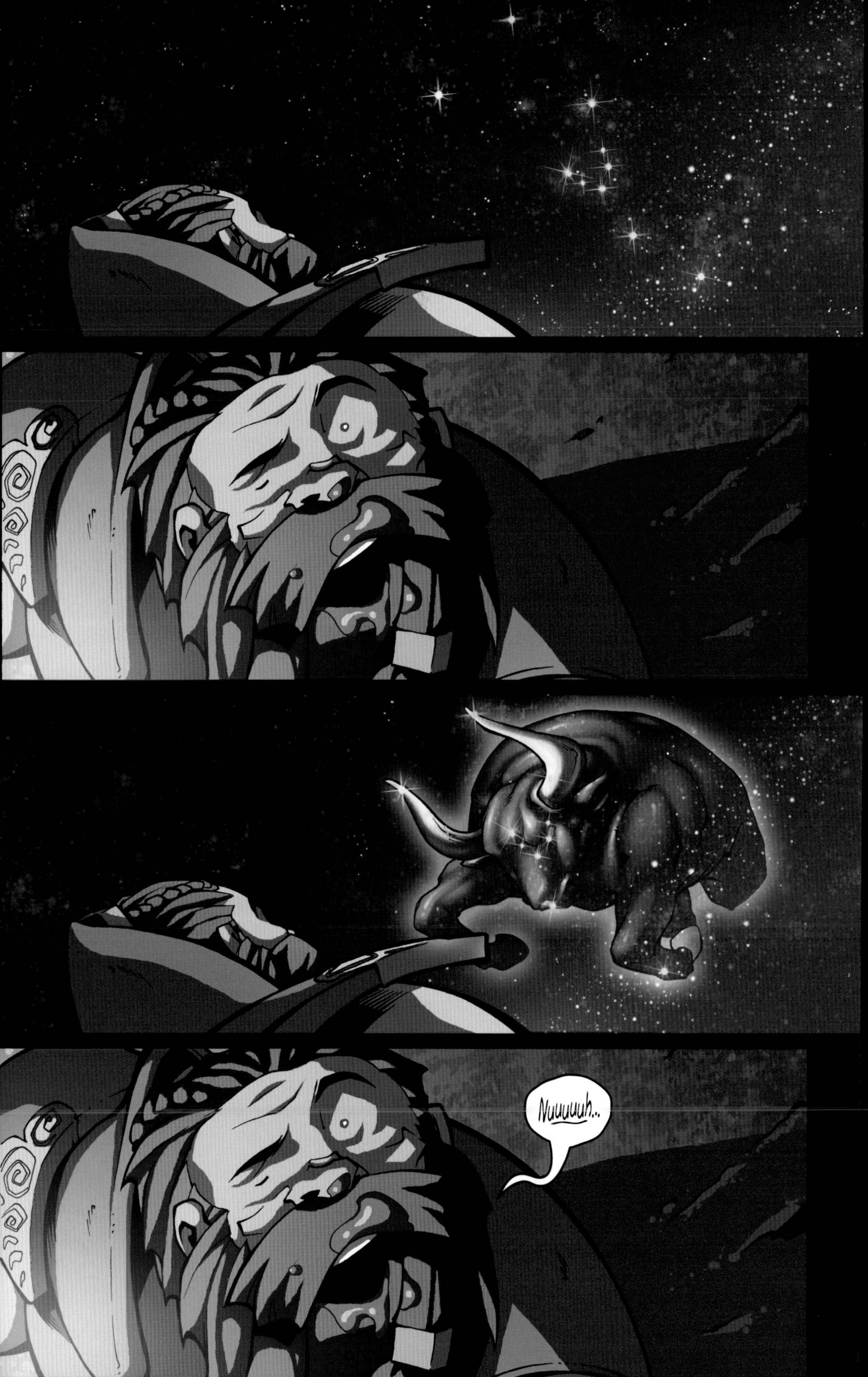
Nuuuuuh...

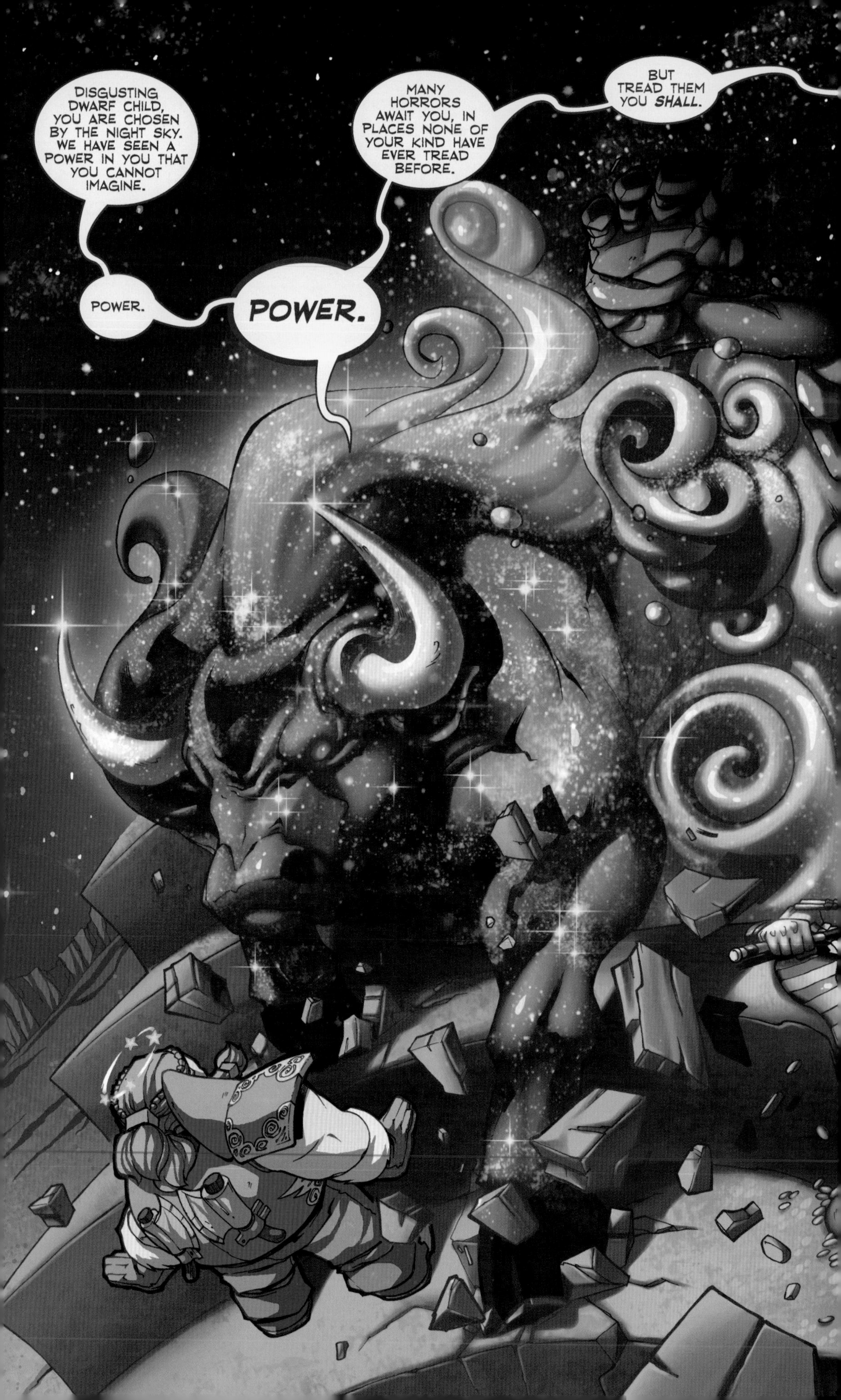
DISGUSTING DWARF CHILD, YOU ARE CHOSEN BY THE NIGHT SKY. WE HAVE SEEN A POWER IN YOU THAT YOU CANNOT IMAGINE.
POWER.
POWER.
MANY HORRORS AWAIT YOU, IN PLACES NONE OF YOUR KIND HAVE EVER TREAD BEFORE.
BUT TREAD THEM YOU SHALL.

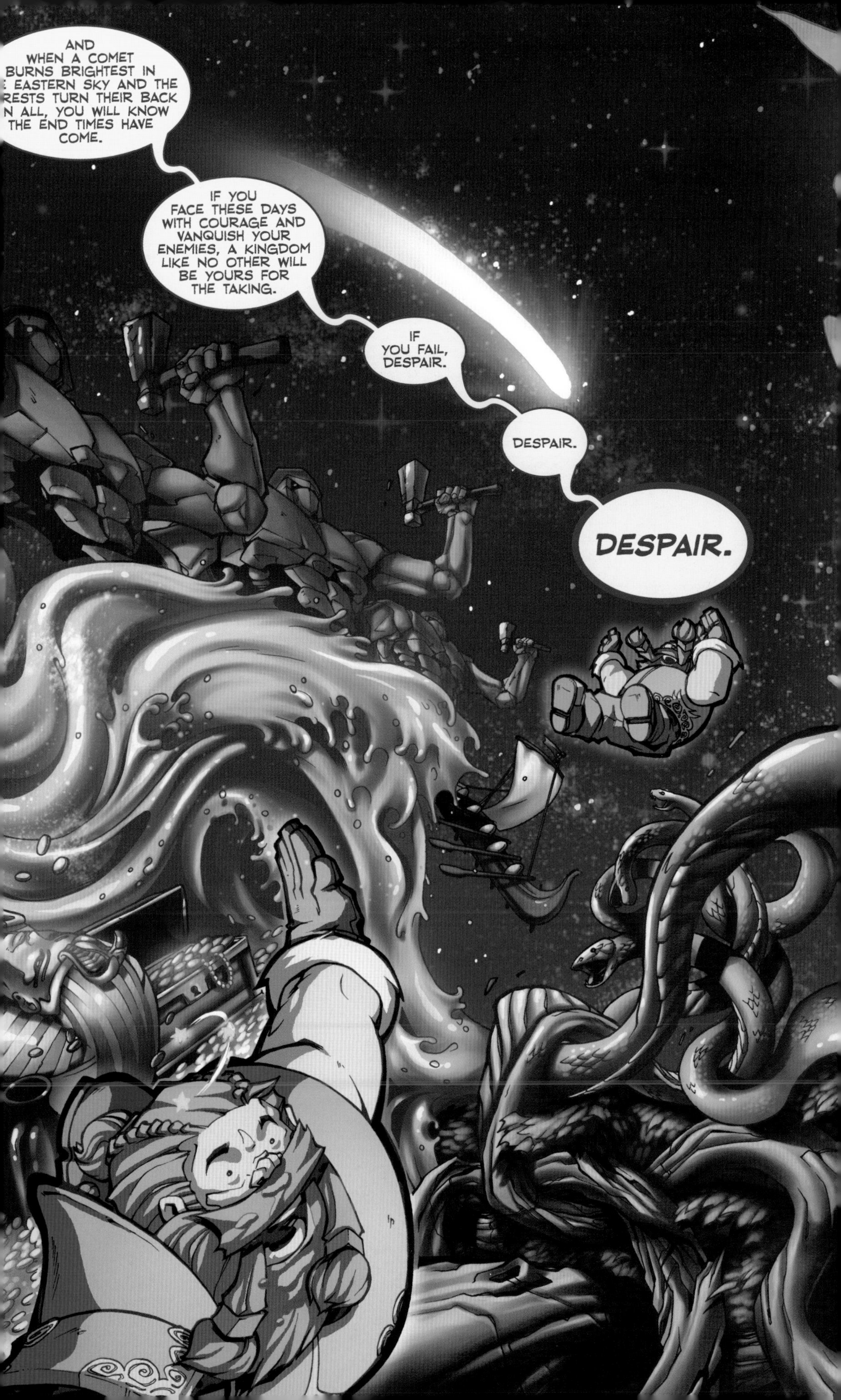
AND WHEN A COMET BURNS BRIGHTEST IN E EASTERN SKY AND THE RESTS TURN THEIR BACK N ALL, YOU WILL KNOW THE END TIMES HAVE COME.
IF YOU FACE THESE DAYS WITH COURAGE AND VANQUISH YOUR ENEMIES, A KINGDOM LIKE NO OTHER WILL BE YOURS FOR THE TAKING.
IF YOU FAIL, DESPAIR.
DESPAIR.
DESPAIR.

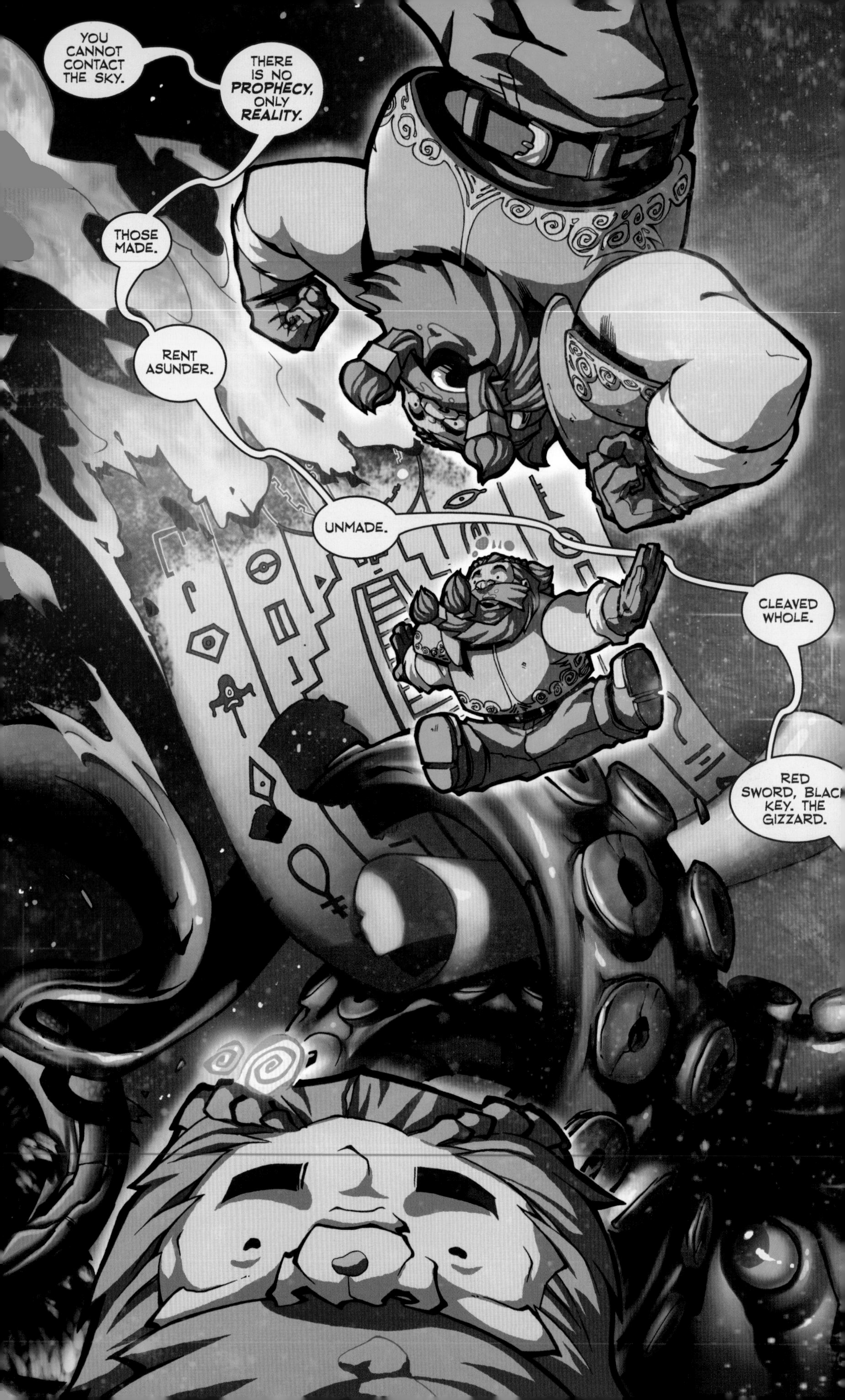
YOU CANNOT CONTACT THE SKY.
THERE IS NO PROPHECY, ONLY REALITY.
THOSE MADE.
RENT ASUNDER.
UNMADE.
CLEAVED WHOLE.
RED SWORD, BLACK KEY. THE GIZZARD.

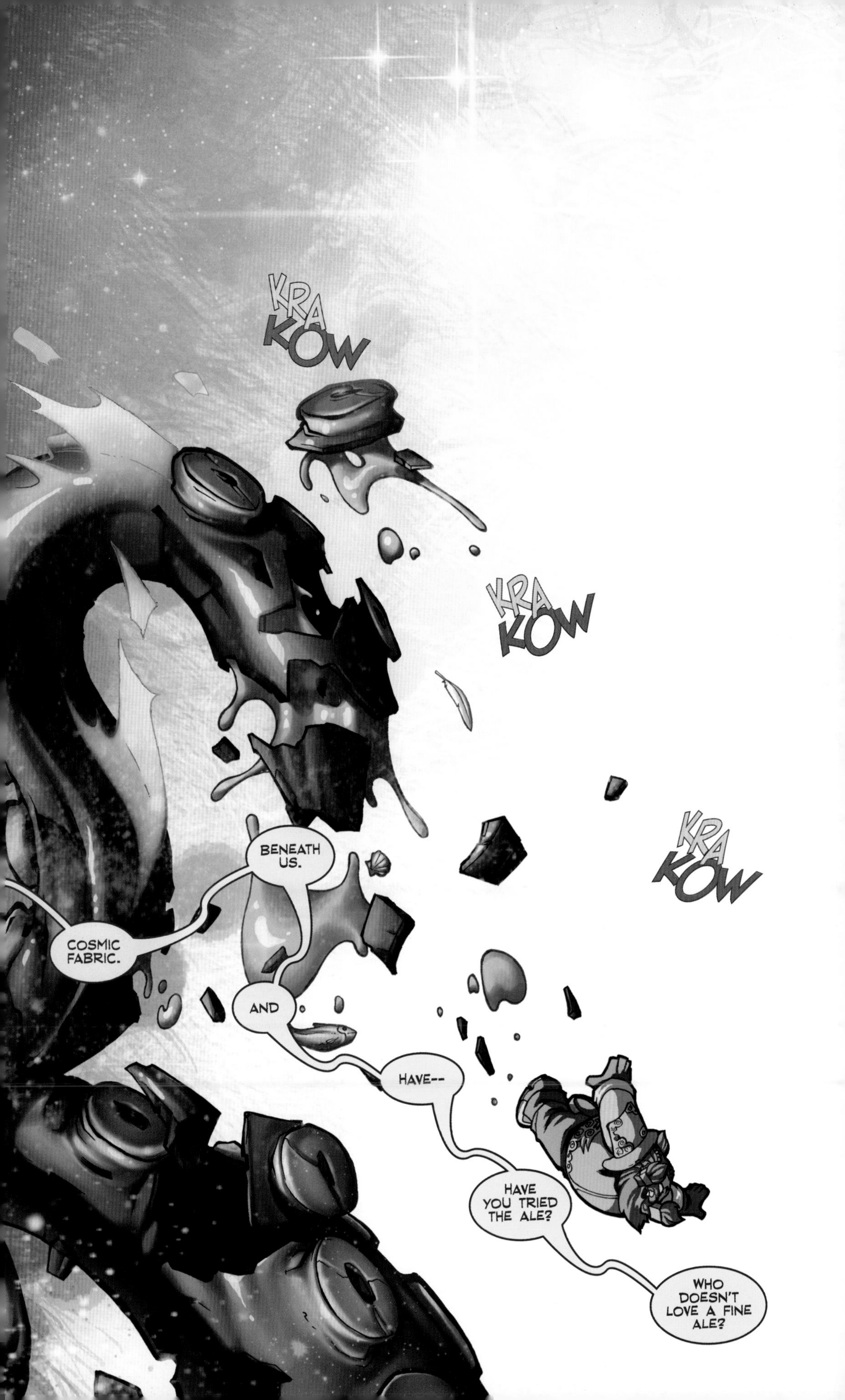
KRA KOW
KRA KOW
KRA KOW
BENEATH US.
COSMIC FABRIC.
AND
HAVE--
HAVE YOU TRIED THE ALE?
WHO DOESN'T LOVE A FINE ALE?

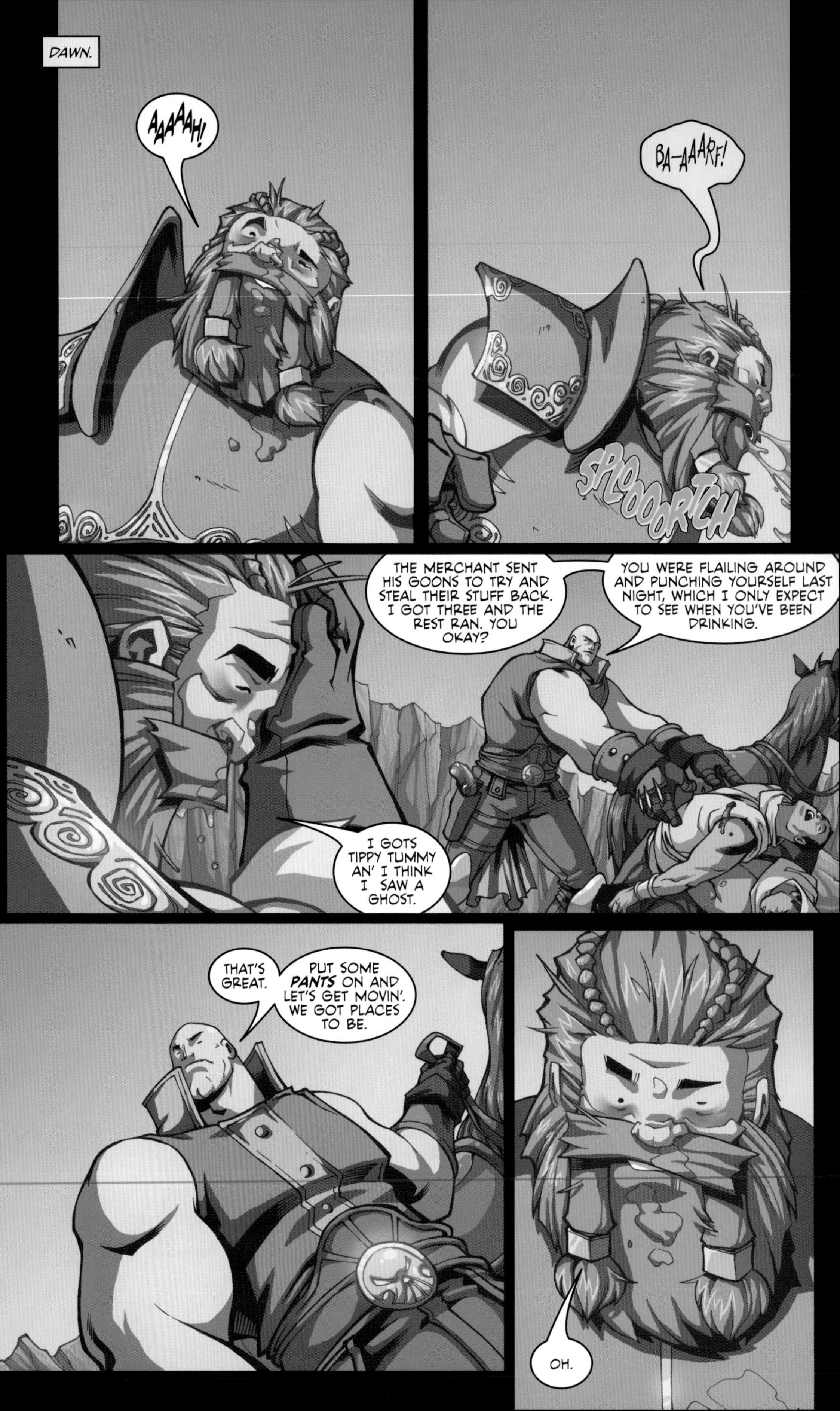
DAWN.
AAAAAH!
BA-AAARF!
SPLOOOORTCH
THE MERCHANT SENT HIS GOONS TO TRY AND STEAL THEIR STUFF BACK. I GOT THREE AND THE REST RAN. YOU OKAY?
YOU WERE FLAILING AROUND AND PUNCHING YOURSELF LAST NIGHT, WHICH I ONLY EXPECT TO SEE WHEN YOU'VE BEEN DRINKING.
I GOTS TIPPY TUMMY AN' I THINK I SAW A GHOST.
THAT'S GREAT.
PUT SOME PANTS ON AND LET'S GET MOVIN'. WE GOT PLACES TO BE.
OH.

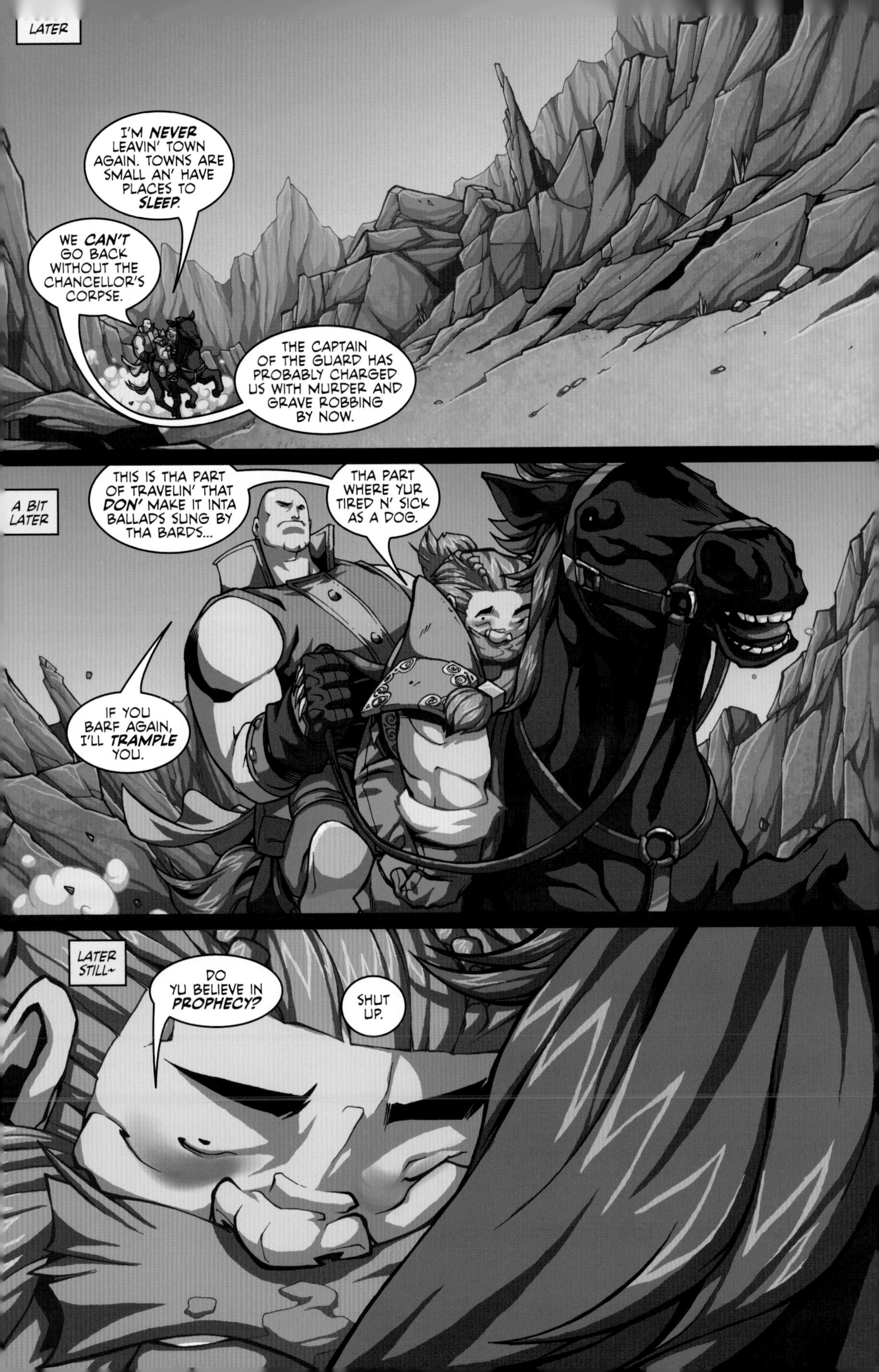
LATER
I'M NEVER LEAVIN' TOWN AGAIN. TOWNS ARE SMALL AN' HAVE PLACES TO SLEEP.
WE CAN'T GO BACK WITHOUT THE CHANCELLOR'S CORPSE.
THE CAPTAIN OF THE GUARD HAS PROBABLY CHARGED US WITH MURDER AND GRAVE ROBBING BY NOW.
A BIT LATER
THIS IS THA PART OF TRAVELIN' THAT DON' MAKE IT INTA BALLADS SUNG BY THA BARDS...
THA PART WHERE YUR TIRED N' SICK AS A DOG.
IF YOU BARF AGAIN, I'LL TRAMPLE YOU.
LATER STILL~
DO YU BELIEVE IN PROPHECY?
SHUT UP.

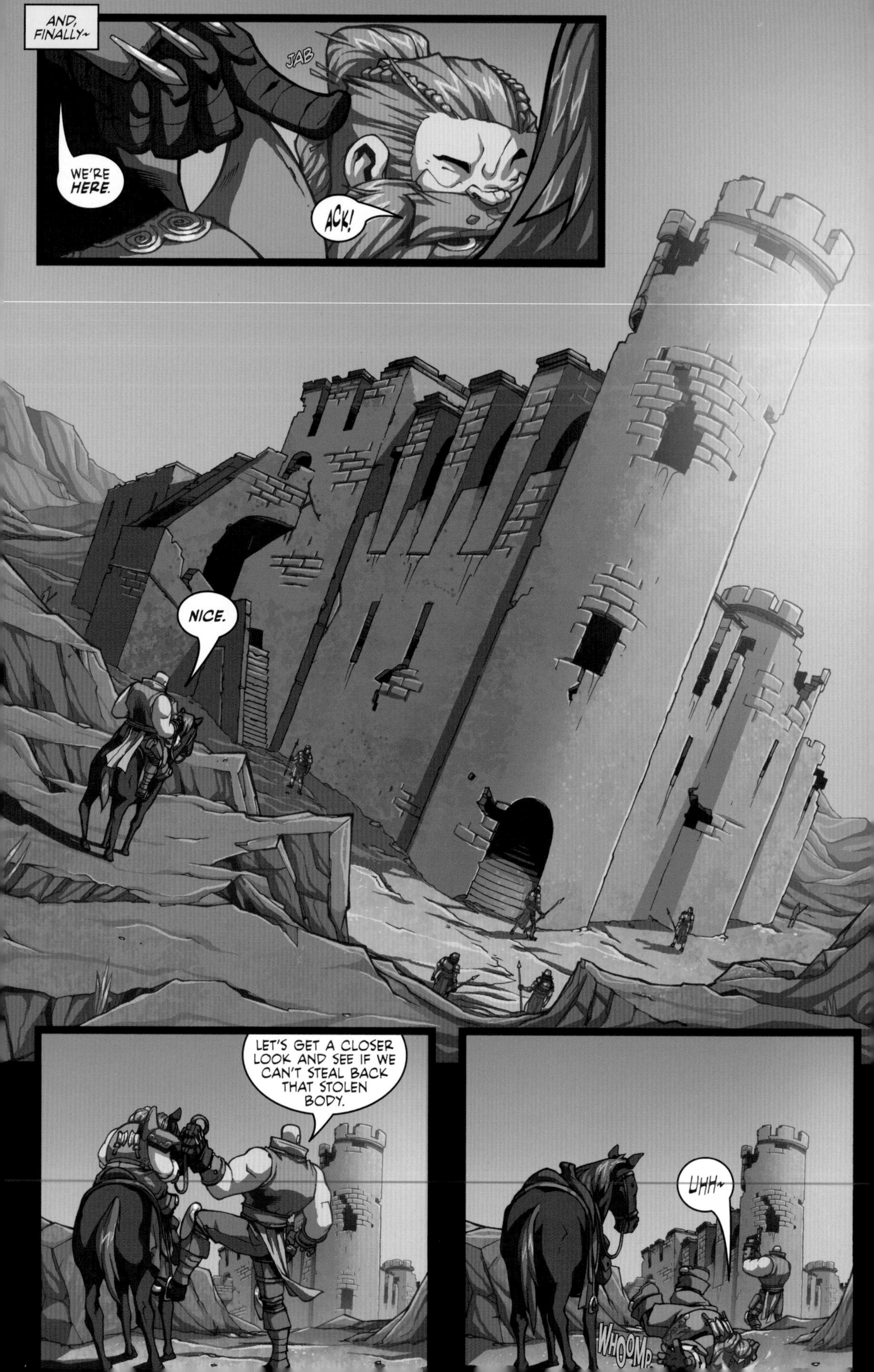
AND, FINALLY~
JAB
WE'RE HERE.
ACK!
NICE.
LET'S GET A CLOSER LOOK AND SEE IF WE CAN'T STEAL BACK THAT STOLEN BODY.
UHH~
WHOOMP

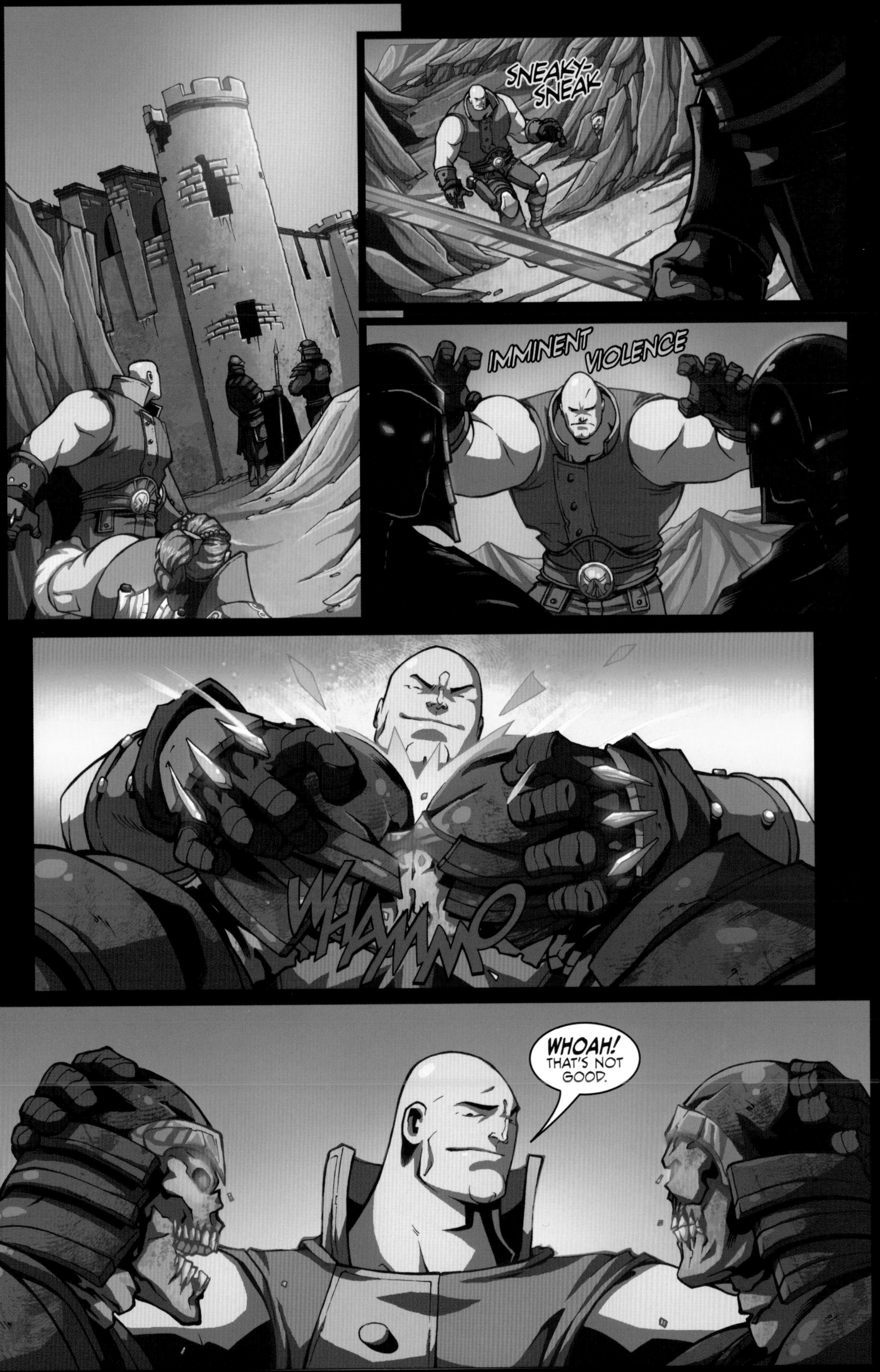
SNEAKY-SNEAK
IMMINENT VIOLENCE
WHAMMO
WHOAH! THAT'S NOT GOOD.

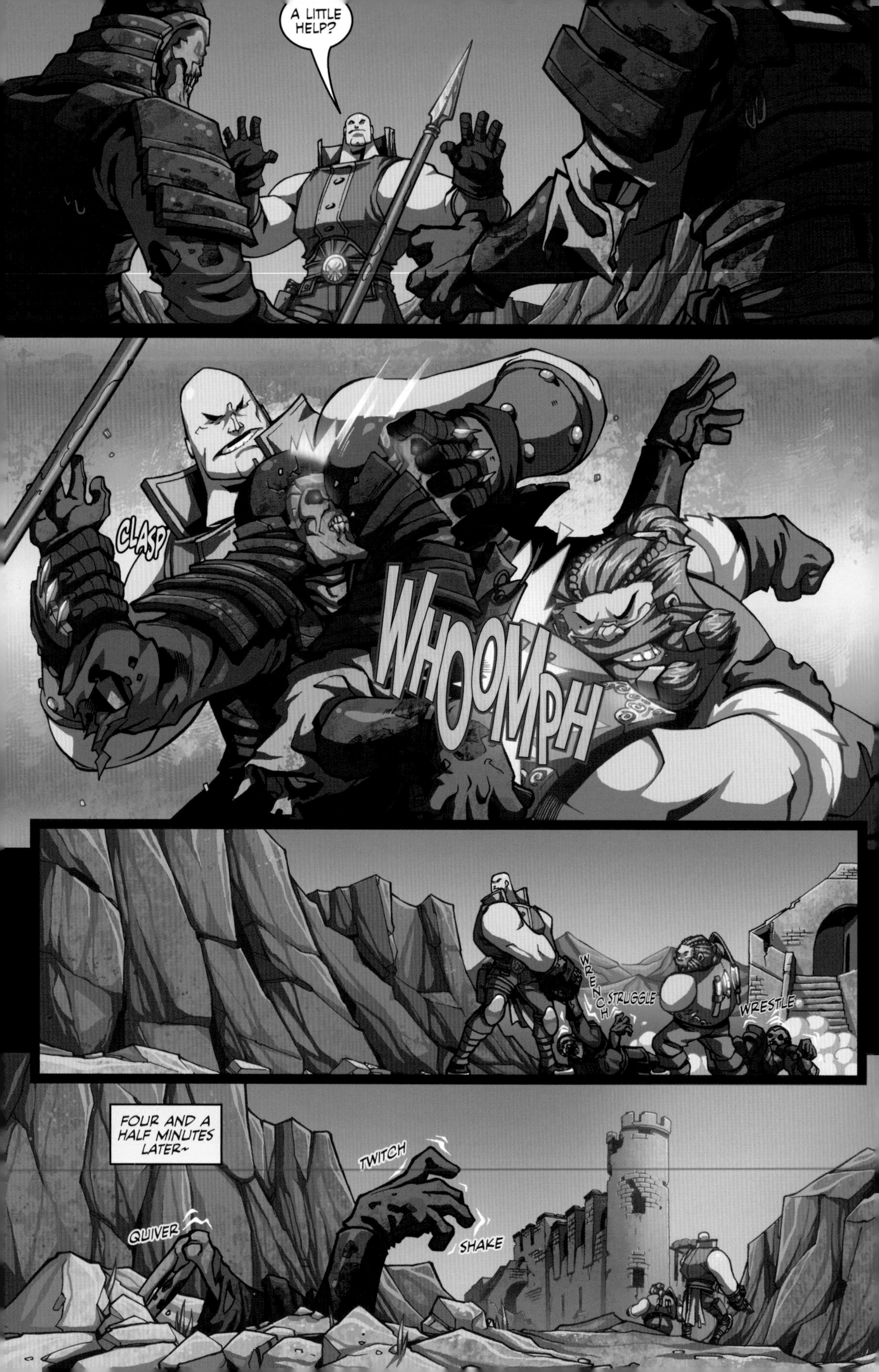
A LITTLE HELP?
CLASP!
WHOOMPH
WRENCH
STRUGGLE
WRESTLE
FOUR AND A HALF MINUTES LATER~
TWITCH
QUIVER
SHAKE

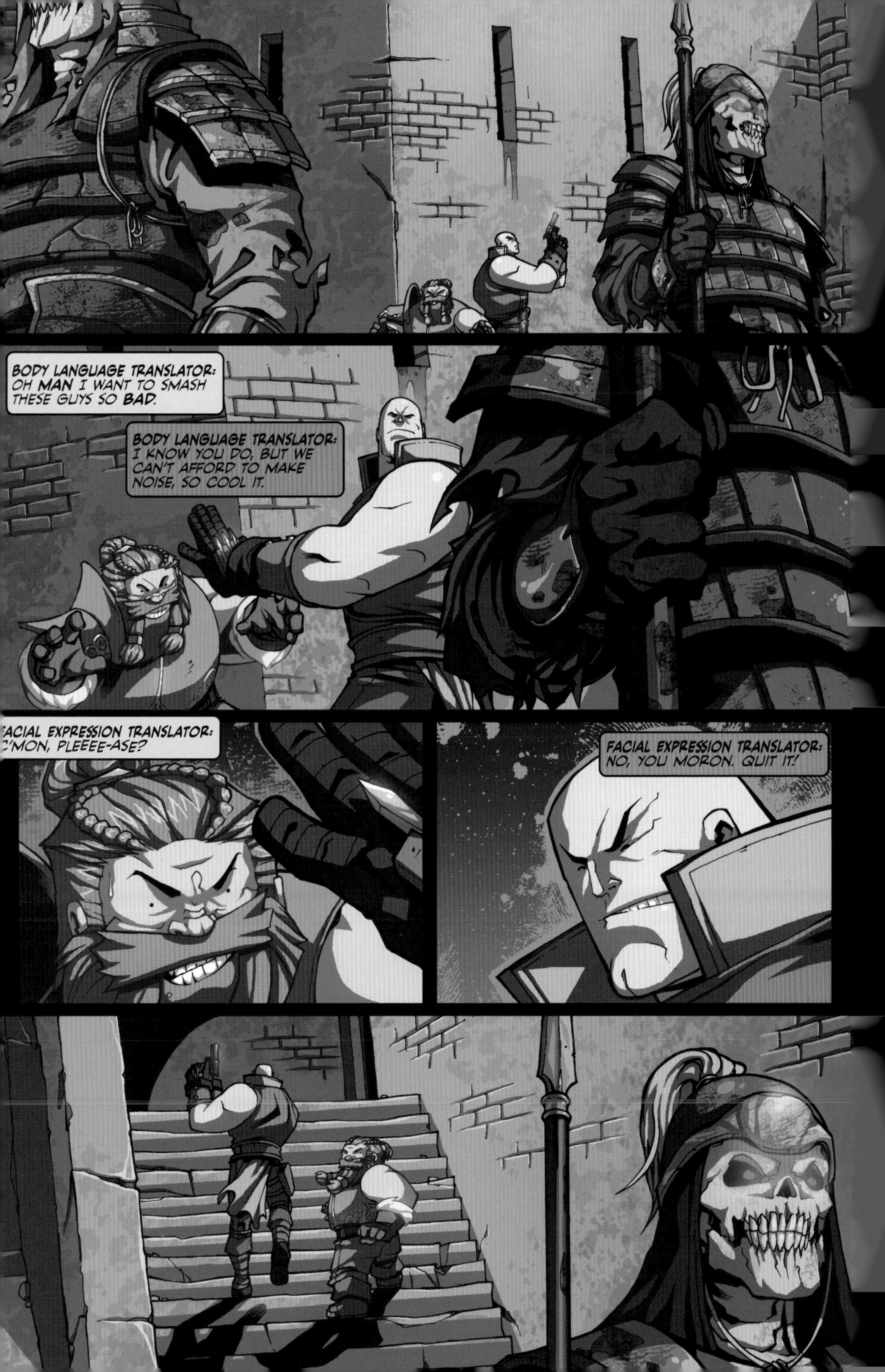
BODY LANGUAGE TRANSLATOR: OH MAN I WANT TO SMASH THESE GUYS SO BAD.
BODY LANGUAGE TRANSLATOR: I KNOW YOU DO, BUT WE CAN'T AFFORD TO MAKE NOISE, SO COOL IT.
FACIAL EXPRESSION TRANSLATOR: C'MON, PLEEEE-ASE?
FACIAL EXPRESSION TRANSLATOR: NO, YOU MORON. QUIT IT!

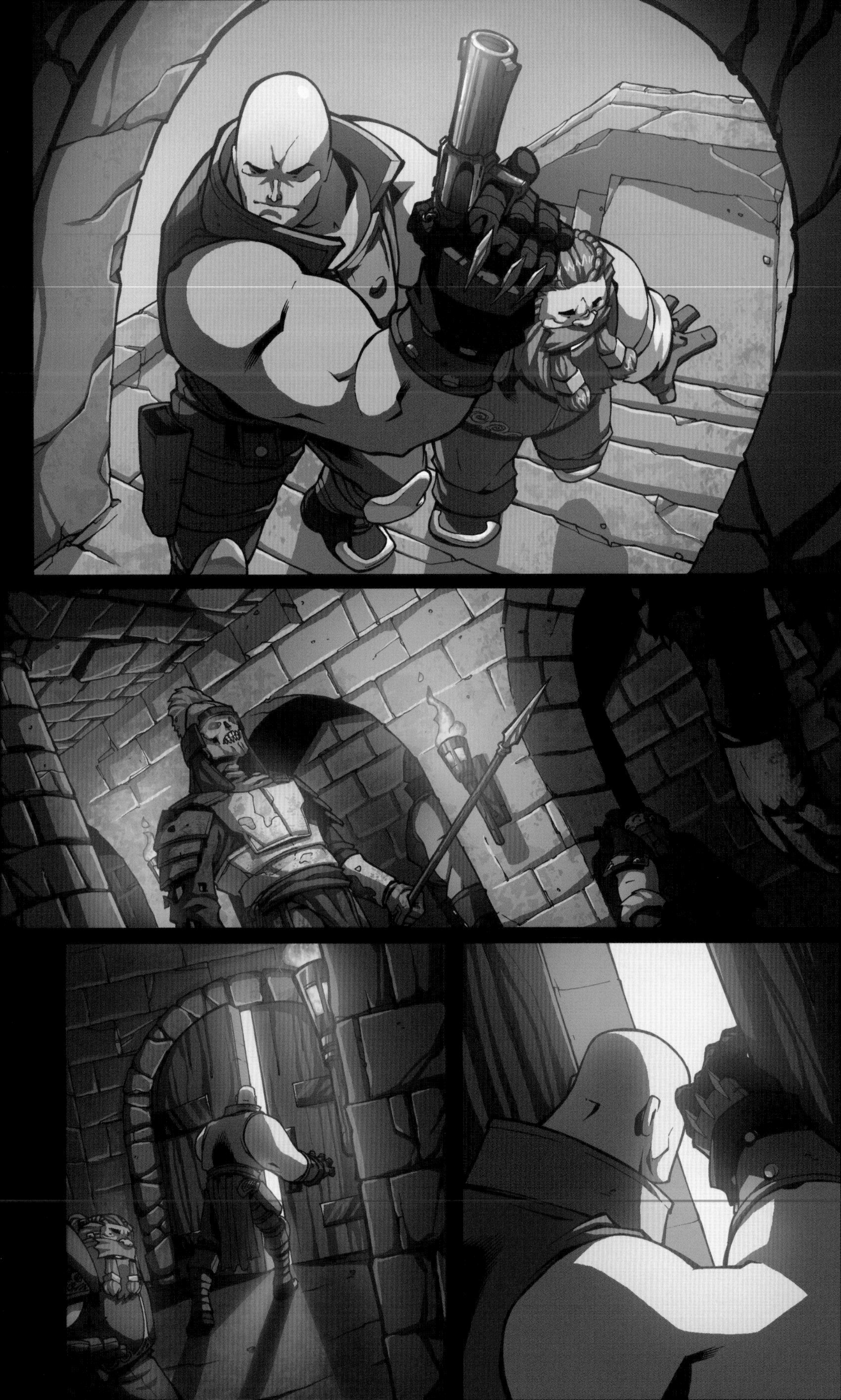

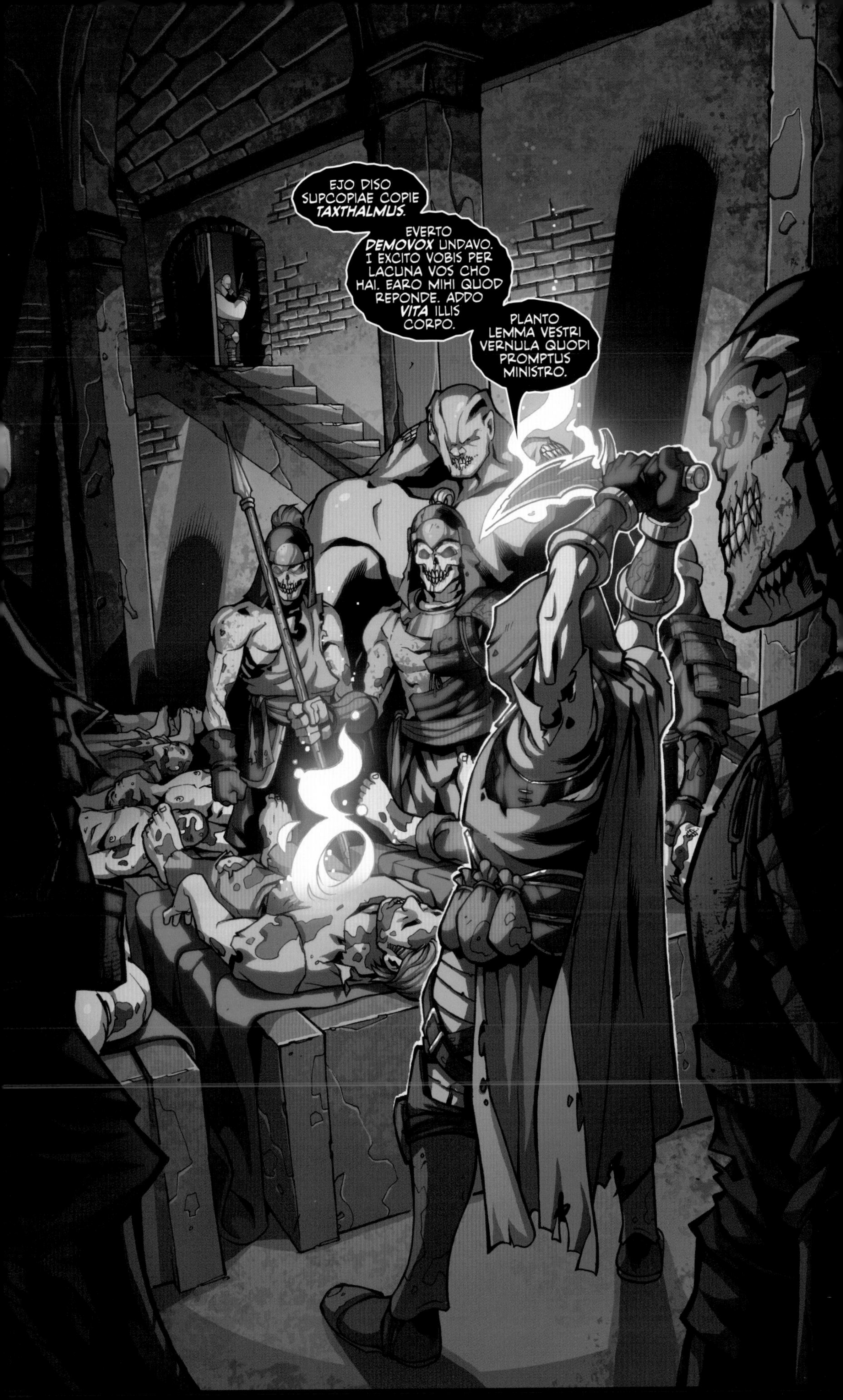
EJO DISO SUPCOPIAE COPIE **TAXTHALMUS.**
EVERTO **DEMOVOX** UNDAVO. I EXCITO VOBIS PER LACUNA VOS CHO HAI. EARO MIHI QUOD REPONDE. ADDO **VITA** ILLIS CORPO.
PLANTO LEMMA VESTRI VERNULA QUODI PROMPTUS MINISTRO.

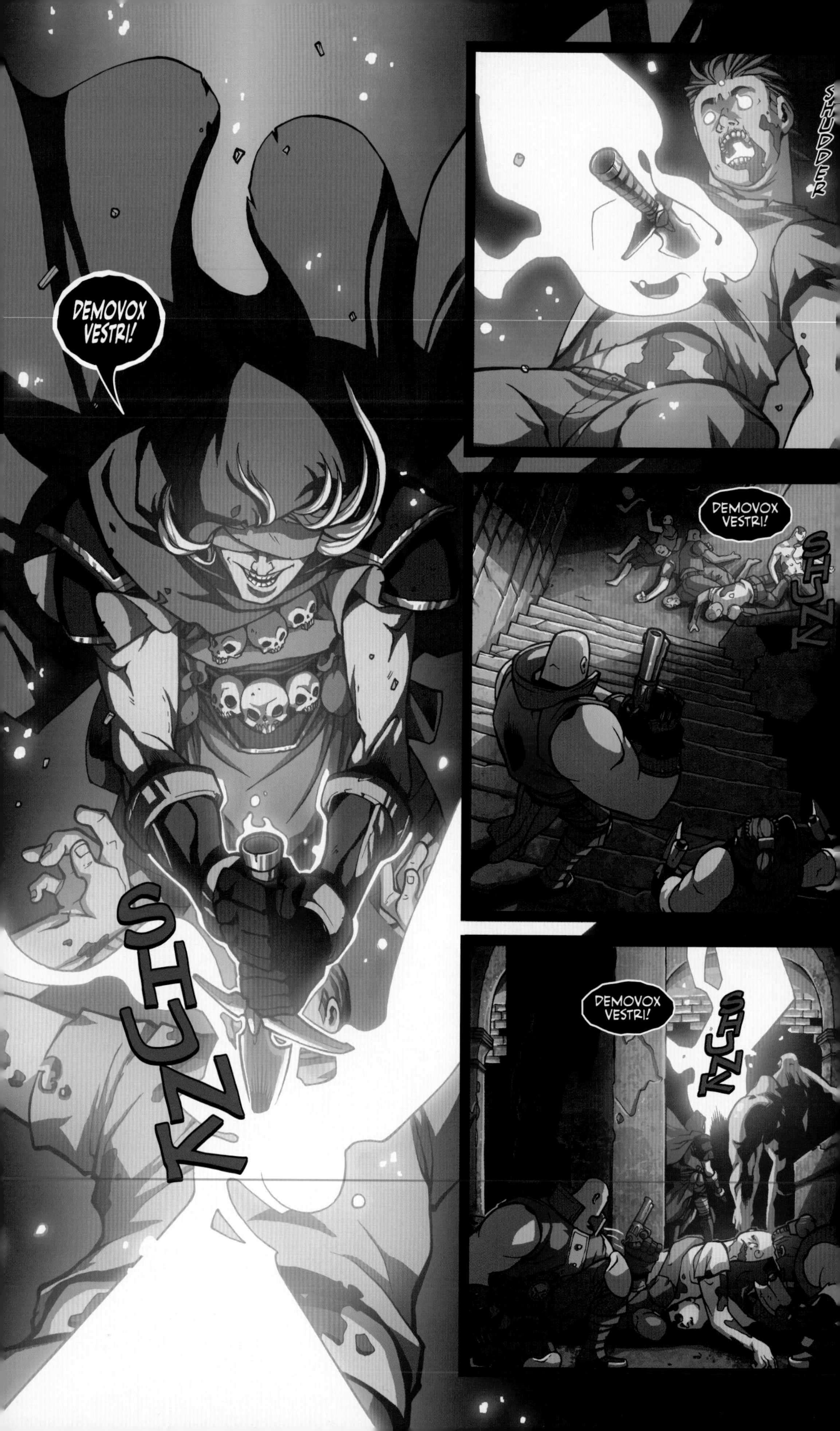
DEMOVOX VESTRI!
SHUNK
SHUDDER
DEMOVOX VESTRI!
SHUNK
DEMOVOX VESTRI!
SHUNK

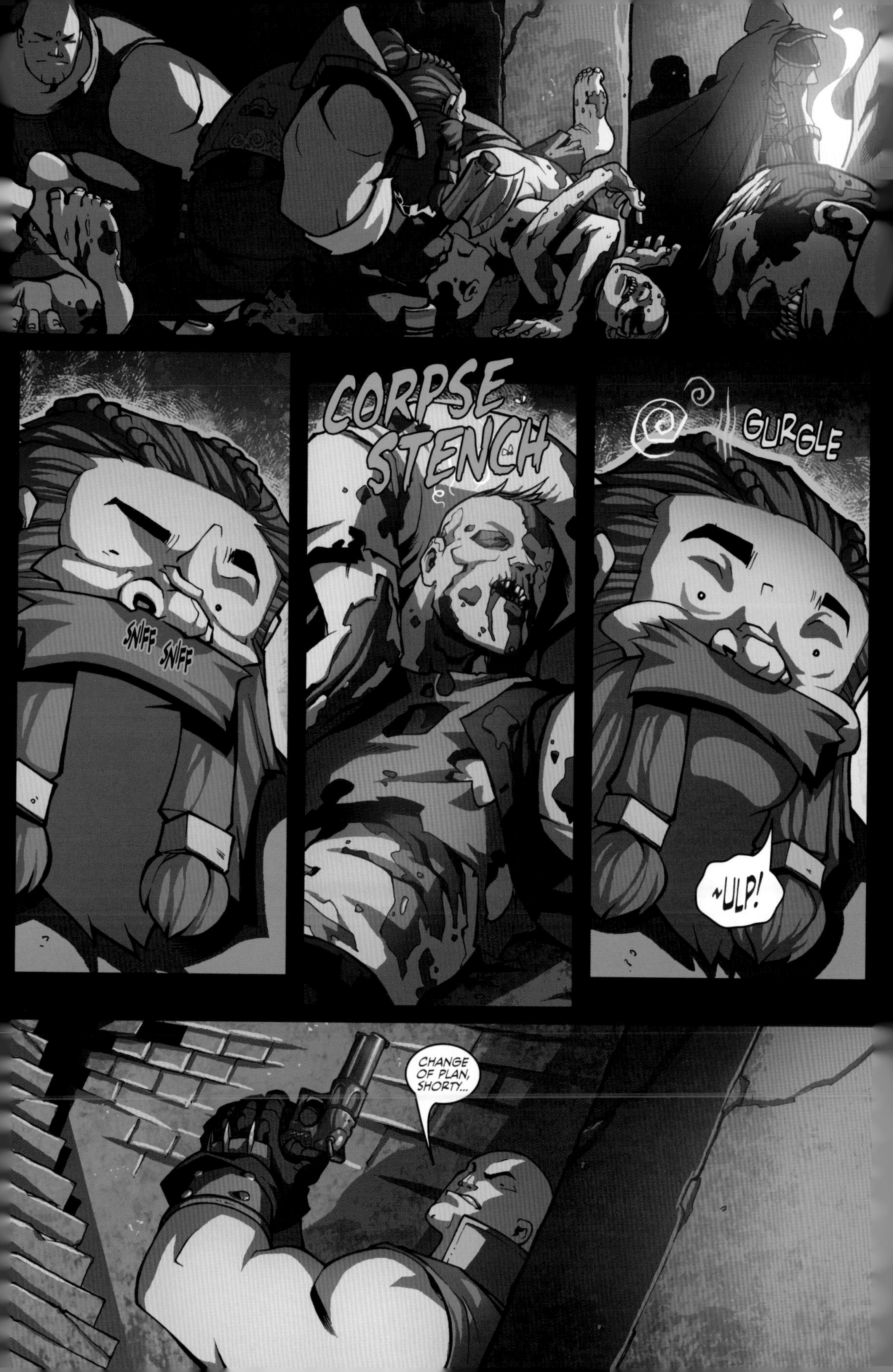
SNIFF SNIFF
CORPSE STENCH
GURGLE
~ULP!
CHANGE OF PLAN, SHORTY...

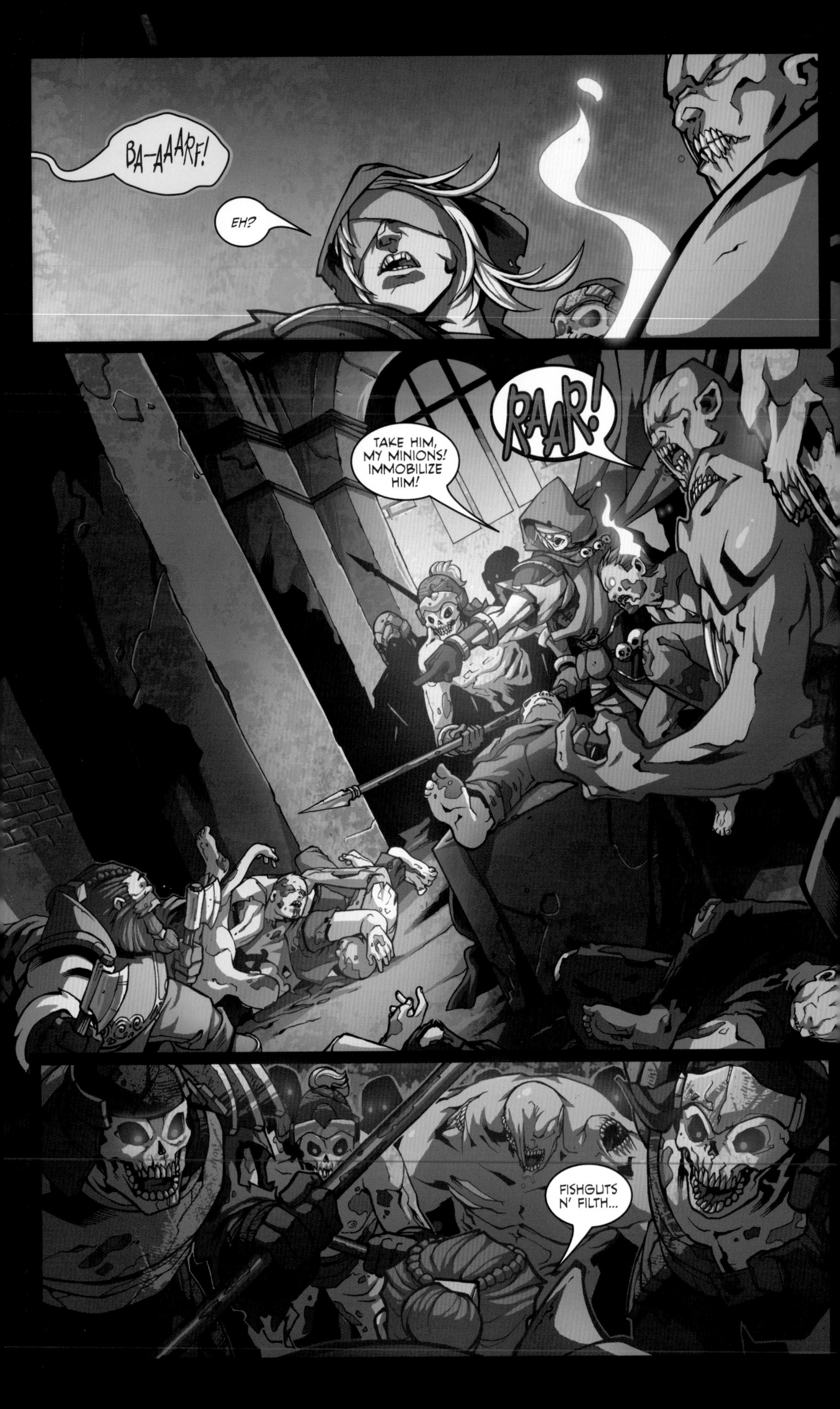
BA-AAARF!
EH?
RAAR!
TAKE HIM, MY MINIONS! IMMOBILIZE HIM!
FISHGUTS N' FILTH...

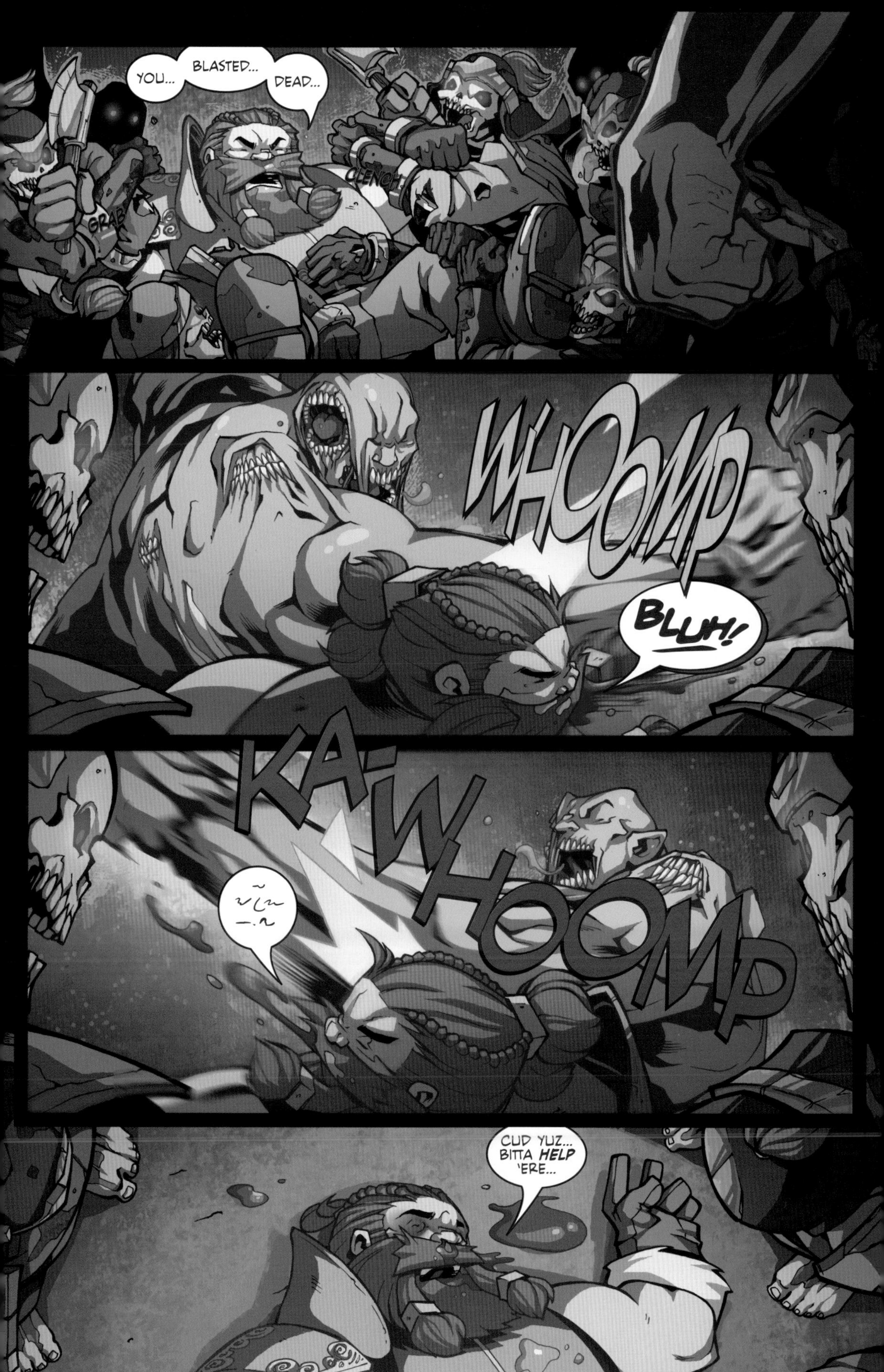

YOU...
BLASTED...
DEAD...
GRAB
CLENCH
WHOOMP
BLUH!
KA-WHOOMP
CUD YUZ... BITTA HELP 'ERE...

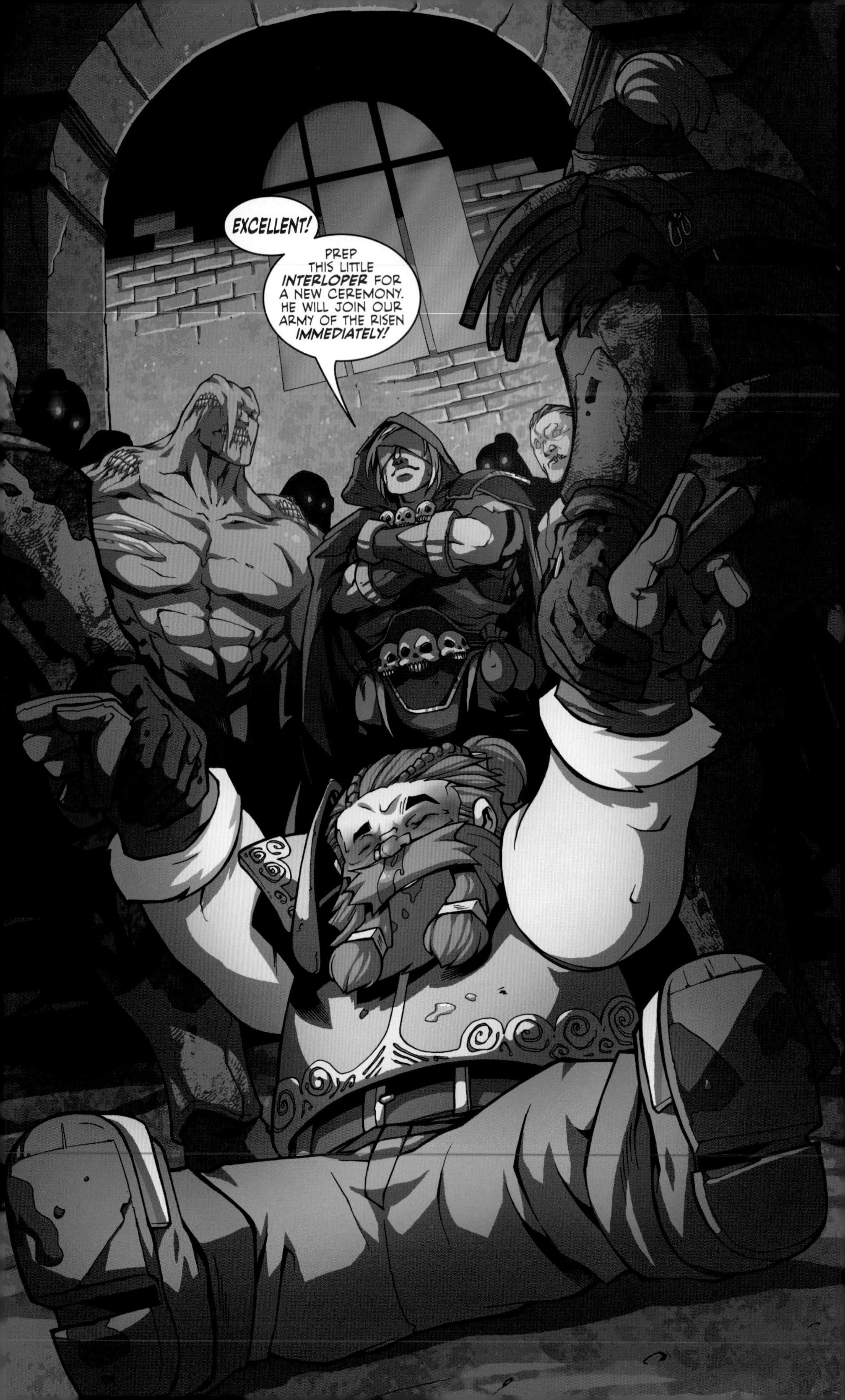
EXCELLENT!
PREP THIS LITTLE INTERLOPER FOR A NEW CEREMONY. HE WILL JOIN OUR ARMY OF THE RISEN IMMEDIATELY!

CHAPTER FOUR

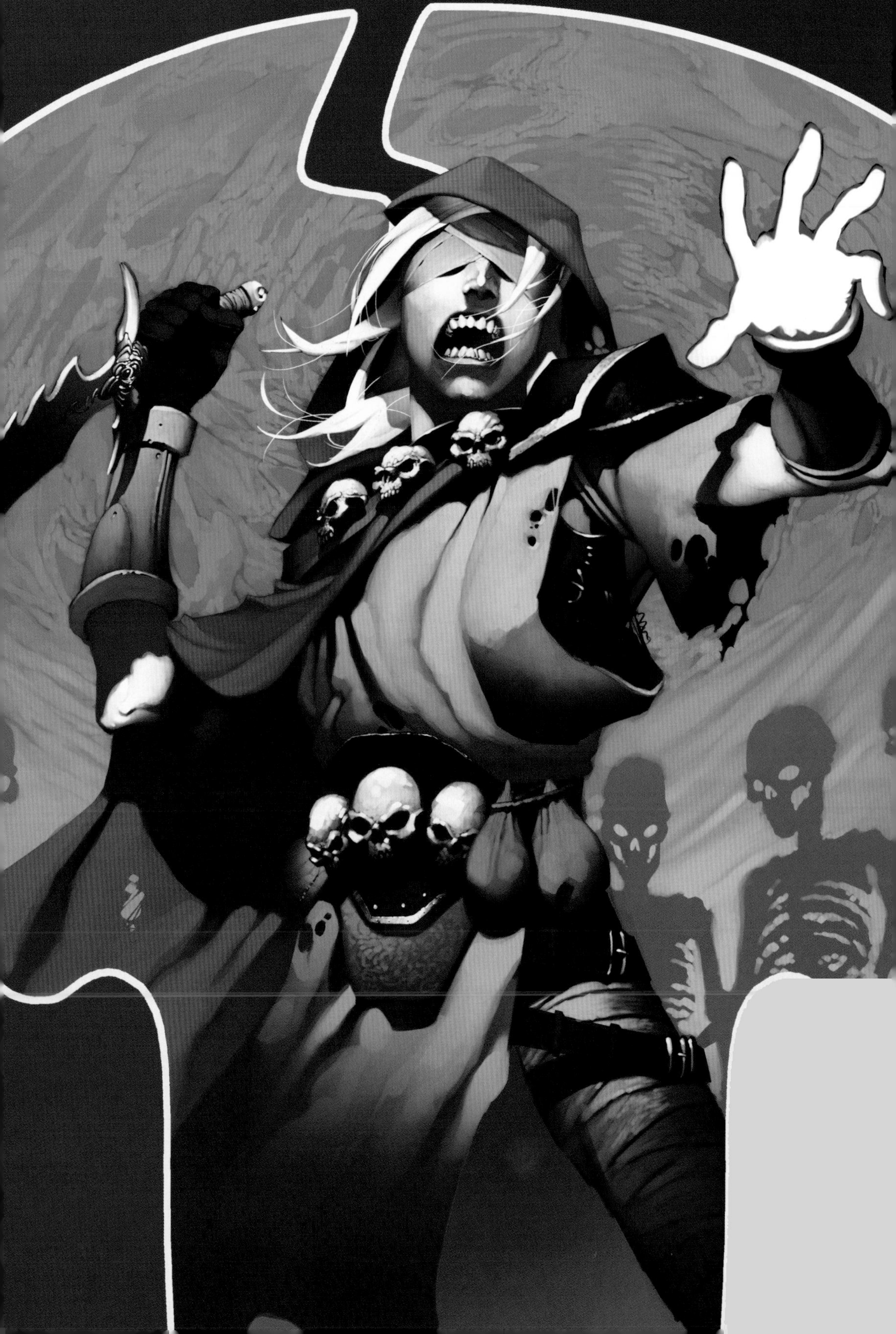

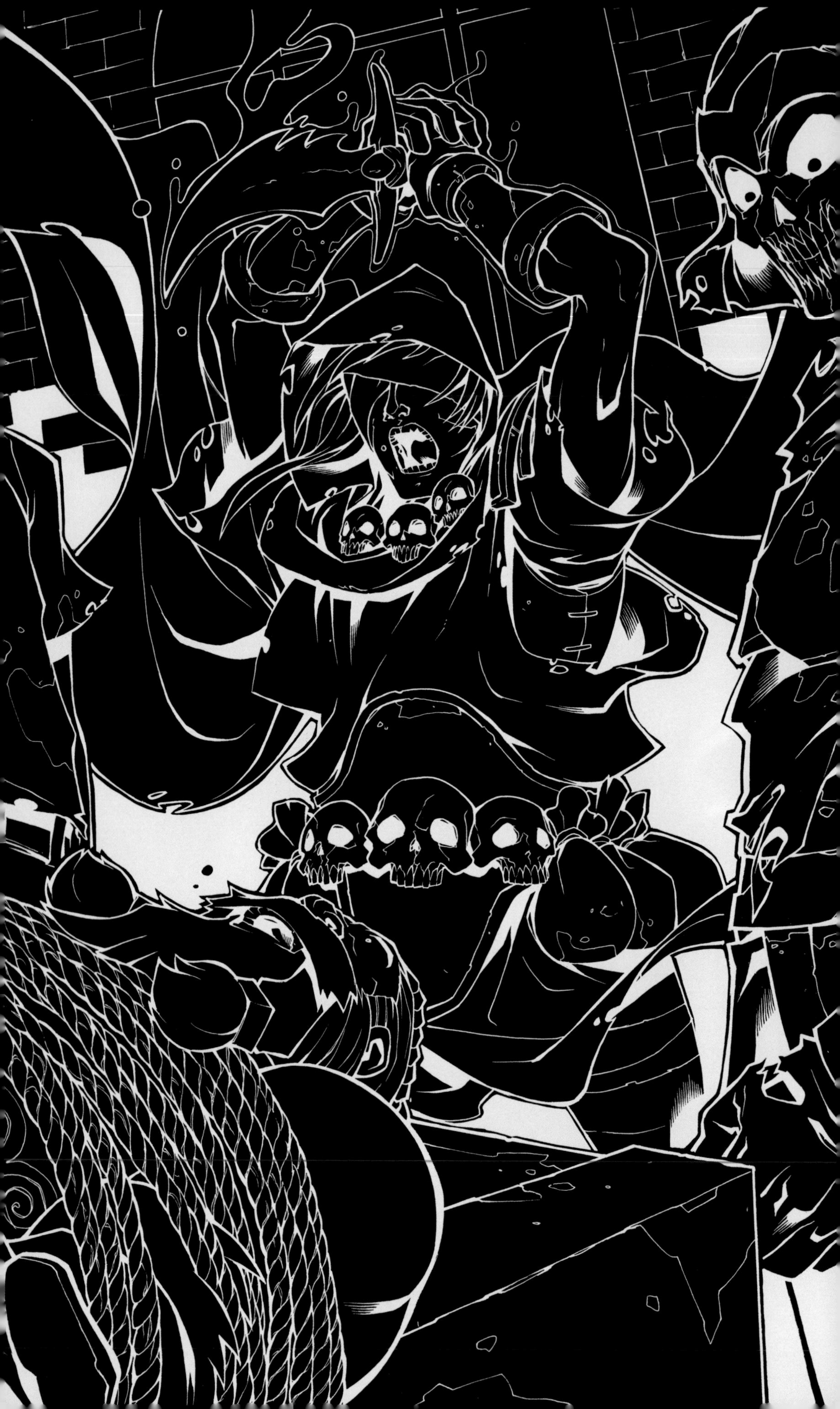

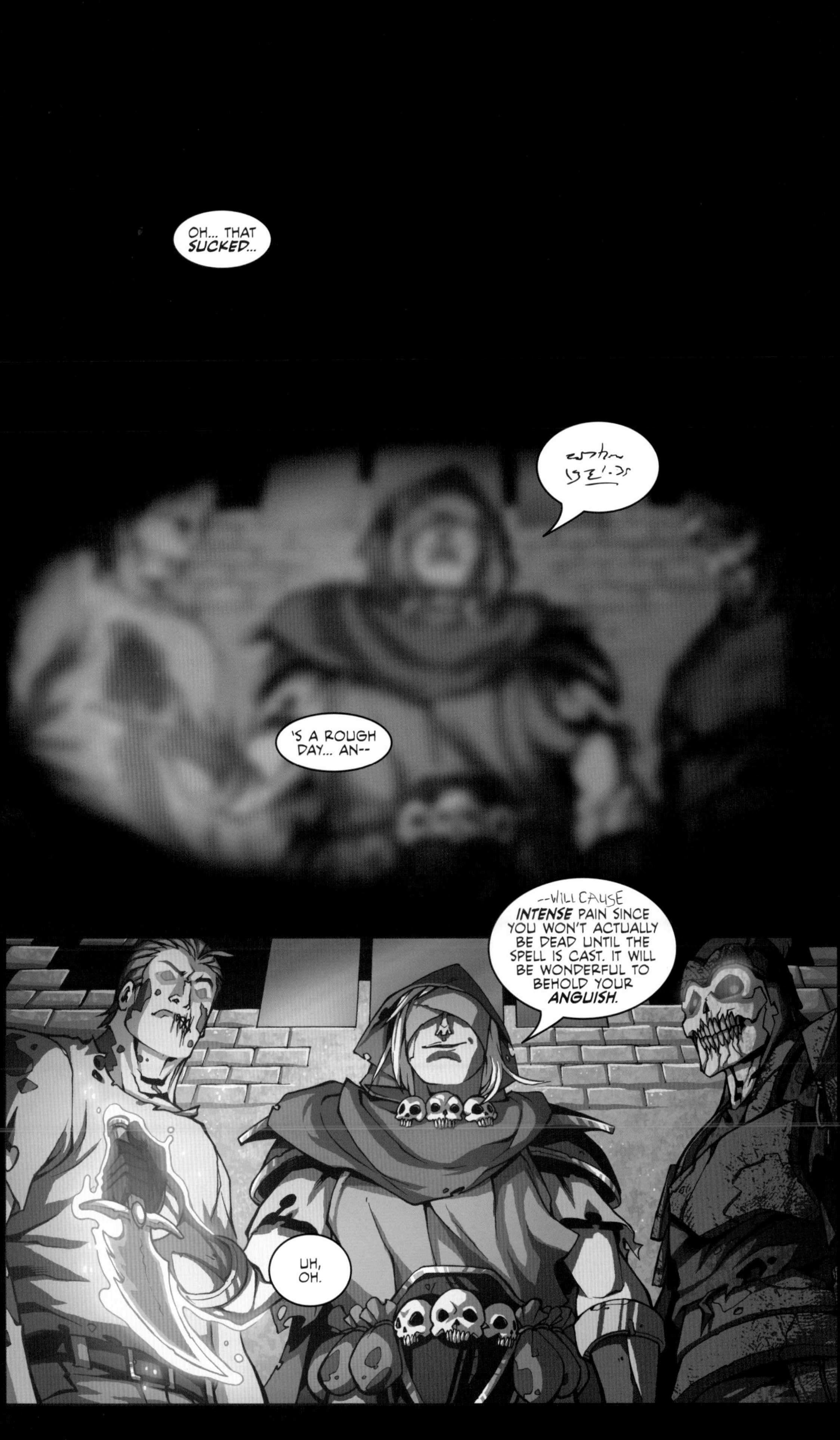
OH... THAT SUCKED...
'S A ROUGH DAY... AN--
--WILL CAUSE INTENSE PAIN SINCE YOU WON'T ACTUALLY BE DEAD UNTIL THE SPELL IS CAST. IT WILL BE WONDERFUL TO BEHOLD YOUR ANGUISH.
UH, OH.

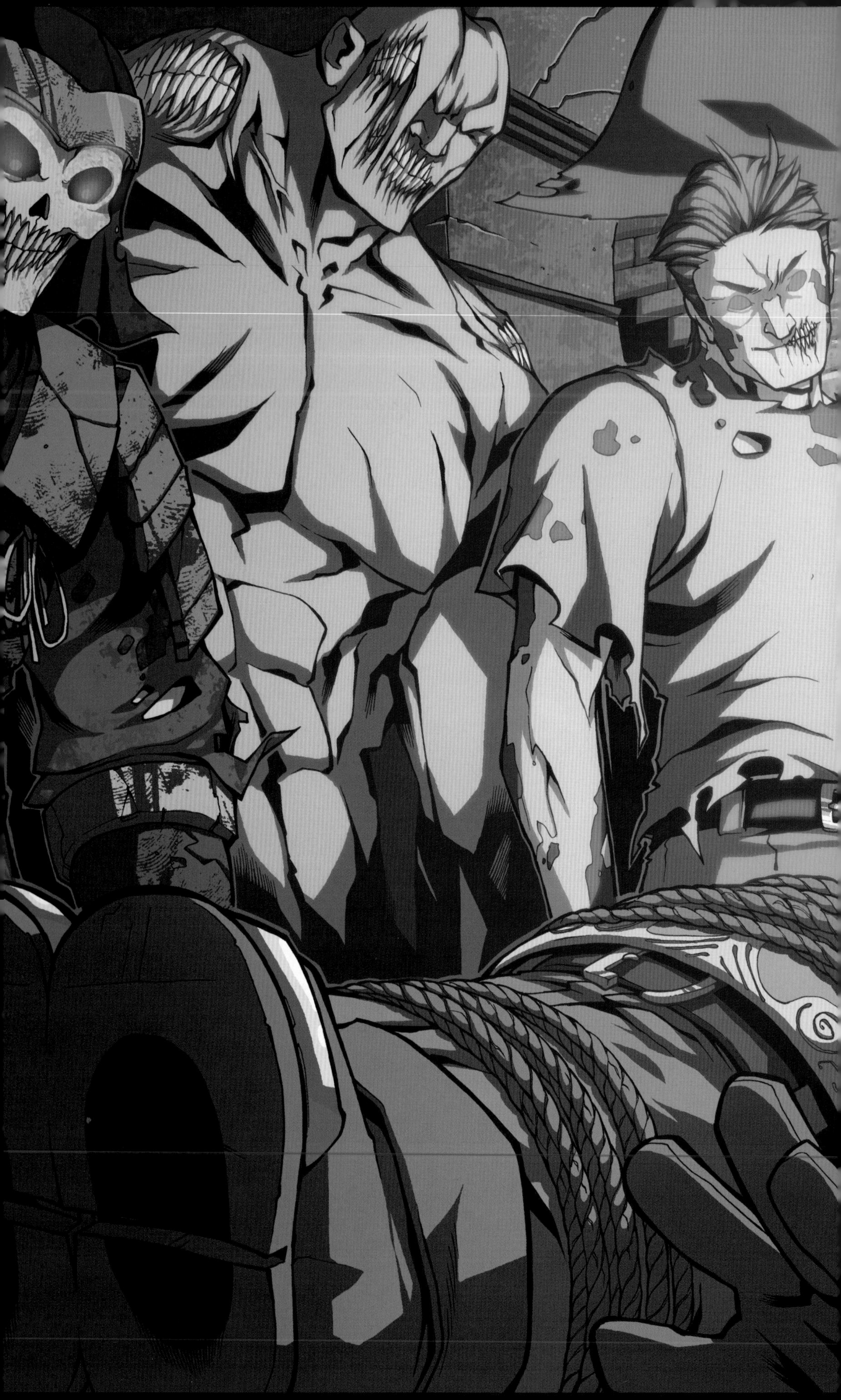

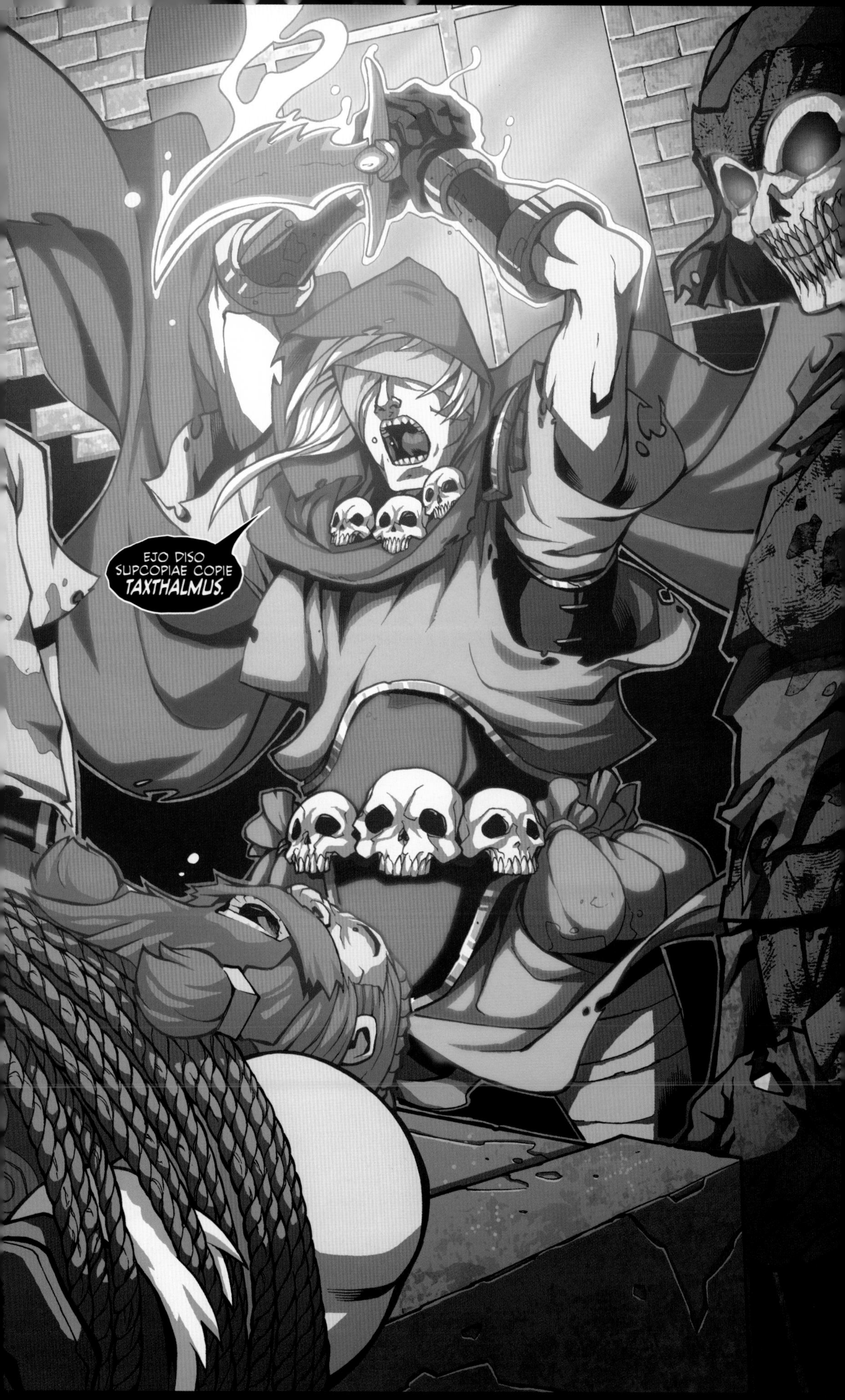
EJO DISO SUPCOPIAE COPIE *TAXTHALMUS.*

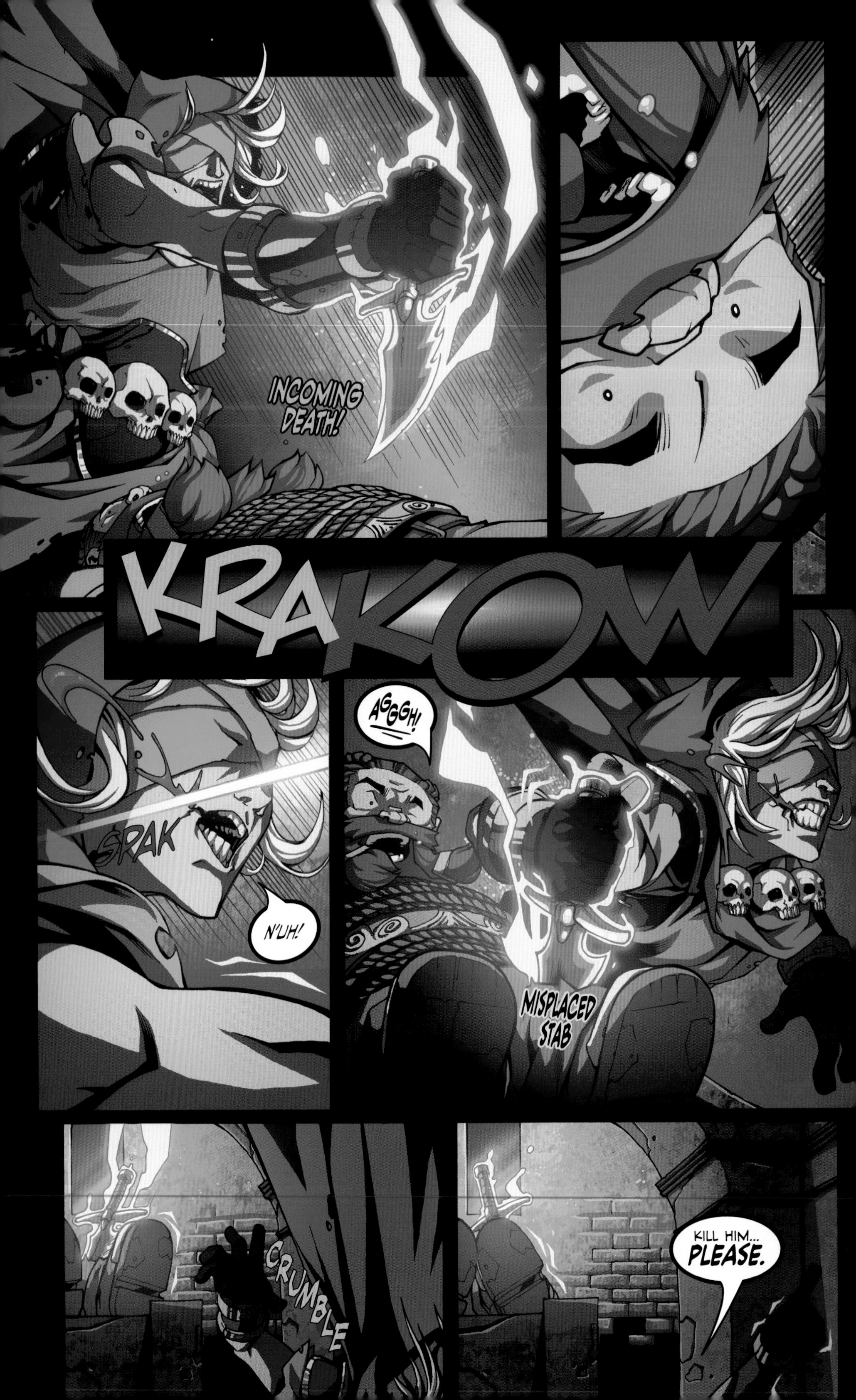
INCOMING DEATH!
KRAKOW
SPRAK
N'UH!
AGGGH!
MISPLACED STAB
CRUMBLE
KILL HIM... PLEASE.

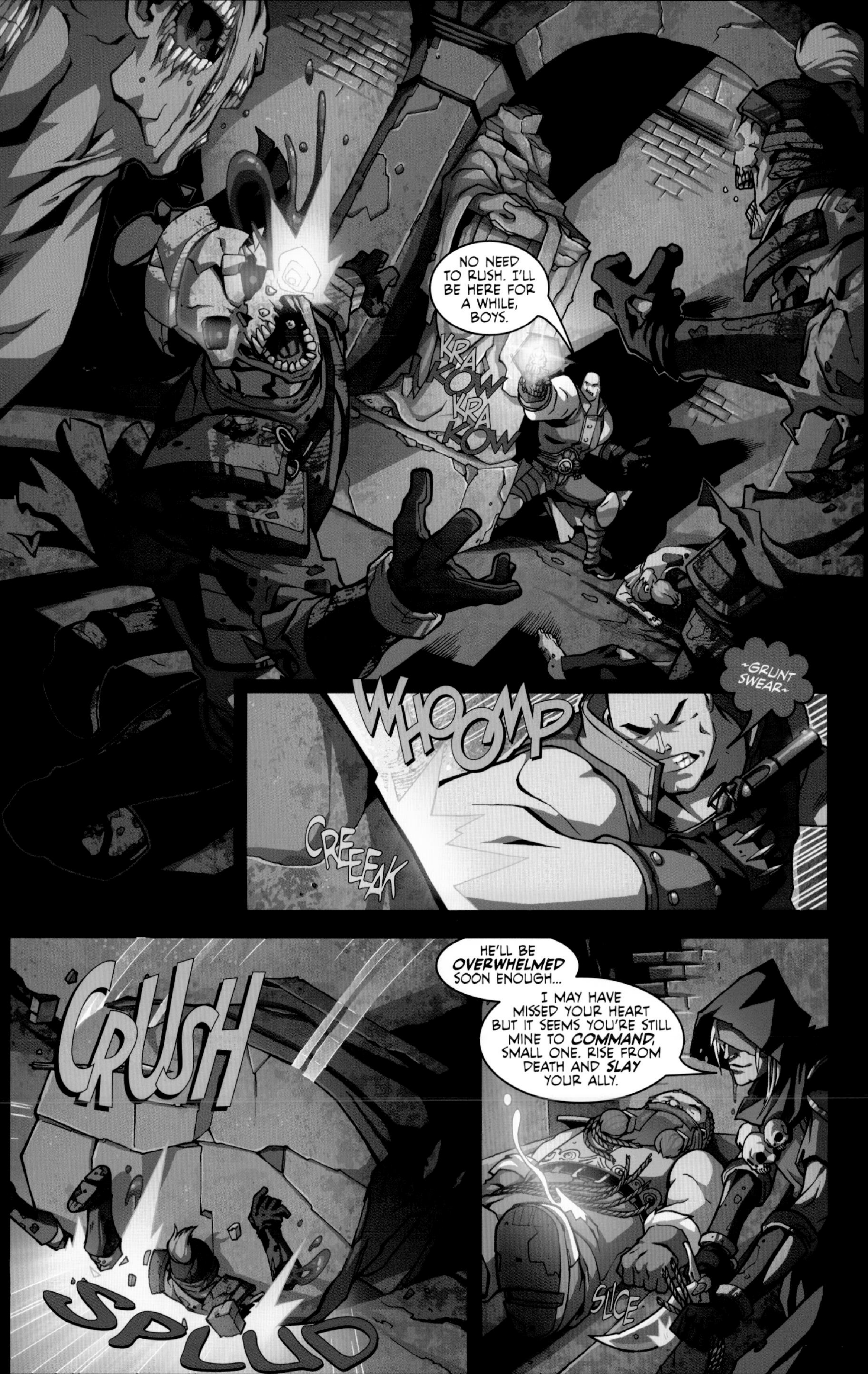
NO NEED TO RUSH. I'LL BE HERE FOR A WHILE, BOYS.
KRA KOW KRA KOW
WHOOOMP
~GRUNT SWEAR~
CREEEAK
CRUSH
SPLUD
HE'LL BE **OVERWHELMED** SOON ENOUGH...
I MAY HAVE MISSED YOUR HEART BUT IT SEEMS YOU'RE STILL MINE TO **COMMAND**, SMALL ONE. RISE FROM DEATH AND **SLAY** YOUR ALLY.
SLICE

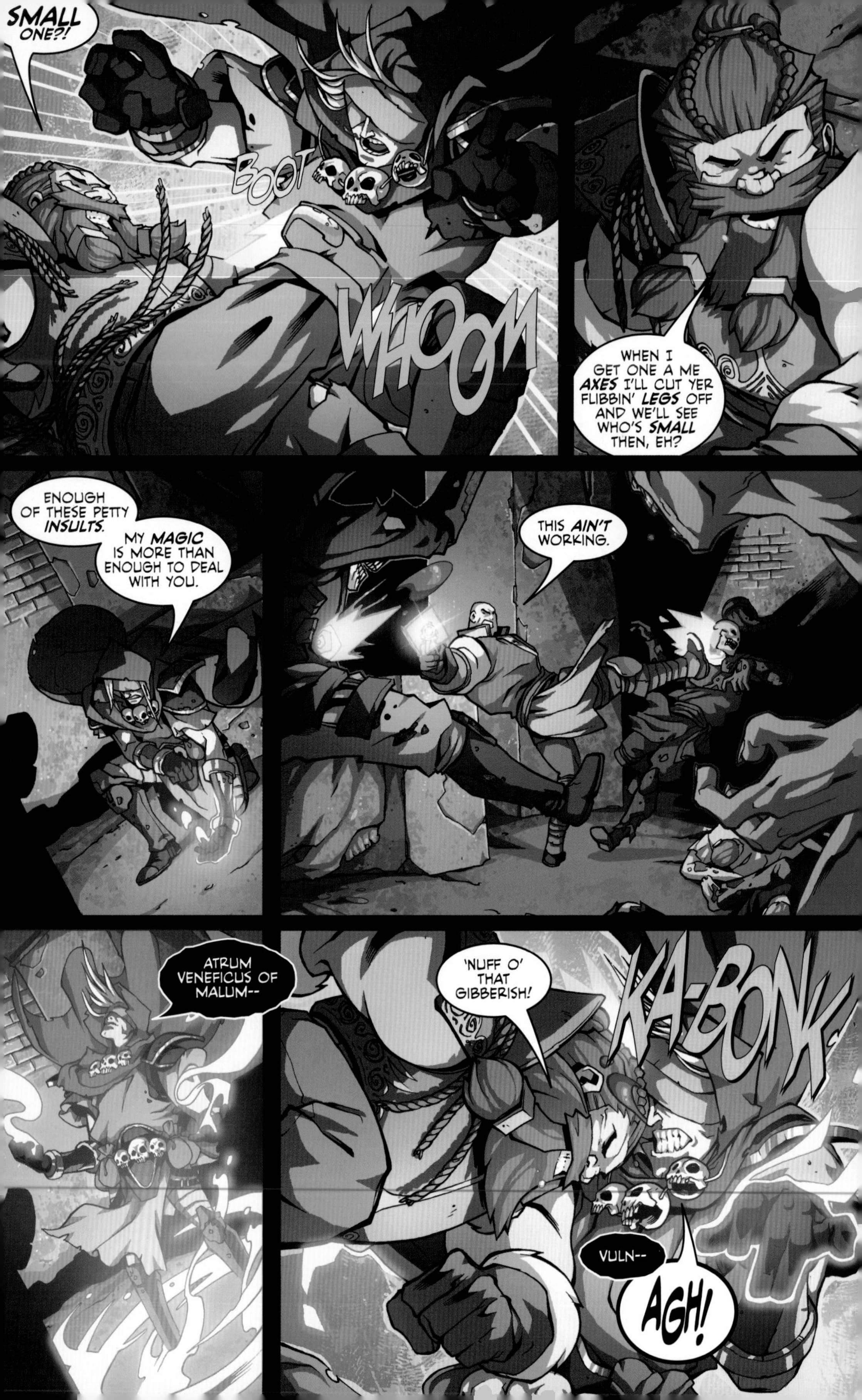
SMALL ONE?!
BOOT
WHOOM
WHEN I GET ONE A ME AXES I'LL CUT YER FLIBBIN' LEGS OFF AND WE'LL SEE WHO'S SMALL THEN, EH?
ENOUGH OF THESE PETTY INSULTS.
MY MAGIC IS MORE THAN ENOUGH TO DEAL WITH YOU.
THIS AIN'T WORKING.
ATRUM VENEFICUS OF MALUM--
'NUFF O' THAT GIBBERISH!
KA-BONK
VULN--
AGH!

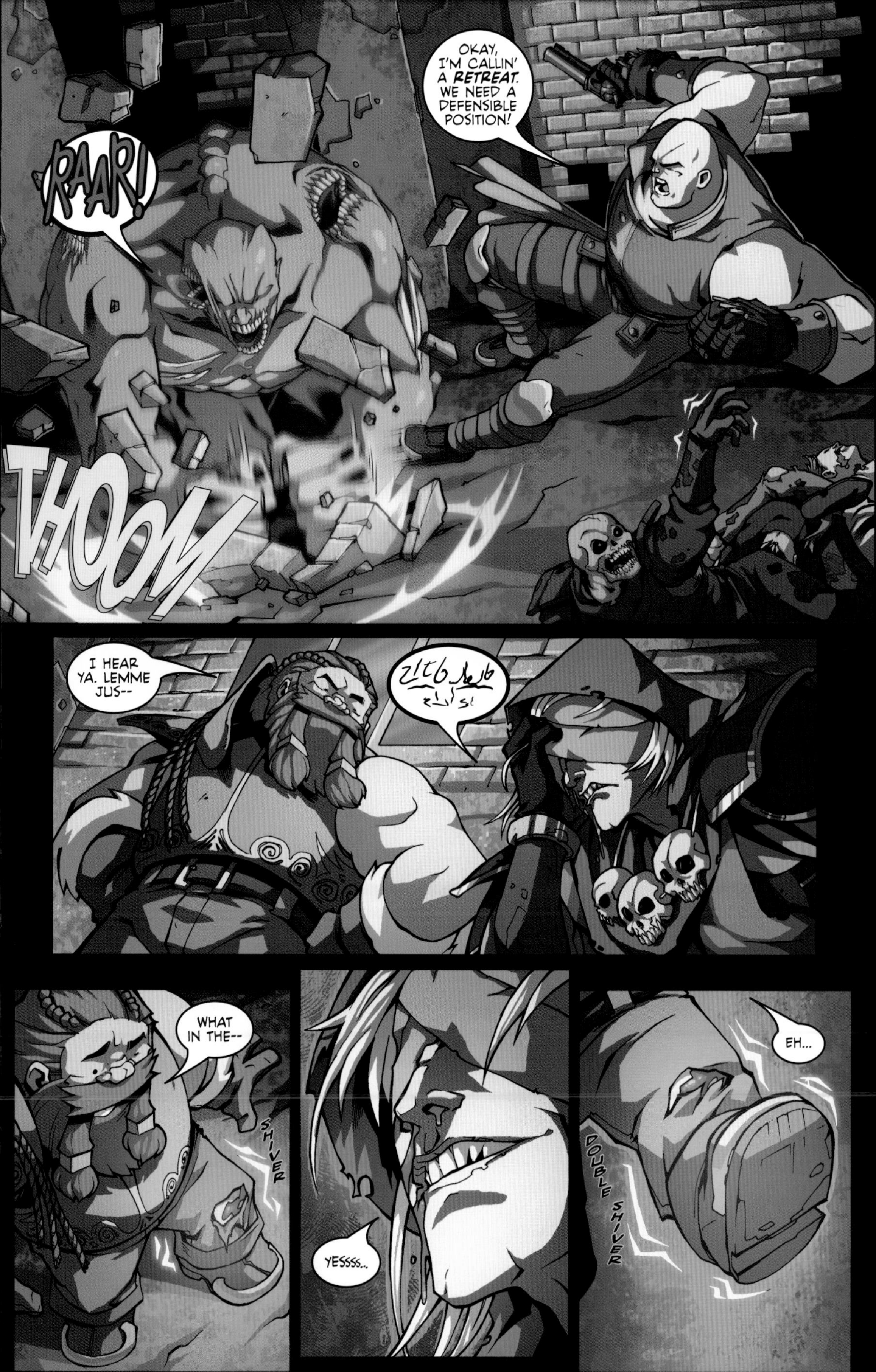
OKAY, I'M CALLIN' A RETREAT. WE NEED A DEFENSIBLE POSITION!
RAAR!
THOOM
I HEAR YA. LEMME JUS--
WHAT IN THE--
SHIVER
YESSSS...
EH...
DOUBLE SHIVER

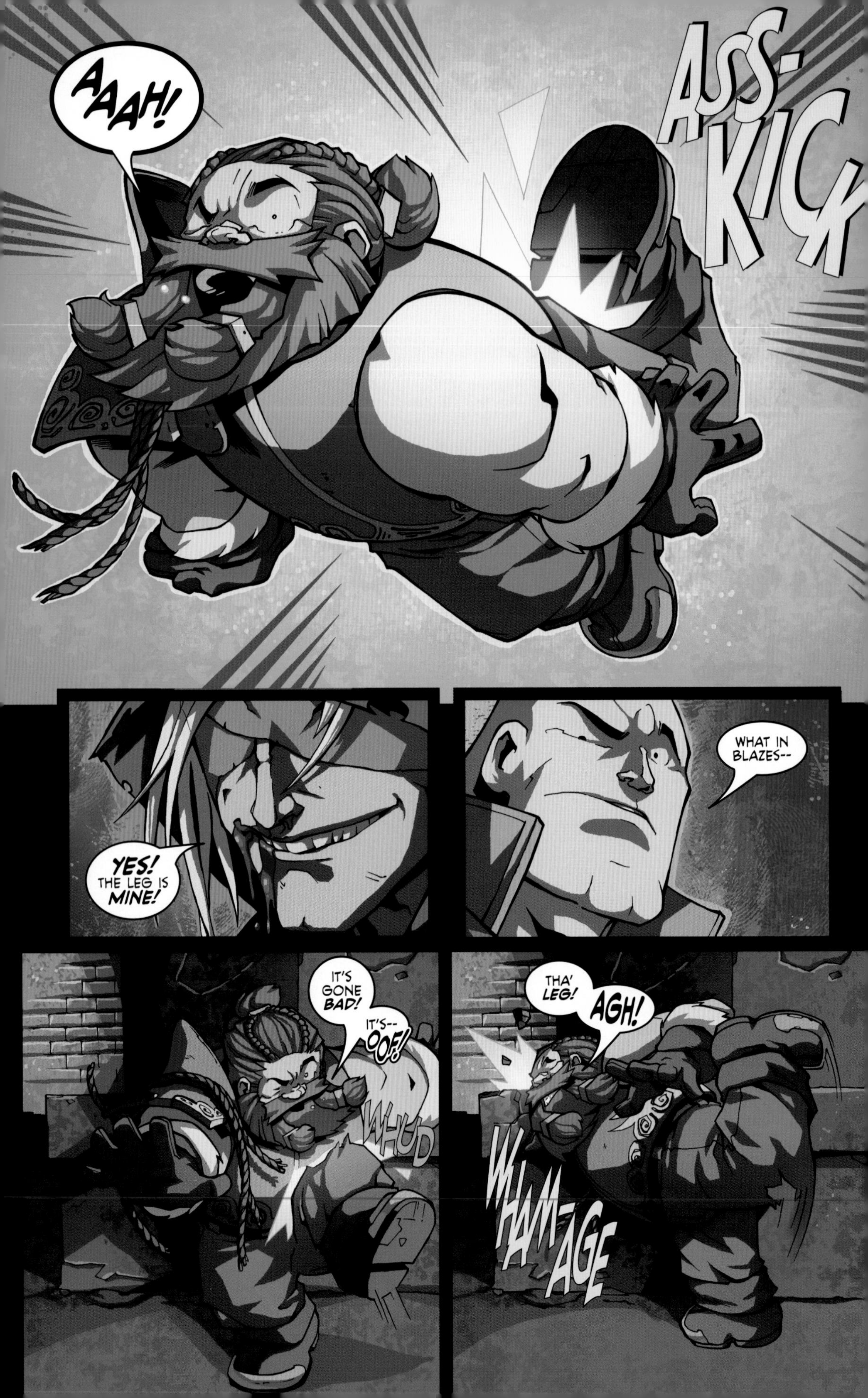
AAAH!
ASS-KICK
YES! THE LEG IS MINE!
WHAT IN BLAZES--
IT'S GONE BAD!
IT'S--
OOF!
WHUD
THA' LEG!
AGH!
WHAM-AGE

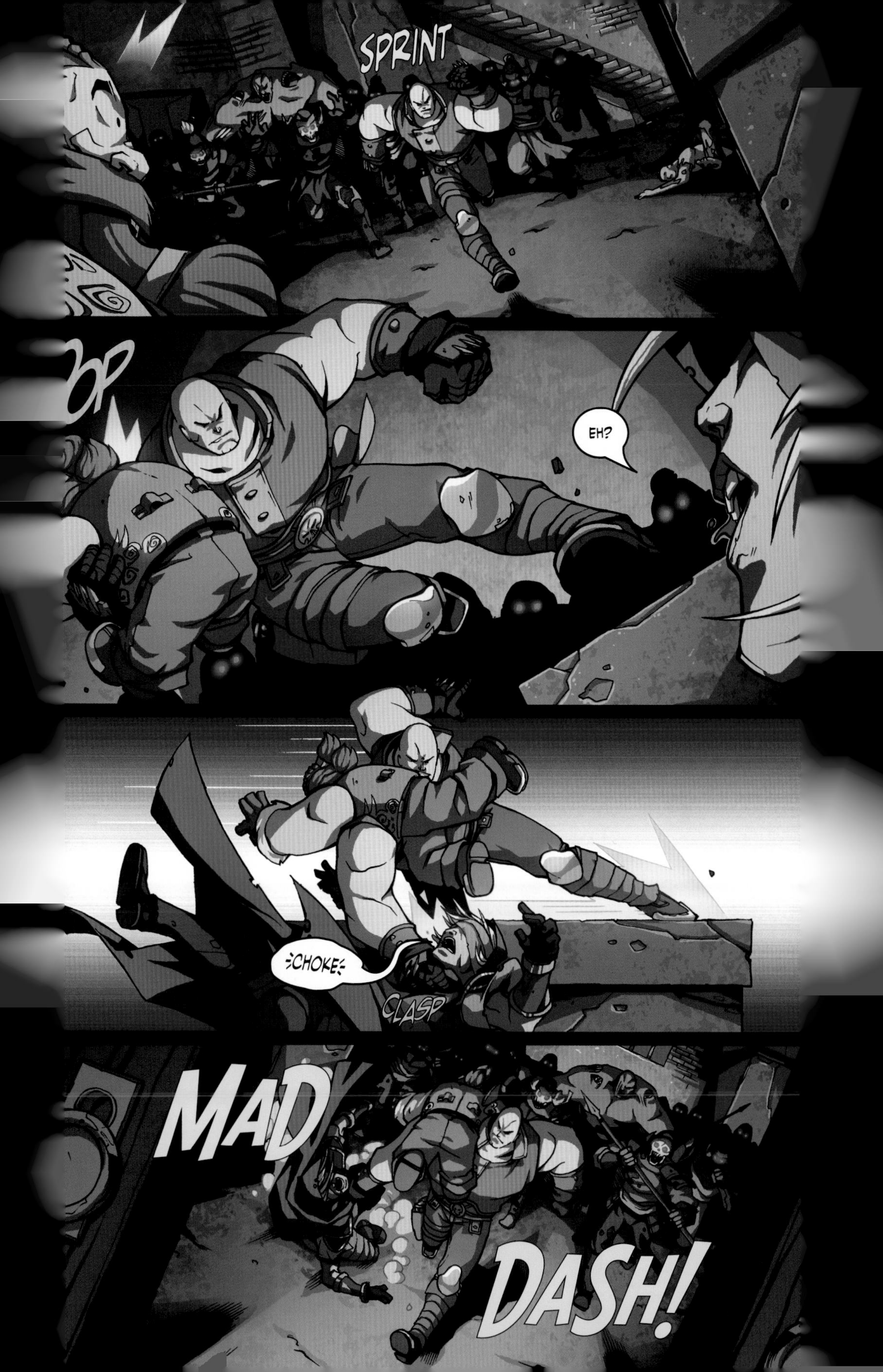
SPRINT
OP
EH?
CHOKE
CLASP
MAD
DASH!

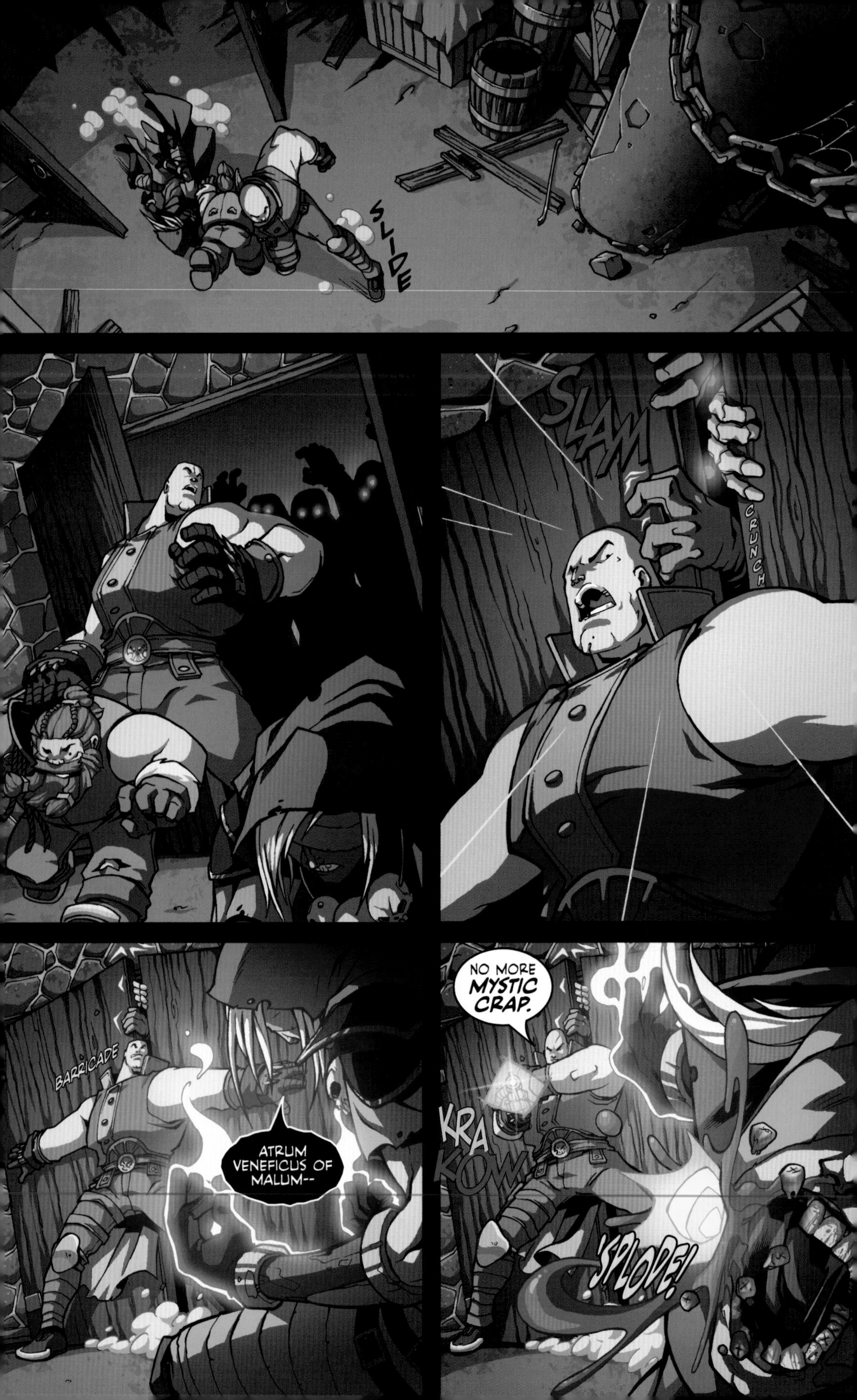
SLIDE
SLAM
CRUNCH
BARRICADE
ATRUM VENEFICUS OF MALUM--
NO MORE MYSTIC CRAP.
KRA KOW
'SPLODE!

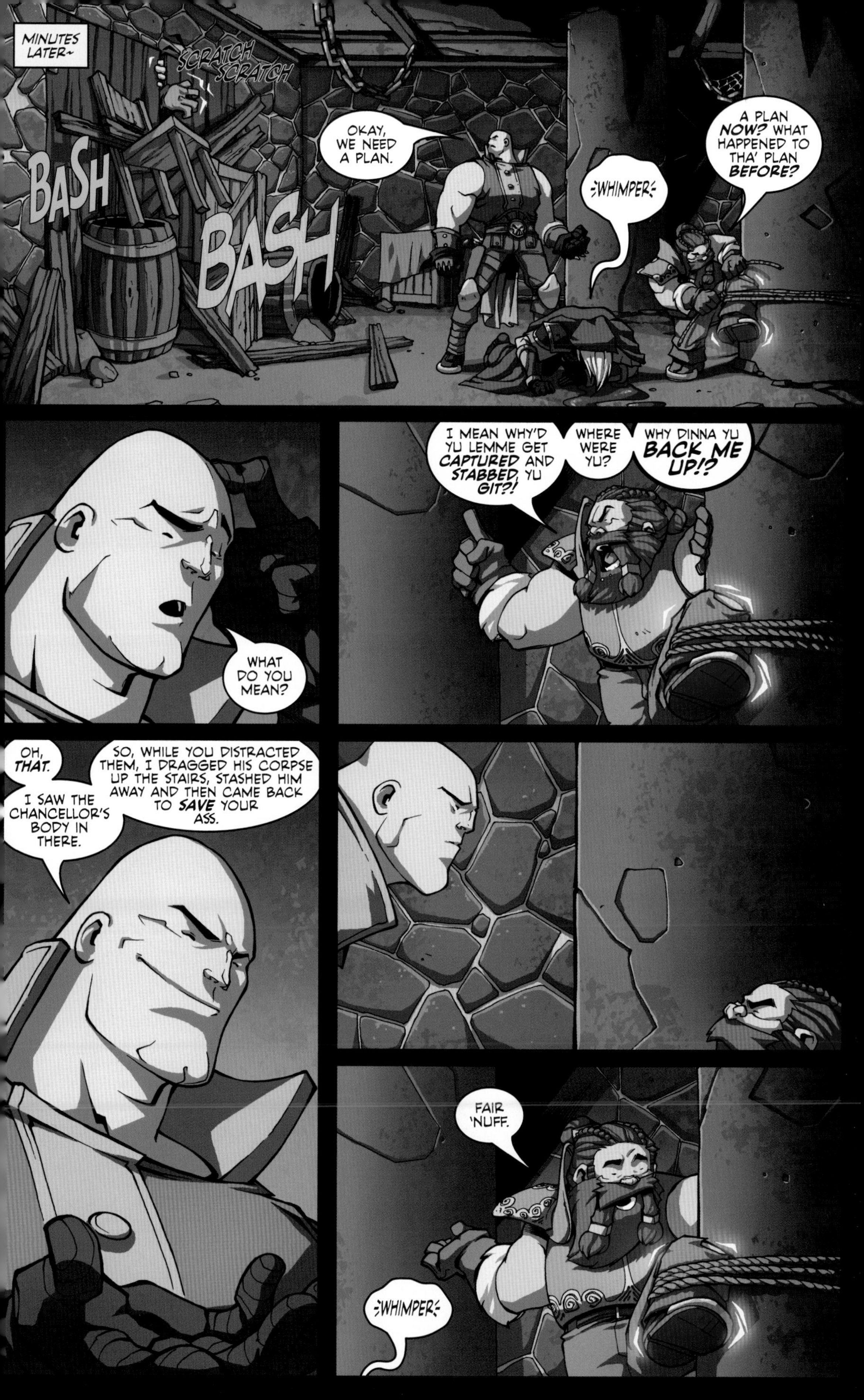
MINUTES LATER~
SCRATCH SCRATCH
BASH
BASH
OKAY, WE NEED A PLAN.
~WHIMPER~
A PLAN NOW? WHAT HAPPENED TO THA' PLAN BEFORE?
WHAT DO YOU MEAN?
I MEAN WHY'D YU LEMME GET CAPTURED AND STABBED, YU GIT?!
WHERE WERE YU?
WHY DINNA YU BACK ME UP!?
OH, THAT.
I SAW THE CHANCELLOR'S BODY IN THERE.
SO, WHILE YOU DISTRACTED THEM, I DRAGGED HIS CORPSE UP THE STAIRS, STASHED HIM AWAY AND THEN CAME BACK TO SAVE YOUR ASS.
FAIR 'NUFF.
~WHIMPER~

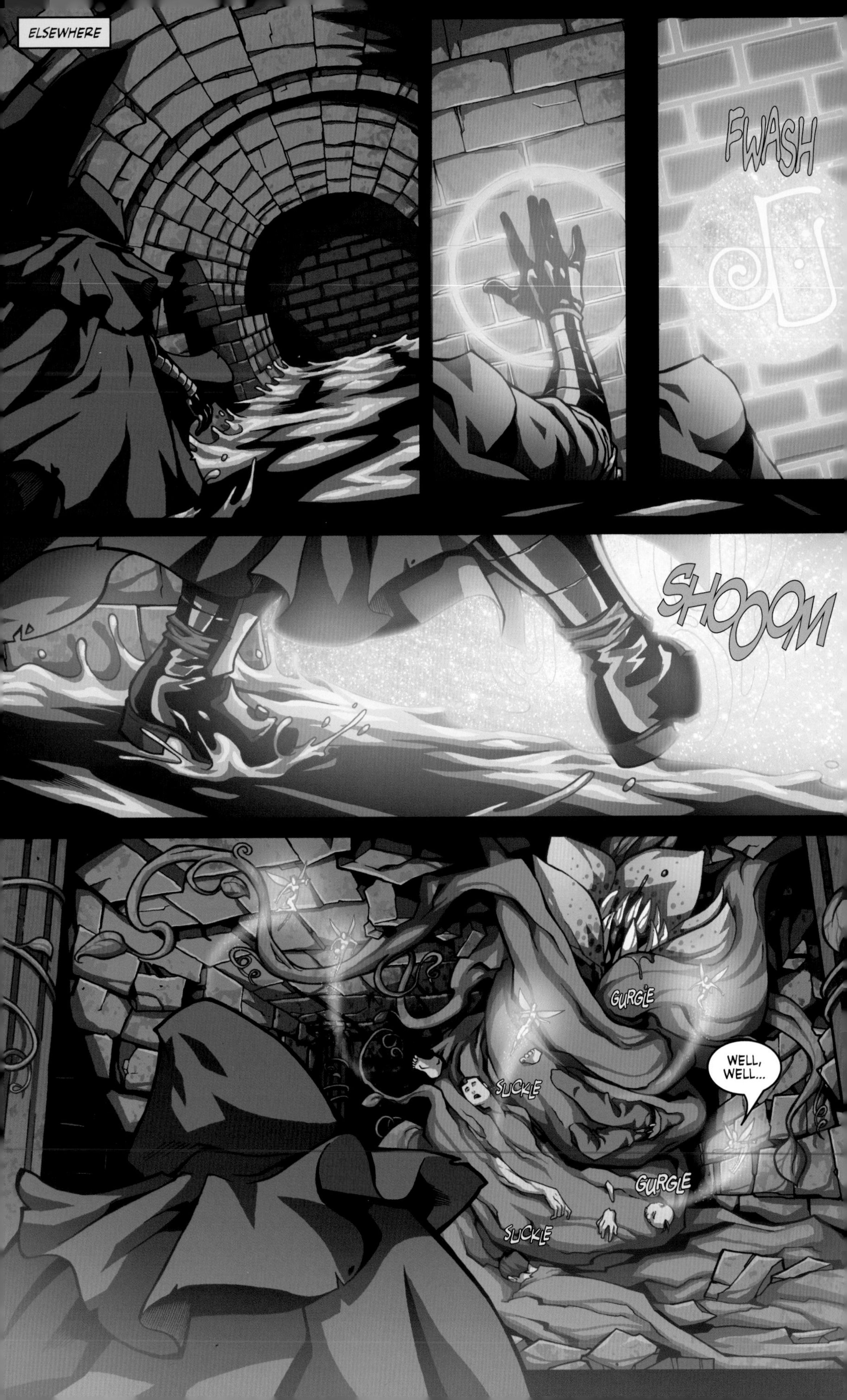
ELSEWHERE
FWASH
SHOOOM
GURGLE
WELL, WELL...
SUCKLE
GURGLE
SUCKLE

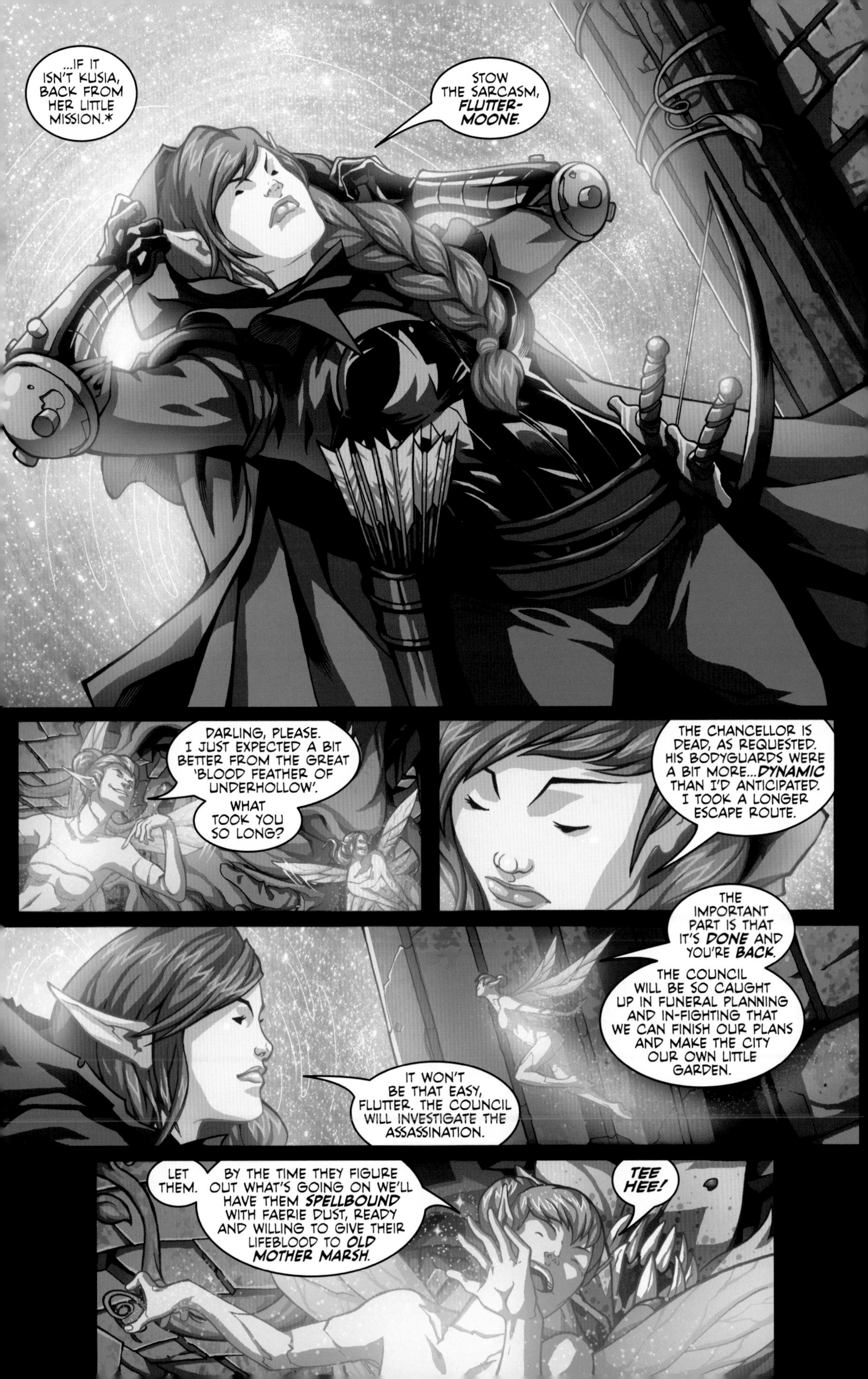
...IF IT ISN'T KUSIA, BACK FROM HER LITTLE MISSION.*
STOW THE SARCASM, FLUTTER-MOONE.
DARLING, PLEASE. I JUST EXPECTED A BIT BETTER FROM THE GREAT 'BLOOD FEATHER OF UNDERHOLLOW'.
WHAT TOOK YOU SO LONG?
THE CHANCELLOR IS DEAD, AS REQUESTED. HIS BODYGUARDS WERE A BIT MORE...DYNAMIC THAN I'D ANTICIPATED. I TOOK A LONGER ESCAPE ROUTE.
THE IMPORTANT PART IS THAT IT'S DONE AND YOU'RE BACK.
THE COUNCIL WILL BE SO CAUGHT UP IN FUNERAL PLANNING AND IN-FIGHTING THAT WE CAN FINISH OUR PLANS AND MAKE THE CITY OUR OWN LITTLE GARDEN.
IT WON'T BE THAT EASY, FLUTTER. THE COUNCIL WILL INVESTIGATE THE ASSASSINATION.
LET THEM.
BY THE TIME THEY FIGURE OUT WHAT'S GOING ON WE'LL HAVE THEM SPELLBOUND WITH FAERIE DUST, READY AND WILLING TO GIVE THEIR LIFEBLOOD TO OLD MOTHER MARSH.
TEE HEE!

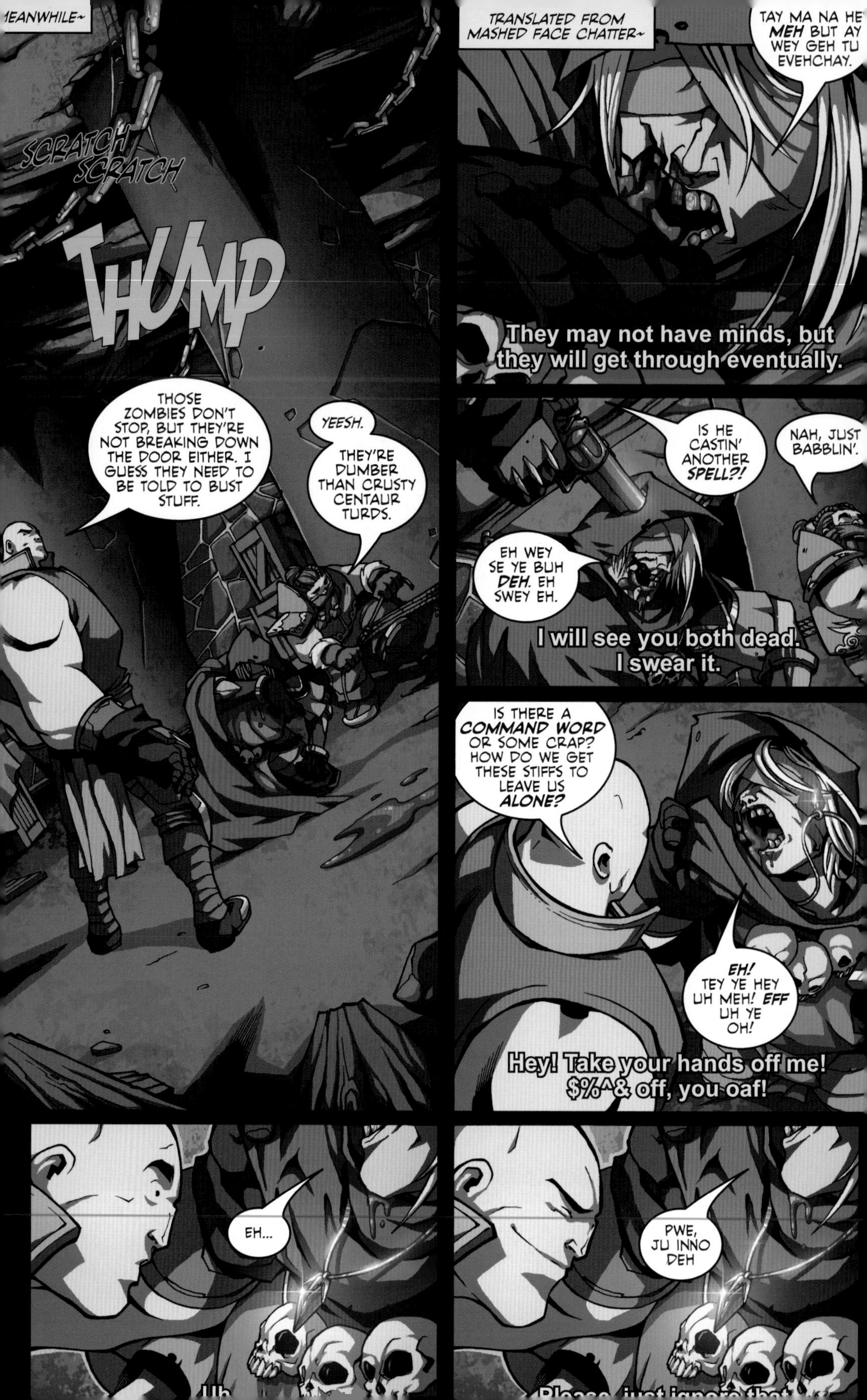
MEANWHILE~
SCRATCH SCRATCH
THUMP
THOSE ZOMBIES DON'T STOP, BUT THEY'RE NOT BREAKING DOWN THE DOOR EITHER. I GUESS THEY NEED TO BE TOLD TO BUST STUFF.
YEESH.
THEY'RE DUMBER THAN CRUSTY CENTAUR TURDS.
TRANSLATED FROM MASHED FACE CHATTER~
TAY MA NA HE MEH BUT AY WEY GEH TU EVEHCHAY.
They may not have minds, but they will get through eventually.
IS HE CASTIN' ANOTHER SPELL?!
NAH, JUST BABBLIN'.
EH WEY SE YE BUH DEH. EH SWEY EH.
I will see you both dead. I swear it.
IS THERE A COMMAND WORD OR SOME CRAP? HOW DO WE GET THESE STIFFS TO LEAVE US ALONE?
EH! TEY YE HEY UH MEH! EFF UH YE OH!
Hey! Take your hands off me! $%^& off, you oaf!
EH...
PWE, JU INNO DEH

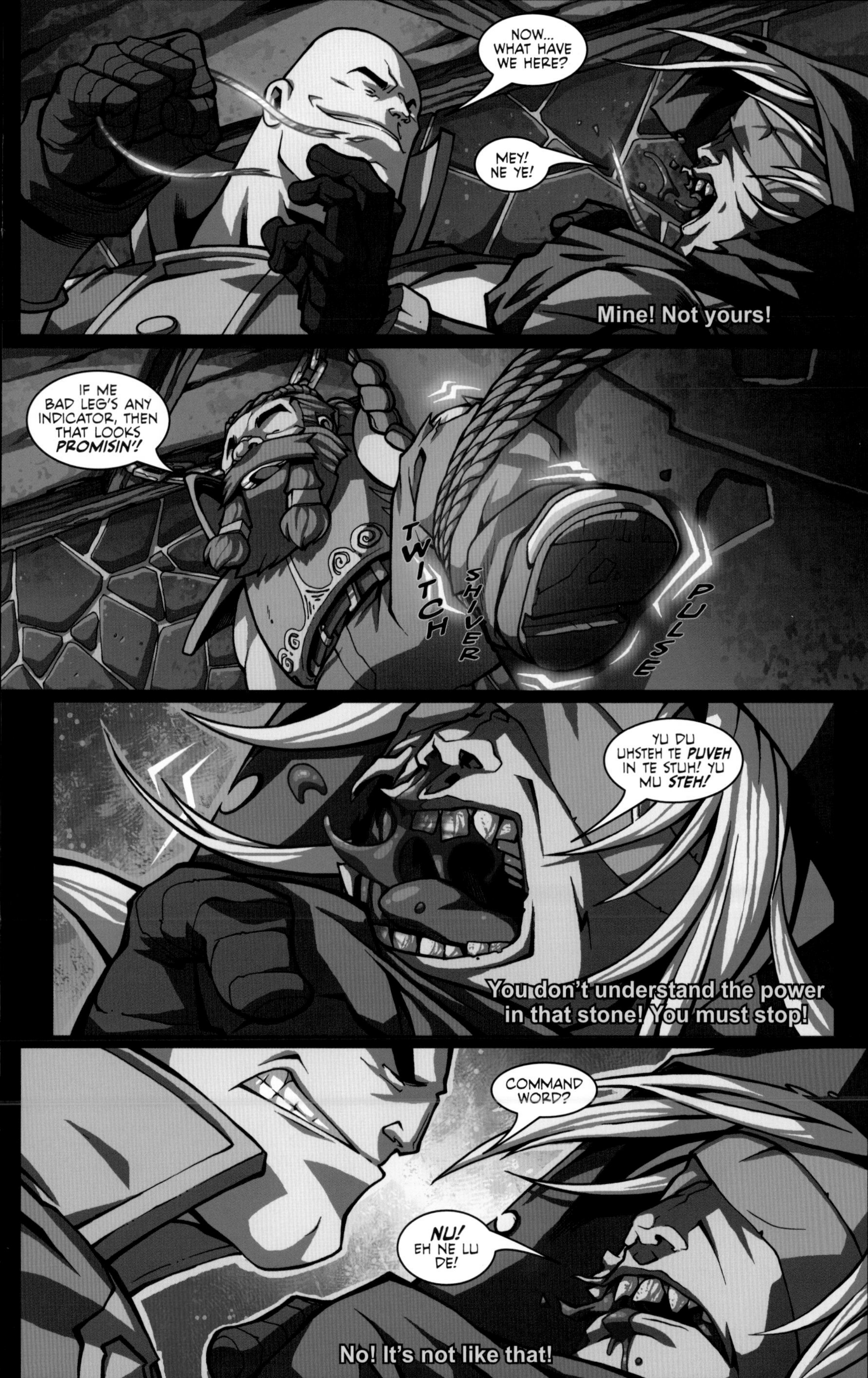
NOW... WHAT HAVE WE HERE?
MEY! NE YE!
Mine! Not yours!
IF ME BAD LEG'S ANY INDICATOR, THEN THAT LOOKS *PROMISIN'!*
TWITCH
SHIVER
PULSE
YU DU UHSTEH TE *PUVEH* IN TE STUH! YU MU *STEH!*
You don't understand the power in that stone! You must stop!
COMMAND WORD?
NU! EH NE LU DE!
No! It's not like that!

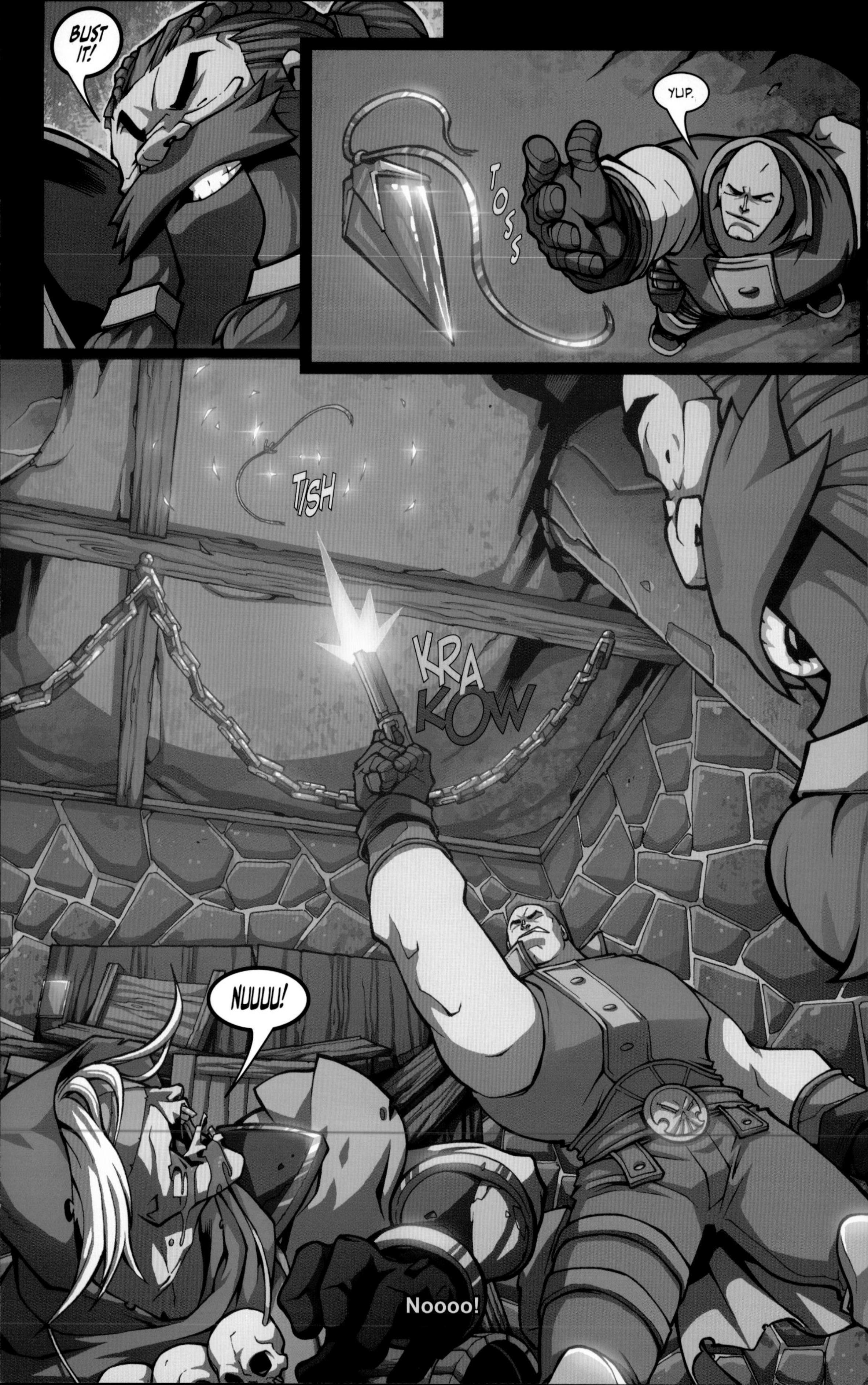
BUST IT!
YUP.
TOSS
TISH
KRA KOW
NUUUU!
Noooo!

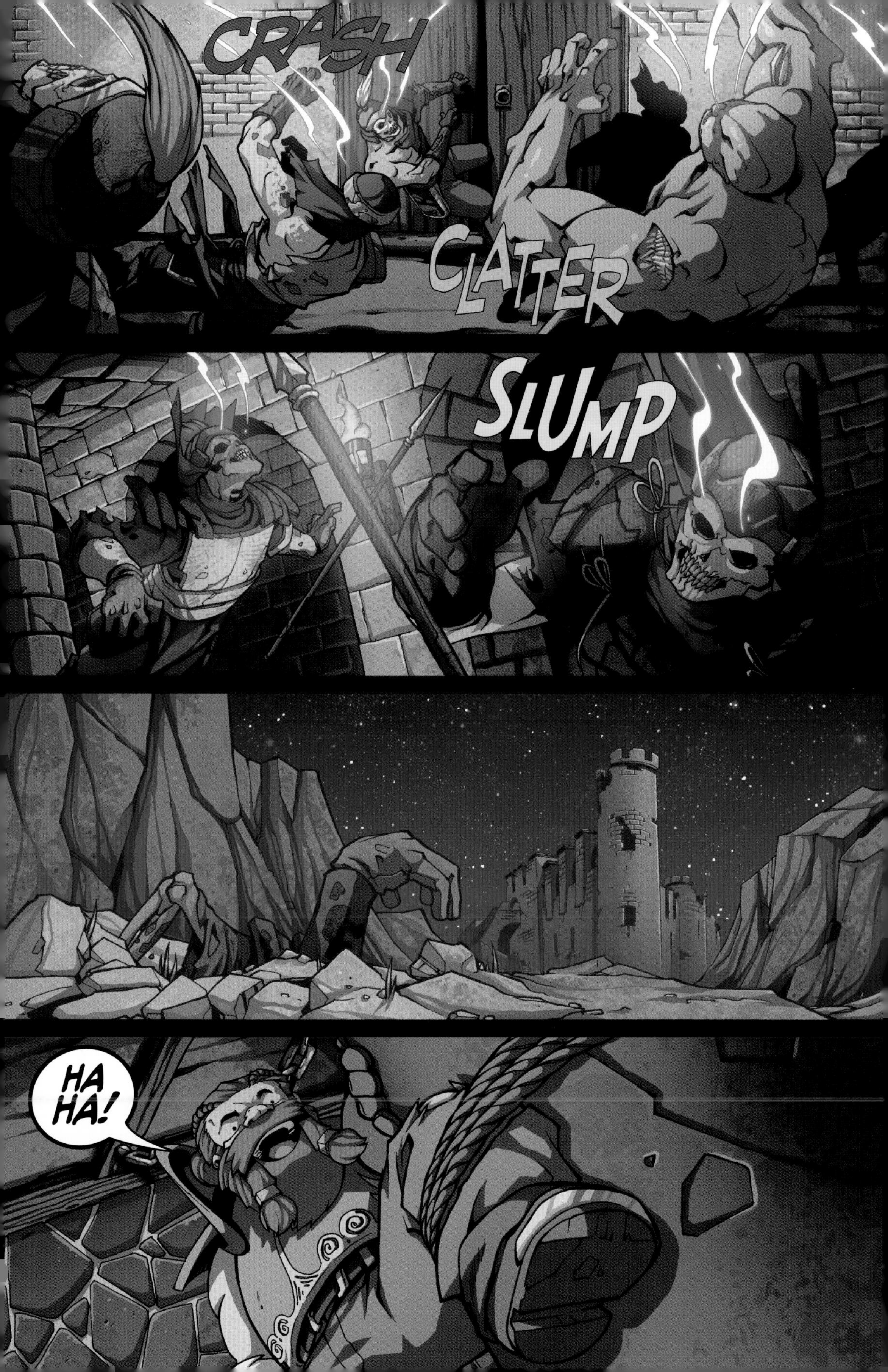
CRASH
CLATTER
SLUMP
HA HA!

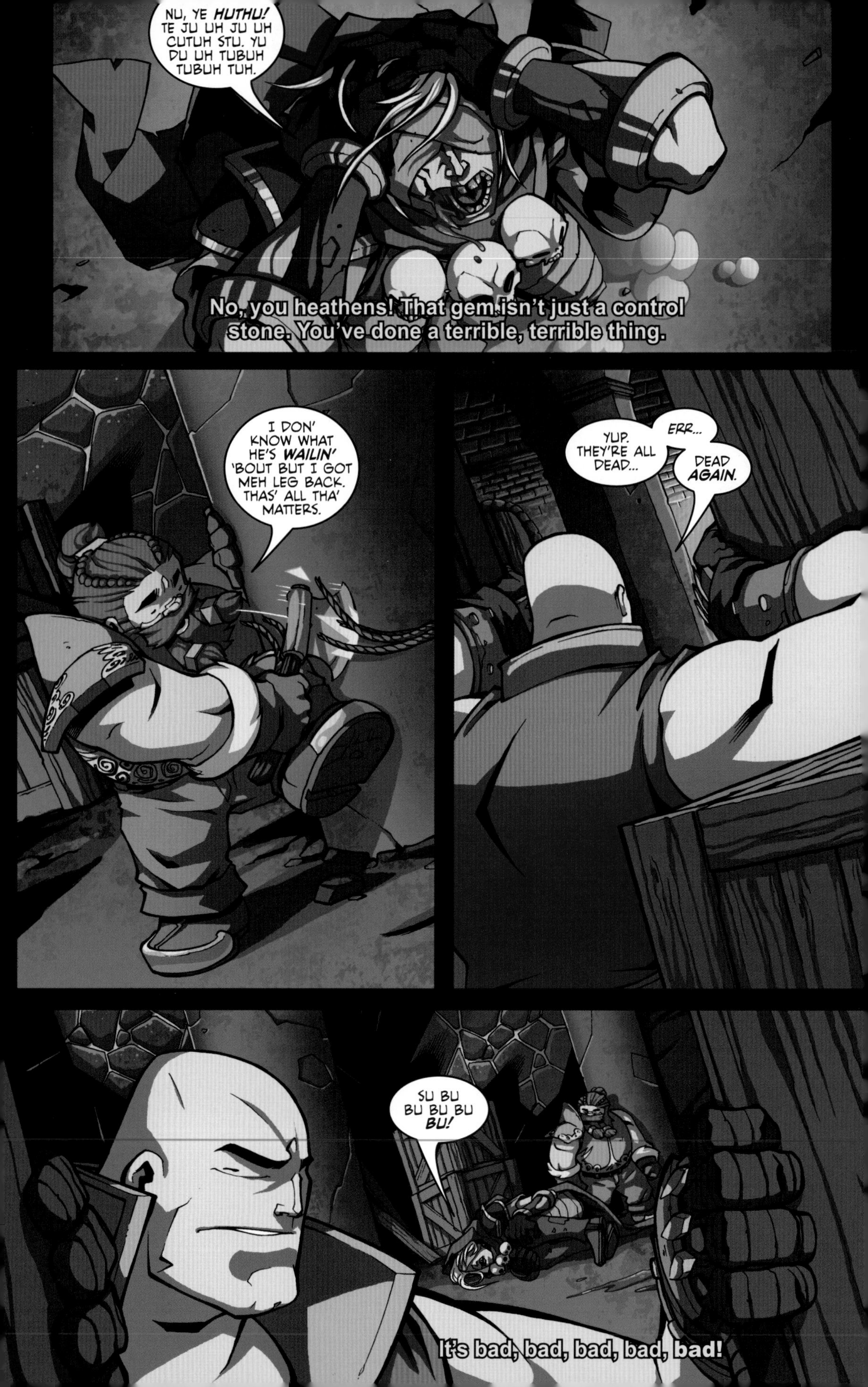
NU, YE HUTHU! TE JU UH JU UH CUTUH STU. YU DU UH TUBUH TUBUH TUH.
No, you heathens! That gem isn't just a control stone. You've done a terrible, terrible thing.
I DON' KNOW WHAT HE'S WAILIN' 'BOUT BUT I GOT MEH LEG BACK. THAS' ALL THA' MATTERS.
YUP. THEY'RE ALL DEAD...
ERR...
DEAD AGAIN.
SU BU BU BU BU BU!
It's bad, bad, bad, bad, bad!

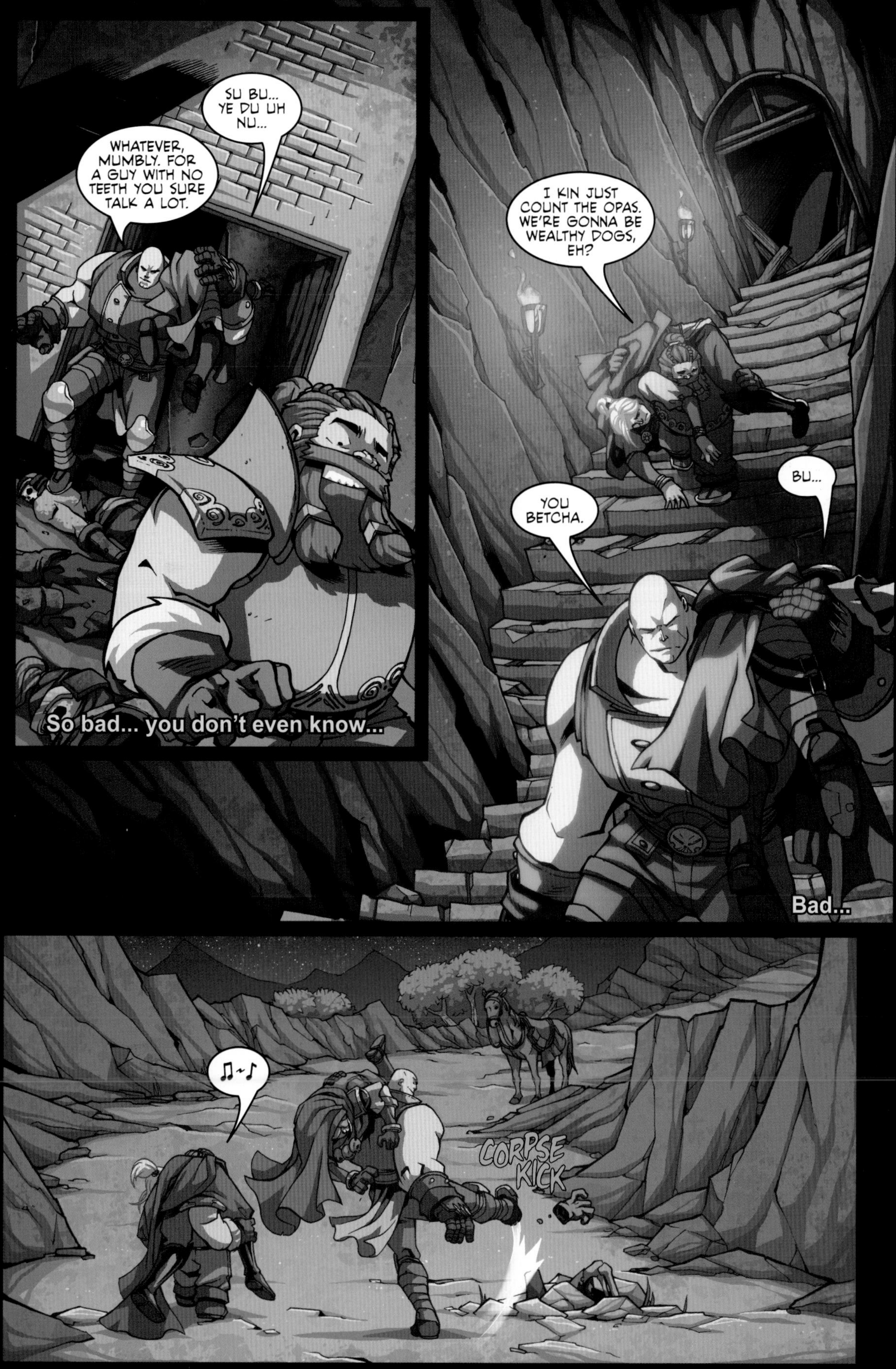
SU BU... YE DU UH NU...
WHATEVER, MUMBLY. FOR A GUY WITH NO TEETH YOU SURE TALK A LOT.
So bad... you don't even know...
I KIN JUST COUNT THE OPAS. WE'RE GONNA BE WEALTHY DOGS, EH?
BU...
YOU BETCHA.
Bad...
CORPSE KICK

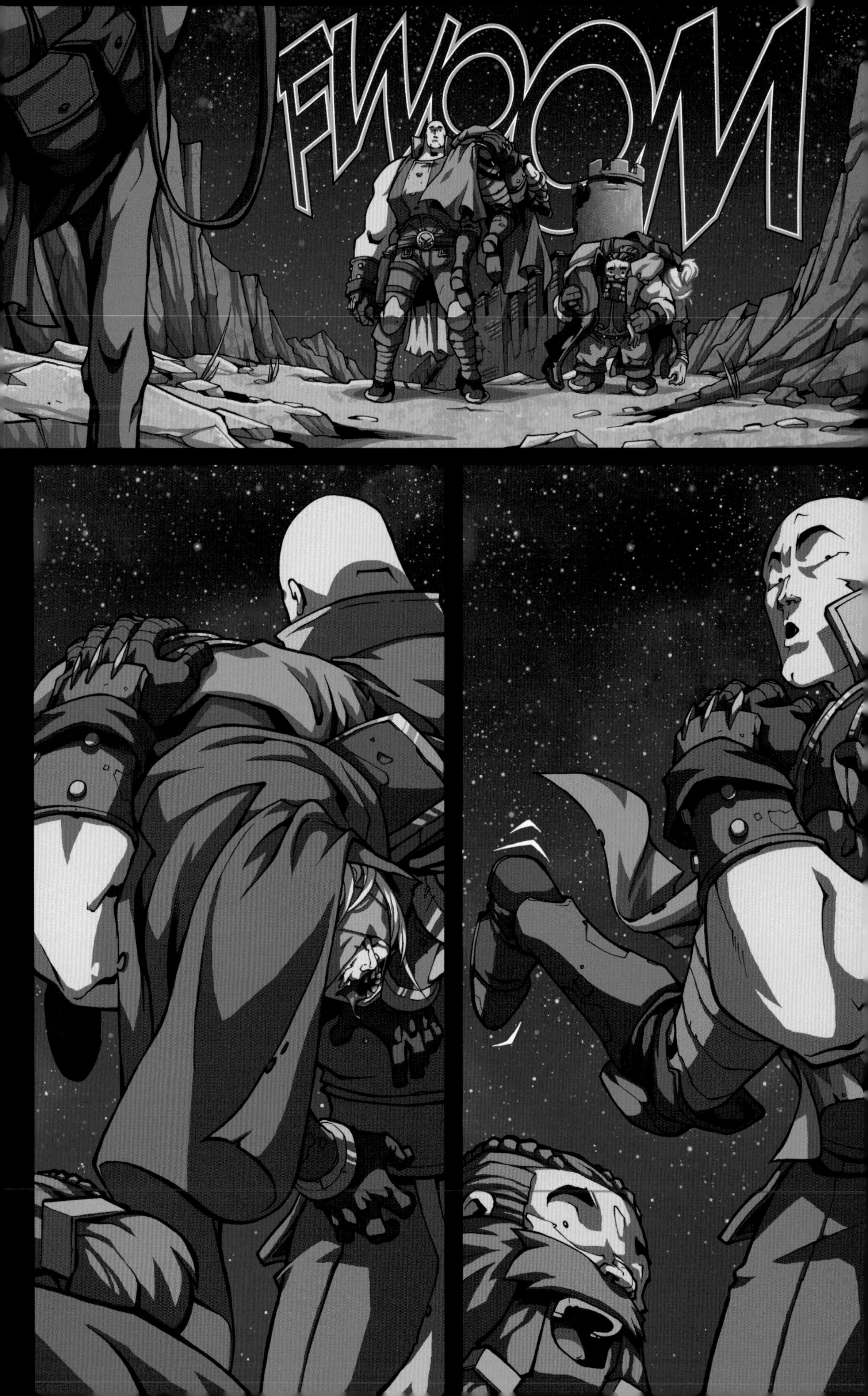
FWOOM

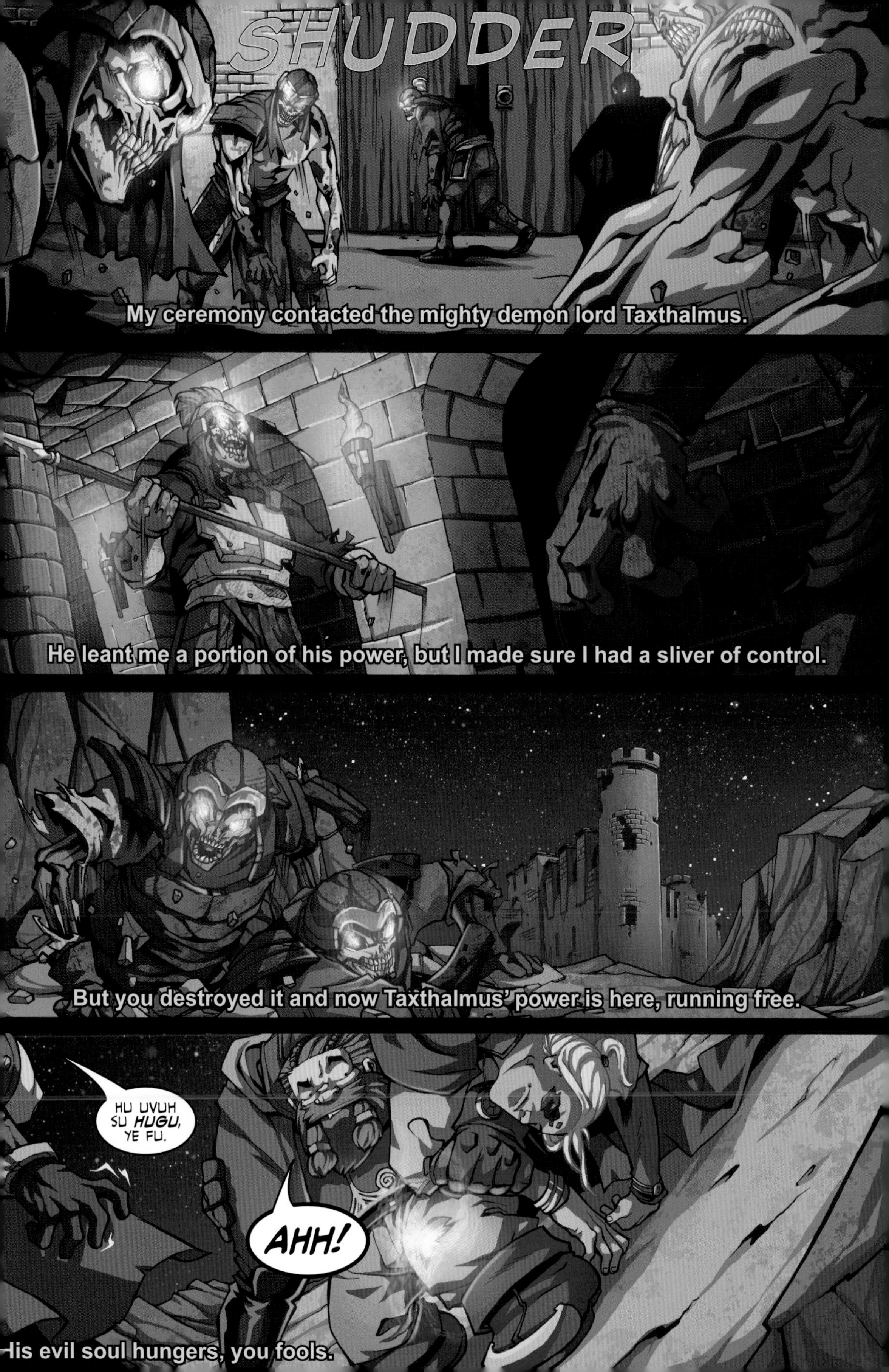
SHUDDER
My ceremony contacted the mighty demon lord Taxthalmus.
He leant me a portion of his power, but I made sure I had a sliver of control.
But you destroyed it and now Taxthalmus' power is here, running free.
HU UVUH SU HUGU, YE FU.
AHH!
His evil soul hungers, you fools.

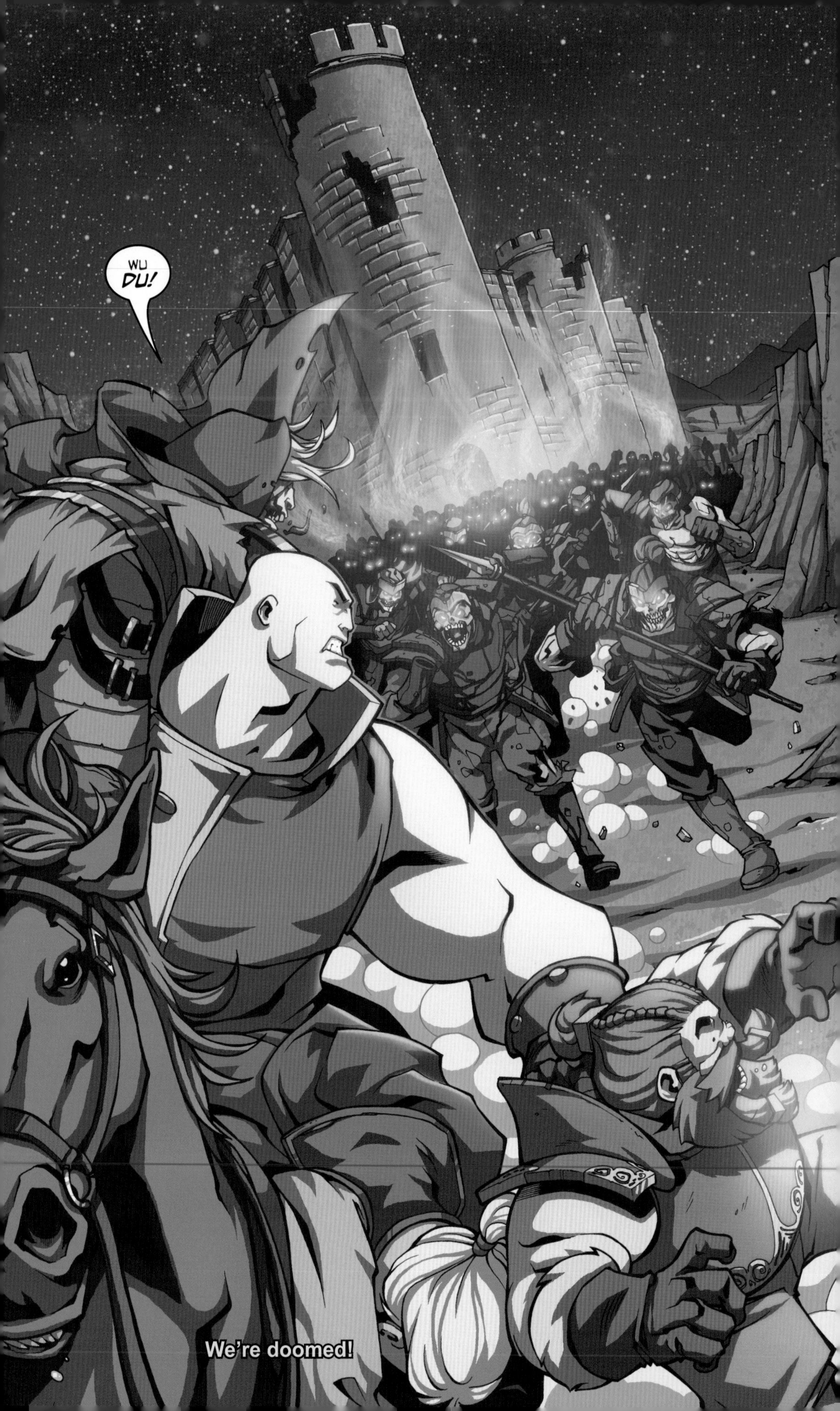
WU DU!
We're doomed!

CHAPTER FIVE

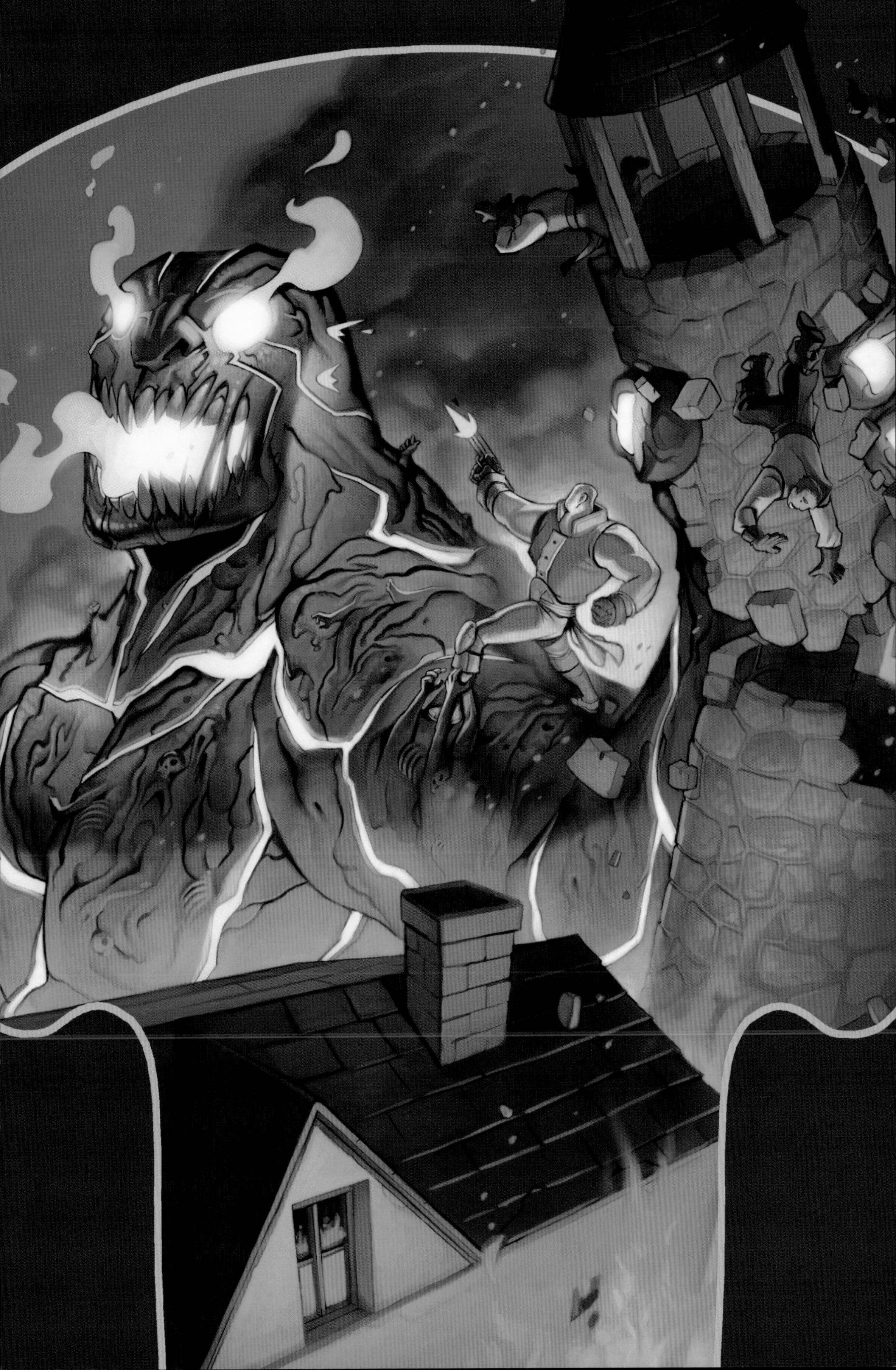

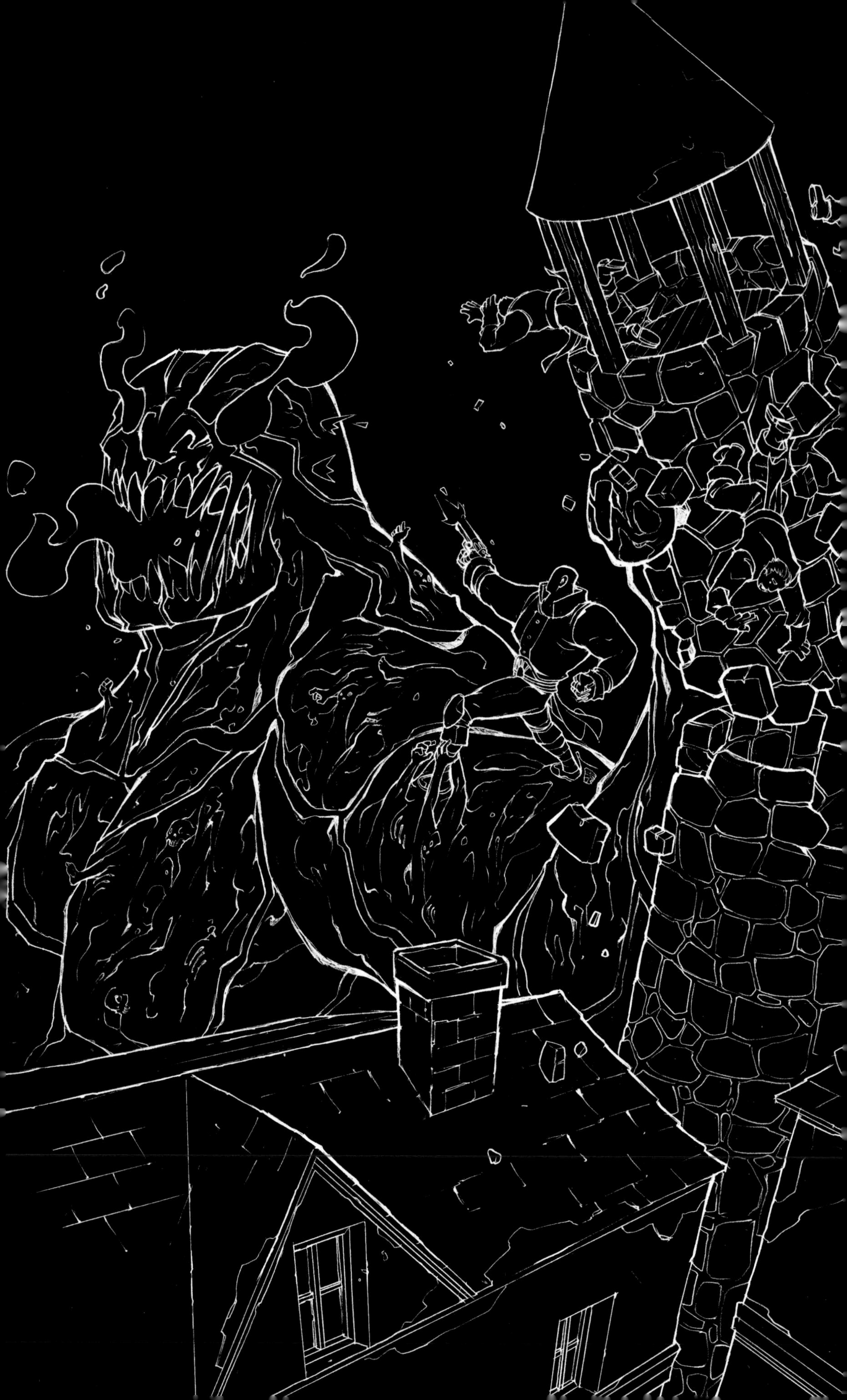

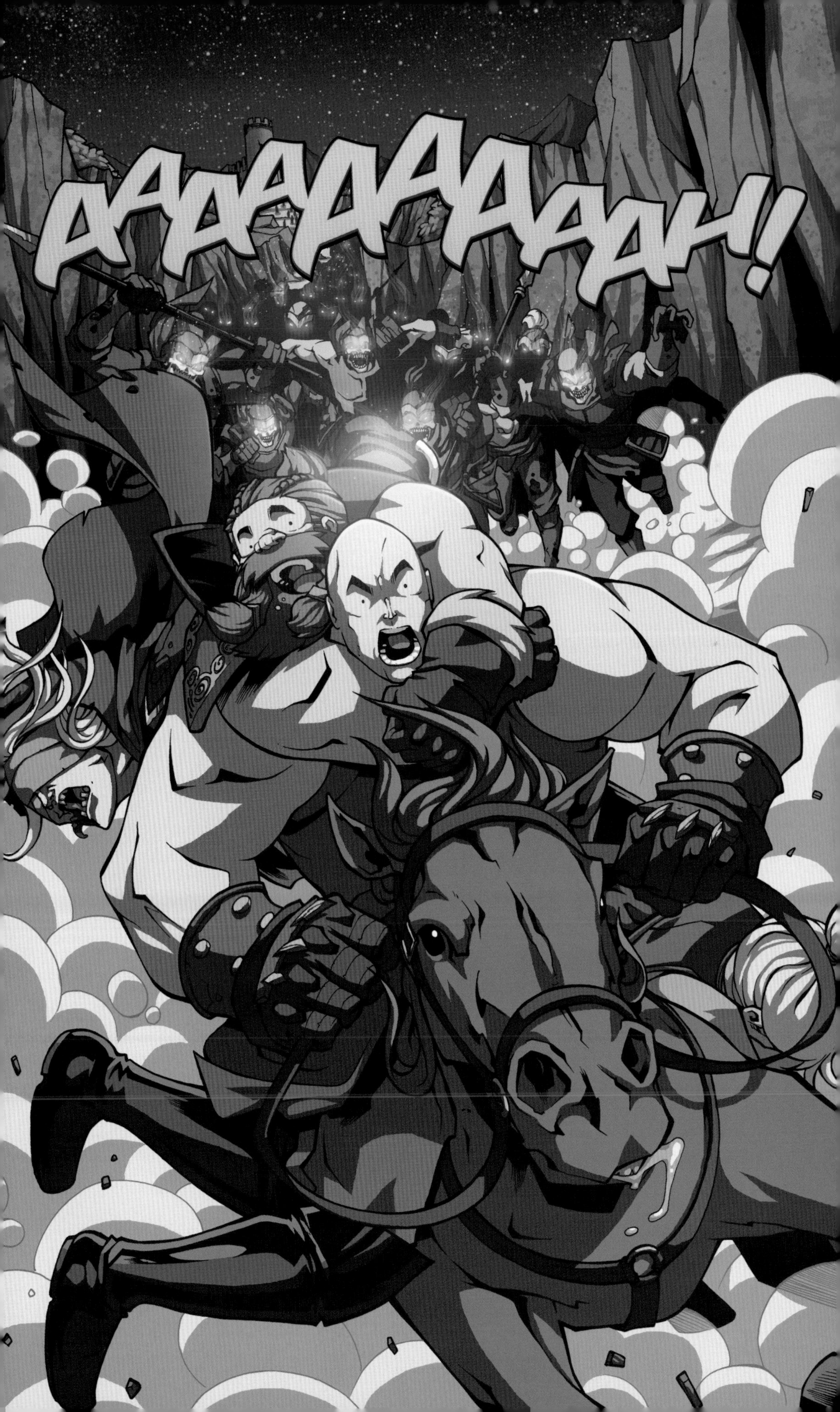
AAAAAAAAAH!!

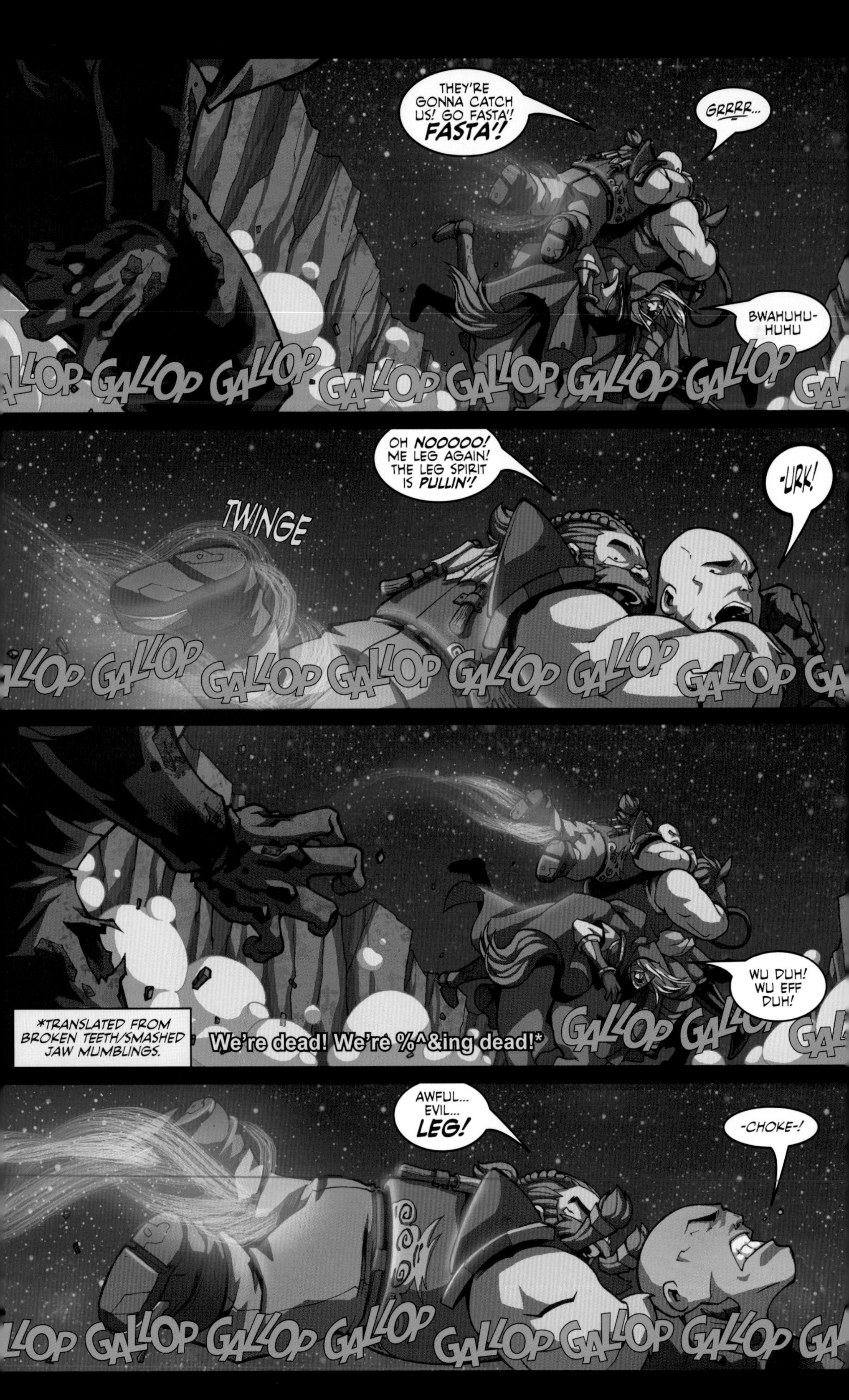
THEY'RE GONNA CATCH US! GO FASTA'! FASTA'!
GRRRR...
BWAHUHU-HUHU
GALLOP GALLOP GALLOP GALLOP GALLOP GALLOP GALLOP
OH NOOOOO! ME LEG AGAIN! THE LEG SPIRIT IS PULLIN'!
-URK!
TWINGE
GALLOP GALLOP GALLOP GALLOP GALLOP GALLOP GALLOP
WU DUH! WU EFF DUH!
We're dead! We're %^&ing dead!*
*TRANSLATED FROM BROKEN TEETH/SMASHED JAW MUMBLINGS.
GALLOP GALLOP
AWFUL... EVIL... LEG!
-CHOKE-!
GALLOP GALLOP GALLOP GALLOP GALLOP GALLOP GALLOP

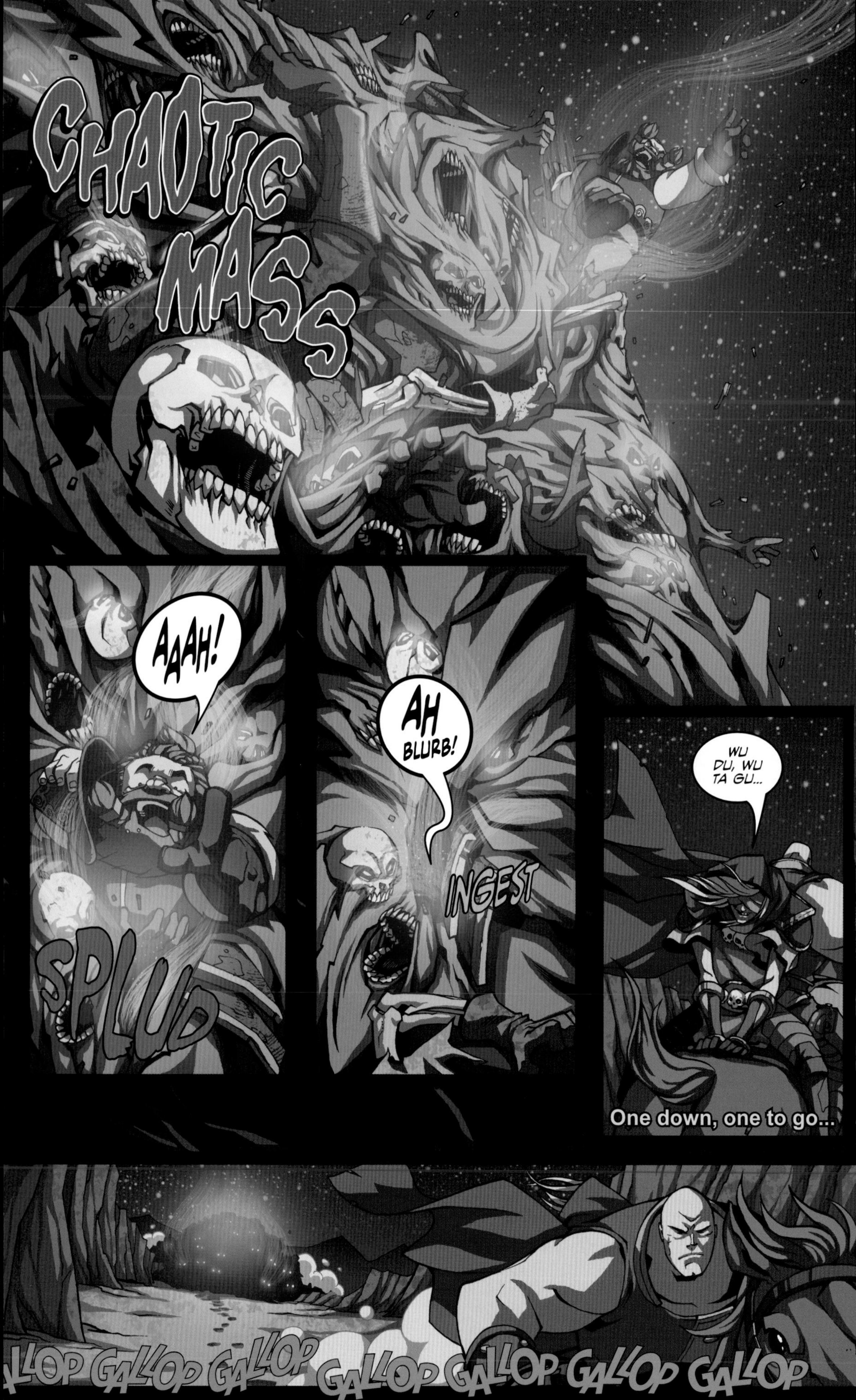
CHAOTIC MASS
AAAH!
SPLUD
AH BLURB!
INGEST
WU DU, WU TA GU...
One down, one to go...
LLOP GALLOP GALLOP GALLOP GALLOP GALLOP GALLOP

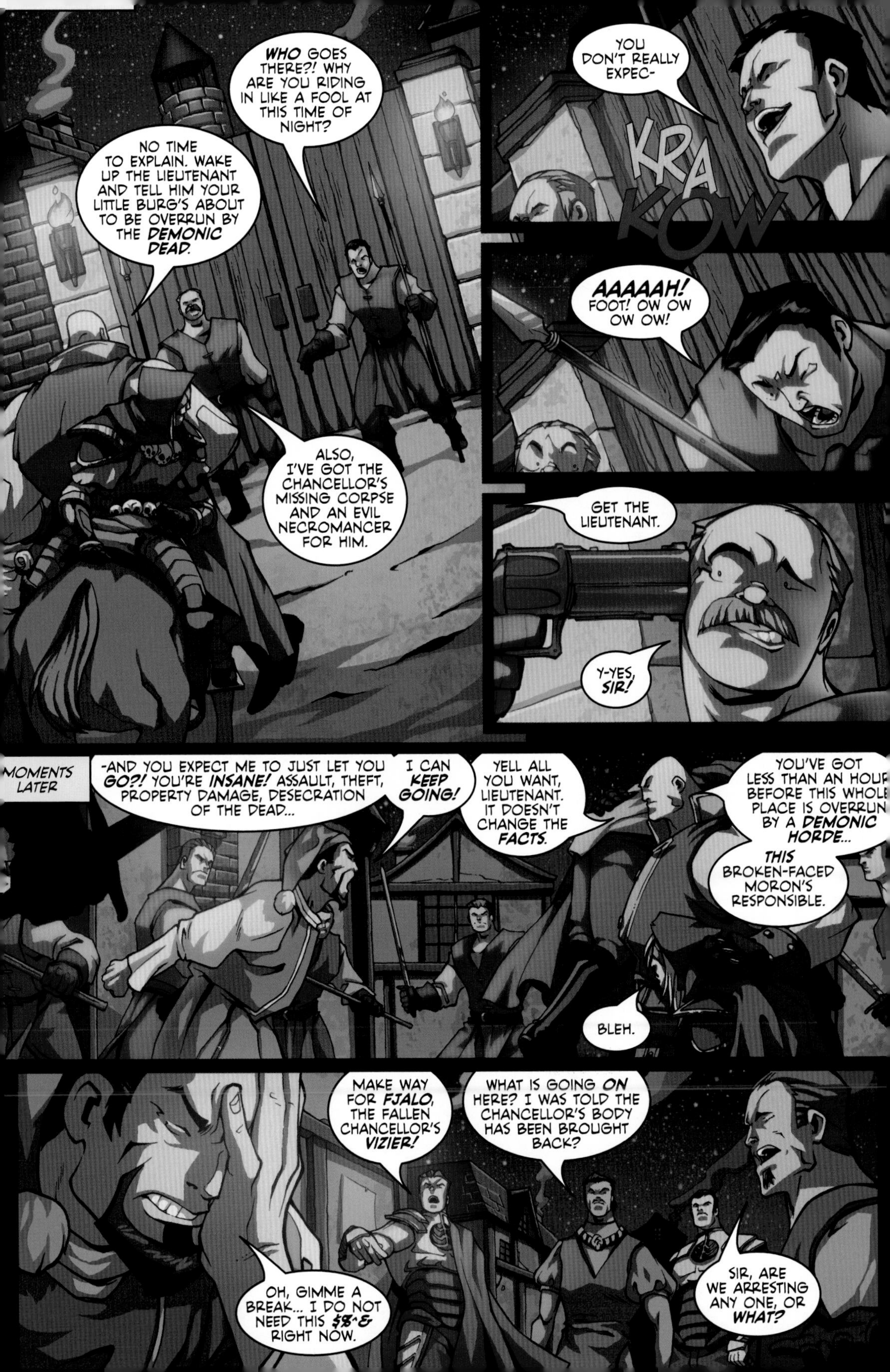
WHO GOES THERE?! WHY ARE YOU RIDING IN LIKE A FOOL AT THIS TIME OF NIGHT?
NO TIME TO EXPLAIN. WAKE UP THE LIEUTENANT AND TELL HIM YOUR LITTLE BURG'S ABOUT TO BE OVERRUN BY THE DEMONIC DEAD.
ALSO, I'VE GOT THE CHANCELLOR'S MISSING CORPSE AND AN EVIL NECROMANCER FOR HIM.
YOU DON'T REALLY EXPEC-
KRA KOW
AAAAAH! FOOT! OW OW OW OW!
GET THE LIEUTENANT.
Y-YES, SIR!
MOMENTS LATER
-AND YOU EXPECT ME TO JUST LET YOU GO?! YOU'RE INSANE! ASSAULT, THEFT, PROPERTY DAMAGE, DESECRATION OF THE DEAD...
I CAN KEEP GOING!
YELL ALL YOU WANT, LIEUTENANT. IT DOESN'T CHANGE THE FACTS.
YOU'VE GOT LESS THAN AN HOUR BEFORE THIS WHOLE PLACE IS OVERRUN BY A DEMONIC HORDE... THIS BROKEN-FACED MORON'S RESPONSIBLE.
BLEH.
MAKE WAY FOR FJALO, THE FALLEN CHANCELLOR'S VIZIER!
WHAT IS GOING ON HERE? I WAS TOLD THE CHANCELLOR'S BODY HAS BEEN BROUGHT BACK?
OH, GIMME A BREAK... I DO NOT NEED THIS $8^& RIGHT NOW.
SIR, ARE WE ARRESTING ANY ONE, OR WHAT?

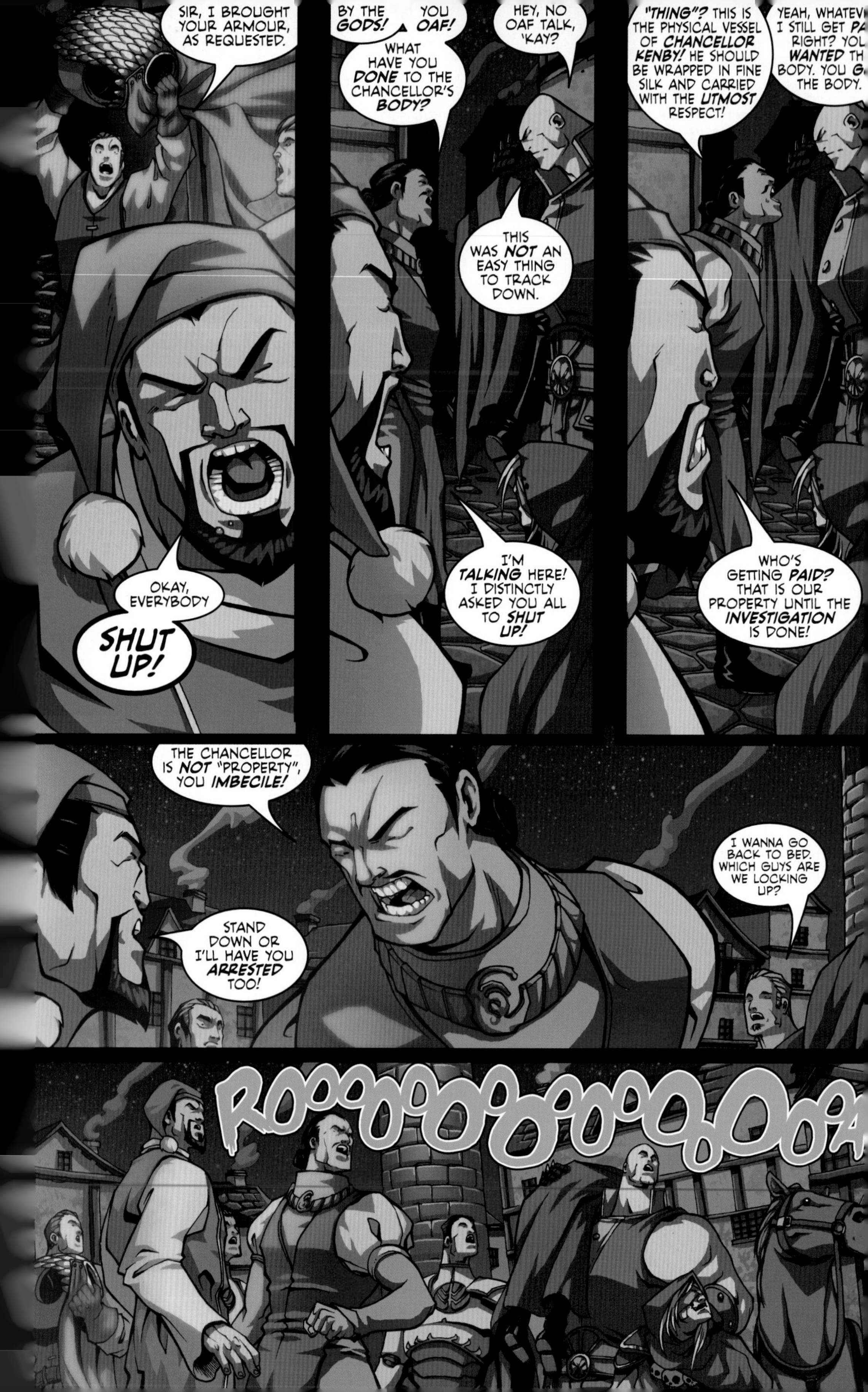
SIR, I BROUGHT YOUR ARMOUR, AS REQUESTED.
OKAY, EVERYBODY
SHUT UP!
BY THE GODS! YOU OAF!
WHAT HAVE YOU DONE TO THE CHANCELLOR'S BODY?
HEY, NO OAF TALK, 'KAY?
THIS WAS NOT AN EASY THING TO TRACK DOWN.
I'M TALKING HERE! I DISTINCTLY ASKED YOU ALL TO SHUT UP!
"THING"? THIS IS THE PHYSICAL VESSEL OF CHANCELLOR KENBY! HE SHOULD BE WRAPPED IN FINE SILK AND CARRIED WITH THE UTMOST RESPECT!
WHO'S GETTING PAID? THAT IS OUR PROPERTY UNTIL THE INVESTIGATION IS DONE!
THE CHANCELLOR IS NOT "PROPERTY", YOU IMBECILE!
STAND DOWN OR I'LL HAVE YOU ARRESTED TOO!
I WANNA GO BACK TO BED. WHICH GUYS ARE WE LOCKING UP?

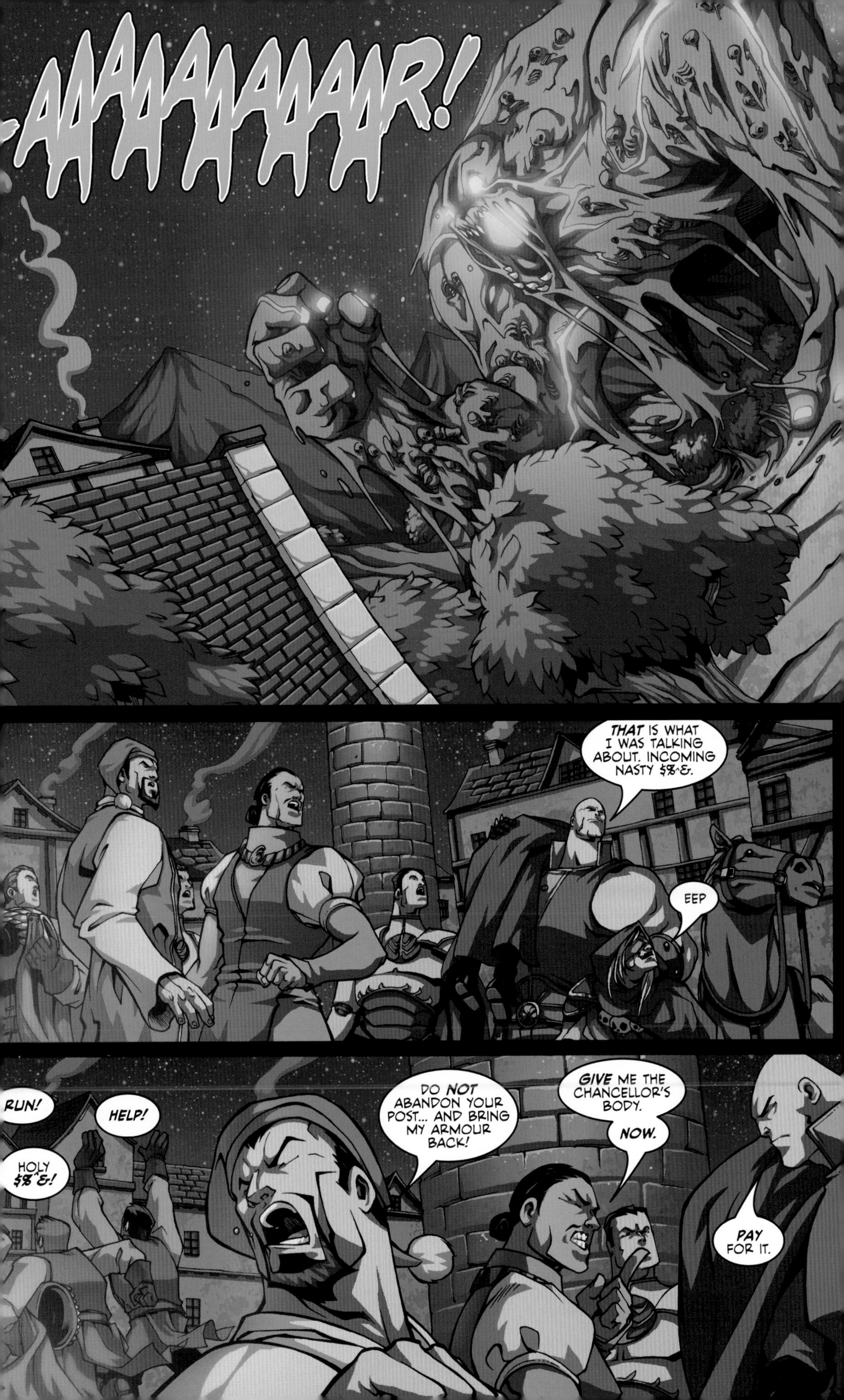
-AAAAAAAAAAR!
THAT IS WHAT I WAS TALKING ABOUT. INCOMING NASTY $%^&.
EEP
RUN!
HELP!
HOLY $%^&!
DO NOT ABANDON YOUR POST... AND BRING MY ARMOUR BACK!
GIVE ME THE CHANCELLOR'S BODY.
NOW.
PAY FOR IT.

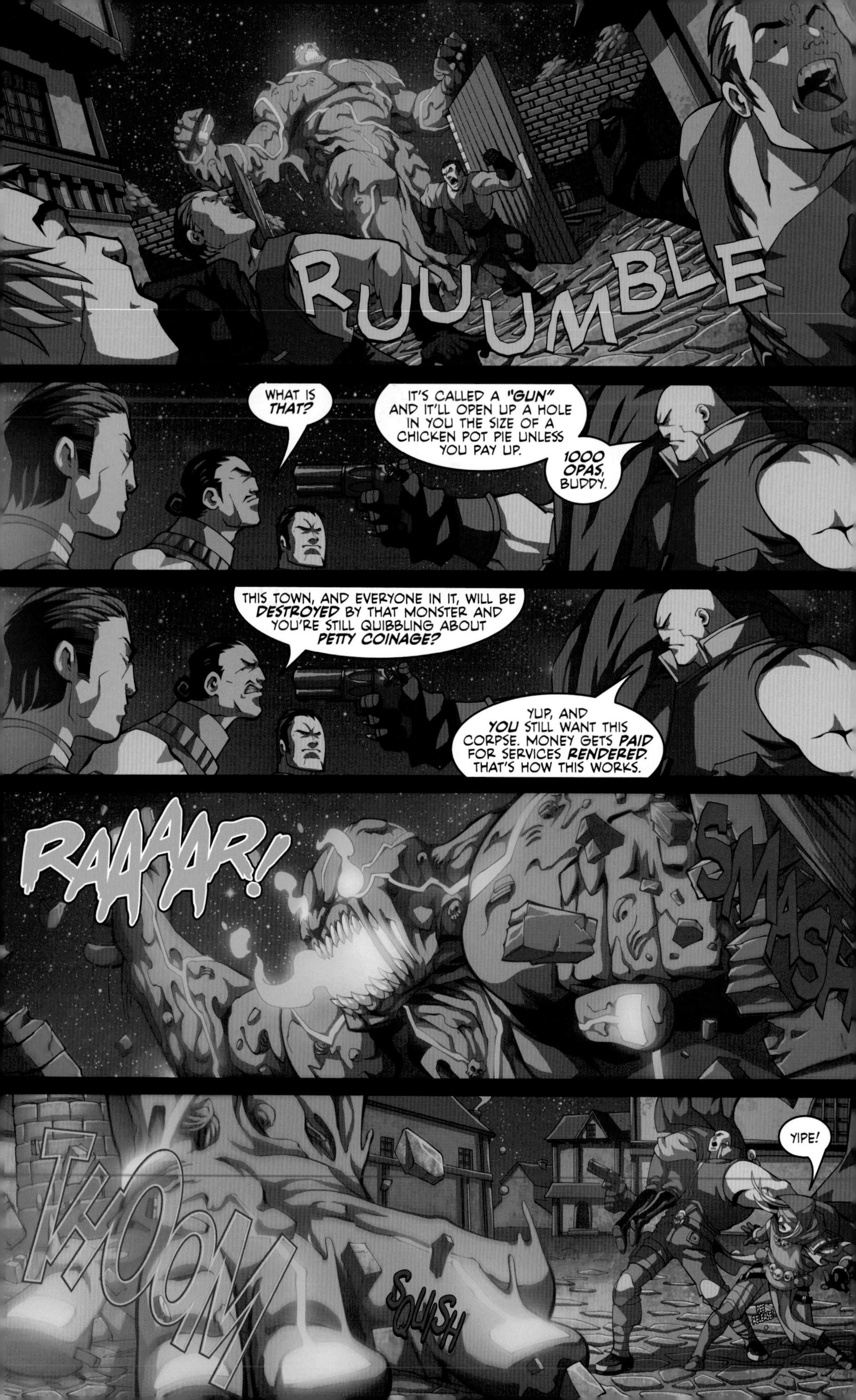
RUUUMBLE
WHAT IS THAT?
IT'S CALLED A "GUN" AND IT'LL OPEN UP A HOLE IN YOU THE SIZE OF A CHICKEN POT PIE UNLESS YOU PAY UP.
1000 OPAS, BUDDY.
THIS TOWN, AND EVERYONE IN IT, WILL BE DESTROYED BY THAT MONSTER AND YOU'RE STILL QUIBBLING ABOUT PETTY COINAGE?
YUP, AND YOU STILL WANT THIS CORPSE. MONEY GETS PAID FOR SERVICES RENDERED. THAT'S HOW THIS WORKS.
RAAAAR!
SMASH
THOOM
SQUISH
YIPE!
PEE RELEASE!

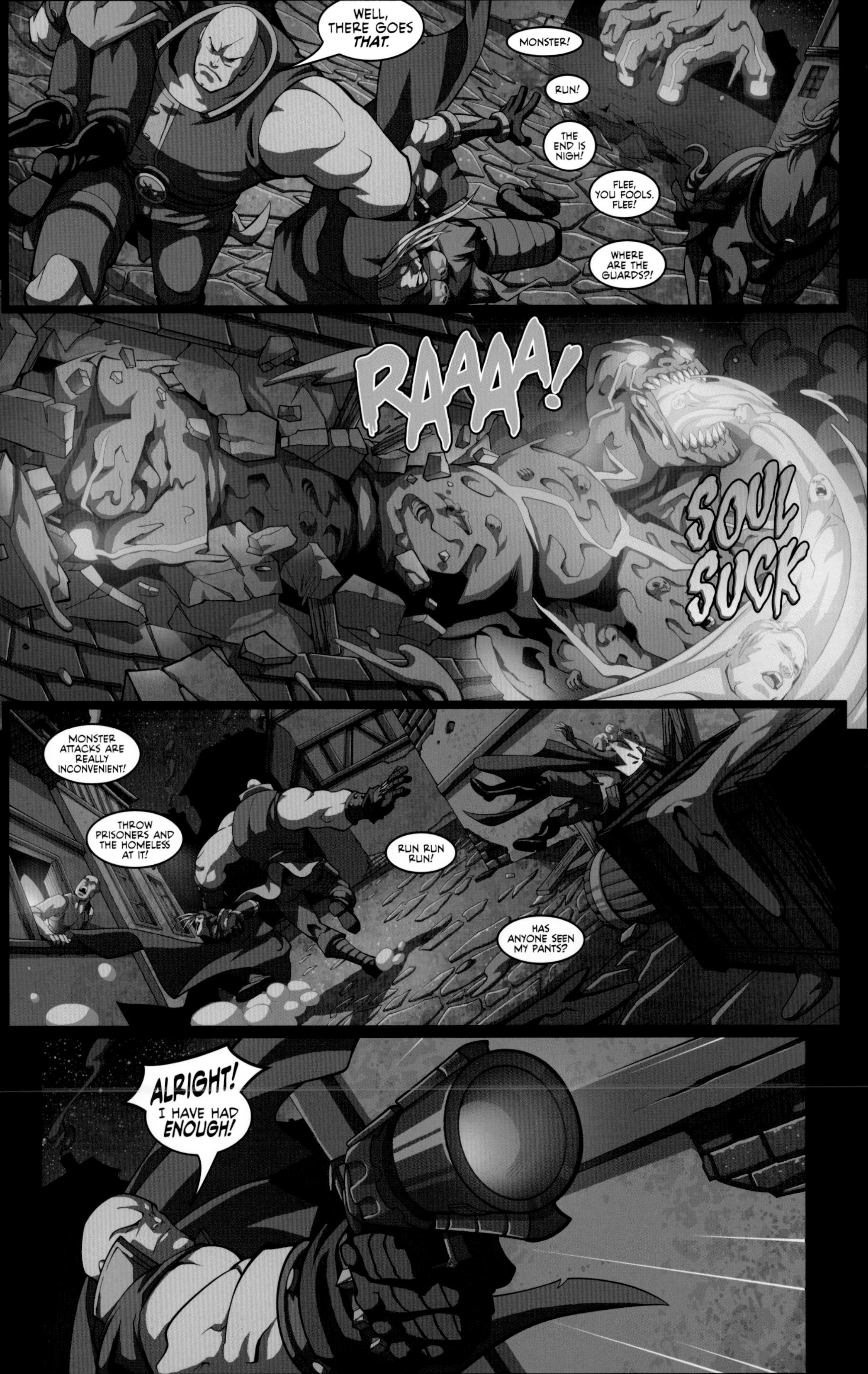
WELL, THERE GOES THAT.
MONSTER!
RUN!
THE END IS NIGH!
FLEE, YOU FOOLS. FLEE!
WHERE ARE THE GUARDS?!
RAAAA!
SOUL SUCK
MONSTER ATTACKS ARE REALLY INCONVENIENT!
THROW PRISONERS AND THE HOMELESS AT IT!
RUN RUN RUN!
HAS ANYONE SEEN MY PANTS?
ALRIGHT! I HAVE HAD ENOUGH!

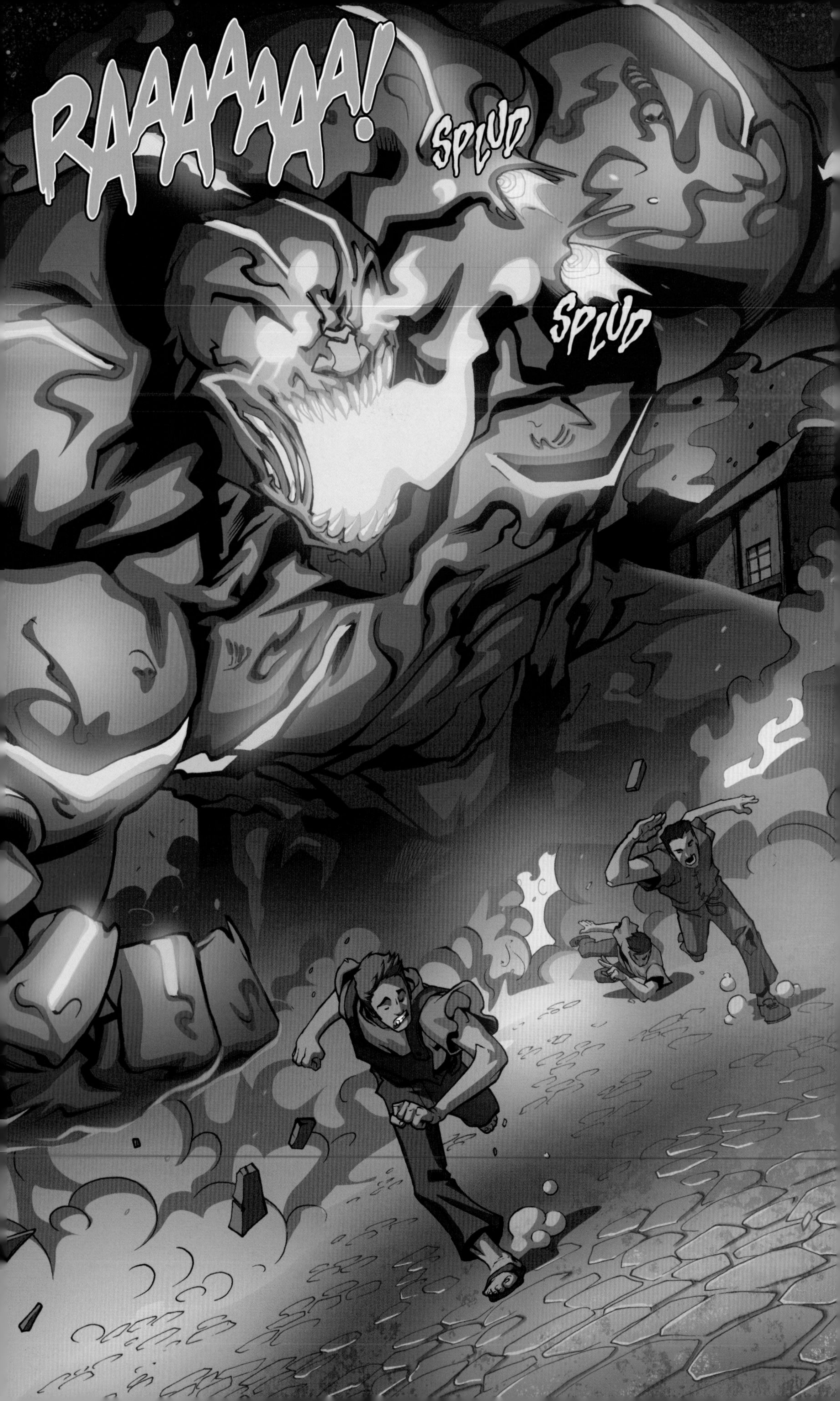
RAAAAAAA!
SPLUD
SPLUD

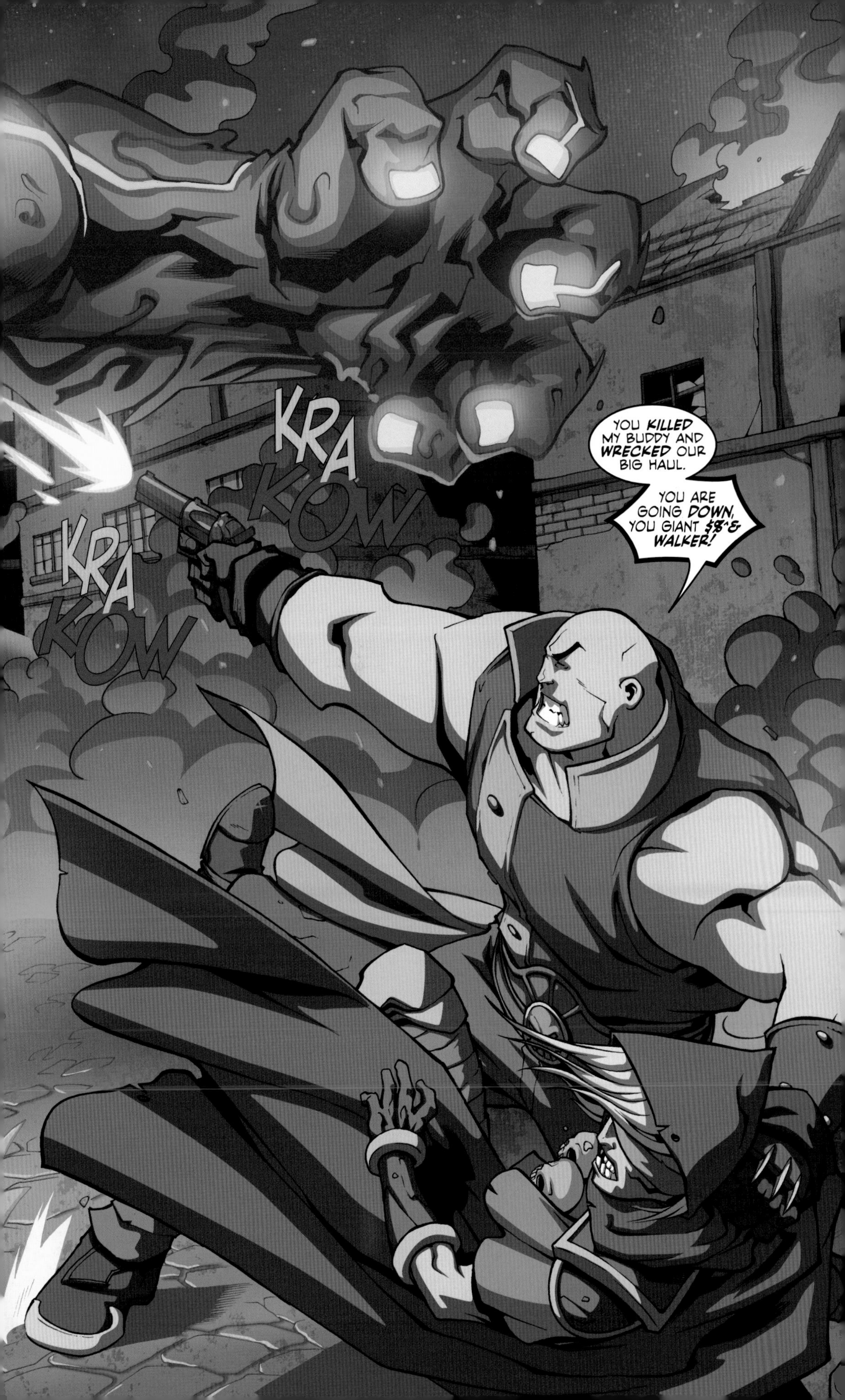
KRA KOW
KRA KOW
YOU **KILLED** MY BUDDY AND **WRECKED** OUR BIG HAUL.
YOU ARE GOING **DOWN**, YOU GIANT **$&^&** **WALKER!**

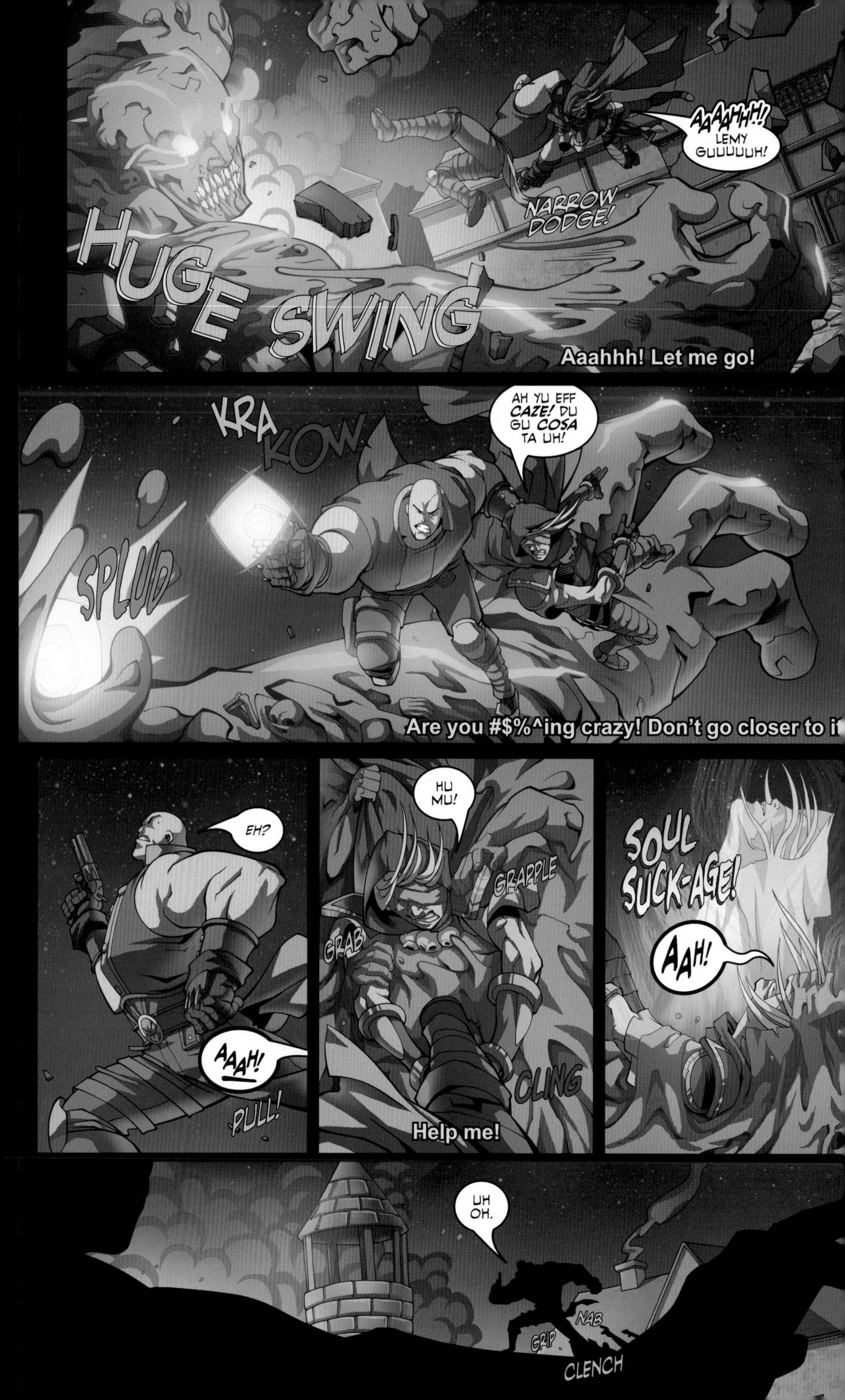
AAAAHH!! LEMY GUUUUUH!
NARROW DODGE!
HUGE SWING
Aaahhh! Let me go!
KRA KOW
AH YU EFF CAZE! DU GU COSA TA UH!
SPLUD
Are you #$%^ing crazy! Don't go closer to it
EH?
AAAH!
PULL!
HU MU!
GRAPPLE
GRAB
CLING
Help me!
SOUL SUCK-AGE!
AAH!
UH OH.
NAB
GRIP
CLENCH

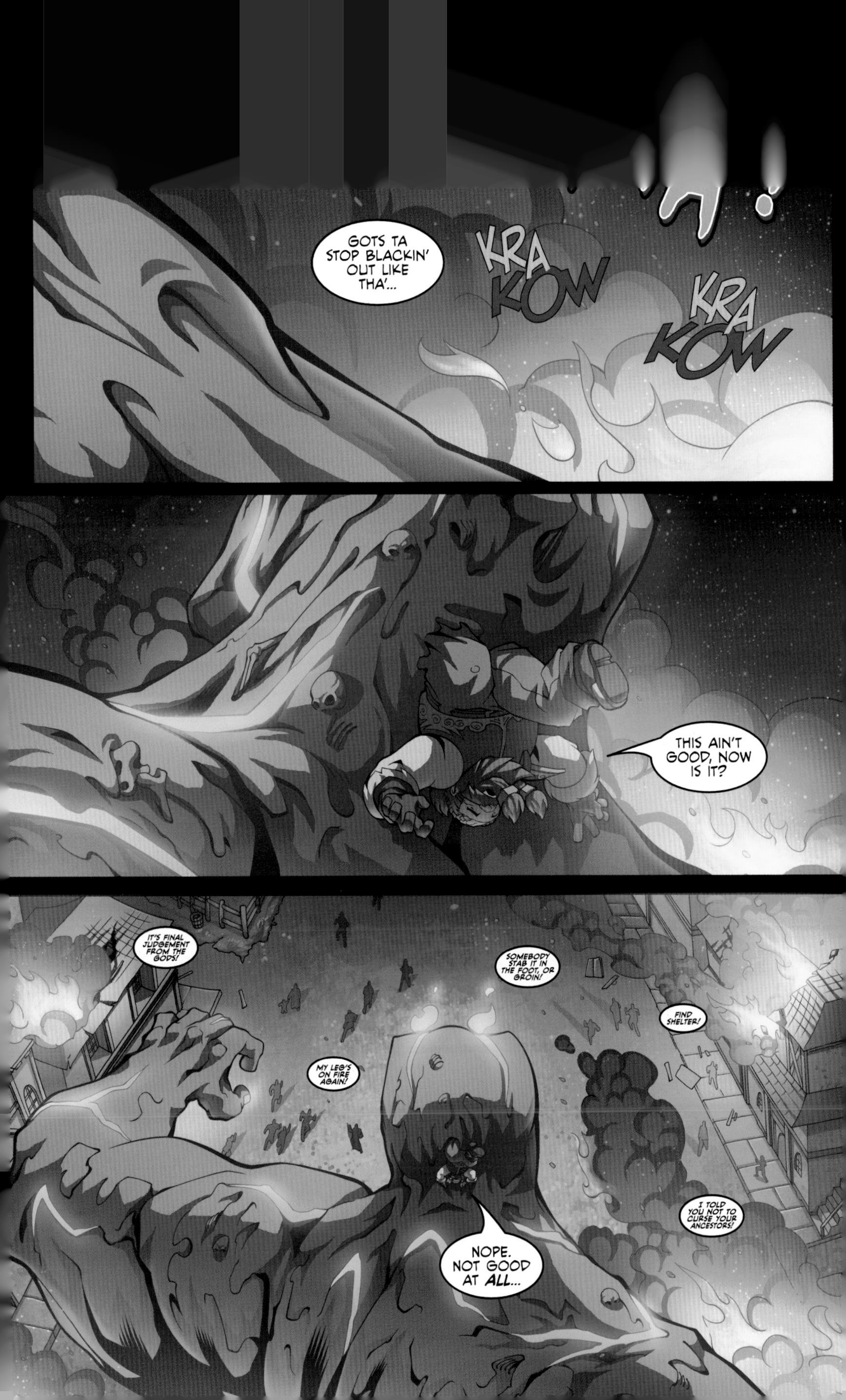
GOTS TA STOP BLACKIN' OUT LIKE THA'...
KRA KOW
KRA KOW
THIS AIN'T GOOD, NOW IS IT?
IT'S FINAL JUDGEMENT FROM THE GODS!
SOMEBODY STAB IT IN THE FOOT, OR GROIN!
FIND SHELTER!
MY LEG'S ON FIRE AGAIN!
I TOLD YOU NOT TO CURSE YOUR ANCESTORS!
NOPE. NOT GOOD AT ALL...

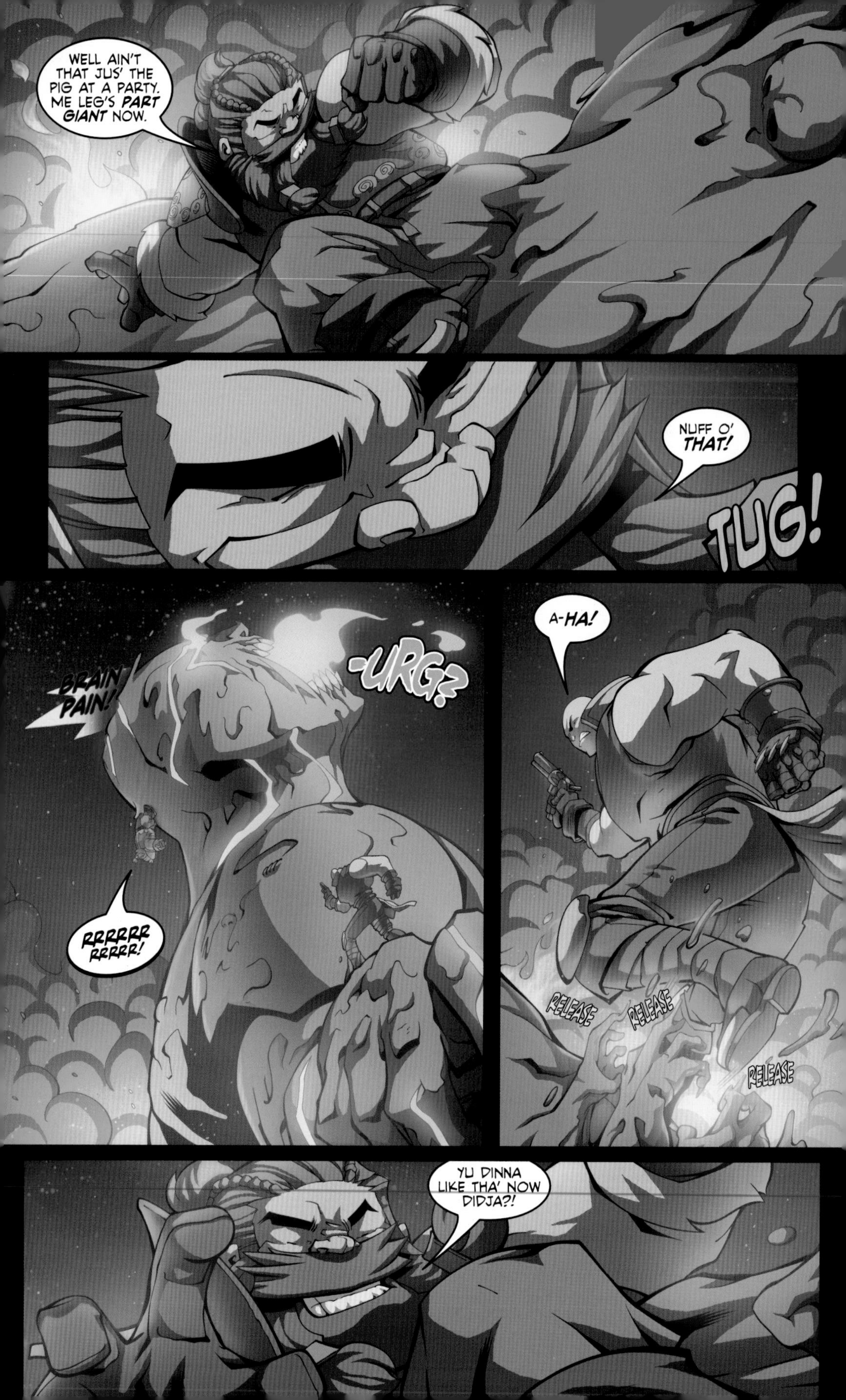
WELL AIN'T THAT JUS' THE PIG AT A PARTY. ME LEG'S PART GIANT NOW.
NUFF O' THAT!
TUG!
BRAIN PAIN!
-URG?
RRRRRR RRRRR!
A-HA!
RELEASE
RELEASE
RELEASE
YU DINNA LIKE THA' NOW DIDJA?!

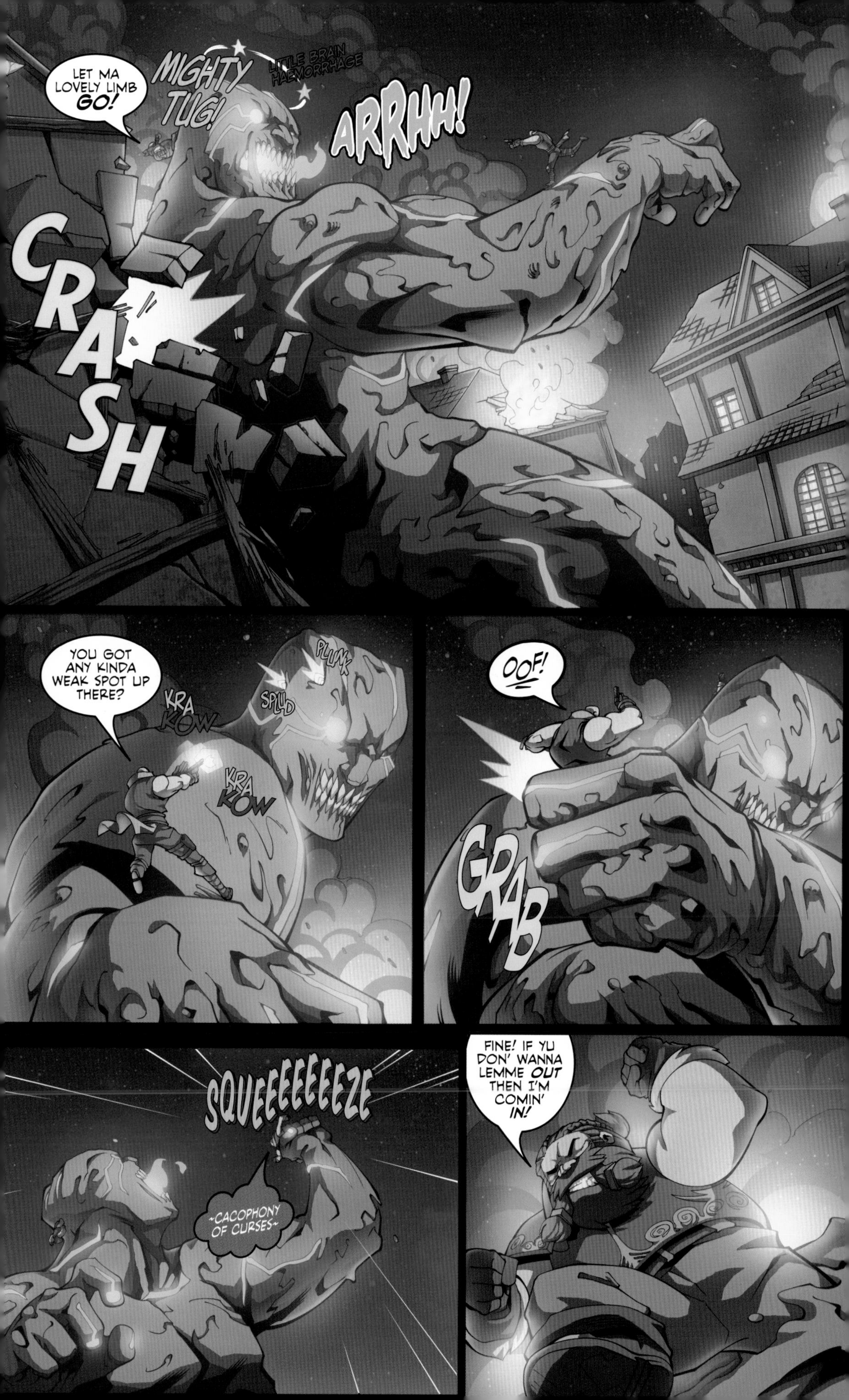
LET MA LOVELY LIMB GO!
MIGHTY TUG!
LITTLE BRAIN HAEMORRHAGE
ARRHH!
CRASH
YOU GOT ANY KINDA WEAK SPOT UP THERE?
PLUNK
SPLUD
KRA KOW
KRA KOW
OOF!
GRAB
SQUEEEEEEEEZE
~CACOPHONY OF CURSES~
FINE! IF YU DON' WANNA LEMME OUT THEN I'M COMIN' IN!

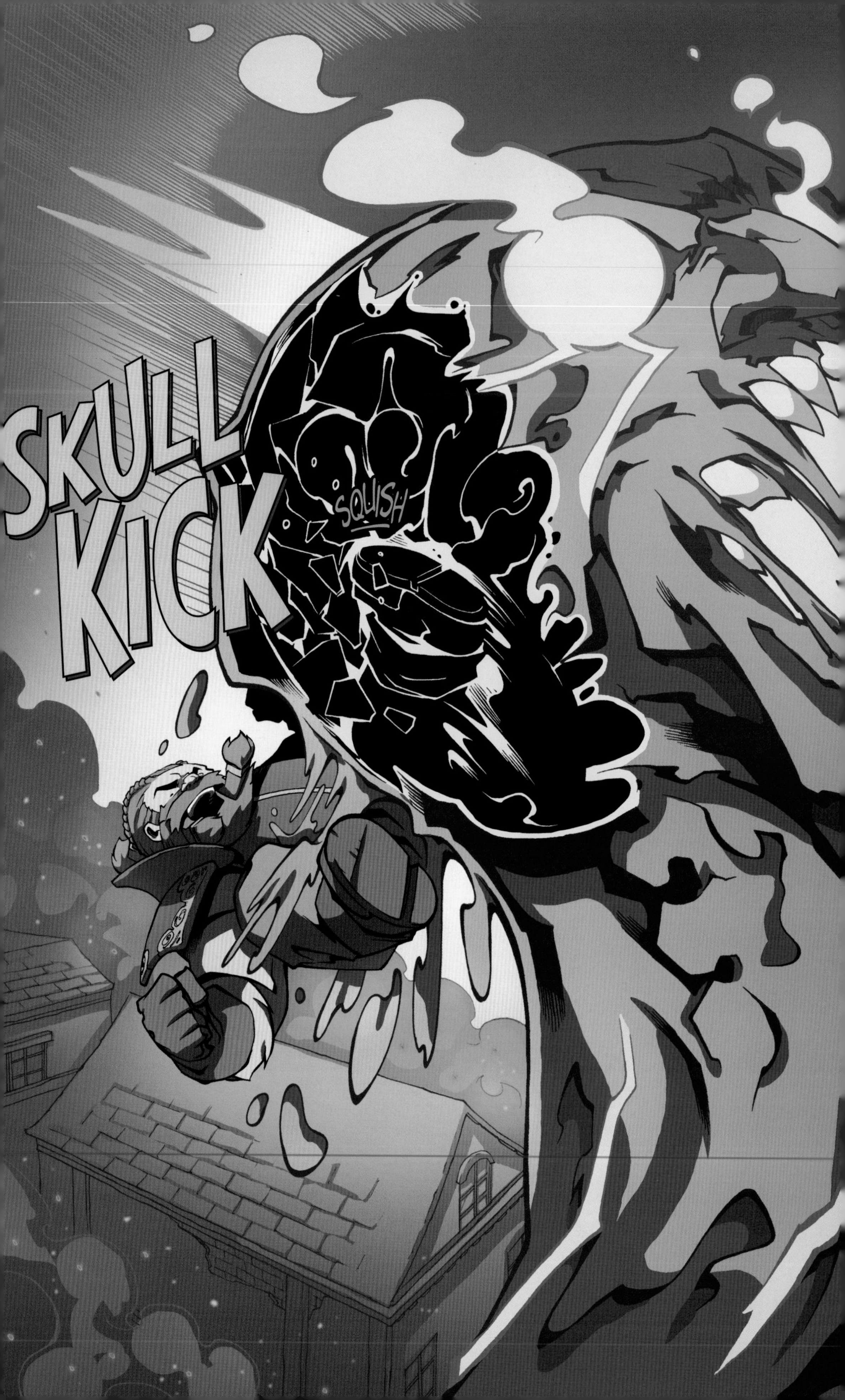
SKULL KICK
SQUISH

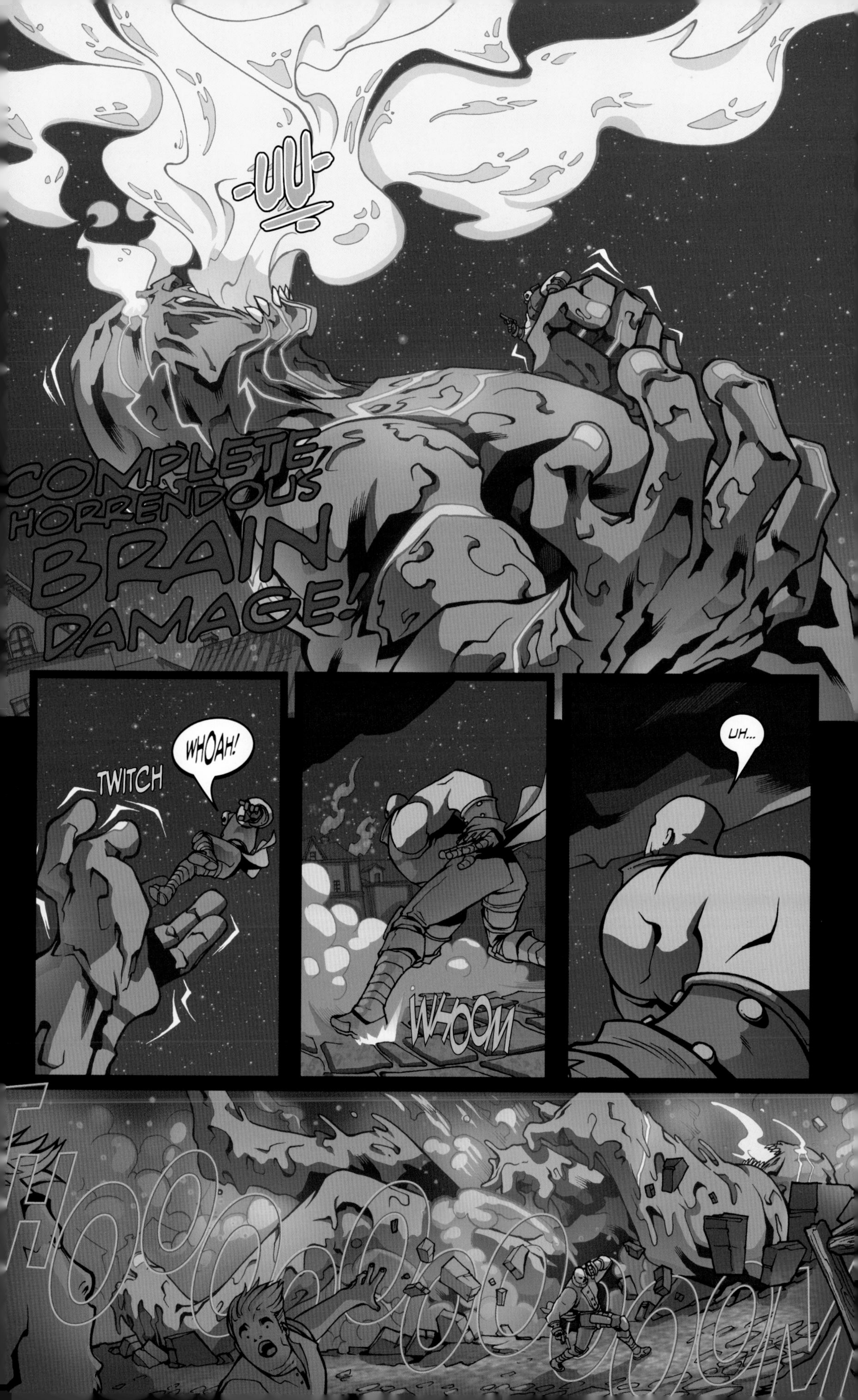
-UU-
COMPLETE HORRENDOUS BRAIN DAMAGE!
TWITCH
WHOAH!
WHOOM
UH...
FOOOOOOOOOOOM

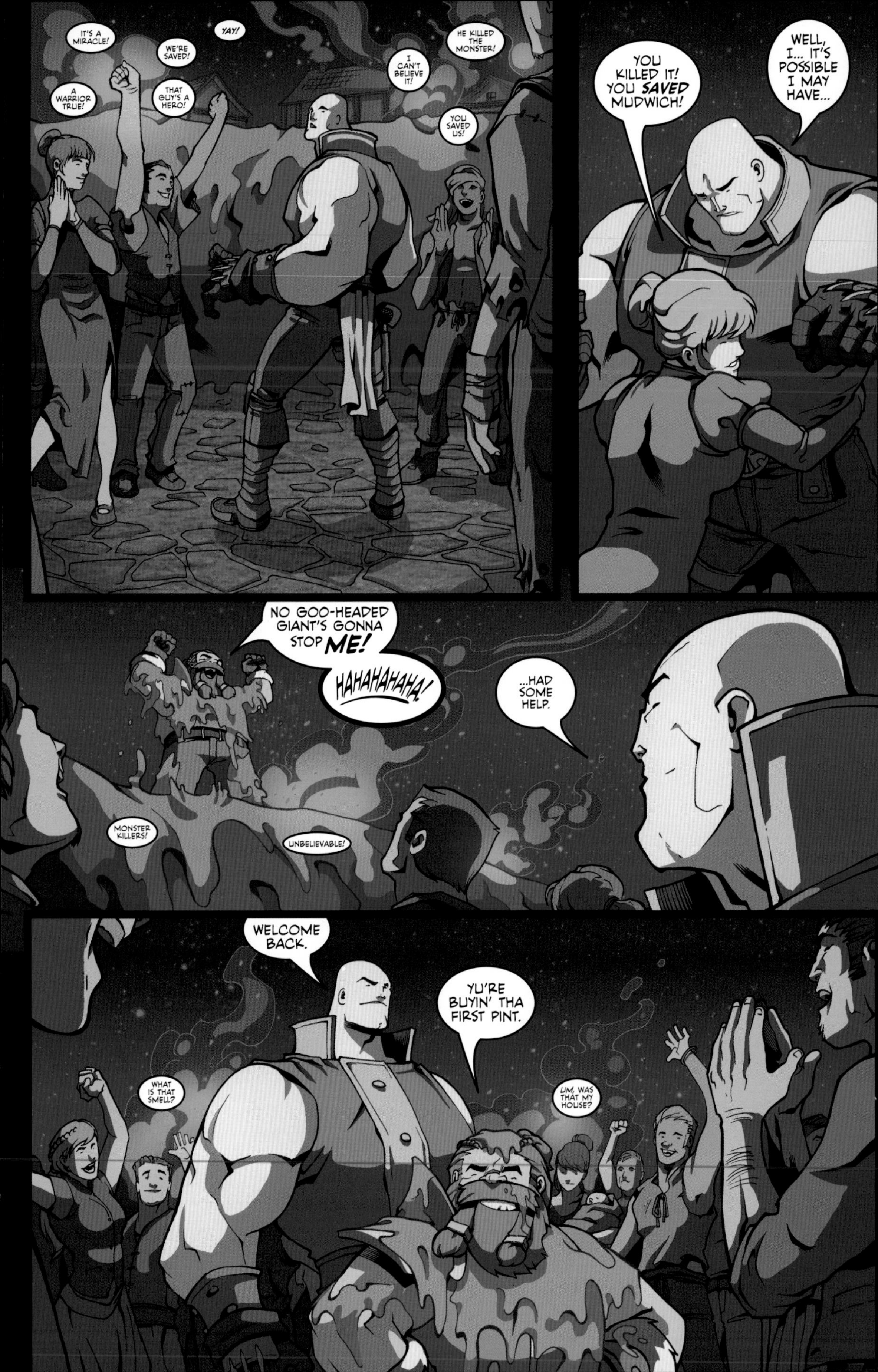
IT'S A MIRACLE!
YAY!
WE'RE SAVED!
A WARRIOR TRUE!
THAT GUY'S A HERO!
I CAN'T BELIEVE IT!
HE KILLED THE MONSTER!
YOU SAVED US!
YOU KILLED IT! YOU SAVED MUDWICH!
WELL, I... IT'S POSSIBLE I MAY HAVE...
NO GOO-HEADED GIANT'S GONNA STOP ME!
HAHAHAHAHA!
...HAD SOME HELP.
MONSTER KILLERS!
UNBELIEVABLE!
WELCOME BACK.
YU'RE BUYIN' THA FIRST PINT.
WHAT IS THAT SMELL?
UM, WAS THAT MY HOUSE?

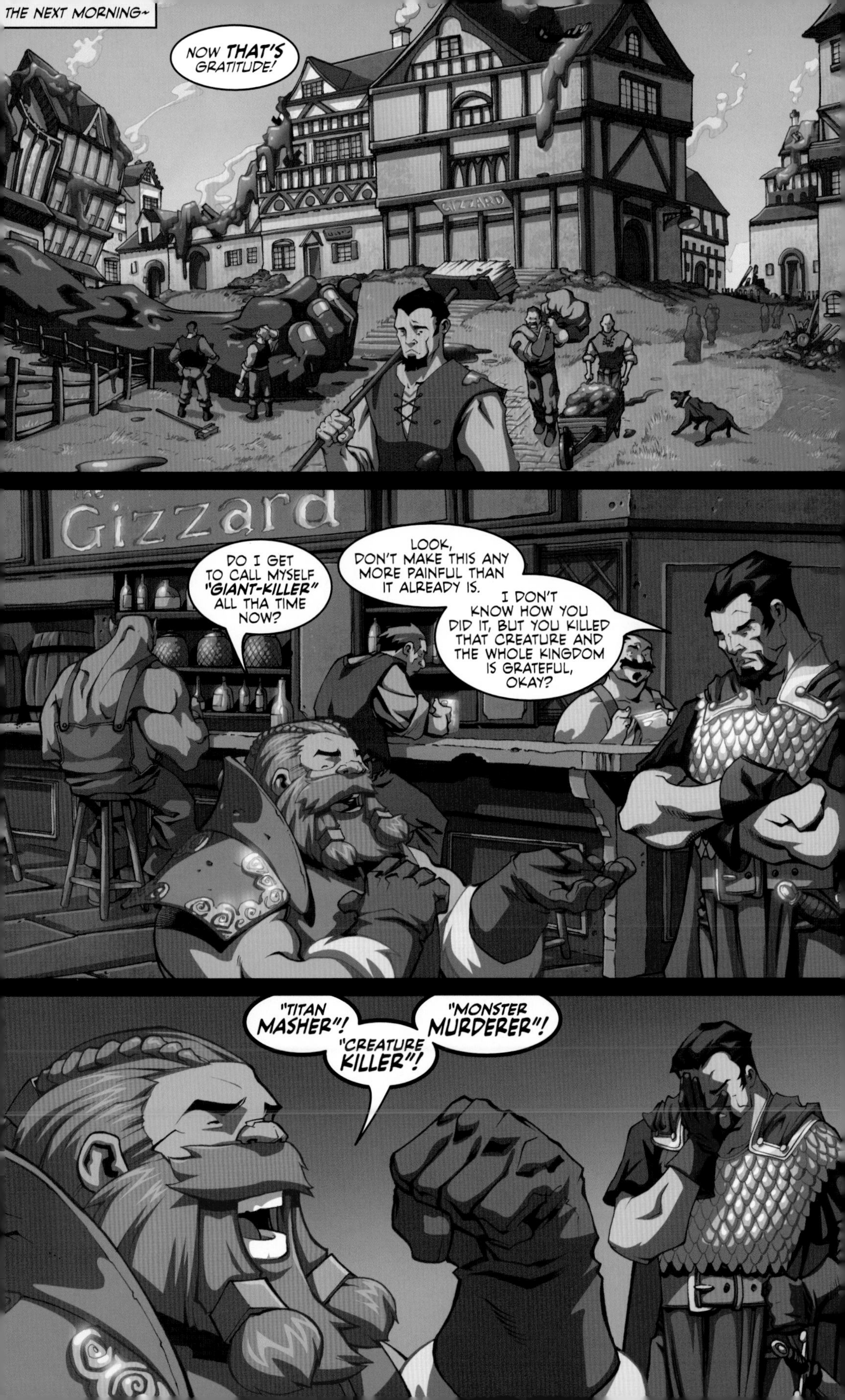
THE NEXT MORNING~
NOW THAT'S GRATITUDE!
GIZZARD
The Gizzard
DO I GET TO CALL MYSELF "GIANT-KILLER" ALL THA TIME NOW?
LOOK, DON'T MAKE THIS ANY MORE PAINFUL THAN IT ALREADY IS.
I DON'T KNOW HOW YOU DID IT, BUT YOU KILLED THAT CREATURE AND THE WHOLE KINGDOM IS GRATEFUL, OKAY?
"TITAN MASHER"!
"CREATURE KILLER"!
"MONSTER MURDERER"!

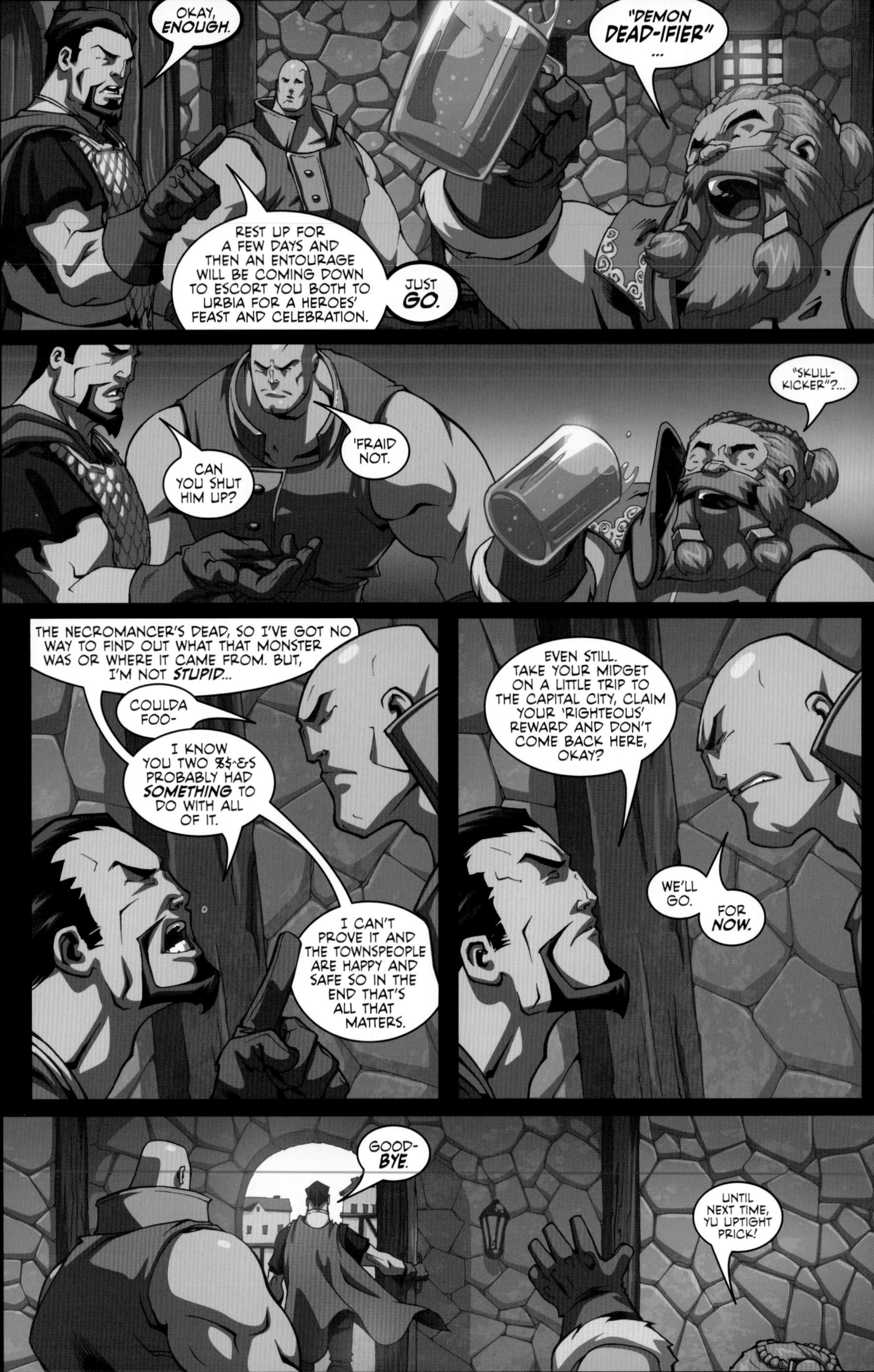
OKAY, ENOUGH.
"DEMON DEAD-IFIER" ...
REST UP FOR A FEW DAYS AND THEN AN ENTOURAGE WILL BE COMING DOWN TO ESCORT YOU BOTH TO URBIA FOR A HEROES' FEAST AND CELEBRATION.
JUST GO.
"SKULL-KICKER"?...
CAN YOU SHUT HIM UP?
'FRAID NOT.
THE NECROMANCER'S DEAD, SO I'VE GOT NO WAY TO FIND OUT WHAT THAT MONSTER WAS OR WHERE IT CAME FROM. BUT, I'M NOT STUPID...
COULDA FOO-
I KNOW YOU TWO %$^&S PROBABLY HAD SOMETHING TO DO WITH ALL OF IT.
I CAN'T PROVE IT AND THE TOWNSPEOPLE ARE HAPPY AND SAFE SO IN THE END THAT'S ALL THAT MATTERS.
EVEN STILL. TAKE YOUR MIDGET ON A LITTLE TRIP TO THE CAPITAL CITY, CLAIM YOUR 'RIGHTEOUS' REWARD AND DON'T COME BACK HERE, OKAY?
WE'LL GO.
FOR NOW.
GOOD-BYE.
UNTIL NEXT TIME, YU UPTIGHT PRICK!

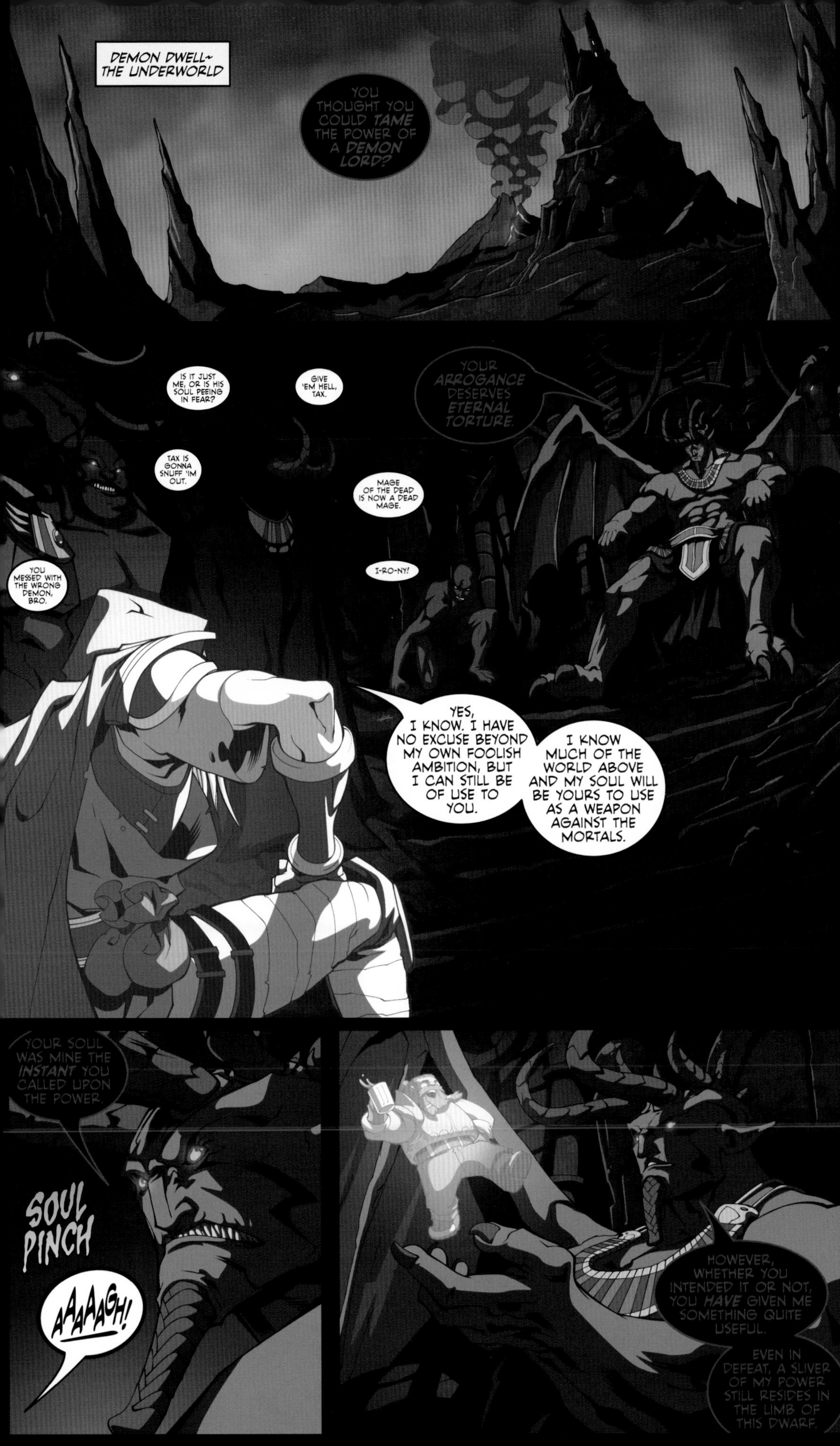

DEMON DWELL~ THE UNDERWORLD
YOU THOUGHT YOU COULD TAME THE POWER OF A DEMON LORD?
IS IT JUST ME, OR IS HIS SOUL PEEING IN FEAR?
GIVE 'EM HELL, TAX.
YOUR ARROGANCE DESERVES ETERNAL TORTURE.
TAX IS GONNA SNUFF 'IM OUT.
MAGE OF THE DEAD IS NOW A DEAD MAGE.
I-RO-NY!
YOU MESSED WITH THE WRONG DEMON, BRO.
YES, I KNOW. I HAVE NO EXCUSE BEYOND MY OWN FOOLISH AMBITION, BUT I CAN STILL BE OF USE TO YOU.
I KNOW MUCH OF THE WORLD ABOVE AND MY SOUL WILL BE YOURS TO USE AS A WEAPON AGAINST THE MORTALS.
YOUR SOUL WAS MINE THE INSTANT YOU CALLED UPON THE POWER.
SOUL PINCH
AAAAAGH!
HOWEVER, WHETHER YOU INTENDED IT OR NOT, YOU HAVE GIVEN ME SOMETHING QUITE USEFUL.
EVEN IN DEFEAT, A SLIVER OF MY POWER STILL RESIDES IN THE LIMB OF THIS DWARF.

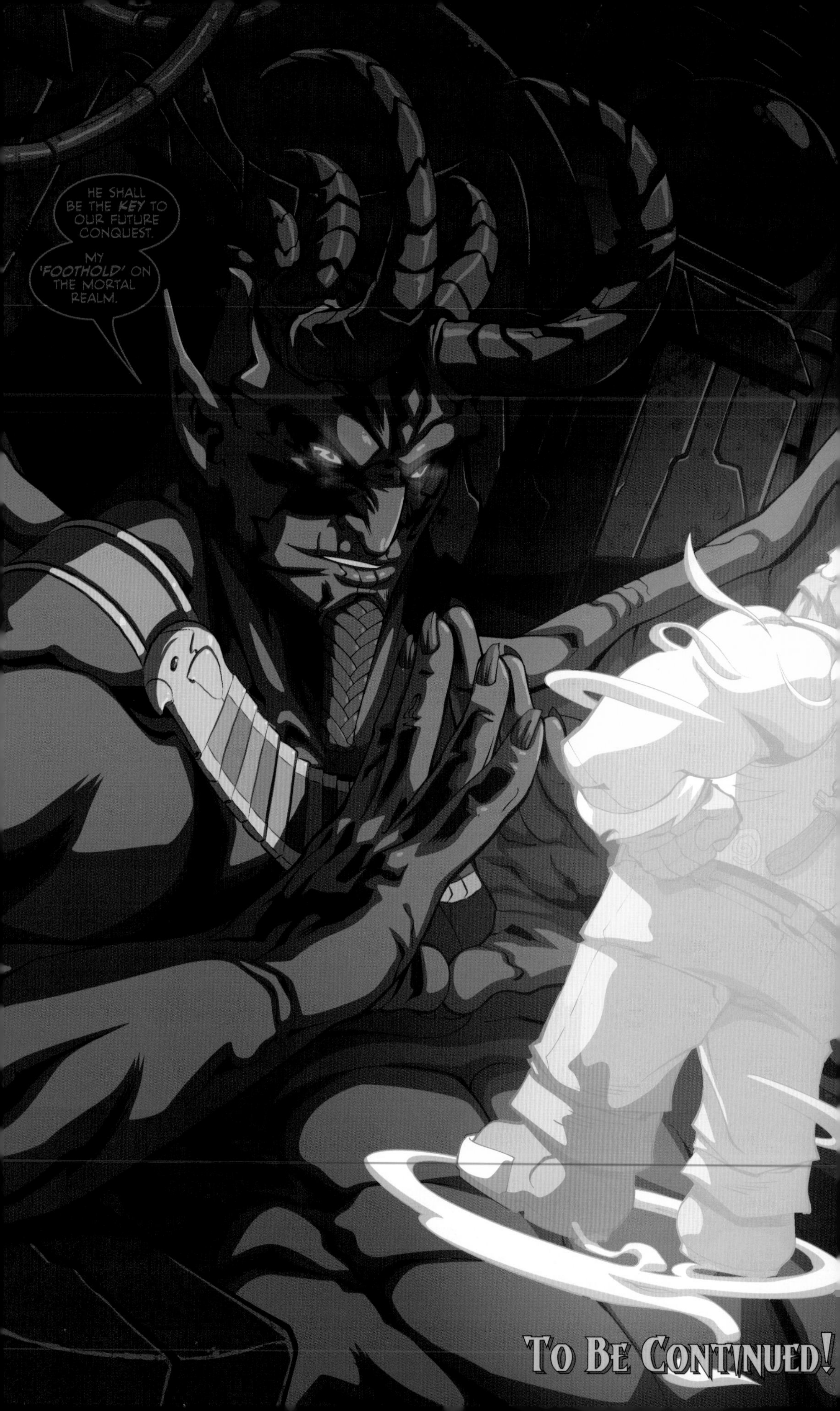
HE SHALL BE THE KEY TO OUR FUTURE CONQUEST.
MY 'FOOTHOLD' ON THE MORTAL REALM.
TO BE CONTINUED!

TWO COPPER PIECES

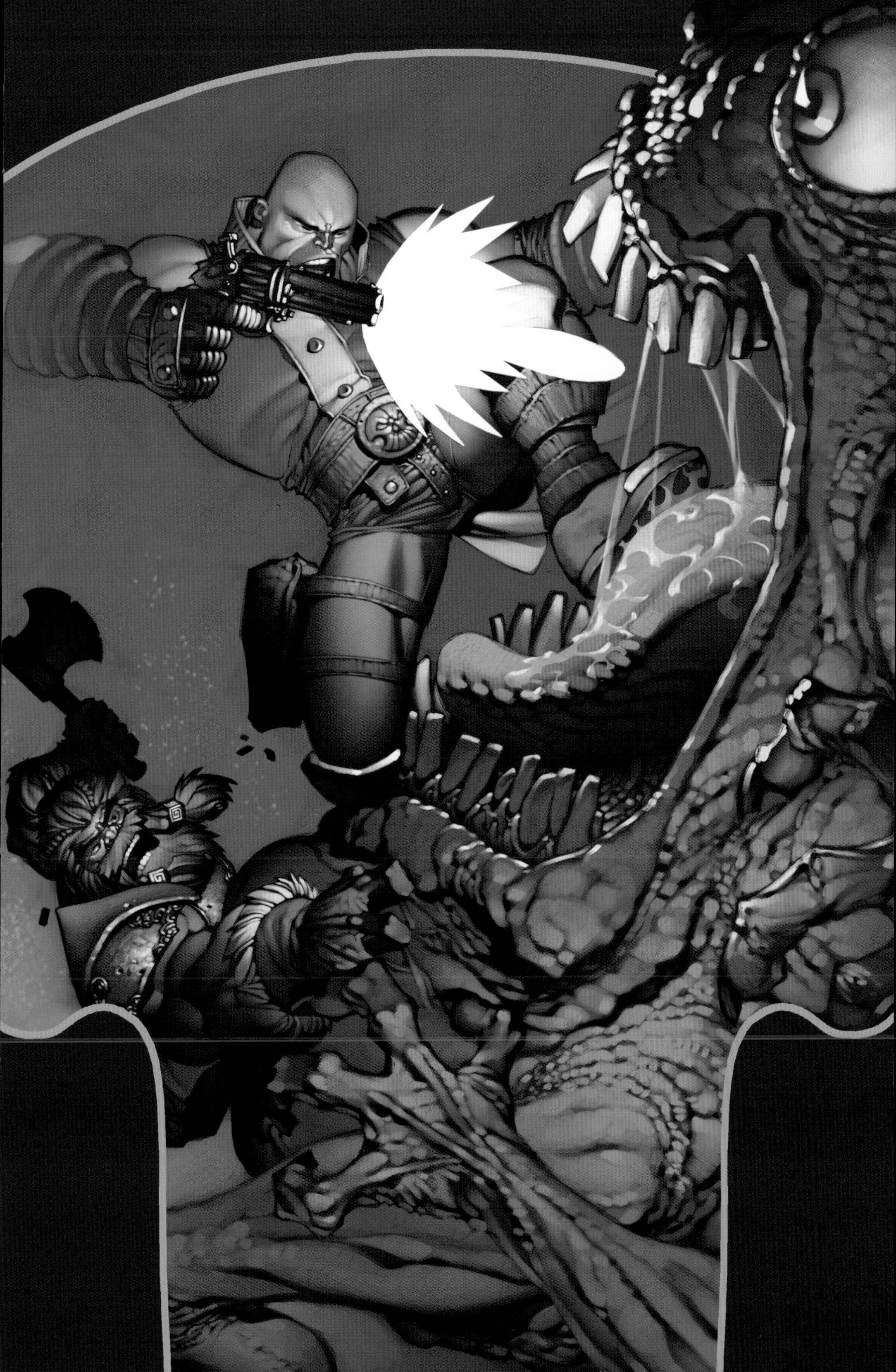

SKULL☠KICKERS
2 COPPER PIECES

Skullkickers started off as two short stories in Image's Popgun anthology series.

Chris Stevens was approached by the editors of Popgun and asked to contribute a short story. When he had trouble brainstorming up something fun to draw, we chatted on the phone and I conjured up the idea of two battle-hardened monster killers who kicked butt and had fun banter between each other. Chris liked it and we were off to the races.

On these next few pages you can read those original Popgun stories and see the origin of what we'd eventually call 'Skullkickers'. The designs are almost identical (though the artwork is more realistic and rendered) and their personalities are intact. The violence is more pronounced and overall attitude is quite a bit more grim, but it's pretty much SK right off the bat.

The original short story is called '2 Copper Pieces' and it's a reference to the fact that these two 'heroes' are less than golden. It's also a bit of a joke about how much they'd charge to kill someone they didn't like. The ending is particularly morbid and, since I didn't think we'd ever use these characters again, I wasn't too worried about their moral standards.

The second story is called 'Gotcha' and I think it delivers on the SK premise quite strongly with tight little banter and then ridiculous violence.

Chris' natural sense of design alongside his atmospheric and earthy locales laid the ground work for the world these two oafs inhabit. The punchy visuals made it easy to come up with more ideas for fantasy clichés run amuck. When Erik Larsen (Image Publisher at the time) asked if we had more stories for these two, I leapt at the chance to flesh things out and take it further. Needless to say, I'm glad it all worked out.

Enough of my blather - read on!

ZUB

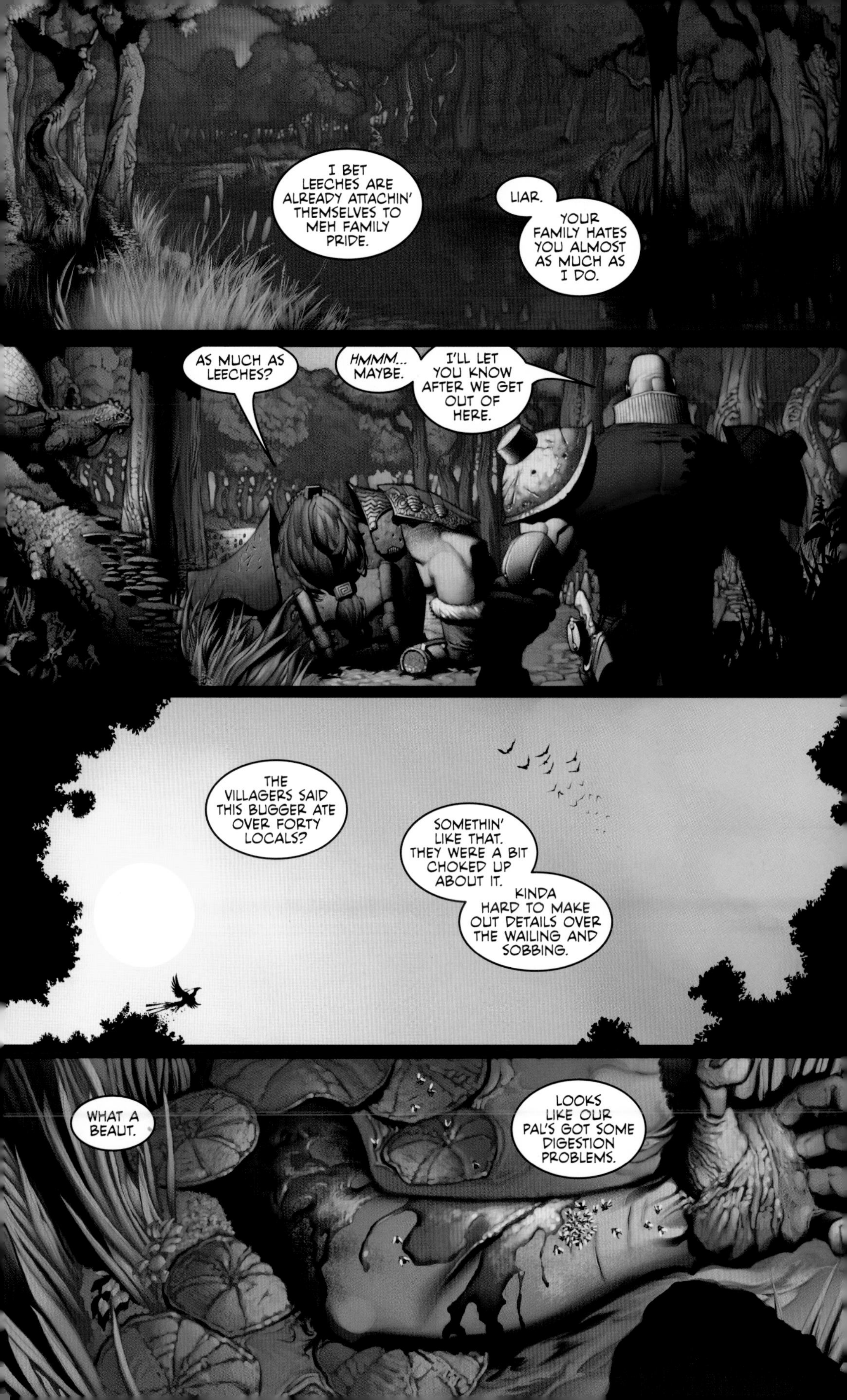
I BET LEECHES ARE ALREADY ATTACHIN' THEMSELVES TO MEH FAMILY PRIDE.
LIAR.
YOUR FAMILY HATES YOU ALMOST AS MUCH AS I DO.
AS MUCH AS LEECHES?
HMMM... MAYBE.
I'LL LET YOU KNOW AFTER WE GET OUT OF HERE.
THE VILLAGERS SAID THIS BUGGER ATE OVER FORTY LOCALS?
SOMETHIN' LIKE THAT. THEY WERE A BIT CHOKED UP ABOUT IT.
KINDA HARD TO MAKE OUT DETAILS OVER THE WAILING AND SOBBING.
WHAT A BEAUT.
LOOKS LIKE OUR PAL'S GOT SOME DIGESTION PROBLEMS.

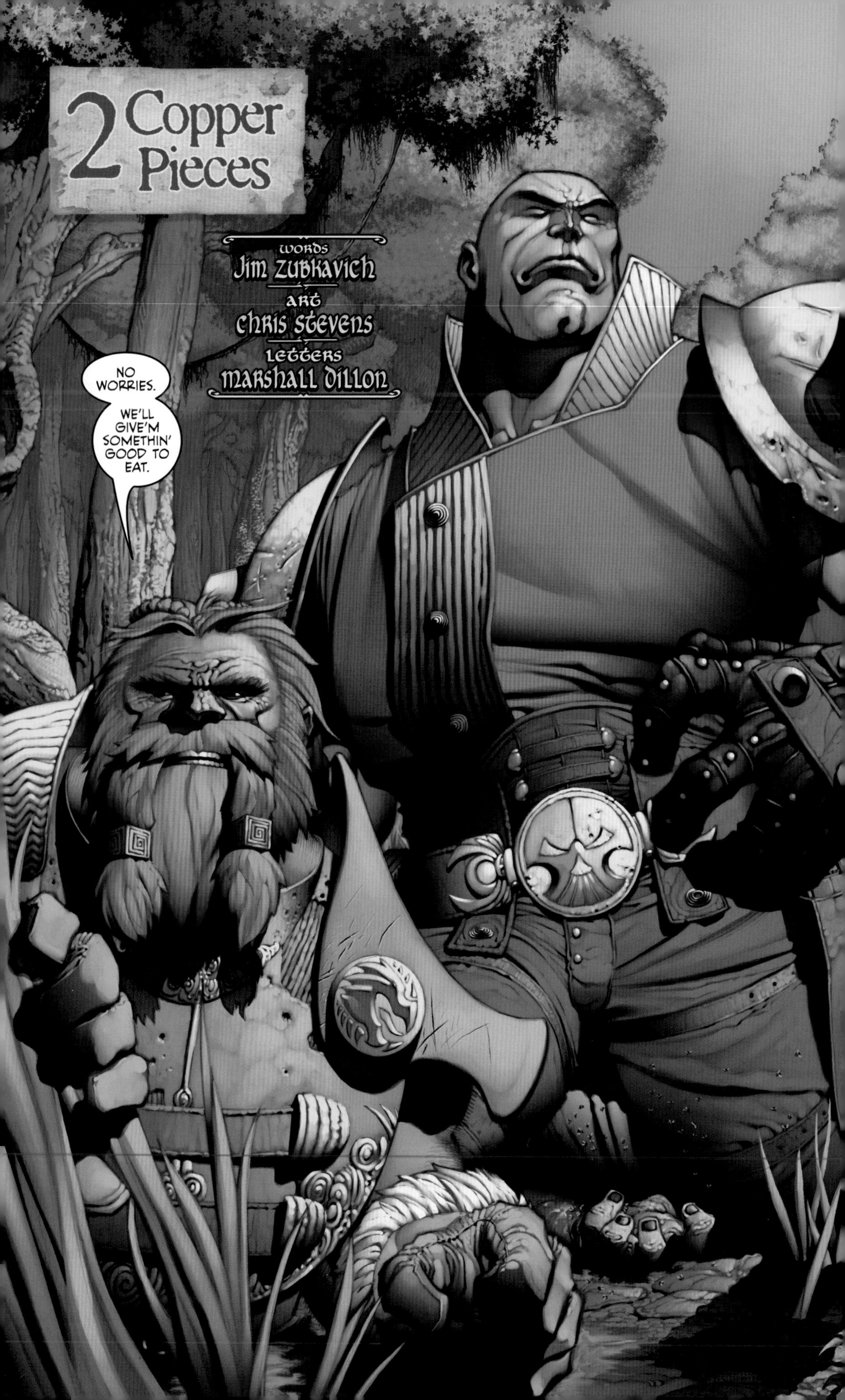
2 Copper Pieces
words
Jim Zubkavich
art
Chris Stevens
letters
Marshall Dillon
NO WORRIES.
WE'LL GIVE'M SOMETHIN' GOOD TO EAT.

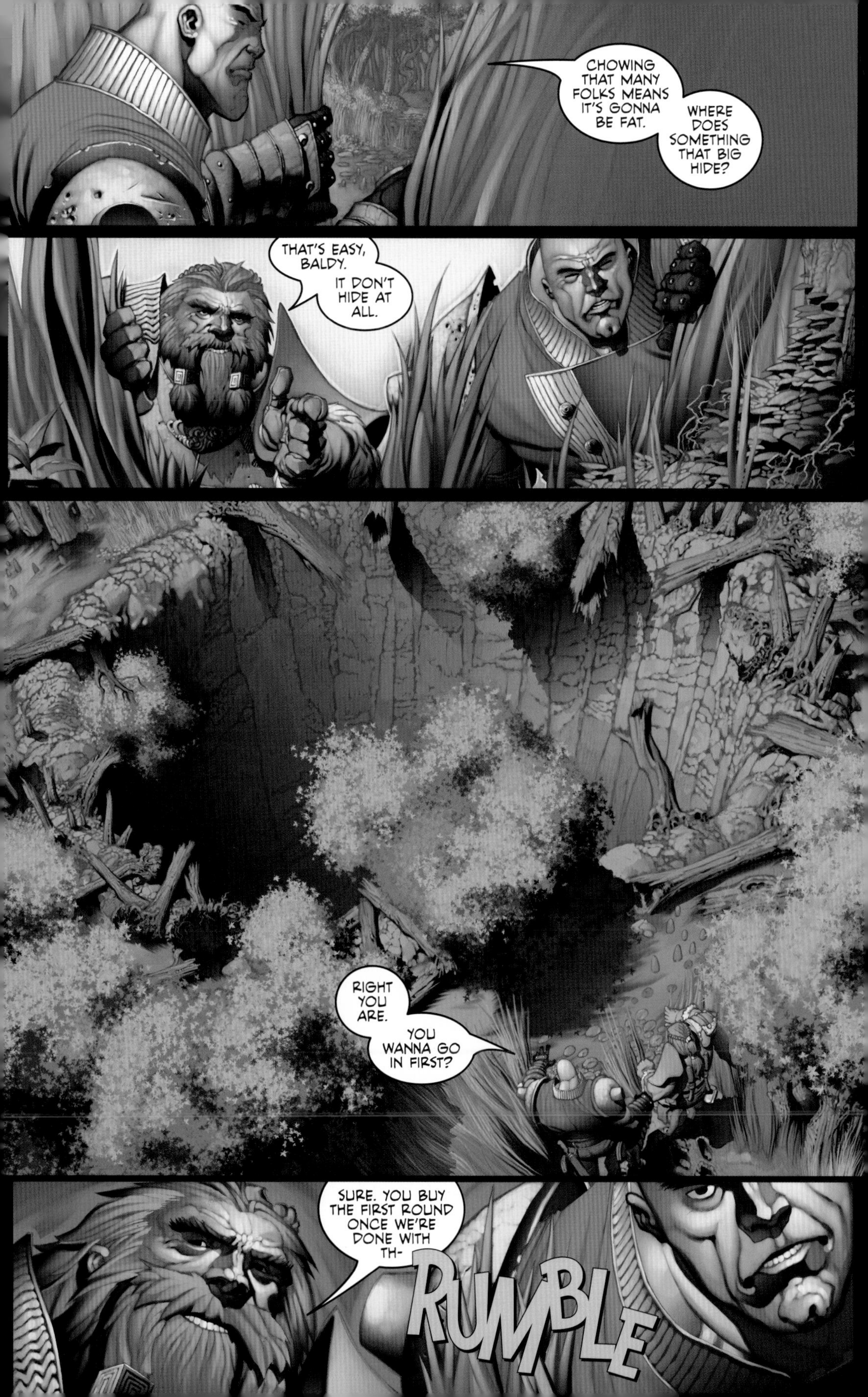
CHOWING THAT MANY FOLKS MEANS IT'S GONNA BE FAT.
WHERE DOES SOMETHING THAT BIG HIDE?
THAT'S EASY, BALDY.
IT DON'T HIDE AT ALL.
RIGHT YOU ARE.
YOU WANNA GO IN FIRST?
SURE. YOU BUY THE FIRST ROUND ONCE WE'RE DONE WITH TH-
RUMBLE

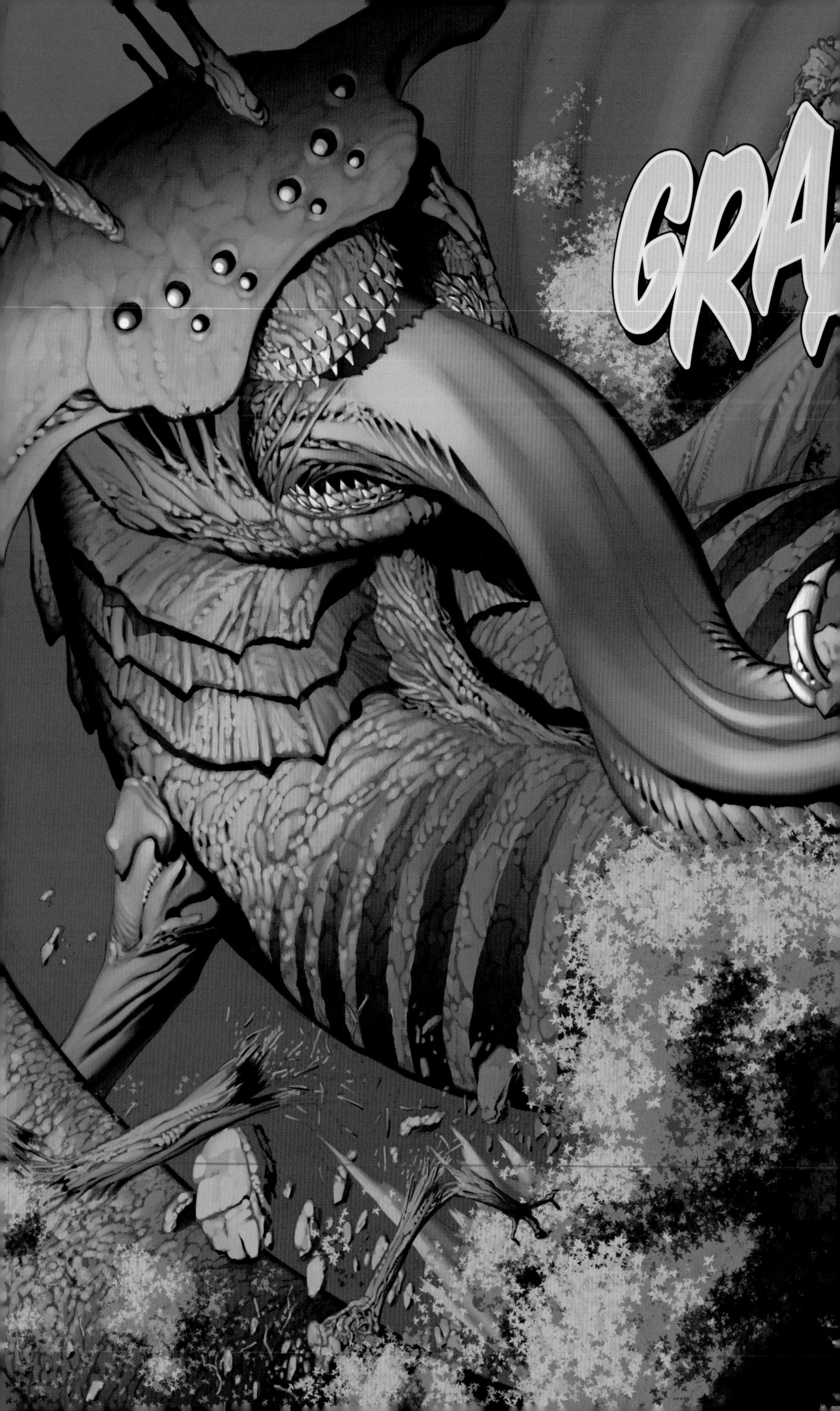
GRA

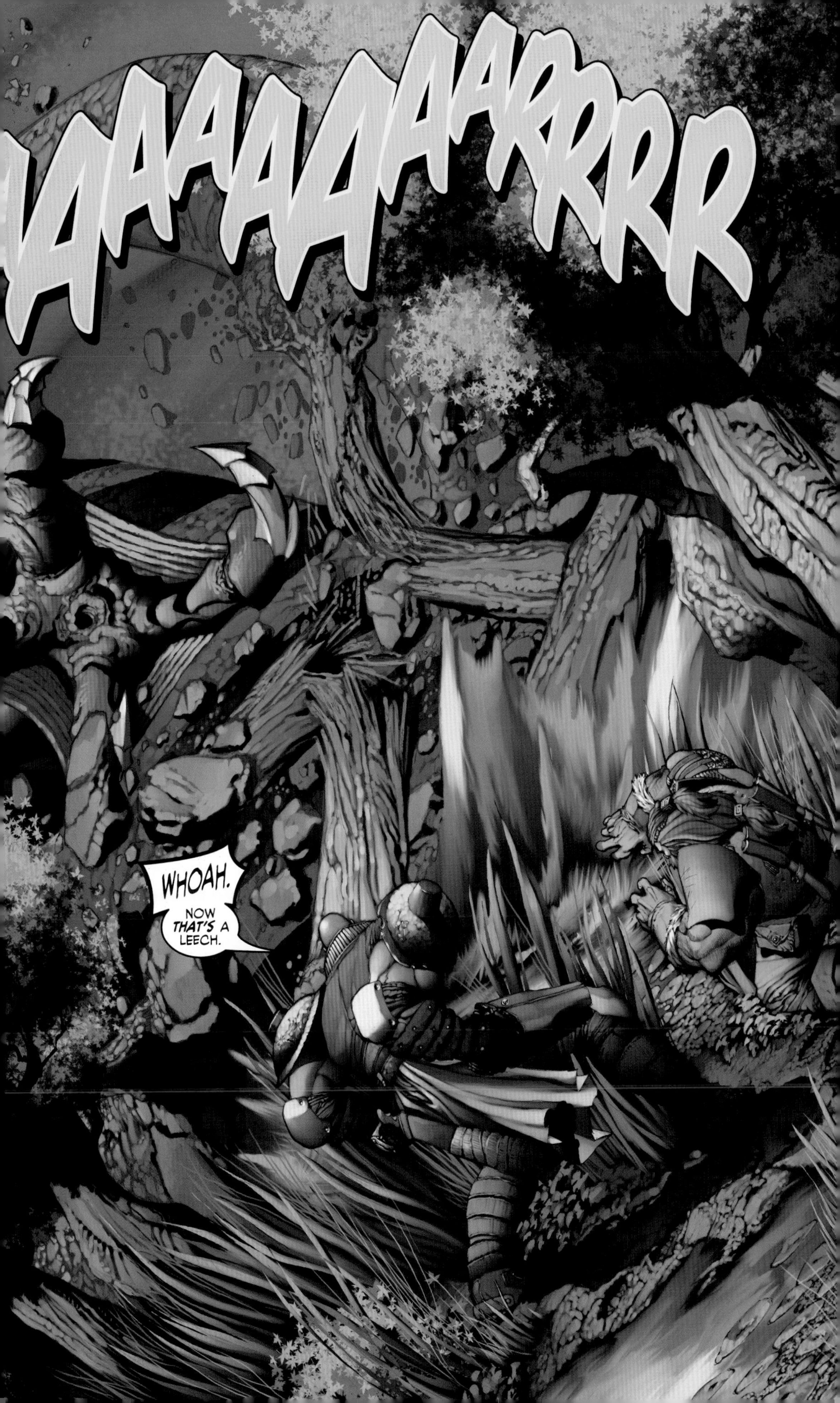

AAAAAAAARRRR
WHOAH.
NOW THAT'S A LEECH.

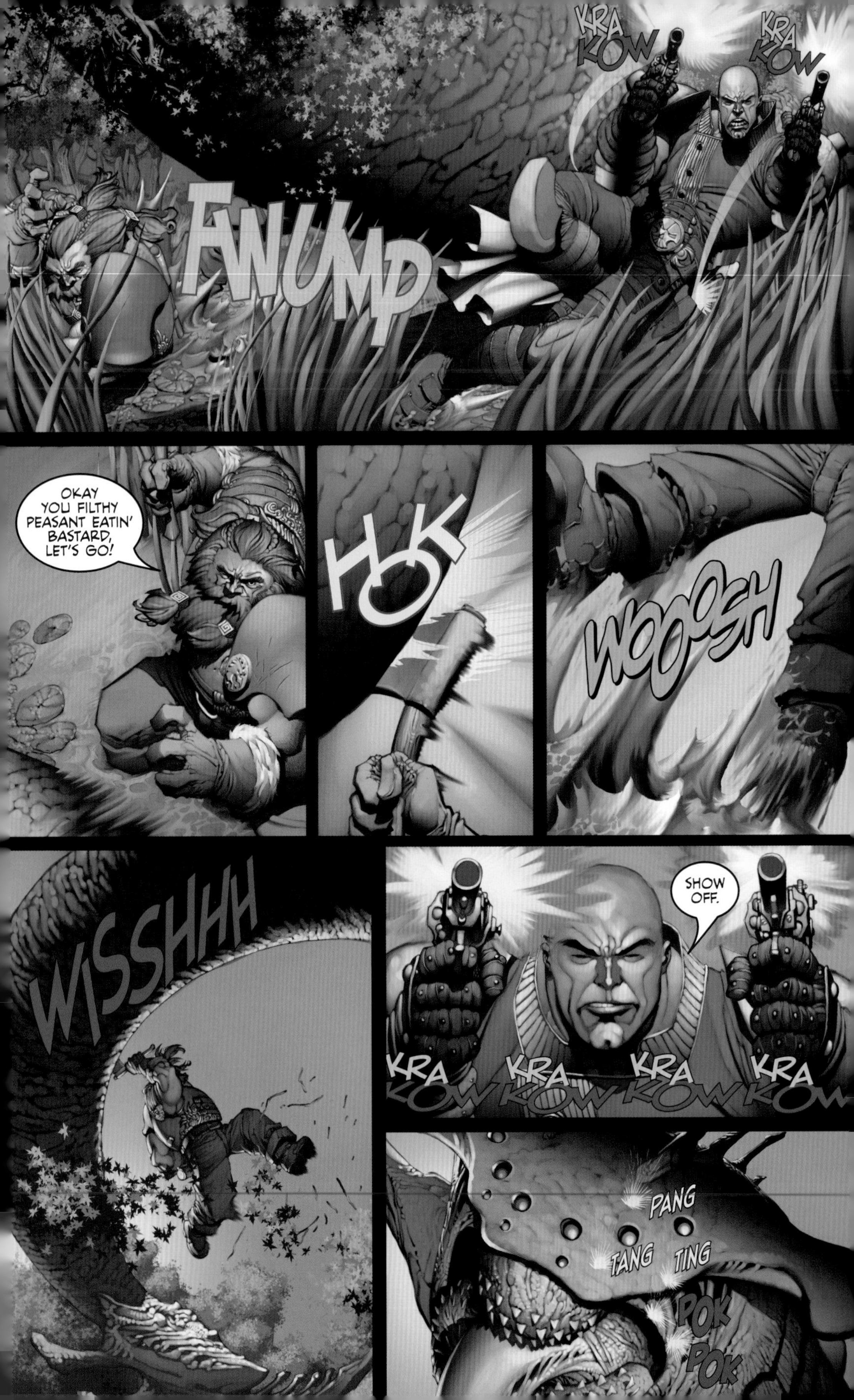
KRA KOW
KRA KOW
FWUMP
OKAY YOU FILTHY PEASANT EATIN' BASTARD, LET'S GO!
HOK
WOOOSH
WISSHHH
SHOW OFF.
KRA KOW
KRA KOW
KRA KOW
KRA KOW
PANG
TANG
TING
POK
POK

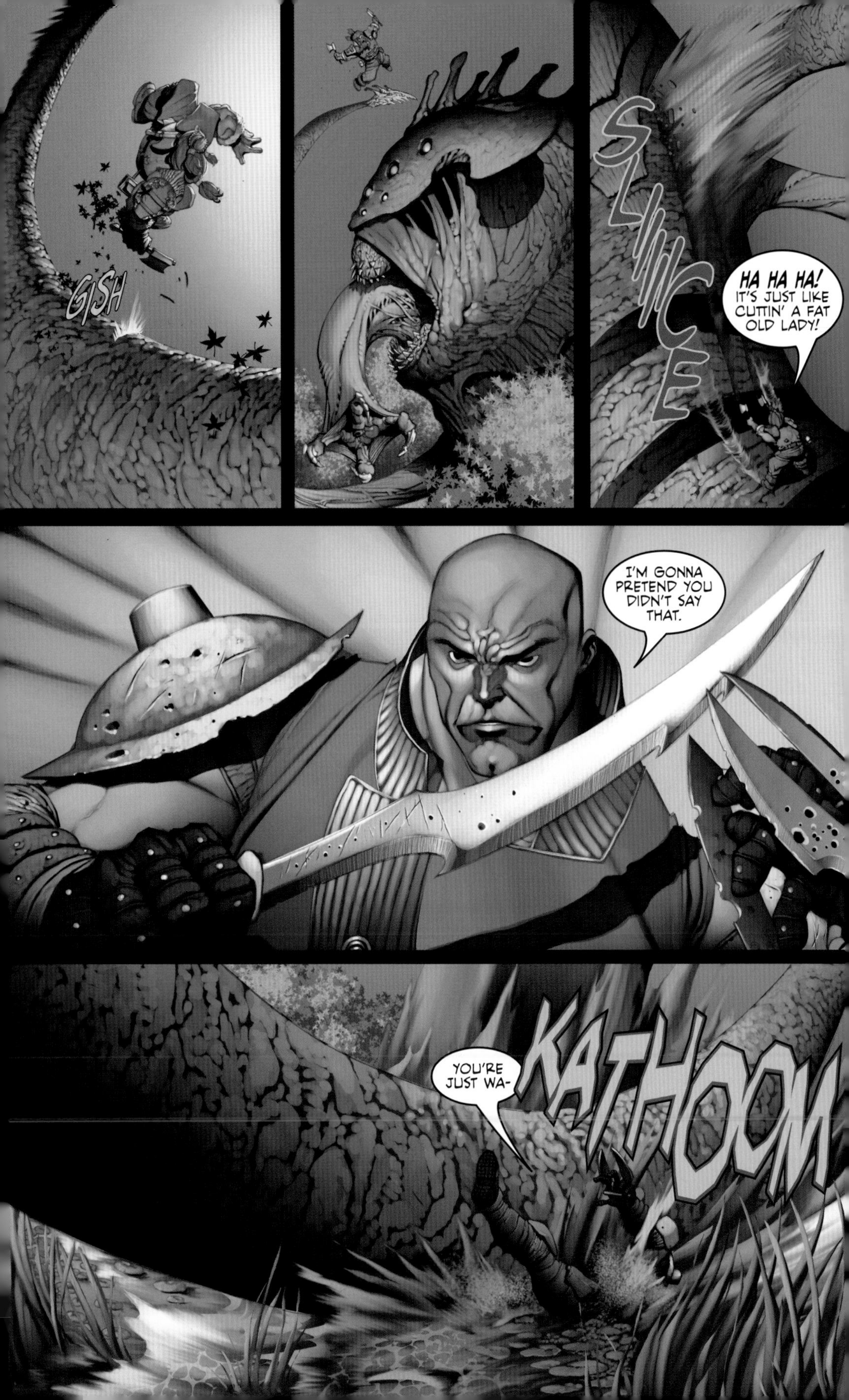
GISH
SLIIICE
HA HA HA! IT'S JUST LIKE CUTTIN' A FAT OLD LADY!
I'M GONNA PRETEND YOU DIDN'T SAY THAT.
YOU'RE JUST WA-
KATHOOM

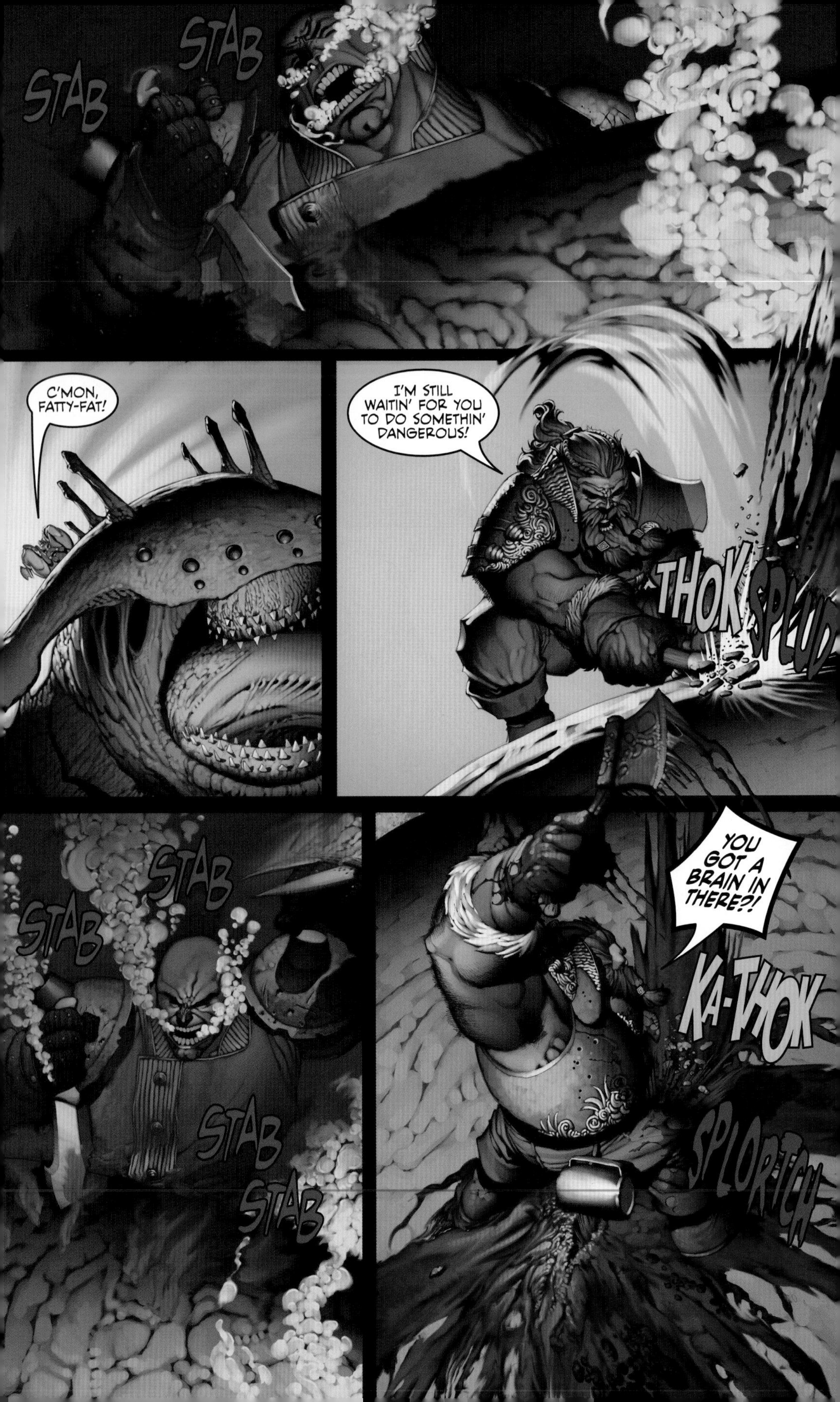

STAB
STAB
C'MON, FATTY-FAT!
I'M STILL WAITIN' FOR YOU TO DO SOMETHIN' DANGEROUS!
THOK
SPLUD
STAB
STAB
STAB
STAB
YOU GOT A BRAIN IN THERE?!
KA-THOK
SPLORTCH

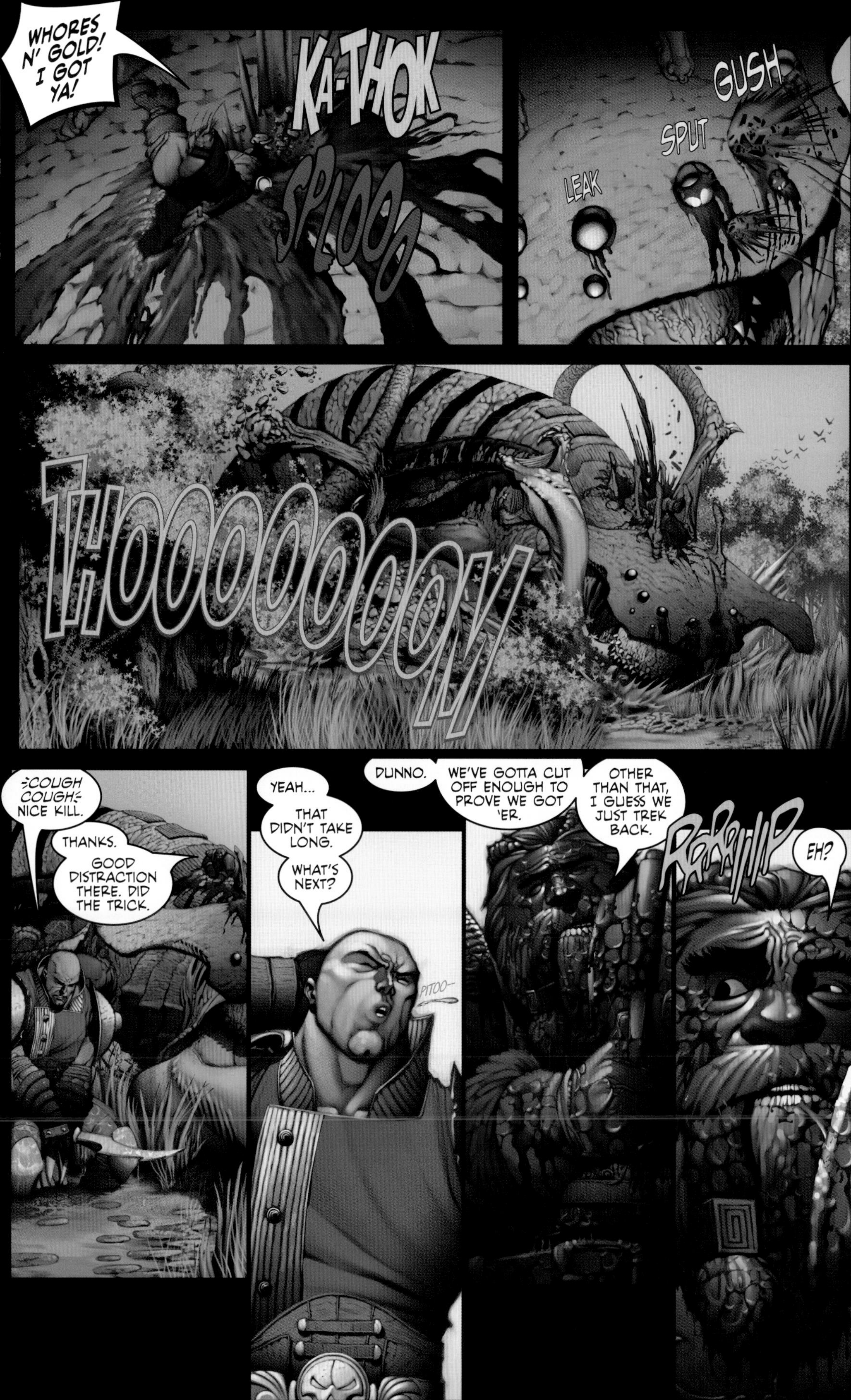
WHORES N' GOLD! I GOT YA!
KA-THOK
SPLOOO
GUSH
SPUT
LEAK
THOOOOOOOM
=COUGH COUGH= NICE KILL.
THANKS.
GOOD DISTRACTION THERE. DID THE TRICK.
YEAH...
THAT DIDN'T TAKE LONG.
WHAT'S NEXT?
PITOO
DUNNO.
WE'VE GOTTA CUT OFF ENOUGH TO PROVE WE GOT 'ER.
OTHER THAN THAT, I GUESS WE JUST TREK BACK.
RRRRIIIP
EH?

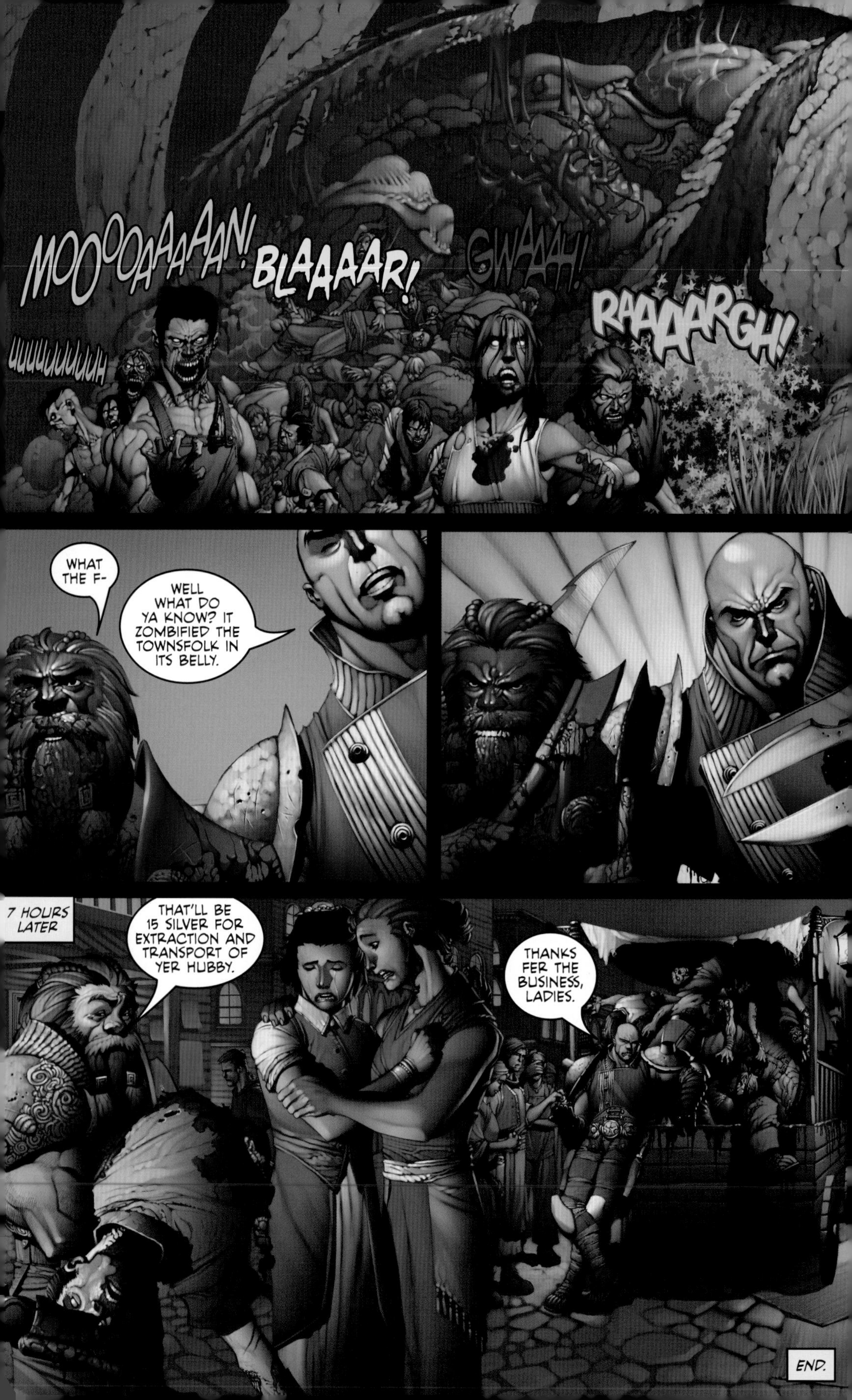

MOOOOAAAAAN!
BLAAAAR!
GWAAAH!
RAAAARGH!
uuuuuuuuuh
WHAT THE F-
WELL WHAT DO YA KNOW? IT ZOMBIFIED THE TOWNSFOLK IN ITS BELLY.
7 HOURS LATER
THAT'LL BE 15 SILVER FOR EXTRACTION AND TRANSPORT OF YER HUBBY.
THANKS FER THE BUSINESS, LADIES.
END.

gotcha!

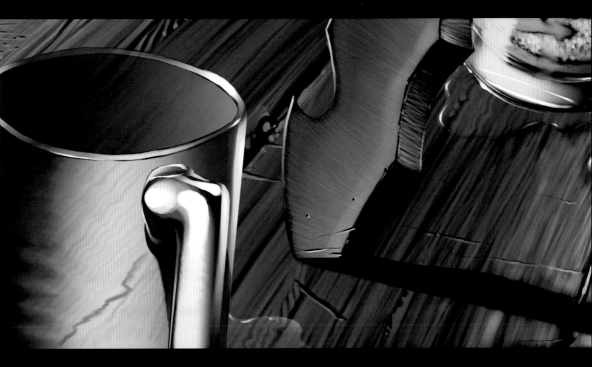

WORDS
Jim Zubkavich
ART
Chris Stevens
LETTERS
Marshall Dillon

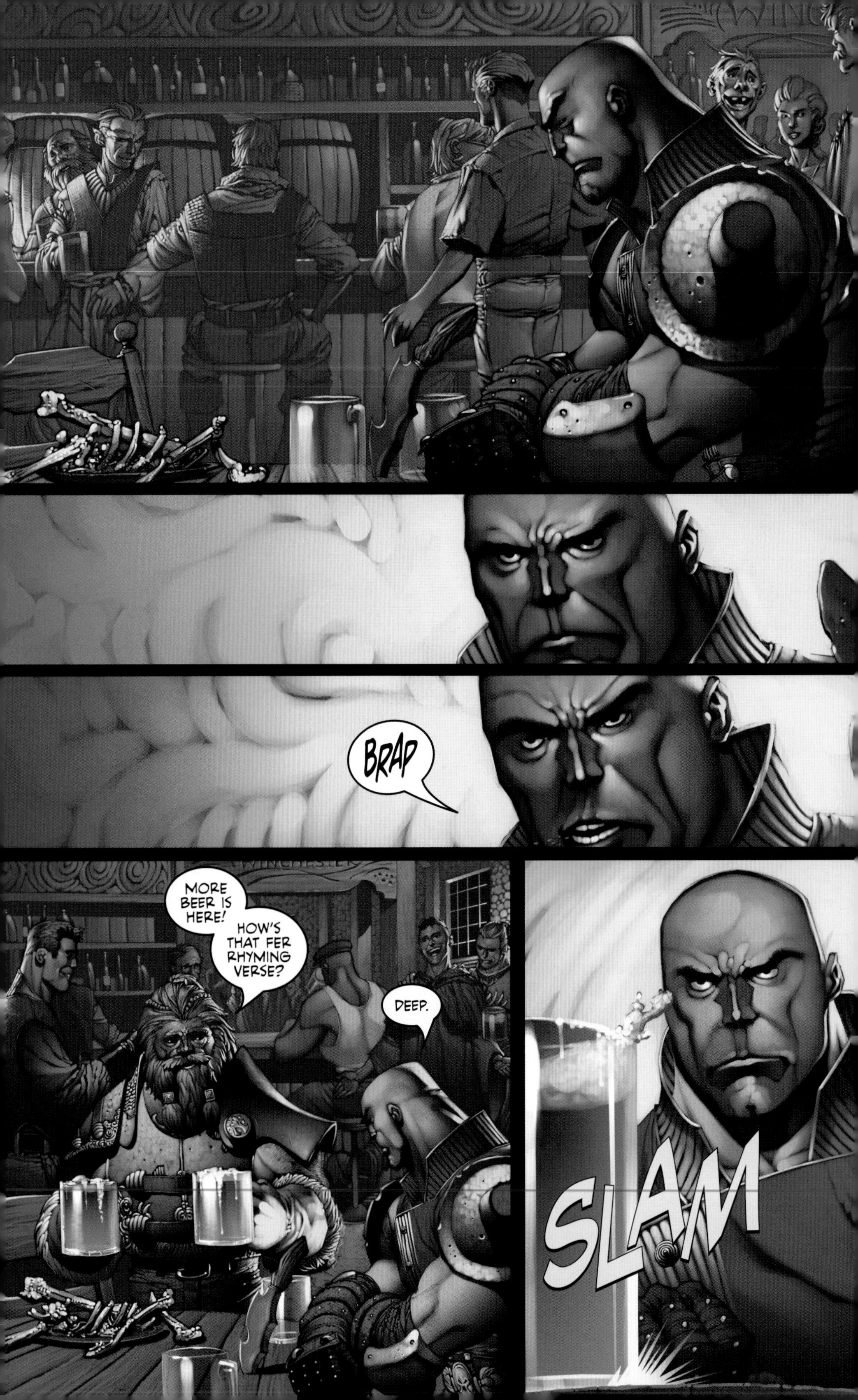
BRAP
MORE BEER IS HERE!
HOW'S THAT FER RHYMING VERSE?
DEEP.
SLAM

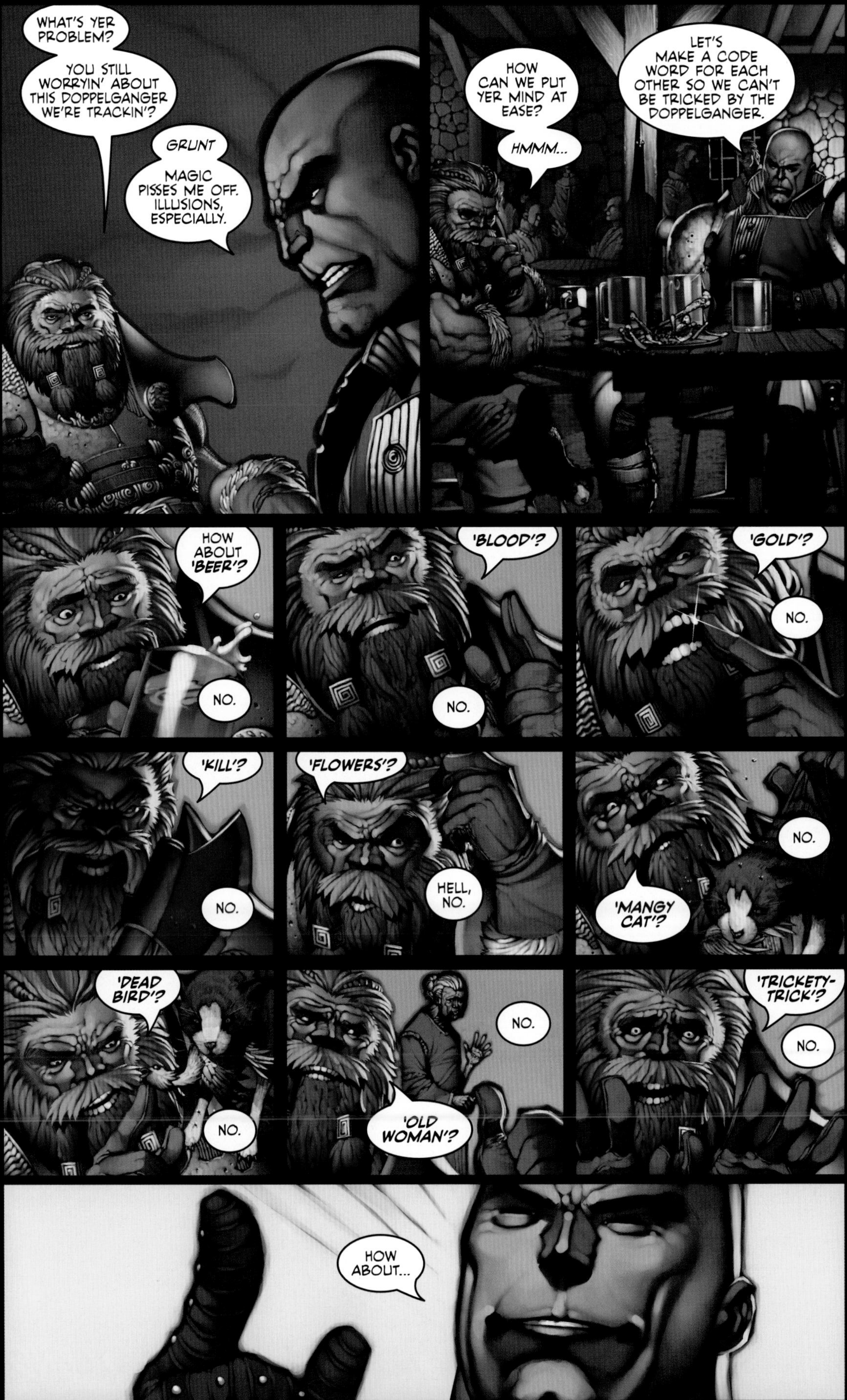
WHAT'S YER PROBLEM?
YOU STILL WORRYIN' ABOUT THIS DOPPELGANGER WE'RE TRACKIN'?
GRUNT
MAGIC PISSES ME OFF. ILLUSIONS, ESPECIALLY.
HOW CAN WE PUT YER MIND AT EASE?
HMMM...
LET'S MAKE A CODE WORD FOR EACH OTHER SO WE CAN'T BE TRICKED BY THE DOPPELGANGER.
HOW ABOUT 'BEER'?
NO.
'BLOOD'?
NO.
'GOLD'?
NO.
'KILL'?
NO.
'FLOWERS'?
HELL, NO.
'MANGY CAT'?
NO.
'DEAD BIRD'?
NO.
'OLD WOMAN'?
NO.
'TRICKETY-TRICK'?
NO.
HOW ABOUT...

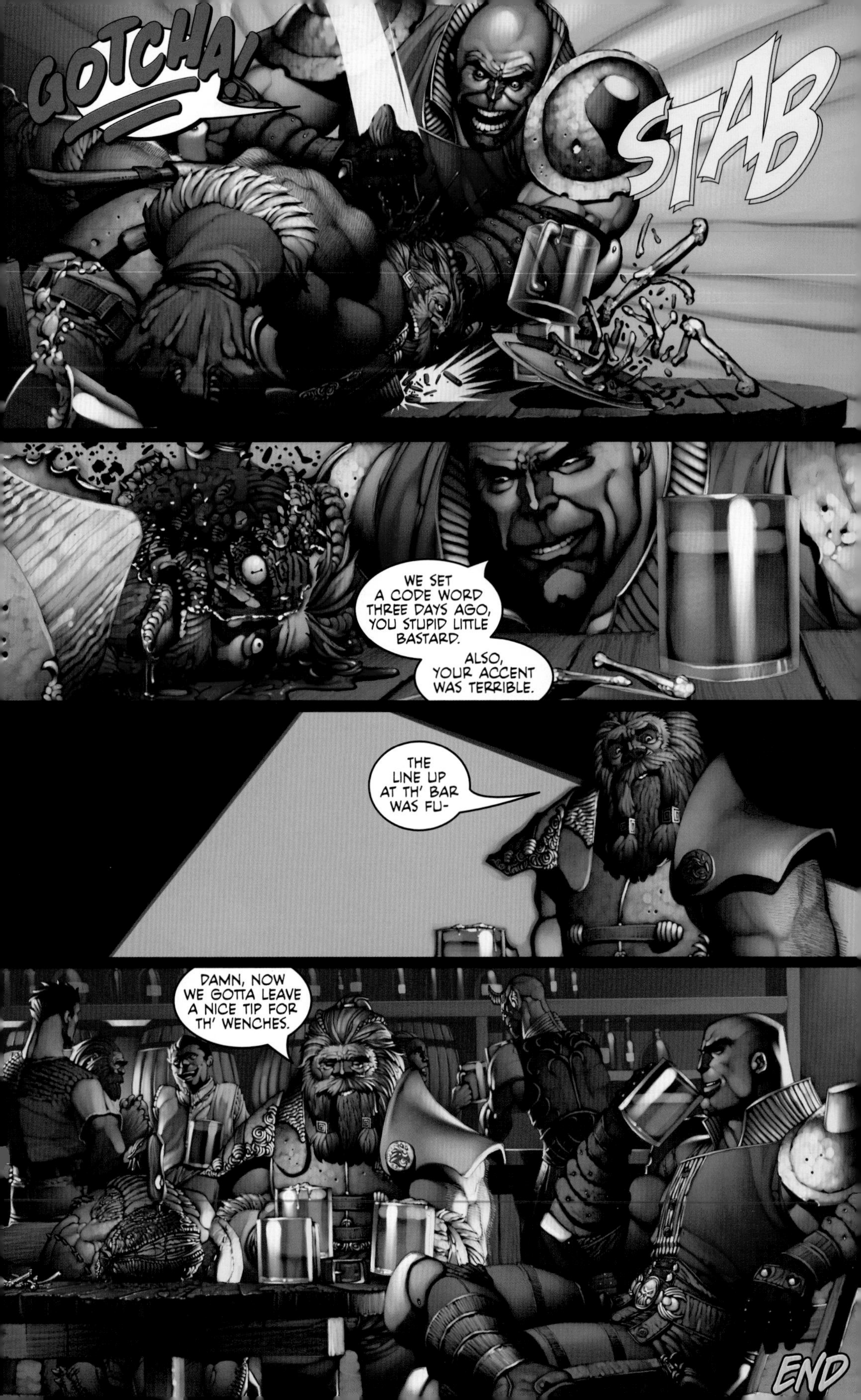
GOTCHA!
STAB
WE SET A CODE WORD THREE DAYS AGO, YOU STUPID LITTLE BASTARD.
ALSO, YOUR ACCENT WAS TERRIBLE.
THE LINE UP AT TH' BAR WAS FU-
DAMN, NOW WE GOTTA LEAVE A NICE TIP FOR TH' WENCHES.
END

SKETCHES

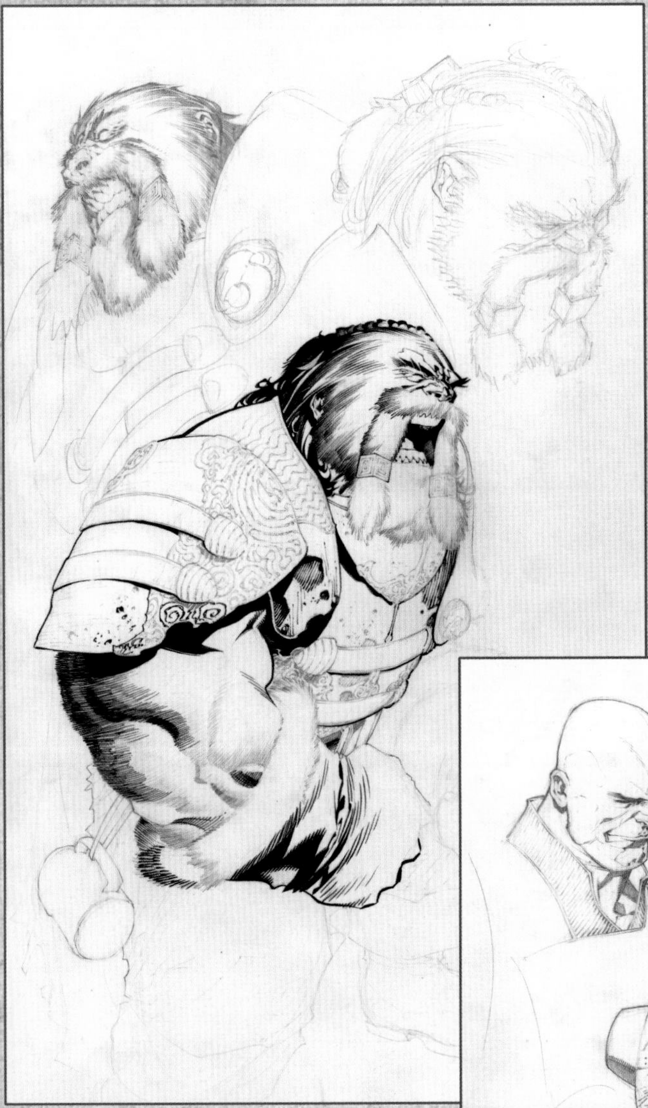

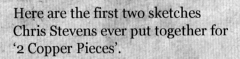

Here are the first two sketches Chris Stevens ever put together for '2 Copper Pieces'.

There's a real ornate design sense to the outfits and although it was detailed and looked amazing, I was a bit worried that these two jerks might be looking too classy for the kind of story I had in mind.

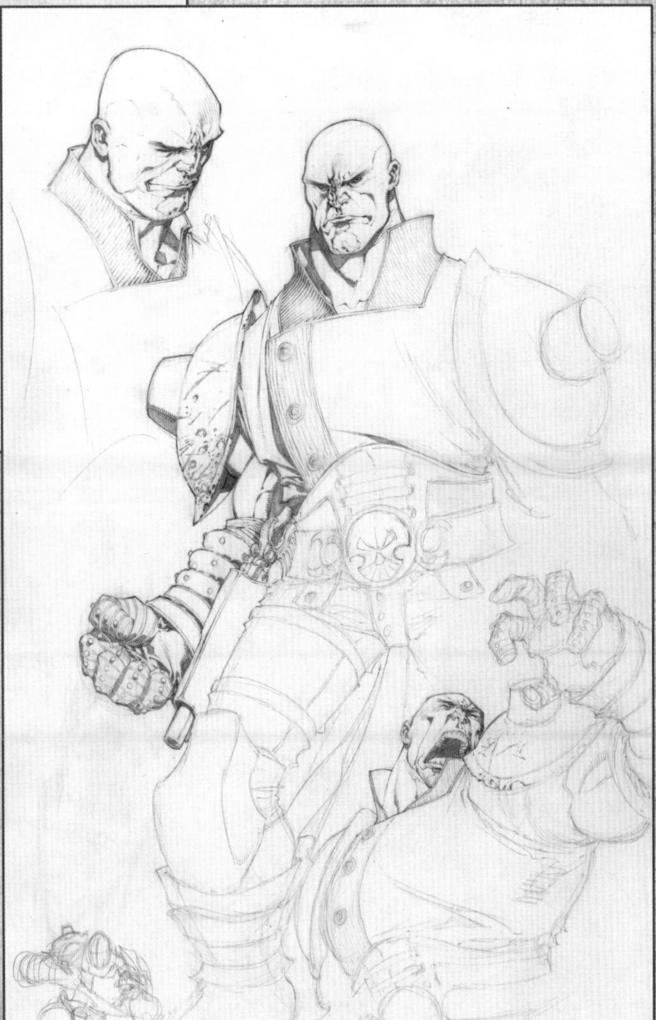

Above and right: original design art by Chris Stevens.

Looking at these again, it's amazing how much from the original designs stayed intact in the final version. They were pretty iconic right from the get-go.

THE DWARF

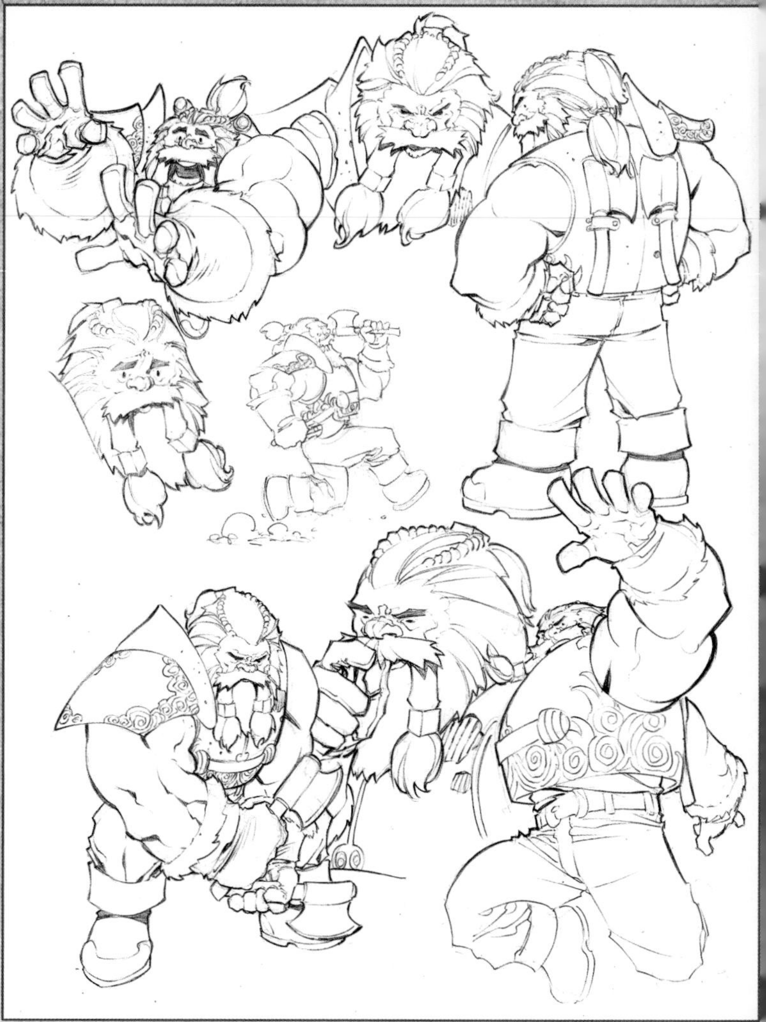

Here's the pint-sized murder machine designed up for the comic series.

The style is streamlined and more expressive when compared to the original short stories, with a clean silhouette reminiscent of an animated cartoon.

The Dwarf is all emotional content - joy &violence always blaring.

He's quick to anger, but almost as quick to forgive. From one minute to the next you don't quite know what you're going to get.

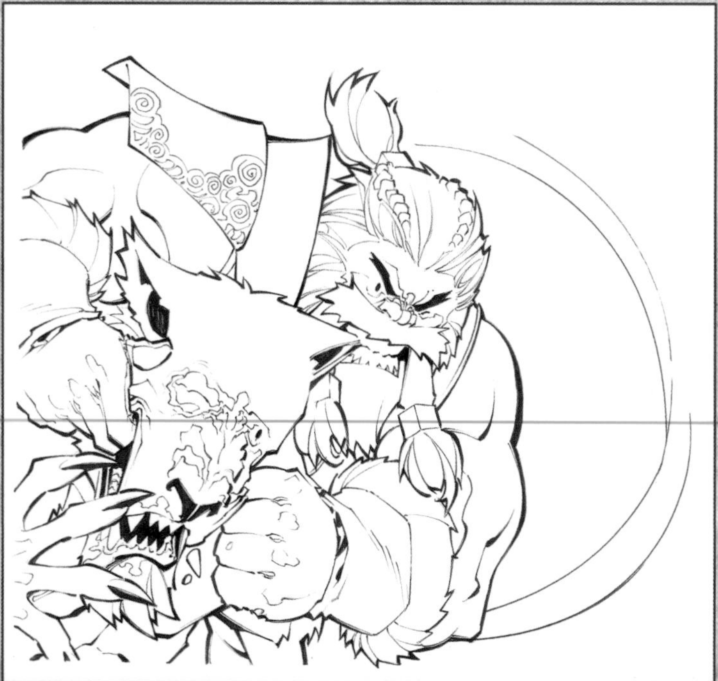

Above and left: Dwarf design art by Chris Stevens.

The werewolf punching piece on the left inspired the pot-bellied werewolf we used in chapter one.

I think I need to use that ear biting attack in a future issue.

THE BIG GUY

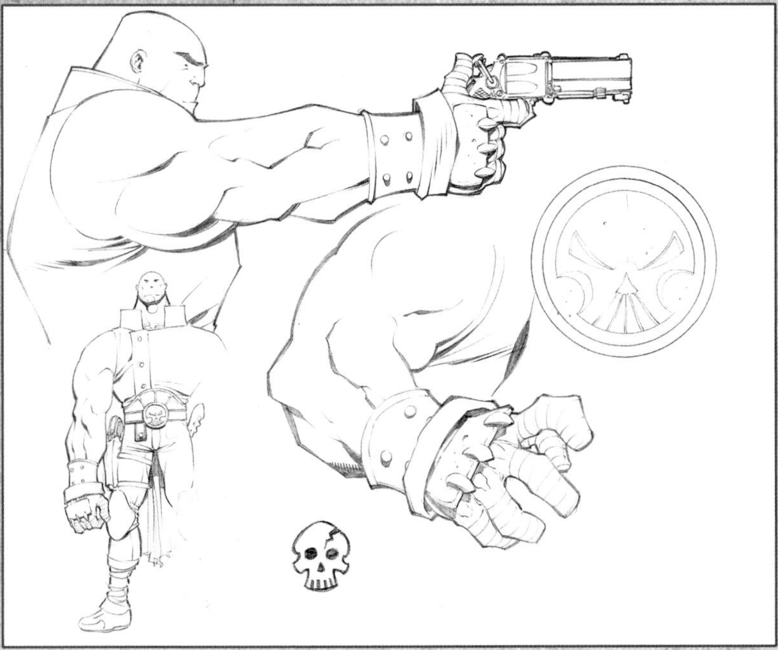

In this first story arc both mercenaries are nameless, like a pair of wandering "Men With No Name".

To compensate, their appearance and distinct personalities had to be easy to describe.

Readers and reviewers would eventually start calling them "Baldy" and "Shorty", which is good enough for now.

Above and right: Human design art by Chris Stevens.

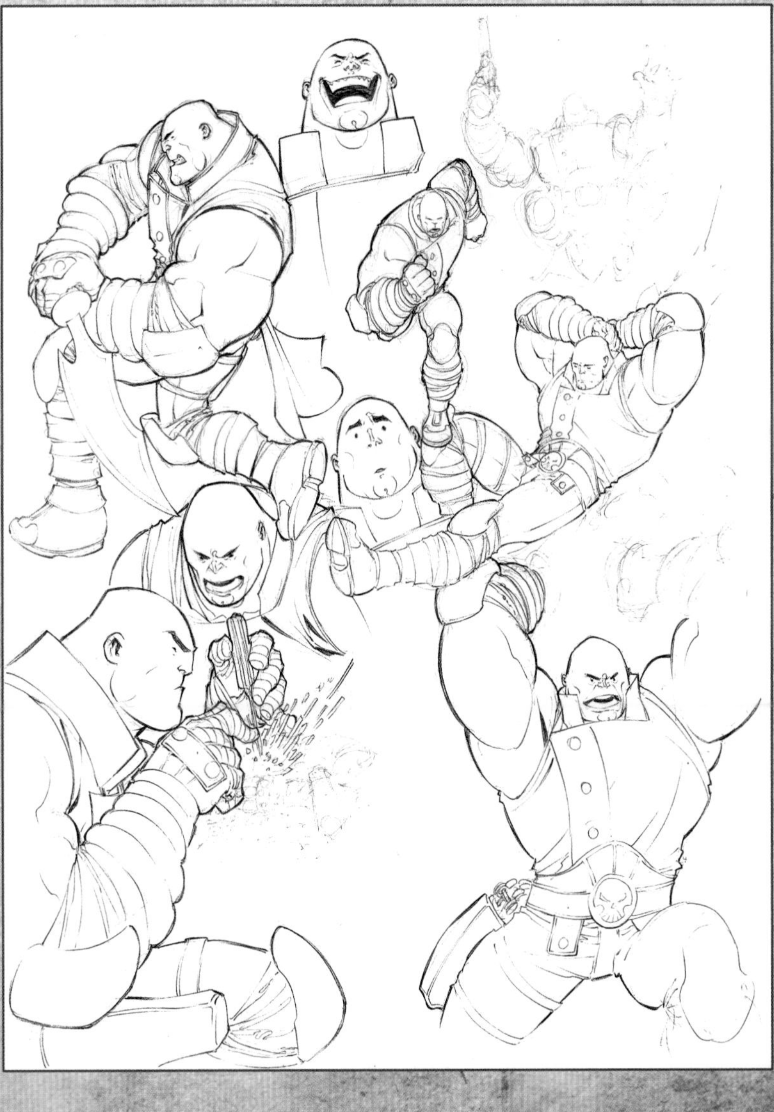

The Big Guy is the more subdued of the two, trying to plan ahead a bit and keep things under control.

His physical size leads you to expect a hand-to-hand confrontation, but he'll hang back and blast you with his pistol instead.

These expression sheets really hit the spot, delivering on the humor I wanted to have wrapped up in the series.

THE NECROMANCER

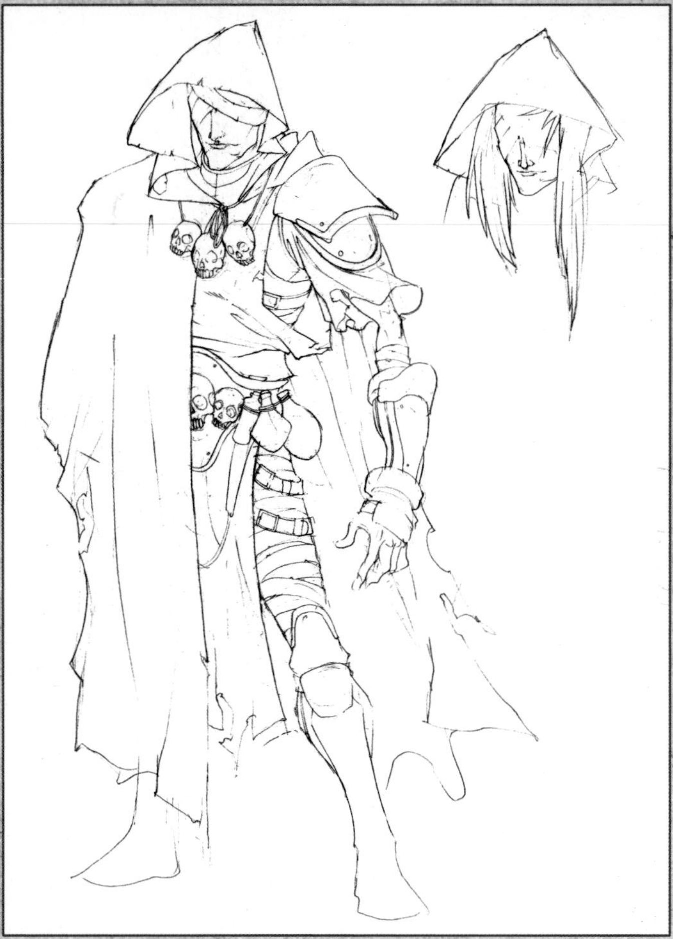

I wanted the Necromancer to look goth, gaunt and intimidating, setting the reader up with the expectation he'd have the skills to match. Obviously, not the case.

Abusing this guy over and over was possibly the most fun part of writing the first Skullkickers adventure.

We haven't seen the last of him.

Above and right: Design sketches by Edwin Huang.

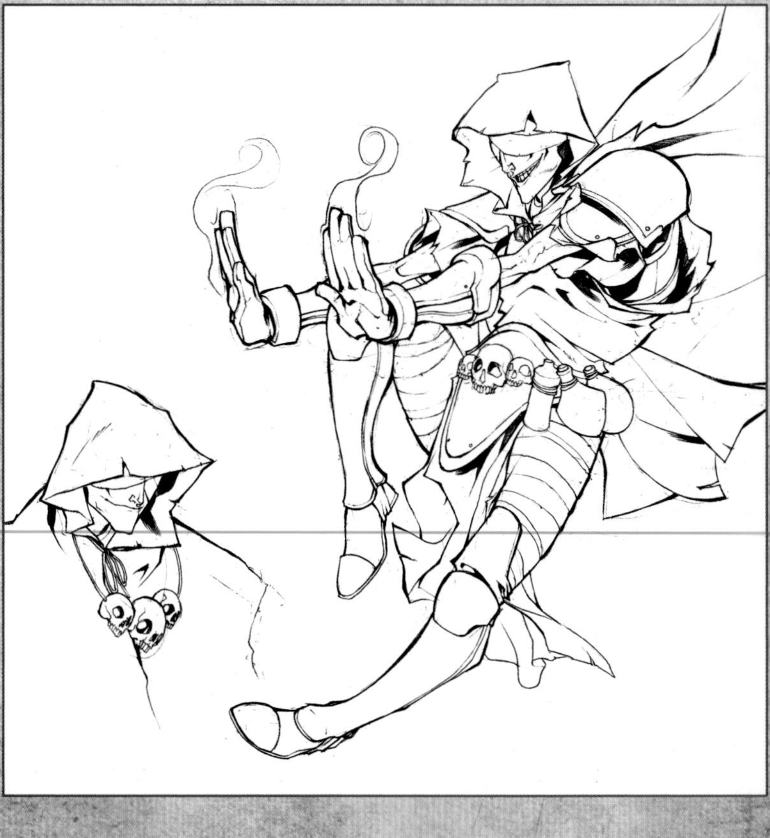

When Edwin came on-board the team he brought his own fantasy design sensibilities.

They were compatible with Chris', and yet were still distinctively his own. I can't wait to see what cool stuff he comes up with for future storylines.